WITH ARMS UNBOUND

Copyright © 2014 Malcolm Ivey
All rights reserved.

This is a work of fiction. The events and characters described herein are imaginary and are not intended to refer to specific places or living persons. The opinions expressed in this manuscript are solely the opinions of the author and do not represent the opinions or thoughts of the publisher. The author has represented and warranted full ownership and/or legal right to publish all the materials in this book.

This book may not be reproduced, transmitted, or stored in whole or in part by any means, including graphic, electronic, or mechanical without the express written consent of the publisher except in the case of brief quotations embodied in critical articles and reviews.

ISBN: 1500483583
ISBN 13: 9781500483586
Library of Congress Control Number: 2014912988
CreateSpace Independent Publishing Platform
North Charleston, South Carolina

WITH ARMS UNBOUND

Malcolm Ivey

Malcolm Ivey also has written

Consider the Dragonfly

Visit him at MalcolmIvey.com

For Sheena
One day…

We are each of us angels with only one wing,
and we can only fly by embracing one another.
—*Luciano De Crescenzo*

Prologue

Once

The stick slid back and forth, running through the groove of his cupped palm and jutting thumb. The chalky blue tip darted straight into the center of the cue ball but pulled away just before contact like the practiced stroke of a teasing lover.

At the end of the table, Bobby drained the last of his Jägermeister and set the glass down hard. "No way you make that," he announced.

Kevin smiled and continued to measure the shot. "Wanna bet?" he challenged, knowing full well that his stubborn little brother would never back down.

"Damn right," said Bobby, unsteadily shoving his hands into the pockets of his jeans, searching for money.

They both knew his pockets were empty. Bobby had been jobless for close to six months. Lately he'd been trying his hand as a small time coke dealer but more often than not, he only ended up snorting his profit. Kevin knew it was only a matter of time before the life swallowed his little brother. He straightened and reached for his beer, studying Bobby under the smoky lamp as he downed the last swallow and set it on the table.

"Want another, Kev?" offered the barmaid.

He shook his head. Two was his limit. He was driving.

Bobby was another story. "Jägermeister please, Donna."

She looked at Kevin questioningly. He shrugged and nodded.

"All right, here's what we'll do," he said. "I make the shot. You don't touch any coke for the rest of this year."

Bobby sniffed his drink and slumped on a stool. "Aw shit, here we go with the war on drugs lecture."

"No lecture," said Kevin. "Straight up. I make the shot, you cut out the stupid shit. Simple."

"And what if you miss?" asked Bobby.

"If I miss," said Kevin, looking him in the eye, "you *still* don't touch any coke for the rest of this year."

"Jeez, I can't win!" his brother drunkenly protested.

Kevin held up his hand, "And … we drive over to New Orleans tonight. Maybe play some blackjack at Harrah's. Hang out on Bourbon. It's been awhile since we've been there."

"But it's already after eleven."

"So what? You got somewhere you gotta be? I'll call in sick to work tomorrow and we'll drive back whenever we feel like it. But," Kevin smiled, "that's only if I miss the shot. Which I won't."

Bobby gulped down his drink and grimaced. "Okay, you're on."

Kevin grabbed his stick while Bobby fired up a cigarette and blew a stream of smoke at the overhead lamp. Van Morrison played from a jukebox in the back of the tavern.

"Eightball, corner pocket," said Kevin.

He tapped the cue ball just left of center and sent it rolling up the side of the table between the remaining scattered balls and the felt banking until it collided with the black eightball at the other end.

"Shit," said Bobby as it crept slowly toward the corner.

Kevin crossed his arms and smiled. When he looked at his kid brother, he didn't see a six-foot-two, two-hundred-twenty-pound man. He saw the same old little Bobby who used to warm his hands by sticking them beneath his big brother's underarms at the bus stop in the winter.

"Wait a second!" said Bobby, leaning over the table.

The same little Bobby that used to pee in the bed and blame him.

"I think it's stopping," he said. "It is. It's gonna stop!"

The same little Bobby who cried and told their foster mother to 'take it back' when she came home from the beauty salon with a new hairdo.

"Yes!" he said, as the eightball crawled to a stop at the edge of the pocket. "Let's go!"

"Damn," said Kevin as he walked over to the bar and dropped a twenty on the counter, winking at Donna. "I almost made it."

Bobby was already in the car by the time Kevin reached it. When he opened the door and slid behind the wheel, he noticed a silver chain hanging from the rearview mirror.

"What's this?" he asked, grabbing it.

"It's your birthday present. I know I'm late but..."

Kevin studied the medallion. "Saint Christopher."

Bobby nodded. "The patron saint of travelers. It's real silver too. Check out the other side."

Kevin flipped it in his fingers. There was an inscription on the back. "M.B.K?"

"My Brother's Keeper."

Kevin smiled and slipped it over his head. "Thanks man."

The neighborhood of Warrington is located on the west side of Pensacola, a coastal town on the Florida Panhandle nestled between the Alabama state line and Escambia Bay. At the ages of seven and four, Kevin and Bobby Freeman were moved into their first foster home in Warrington and continued to call the west side home seventeen years later.

A perk to living on the Redneck Riviera was its close proximity to surrounding major cities. Jacksonville, Atlanta, Birmingham, and Memphis were all a half-day's drive. New Orleans was even closer at less than three hours away. Kevin nosed his Monte Carlo out into the evening traffic on Highway 29 and headed north to Interstate 10.

Bobby slid a CD from its case and popped it in the deck. The voice of Bradley Nowell and Sublime filled the car. Kevin tapped his fingers on the steering wheel in time with the music.

It was almost midnight. The fluorescent lights of passing car dealerships gave way to seedy motels. A strolling prostitute moved down the sidewalk. A grizzled hobo with a bedroll strapped to his back watched the traffic from a bus stop. There was a fight going on in the Waffle House parking lot.

"Whoa, check that out," said Bobby, looking over his shoulder at the fading street scene.

Kevin's eyes flicked to the rearview. A cop car's blue lights flashed as it crossed the median to quell the disturbance.

"Watch out!" screamed Bobby.

A red SUV shot in front of them from a side street, cutting across to the southbound lane. Kevin stomped the brake pedal into the floorboard and the Monte Carlo trembled and shrieked as it attempted to do the impossible. There simply wasn't enough space or time to react.

For a brief moment the blurred faces of the passengers in the SUV came into focus, frozen in horror, then the world exploded in a cacophony of shattered glass and crunched metal. Tires screeched. Horns blared. Lights flashed. **CRACK!** Another car hit them and the Monte Carlo tumbled sideways across the highway like a toy flicked by a child.

Then, stillness. Kevin Freeman opened his eyes. He was upside down, pinned to the seat by the safety belt. The Sublime CD continued to play as the car groaned and shifted in the ditch.

"By the rivers of Babylon
Where he sat down
And there he wept
When he remembered Zion…"

He looked over for Bobby, but the passenger seat was empty. The night air blew in from the gaping hole in the shattered windshield.

PART I
August, 10 years later

1

Training Day

Her trainee was huge, easily double her one-hundred-twenty pounds and a good foot taller. Tribal tattoos peeked from beneath his tight shirt sleeves and his polished black boots were the size of toilet seats. He wore a bald head, a sculptured beard and a natural scowl. *Some people are just born for this,* she thought as she pulled her keys from the cargo pocket of her brown DOC uniform.

"Wings one and three are open pop," she explained. "Two is disciplinary confinement."

The trainee grunted as she unlocked the door and pulled it open. Blaring white noise, oppressive heat, and the stench of unwashed flesh assaulted them. After six years on the job, Rayla Broxson was used to it. She glanced at the massive cadet to see his reaction. His face was stone. She held the door open as they stepped inside and slammed it shut behind them.

The dayroom television presided high above the slamming dominoes and slapping cards below. "*You are not the father,*" announced Maury Povich as the studio audience erupted and the guests argued beneath a sequence of ear-splitting bleeps.

"One time!" somebody shouted. "Comin' in!"

The loud volume of the TV diminished as they moved from the dayroom to the living area. A skinny, stoned-looking kid stepped around them. Shirtless musclebound men watched them pass from the second tier. A sissy leaned against a doorway across the hall, "Hey Ms. B!"

"There are forty-four cells on this wing," she said, "twenty-two on each floor. All two-man except for twenty-one and twenty-two over there, those are handicapped cells."

The trainee nodded.

"You've probably already noticed that this is the only dorm with two-man cells on the compound," Rayla pointed out. "These inmates have a higher custody level. Many of them are lifers, murderers, sex offenders, habitual violent offenders. Stuff like that. The only other dorm where you'll find lifers is Alpha, that's our spillover dorm."

A Muslim with a prayer rug draped over his shoulder squeezed by them carrying an armload of books. "Ms. B. whatchu' doin' workin' down here in the dungeon?" he asked, smiling broadly at her.

Rayla nodded but didn't answer. She turned to the trainee. "This isn't my normal post," she said before pausing and looking in a cell above them. "Munoz, I *know* you're not smoking up there."

A tattooed Hispanic came to the door. "No ma'am."

They continued. "I usually work the gun towers or inside security," she explained, "sometimes Alpha, but not often."

As they walked down the row of open cells Rayla Broxson maintained an air of unconcerned confidence. To the untrained eye, she was just another guard making a security check, showing the ropes to a new recruit. Comfortable with the routine to the point of boredom. But behind her mask of cool detachment she was hyperaware of her surroundings:

a flushing toilet in an upstairs cell, the drone of overhead exhaust fans, hollow laughter, heavy footsteps and leering eyes from every direction. She was not naïve to the fact that under different circumstances – a dark alley, an empty parking lot, a stalled car – some of these same men would attempt to rape her, kill her, a few might even try to *eat* her. But she generally ignored that line of thinking. She was well trained and knew that in the event of a situation, the distress button clipped to her belt would signal every available officer to come to her aid in a matter of seconds.

As they neared the end of the cellblock a guttural roar caused their heads to turn. A bald, fiftyish white man covered in tattoos was curling a mesh laundry bag full of books. Rayla watched him for a moment before turning and walking up the steps to the second tier.

The trainee rushed to catch up. "Officer Broxson," he said, speaking for the first time, "doesn't the rulebook say that exercising in the cells is prohibited?"

She fought off a smile as a malnourished-looking Mexican with a wine stain birthmark covering half of his face slid by them.

"Could you smell him?" she asked.

"Who?" he frowned.

"The inmate who just walked by. With the birthmark."

The trainee turned to look.

"Didn't he smell terrible to you?" she asked.

"I … well, I guess. Maybe," he said. "The whole place smells."

"Right," she said. "It's 100 degrees outside and these dorms aren't air conditioned."

"I don't see what this has to do with the rulebook."

She held up a hand. "Right now he's in violation of rule eight-dash-one. Failure to maintain personal hygiene. It carries ten days in confinement and fifteen days loss of gain time.

You could write him a disciplinary report for that, but the state doesn't supply deodorant and he's probably broke by the looks of him. Kind of petty. Don't you think?"

The trainee crossed his arms and leaned against the railing.

"He could ask a friend to buy him some from the canteen but that would also be a violation of rule nine-dash-six, bartering, which carries fifteen days in confinement, sixty days loss of gain time."

"Are you going to quote the entire rulebook?" the trainee asked with a smirk as he turned to walk away.

She followed. "My point is that there are literally hundreds of rules on the books and anything that isn't a rule is covered under six-dash-one, disobeying a verbal order."

"You make that sound like a bad thing," he said as he strode down the cell block, glancing in each cell as he passed.

Rayla stared at his wide back as she searched for the right words. He was at least Lance's size, maybe even bigger. She felt stupid giving him tips on the job. He'd probably be her superior within a year or two. The department loved promoting the big ones, especially those with a mean streak.

"Not at all," she said. "I guess what I'm saying is to pick your battles."

The trainee paused to glare into a cell. A young black kid was beating on his locker and rapping. The music suddenly stopped. The trainee continued down the tier. Rayla followed.

"Look," she said, "everybody has their own approach. I'm not here to punish. Prison is its own punishment. Some of these guys will die in here."

He shot her a look over his shoulder. "I'm heartbroken."

She ignored his sarcasm. "As long as they don't hurt themselves or a staff member and they show me respect, I can overlook some of the small stuff."

Movement in her peripheral piqued her attention, causing her to double-take and freeze as the trainee continued to saunter down the cell block unconcerned.

The inmate in 208 was shirtless and standing two feet from the doorway, his eyes glowed against the shadowy backdrop of his cell, his fingers curled around the bulbous veiny stump of his erect penis. He *could* have been urinating except that the toilet was behind him in the corner of the cell. *Scratching himself? Applying jock itch cream?* She quickly ran through and discarded every potential explanation as she turned to face him.

Emboldened by her silence, he took a small step forward, locking eyes with her as he continued to stroke himself. The wet rhythmic slapping of lotion and friction, mixed with the sound of his heavy breathing filled the cell. The smell of cocoa butter wafted toward her. Sweat trickled down his tattooed chest.

She glanced in the direction of her backup. He was almost to the end of the tier. *No help there.* Suddenly her training took over. She jammed her left thumb into the panic button fastened to her belt while her right hand unsnapped the canister of pepper spray. She held it out in front of her.

"Really?" she hissed. "You're gonna try me like that? Put it away!" she ordered. "Now!"

His voice was like a snake sliding through the undergrowth. "Come on baby, you know you like it."

She fumbled for her radio. "Hotel Dorm to Nine Alpha and all available units. I've got a one-dash-six in progress on wing one, requesting immediate assistance."

"Aw baby, don't be like that …" he said, taking another step forward and stroking furiously.

She aimed the pepper spray at his contorted face. "Cut it out!" she demanded.

"Just ten more seconds," he pleaded, "stand right there."

She hit him with three successive bursts, all to the face. The chemical agent caused him to stagger backwards and blink. He was supposed to fall to the floor screaming and clawing at his eyes. Instead he shook his head and smiled.

"Spray some of that down here," he said, his fist still clenching his erection, pulling it wildly and aiming it at her.

"They'll be here any second," she said, clutching the radio in one hand and the canister of pepper spray in the other. Her own voice sounded shrill in her ears.

"You're right," he said, releasing his penis and wiping his face with the back of his hand.

She couldn't believe he was so unaffected by the gas. She'd witnessed men crying and screaming for help from a lot less.

"I'm wastin' my time jackin' off." He paused and spat on the cell wall. "I'm going to lock-down anyway, might as well make it worth somethin'."

He sprang forward, pulling her into the cell by her hair. She repeatedly mashed the spray button, holding it where she thought his eyes were. He grunted and knocked the canister from her hand. She swung her radio and caught him square in the temple. He stumbled to one knee, blind from the pepper spray and disoriented from the headshot.

She sensed the presence of someone behind her, filling the doorway to the cell. She jumped, thinking it was another inmate.

"What's all this?" the trainee asked, blinking repeatedly.

Suddenly the overpowering chemical taste of the gas was in her mouth. She leaned over and coughed, almost puked, then straightened and launched a vicious kick into the downed inmate's nuts. He whimpered and fell to his side.

"Hey!" the trainee shouted, unsure of what to do.

The sound of jangling keys, shouting voices and pounding footfalls filled the dorm.

She leaned against the wall and brushed a sweaty strand of hair from her face. "Cuff him," she said.

The trainee removed the handcuffs from his belt and knelt next to the inmate, forcing him to his stomach and twisting his arms behind his back. She was relieved to hear the loud clicking of the cuffs tightening around his wrists.

"Everybody in their cells! Move! Now!" a voice thundered. "Officer Broxson, what's your 20?"

Rayla walked to the doorway of the cell and waved before lapsing into another coughing fit.

"208," a voice called over the squawking radios and slamming cell doors. "She's in 208."

Suddenly her coworkers stormed past her into the cell. She walked to the railing of the tier and willed herself to breathe. Behind her the muffled sounds of kicks and punches echoed from the cell walls. The roar of unchecked testosterone swelled. She understood that this wasn't simply about a female officer being disrespected. This was about the wife of Sergeant Lance Broxson being disrespected.

A white shirt appeared beside her and leaned against the railing; her shift supervisor, Captain Holland. He allowed the violence to continue for a few moments before finally putting a stop to it.

"All right that's enough," he announced with a voice like a cement mixer. "Let's get him over to confinement."

The dull thudding and oomph of blows ceased and was replaced by heavy breathing as the inmate was dragged to his feet. His swollen face was covered in the orange chemical agent and bright red blood. He was pulled roughly from the cell.

"Aw, hell," said the captain, "somebody shove his dick back in his pants."

Rayla turned away.

"You okay?" asked Captain Holland.

She nodded.

"How'd the rookie do?" he asked.

She glanced over at the trainee who was still standing inside the cell. "He did fine," she said. "The 10-15 was cuffed and subdued by the time our backup arrived."

The captain gave a thumbs up to the trainee. "Good work," he said before turning back to Rayla. "Who sprayed him?"

"I did," she said.

"Make sure you do the 'use of force' paperwork. Might as well show the rookie how to do it while you're at it."

"Yes sir," she said.

He turned to leave. "And write the disciplinary report before you go home. One-dash-six, right?"

She nodded.

"Fucking pervert."

She watched him go.

"Thank you," said the trainee from behind her.

"For what?" she asked.

"For not telling him I left you."

She shrugged. "Just don't do it again."

"I won't," he assured her.

Suddenly her churning stomach sent a surge of vomit up her throat. She pushed past the confused trainee and went back in the cell. She gripped the stainless steel toilet and emptied her lunch into the dirty water below, dry heaving when there was nothing left. Rayla hated to throw up. It was the main reason she didn't drink. There was something about the lack of control that was frightening, the body taking over, imposing its will.

Finished, she tucked a sweaty strand of hair behind her ear and rinsed her mouth in the sink.

"Now we have two secrets," she said as she walked past the massive trainee and made her way down the tier.

He rushed to catch up. "So, what is a one-dash-six?"

She paused on the first step of the stairwell and looked up at him. "Masturbation or intentionally exposing the genitals to a staff member. Sixty days in confinement and ninety days loss of gain time."

2

Strawberry Wine

She was cooking dinner when headlights flashed across the windows of their double wide. She heard the engine cut, a door slam and the familiar sound of boots on the deck. The door squeaked open and Lance ducked beneath the frame.

"Hey beautiful," he said.

"Where were you?" she asked.

He held up a six-pack of Bud Light. "Walmart."

"I was worried," she said.

He smiled and opened the fridge. "You worry too much."

She stirred the mashed potatoes. "I had to deal with a gunner today … in H-Dorm."

He walked behind her and gathered her in his strong arms. He smelled like coffee and cigarettes. He gave her a squeeze and kissed the top of her head. "I heard you did real good, baby. I'm proud of you."

His hands began to wander. She allowed herself to enjoy it for a moment before wiggling free of his grasp. He groaned behind her as she walked over to the kitchen table and emptied the steaming potatoes into a bowl.

She sat down and smiled at him. "Hungry?"

He grabbed a beer and pulled out a chair. "Starvin'."

They ate in silence. The *Jeopardy* theme song on the living room TV meshed with a far off barking dog and the remaining neighborhood kids playing in the street. She felt her husband's eyes on her as she forced herself to eat.

The Broxsons resided on a dead-end street, one block past the training building. The bright lights and gun towers of Pine Grove Correctional Institution were visible from the bedroom window of their trailer.

Rayla hated living in staff housing. When she first became a correctional officer she vowed to keep her personal life and her professional life separate. Six years later, she was married to a sergeant and living in a trailer park on the prison grounds. It had its advantages. Low custody inmates cut the grass, rent was dirt cheap and the crime rate was non-existent. But then so was the privacy.

"So who told you?" she asked.

He lit a cigarette. "Huh?"

She set down her fork. "When I told you about the gunner in H-Dorm you said 'you heard.' Who told you?"

He drained his bottle and belched loudly before wiping his mouth on the back of his hand. "Jessie," he said.

She fought off her initial response. Jessica Maldonado lived two lots over in a rusty dilapidated trailer with toys and bikes strewn carelessly over the front yard. A notorious hard partier, a pill head and a slut, most of the male officers at the prison eventually made their way through Jessie Maldonado's bedroom. Her last husband, the fourth by Rayla's count, returned home from Afghanistan to find her in bed with his best friend. Needless to say, she was single again. Rayla bristled at the thought of her talking to Lance.

"Oh," she said. "When did you talk to Jessie?"

He took another drag, "This afternoon."

She rotated the small gold watch on her wrist, a graduation gift from her Mema. Rayla hated the fact that she was jealous, especially of someone like Jessica, but she and Lance had barely been married a year and he did have a reputation as a ladies' man before they began dating.

"Where?" she asked in a small voice, hating the way she sounded.

He didn't respond.

"Where?"

"Where what?" he asked, stubbing his cigarette out in the leftover mashed potatoes.

"Where did you talk to her?"

"By the goddamn mailbox. What the hell does it matter?" He stood up abruptly, knocking his chair over and stomped down the hall to their bedroom.

Rayla flinched as the dresser drawers were flung open then slammed shut. She got up and began to clear the table, silently berating herself for starting another argument. She glanced at her wedding ring as she set the dishes in the sink.

Two years ago if someone had told her that she would, one day, be Mrs. Lance Broxson she would have laughed in their face. She was not some naïve little bumpkin fresh off the turnip truck. Lance was not her type. Tall and broad shouldered with intense blue eyes and dark wavy hair, he was beautiful to look at but then so were tigers and other predators in the wild. She knew better.

It was hard to keep secrets in a tight knit community like Corrections. Lance never bothered trying. During her first years at the prison she heard all the rumors. Lance Broxson was a player, a heartless, self-centered ladies' man that darted from conquest to conquest like a toxic butterfly leaving a trail of broken homes and hearts in his wake.

She dampened a rag and began to wipe down the kitchen table. *Jeopardy* transitioned to *Wheel of Fortune* in the living room. The bathroom door slammed down the hall and the muffled sound of the shower rushed in the background.

WITH ARMS UNBOUND

It had taken Lance the better part of four years to get around to her, not that she cared at the time. It was partly because they worked on different shifts but Rayla knew it was also because it had simply taken him that long to notice her. Lance gravitated toward big hair, big busts, and lots of makeup. Rayla was plain in every way.

She hung the dishcloth on the oven door and brushed her hands on her shorts before walking through the living room and out the front door. Although it was dark out, the air was still thick and humid. She sat down on the top step and listened to the crickets.

The first time Lance asked her out she politely sidestepped the question and left him standing in the parking lot at shift change. She would always remember the befuddled look on his face in the rearview of her Honda as he watched her pull off. She wanted nothing to do with Lance Broxson but she didn't want him for an enemy either. He was a rising star in the Department and his circle was the "in" crowd. While Rayla had no aspirations of being a part of that circle, she also did not want to draw its ire. Things like promotion, post assignment, and shift designation inevitably came down to whether the brass liked you or not and the brass hunted, fished, and drank with Lance Broxson. Rejecting him would have to be handled delicately.

The problem was that he wouldn't take no for an answer. After grilling her coworkers to ensure that she was, in fact, not a lesbian, he began pursuing her relentlessly. There were flowers constantly appearing on her windshield after work. He had somehow gotten her number and ambushed her answering machine. There were teddy bears and chocolate and embarrassingly bad attempts at poetry.

In the end, it was a scene straight from a Hollywood script that did her in. Her car had died in a torrential downpour two miles from the prison. She couldn't get a signal on her cellphone and the occasional passing cars flew by unconcerned. Suddenly Lance's Silverado burst through the storm like a hero galloping to the rescue. She slunk deeper in her seat as he slowed his truck and made a U-turn. He swaggered up to the passenger side of her car and tapped on the window. She reached over and unlocked the door. He was smiling as he climbed in. A day's growth of stubble peppered his strong jaw and the rain plastered his white t-shirt against his chiseled body. "Need a hand?"

He fixed her car himself. He even bought the parts. But as the saying goes, 'Nothing in life is free.' His price was a date.

She tried not to like him. She fought to maintain her perception of him as a pompous, selfish asshole. But five minutes into their first evening together, at a small Italian trattoria on the outskirts of Tallahassee, her resolve began to crumble. The most handsome man in the restaurant was sitting across from her. His sapphire eyes sparkled as he sipped his wine, his southern voice was rich and deep as he complimented her dress, his teeth flashed white against his tan skin when he smiled. She braced herself for cocky arrogance when he spoke but instead found a quiet humility. She was surprised by how comfortable and natural it felt to be alone with him and how quickly the hours flew by. When the restaurant closed and they walked to his truck, she had a new understanding of Lance Broxson.

They kissed on the next date. She had spent the entire week convincing herself and anyone who would listen that they were just friends, but his warm lips and strong arms put an end to that. She still maintained a token resistance for the next few dates, but they both knew it was futile. The walls were crumbling.

They made love for the first time by the river in the bed of his pickup. Even now, eighteen months later, the memory was fresh, each scene vivid. She could still smell the pines and hear Deana Carter singing Strawberry Wine on the radio. His kiss was somehow gentle and overpowering at the same time. She could feel the lust and hunger pulsating through his embrace, humming in his powerful biceps, hot in his fingertips. She remembered his lips brushing against the skin of her throat, then soft kisses on her collarbone; the sight of her own breast, pale in the moonlight, her nipple pink and upturned, suddenly disappearing under his warm mouth. She remembered her skirt around her waist, his hand cupping her through the moist material of her panties, pushing him away only to feel him return, again and again, until she finally surrendered...

The door opened. She jumped.

Lance frowned at her. "You know I've gotta go in at 11 tonight. Are you gonna go to sleep mad?"

Rayla stared at the porch light across the street. "I'm not mad. You're the one who stormed off."

"I just hate it when you accuse me."

"Accuse you of what?" She turned toward him. "I haven't accused you of anything."

He exhaled. "Look, I know you've had a rough day. Why don't you let me give you a back massage before I go. Help you sleep good." He held out his hand to help her up.

She rolled her eyes but accepted it. In their entire year of marriage she had never received a back massage that lasted more than three minutes. Lance was horny. Fine.

3

The Visit

It was after two in the morning when Lance left his post and walked across the compound toward the confinement unit. The bright searchlight from tower two tracked his movement.

He smiled up at the new girl as he passed. "Momma always said I'd be in the spotlight someday."

He heard her giggle through the open window as she popped the center gate and allowed him passage. He slammed it shut behind him.

The Administrative Confinement Unit was a flat, two wing, one story structure that sat between the medical building and perimeter fence. The hallways were dark, narrow and poorly lit. Unlike the reinforced steel doors of Disciplinary Confinement, the animals on administrative lockdown resided behind bars. In the 90s the building was named X-Dorm, but after an inmate was beaten to death in another X-Dorm down in the triangle and the five guards who killed him were acquitted, the bigwigs in Tallahassee decided it would be a good PR move to rename all X-Dormitories in the state. Lance smirked at the stenciled black "Y" over the front door of the building.

Y-Dorm, he thought, *what a load of shit.* The door buzzed and he stepped inside.

Jarvis met him in the hall. "Hey Sarge."

Lance nodded. "Where's he at?"

"Wing two."

"Let's go," said Lance.

Lance Broxson and Clayton Jarvis had known each other since kindergarten. They grew up exploring the endless acres of woodland in Conrad County. Lance still had the tent they camped in as boys and the arrowhead Jarvis had given him for his twelfth birthday.

By their senior year in high school they had both grown tall, but Jarvis was a small mountain at six-foot-five, three hundred ten pounds. When Lance was named quarterback of the football team, Jarvis played left tackle and protected his blindside. Fifteen years later, Clayton Jarvis was still fiercely loyal to Lance. They were like brothers.

The whine of the exhaust fans camouflaged their footsteps. The exit light at the end of the hall splashed red over the cinderblocks beneath it. Jarvis stopped twirling his Maglite and began shining it in the passing cells. Breakfast was still a few hours away and most of the inmates were sleeping. Those still awake glared back defiantly into the harsh beam of the flashlight but none uttered a complaint. They knew better.

Lance paused to pull the black leather gloves from his pocket. He was tightening the Velcro straps when Jarvis stopped in front of the last cell on the wing and began to chuckle. His immense belly convulsed with stifled laughter as he turned to Lance and shook his head. "Told you he was plum crazy."

Lance stood next to his friend and looked through the bars. The inmate sat Indian style on the floor beside the toilet, wearing only a pair of boxers. He held a toothbrush in both hands, extending it out over the commode. A string was tied to the end and hung down into the water.

"What the hell is he doing?" asked Lance.

Jarvis kept the flashlight pointed in the cell. "He's fishin' Sarge, can't ya tell? Shhh, don't talk too loud. You'll scare them off."

Lance watched him for a moment longer before nodding to Jarvis who reached behind his back for the handcuffs.

"Hey Hemingway," Jarvis called, "set down that fishin' pole and come over here and cuff up."

The inmate continued to stare into the toilet.

"Hey dumbfuck!" said Jarvis. "Did you hear me? You've got about two seconds to get your ass to these bars."

"For what?" the voice in the cell rasped. "To make it easier for you to beat me down? To kill me? Fuck that."

"Open the door," Lance growled.

Jarvis glanced at him uncertainly.

"Now," ordered Lance.

The inmate leapt to his feet as the keys jingled. Facing them, gripping the toothbrush like a weapon, Lance could see the filed pointy tip in the beam of the flashlight. The bars swung open.

He shook his head as he entered the cell, smiling.

"Careful," said Jarvis from behind him.

Lance ignored him, focused instead on the danger in front of him. He lived for this shit. "So let me get this straight," he said, smiling at the inmate, smelling his fear, reveling in it. "First you jack off in front of my wife, then you disobey Officer Jarvis's verbal order to cuff up, and now you threaten me with a weapon." He paused and shook his head. "You ain't too bright are you boy?"

"I wanna see the psych doctor," the inmate said. "I gotta psych emergency."

Even from across the cell Lance could smell his rancid breath, the stench of his body, his sour feet. "Doctor's gone for the night," he said, taking a step forward.

"Well then I wanna see the captain!"

"Yeah, well, the captain don't want to see you." Another step.

The man was a cornered rat. His eyes glowed in the dark cell as he clenched the sharpened toothbrush. Lance could have easily incapacitated him with the canister of mace that hung from his belt, just as his wife had done earlier in the afternoon. But mace was for weaklings and frightened women. It was an odds evener, a playing field leveler. He had used it before. Many times. But never in self-defense. Lance Broxson only used pepper spray to break, to torture, and even then, only after he had physically imposed his will.

He snatched the pillow from the empty top bunk and took another step. "Officer Jarvis," he called over his shoulder, "close the door."

"Come on Lance," Jarvis protested.

"Do it."

The cell door slammed shut.

"Please," begged the inmate, the shank still clutched in his trembling hand. "I don't want no problems."

"You don't want no problems?" said Lance. "Now that's not very *gangsta*. I bet you've bragged a thousand times to your homeboys about a situation just like this. How you wish you could just get five minutes alone with some asshole guard. Man to man, toe to toe." Lance took another step. "Now here we are, locked in this cell, opportunity of a lifetime, *and you don't want no problems?*"

The inmate raised the shank. "Back the fuck up, man."

"That's it," said Lance. "Stab me."

Suddenly he sprang forward, ripping downward with the shank. Lance met him with the pillow and drove him backwards into the wall. The toothbrush fell to the floor. Lance hammered him into the corner in a torrent of elbows, knees, and fists, feeling the rush of rage surge throughout his body. He then dragged him to the toilet and forced his head down in the water. He barely moved.

Keys jingled, the door opened and Jarvis was pulling him back. "Jesus Christ, Lance! You're gonna kill him!"

He slumped against the wall and caught his breath as the pounding rage subsided. Jarvis was standing over him. His eyes flicked to the inmate, broken and draped over the toilet like a hung-over drunk. The sound of blood dripping from his face down into the dirty toilet below ticked like the second hand of a clock. His groans, hollow and muffled, reverberated in the bowl.

Lance straightened and took a deep breath. "I'm okay."

Jarvis removed his cap and mopped the sweat from his brow with a forearm. "You sure?"

Lance nodded and reached in his uniform pocket for his buck knife. With a flick of the wrist it was open.

"Aw shit," said Jarvis.

"I just need you to hold him still," said Lance, kicking the inmate from the toilet and rolling him over with a polished black boot.

"You're taking this too far."

"I've got it under control."

"We could lose our jobs ... or worse."

"Clayton, shut the hell up and do like I tell you so we can get the fuck out of here."

Jarvis reluctantly lumbered over to where the inmate lay groaning on the floor. He shined the flashlight on him. His swollen face was smeared with blood. "I think he's dying."

"He'll be all right," said Lance. "Hand me that flashlight."

"Why?"

"Because, goddamn it, you can't hold him and the flashlight at the same damn time. Now quit being stubborn and get with the program!"

Jarvis handed him the Maglite and he positioned it on the bed so that its beam illuminated the cell floor. "Now get behind him and hold him still."

The man mumbled and coughed as Jarvis slid behind him and sat him up, wrapping a massive arm around his throat.

Lance straddled his legs and dug his hand down the front of his boxers, pulling out the inmate's uncircumcised penis.

"Jeez Lance!" whispered Jarvis. "Have you gone crazy?"

Lance ignored him, staring instead into the wide open terrified eyes of the man they were restraining, the man who disrespected his wife. He laid the blade against the shaft. "Can you hear me, you fucking piece of shit?"

The inmate nodded vigorously.

"That was my wife you assaulted today. Did you know that?"

He shook his head.

Lance pushed the teeth of the blade harder into his flesh. "The world would be a better place if I cut you into little pieces and flushed you down that toilet." Lance paused and stared at him for a few long seconds. "But I'm not going to do that."

Jarvis exhaled. "Oh, thank God."

"But if I ever hear about you exposing yourself to a female employee again," the knife pressed harder, "I promise I will transfer to whatever prison you're at, cut this off and stick it up your ass. Do you understand me?"

More vigorous nodding.

"Good." Lance released him and stood. "Let's go Jarvis."

The inmate remained on the floor trembling violently as they exited the cell.

"Oh," said Lance, "one more thing. If you ever mention this to anyone, Officer Jarvis here will kill you." He slammed the door. "Sleep tight."

4

A Sensitive Man

Rayla checked her makeup in the rearview before opening the car door. The midnight shift had begun trickling through the front gate of the prison. She looked for Lance.

The worst part of working different shifts was having to sleep alone. Ever since Lance had been assigned to midnights Rayla had trouble sleeping. She was grateful that they at least shared the same days off, but recently Lance had been using that time to go hunting with Jarvis. She didn't get to see him enough.

She hated being so clingy. Before Lance, she was disgusted by that type of behavior in other women and vowed never to act that way. Yet here she was, not even a full year into marriage, needy and emotional as hell.

It was just that there were only twenty-four hours in a day and after her eight hour shift and his eight hour shift were subtracted, the remaining hours flew by too fast, especially if there were errands to run or, *God forbid,* Lance wanted to go drink at The Spur.

A nurse waved as she passed Rayla's car. Rayla smiled and waved back.

She hated herself for exposing her jealousy regarding Jessica Maldonado the night before, for pressing him on the issue. *That bitch*, she thought.

The parking lot came to life around her. Cars were pulling in and out. Many of her coworkers were making their way to the gate. She remained in her car, door open, one boot on the asphalt, one on the floorboard, waiting for her husband.

She did not regret falling for Lance. She knew people were whispering when they started dating but now, after almost a year of marriage, his playboy past was buried. He deserved her trust. He fought for it and earned it. More than anything, she felt guilty when she was jealous. And weak.

But Lance had been acting strangely lately. Especially in the bedroom. He used to be so gentle and passionate and attentive. Lately he was rough. And quick. *No Rayla*, she thought. *Not lately… just last night and he was probably in a rush to get the hell out of there before you started interrogating him again.*

"Excuse me, Officer Broxson?"

She jumped. It was the trainee from H-Dorm. His uniform shirt was tight and his muscles bulged beneath the light brown material. Even the ripples of his abs were evident. She looked away.

He rested an arm on the roof of her car and leaned over her. "I just wanted to apologize once more. I … I underestimated you."

"It's fine," said Rayla.

"No," he said, "it's not. I just figured that you were still behind me and when I turned around, you weren't there. If something would have happened to you, I–"

"Hey," said Rayla, "I've been doing this awhile. I can handle myself."

"Oh I know you can," he said. "You're… you're amazing."

Rayla felt her face redden.

"I think she's pretty amazing too," said a deep clear voice. "That's why I married her."

Rayla turned and saw her husband's belt buckle pressed against the passenger window of her car.

"Now is there a reason why you're hovering over my wife?" Lance asked.

The trainee backed away from the car and raised his palms. "Hey man, I didn't–"

"Man?" Lance snarled. "My name is Sergeant Broxson, *Boy*, and I'm a little sensitive about people trying to fuck my wife."

"Lance!" Rayla exclaimed.

"Sir, I'm sorry, I wasn't trying to–"

Lance pounded the roof of her car. "Shut up!"

Rayla had enough. She grabbed her bag and slammed the car door, glaring at Lance. The trainee was already hurrying off toward the gate.

"If I ever catch you talking to Rayla again, I'm going to show you how useless all those steroids are!" Lance called behind him.

"You're making a scene," said Rayla.

"And you're late for work," said Lance as he headed to his truck. "I'll deal with you later."

5

A Visit from Hollis Fretwell

Like most Florida prisons built during the War on Drugs era, Pine Grove Correctional Institution had three gun towers. Tower one presided over the front gate of the prison, tower two sat in the center of the compound, and tower three was located on the opposite end of the property at the entrance to the rec yard.

Many officers dreaded being assigned to the towers, preferring the freedom of inside security or a dormitory post; Rayla loved it. There were no inmates to nag her for request forms or ibuprofen every five minutes, no psychotic predators exposing themselves (at least none that she could see), no trainees, no boss looking over her shoulder. Just the occasional curious bird, the sound of her own thoughts and the endless miles of trees and sky. On a clear day she could almost see the Gulf of Mexico.

Of course, the cold reality of her job description was that it was her responsibility to shoot any inmate who attempted to scale the fences that surrounded the prison.

With an assault rifle.

Deep down she wasn't sure if she could pull the trigger on another human being, but she doubted she'd ever have to. The lone inmate who ever attempted to hit the fence in the entire history of the prison got so hung up in the razor wire that by the time they finally extracted him, he looked like he'd been attacked by mountain lions. And that was long before she worked there anyway.

The overwhelming majority of correctional officers in the state of Florida would only get to fire their weapons at the shooting range. Rayla was fine with that. In fact she was certified as an expert marksman.

It was the middle of summer and the rec yard was bustling with activity. The basketball and volleyball courts were all in use. Loose lines formed behind the pull-up and dip bars. Joggers weaved their way past walkers on the track. The tables were full of card players. Loners and lovers dotted the sea of grass that was once the softball outfield. Rayla watched it all through binoculars and saw none of it. Her mind was on Lance.

Wishing she hadn't left her cell in the car, she picked up the phone.

"Control room," said a female voice.

"Hey Dottie, this is Rayla. Will you give me an outside line?"

"Sure baby," said Dottie, "hang on a sec."

There was a click followed by a dial tone. Rayla tried the house phone first, then Lance's cell.

Nothing.

She placed the phone in its cradle and chewed on her bottom lip. *Where is he?* She wanted to explain to him that her conversation with the trainee in the parking lot was innocent and harmless. That he was being silly, that she had no interest in anyone else.

She thought about the scene from that morning, the squiggly vein on his temple, the way his blue eyes darkened and narrowed, the trainee almost tripping over a parking bumper as he hurried away. She began to giggle.

She knew it was mean and she did feel bad for the poor trainee who was dumb enough to call her *amazing* in front of

Lance. But at the core of her husband's embarrassing overprotective jealous tirade, she found reassurance. At least she wasn't the only insecure one in the relationship.

"Officer Broxson," a voice cut through her thoughts.

She stood and opened the window. There at the foot of her tower, shielding his eyes from the sun as he looked up at her was Hollis Fretwell, the institutional inspector.

He waved.

She held up a finger then grabbed her keys from the peg. She fastened them to a clip, double checked them to ensure they wouldn't slip off, then lowered them on a cable down to the waiting inspector. There was only one set of keys to each tower, for security purposes.

Fretwell quickly removed the keys from the cable and she pulled it back up. She could hear his feet on the spiral staircase as she straightened her desk.

The Office of the Inspector General and its institutional designees operated independently of the Department of Corrections. Similar to internal affairs, they had the power to suspend, fire, and place officers under arrest, as well as lock up inmates in administrative confinement for long stretches of time. They had snitches in both blue and brown and were equally distrusted and disliked by both sides.

"I hear you had a little problem in Hotel Dorm yesterday," he said as he reached the top of the stairs.

She shrugged. "Just a gunner."

He shook his head. "Sick bastards. Seems like we're seeing more and more of that every year."

She nodded and handed him the log book.

He glanced at his watch before signing it. "I also hear that you didn't get much help from the new guy. What's his name? Redmon?"

She looked at him sharply. "Where'd you hear that?"

He smiled as he passed the log book back to her. "A little birdie."

She watched as he leaned forward on his knuckles and surveyed the sprawling rec yard below. His shoulder blades jutted from his narrow back and strained against his polyester shirt. His underarms were dark with rings of moisture that seemed to expand as she watched. His khaki pants were wrinkled and ended just above his scuffed loafers where a swath of white from his socks was visible. She could feel his cold eyes assessing her in the reflection of the tower window.

"Nice view," he said.

"Am I in trouble for something?" she asked.

He turned and smiled. "Spoken like a true Broxson. Screw the pleasantries and cut straight to the red meat of the matter."

She didn't respond.

"Okay, fair enough," he said. "No, you're not in trouble. I just need to ask you a few questions. About Lance."

"Is Lance in trouble?"

He studied her for a long moment. "Not yet."

"Why not talk to him?"

"I plan on it," he said, obviously annoyed. "Now, yesterday, when you told your husband about the incident in H-Dorm. How did he react?"

"We didn't talk about it."

"I find that very hard to believe," he said, hopping up on the counter and leaning against the tower window. "By now every inmate and every officer on this compound are buzzing about it. Surely it was a hot topic at the dinner table last night."

"I may have mentioned it in passing," she said.

"*In passing,*" he echoed, a smile in his voice. "You get attacked by a masturbating psychopath and end up having to take him down single-handedly because your backup is off chasing butterflies and you 'may have mentioned it in passing' to your husband? Come on now, Rayla."

"I don't know where you're getting your information, but somebody's lying to you."

"You're right about that," he interrupted, "somebody's definitely lying."

"The trainee, Officer Redmon, actually subjugated the inmate. He's the one who cuffed him, and as far as my conversations with my husband are concerned, we try not to discuss work at home. Not that it's any of your business."

Hollis Fretwell laughed. "Subjugate, huh? Now there's a word you don't hear too often. Not around here at least."

"It's in the training manual," Rayla said quietly.

"I bet it is," said Fretwell, his laughter trailing off. "You know what else is in the manual? Rules that prohibit abuse."

He stared hard at her. She didn't look away.

"Are you accusing me of abuse?" she asked.

"No," he sighed, running his fingers through his brown thinning hair. "Look, Rayla, the nurse found your secret admirer on the floor of his cell this morning. His jaw was broken, his ribs were cracked, and apparently there was some internal bleeding."

Outside the window, a whistle blew. The perimeter truck moved slowly along the fence line, a far-off jet carved a thin white line into the cloudless sky.

"The inmate said he was roughed up yesterday afternoon before he was taken to confinement. I think he's full of shit. I think your husband may have paid him a friendly visit sometime after midnight. Do you know anything about that?"

Rayla shook her head.

"Last night, when you told him what happened, did he get angry? Maybe he mentioned getting revenge?"

"I told you we didn't discuss it."

"You said you mentioned it in passing."

"Yeah, well I don't remember his response," said Rayla, "so I guess you're going to have to ask him."

Hollis Fretwell's face reddened and his thin lips pursed into a tight white circle of lines.

"You know," he said, sliding off the counter and smoothing his rumpled khakis, "even if I prove this, the worst thing that'll happen to Lance is a reprimand. Maybe a probationary period."

Thank God, she thought, willing her face to remain expressionless.

"But I won't forget your flippant disrespectful attitude. I would have never expected this from you."

"I told you the truth," she said, rising to her feet. She suddenly realized he was only a few inches taller than she was. She had always thought of him as taller.

"You are willfully impeding an investigation," he said as he moved toward the stairs. "You better hope your name never comes across my desk because if it does, for even the slightest infraction, I promise you'll be back to bagging groceries at the Piggly Wiggly and not even your husband will be able to save your job."

She listened to his footsteps disappear down the metal staircase.

"IGA," she mumbled under her breath. "I worked at the IGA, asshole."

6

Coke Slurpees and Bologna

After work, she made her way to her car and was the first one out of the parking lot. She drove slowly past the turn-off to the row of trailers where she lived, but when she didn't see Lance's truck in the driveway, she smashed the gas. The car leaped forward. She pulled the scrunchy from her ponytail and let her hair whip in the wind as she roared toward Highway 20.

Gretchen Wilson was on the radio. She turned the volume knob as far as she could to the right and sang along at the top of her lungs.

She swung into a convenience store in Pine Grove and bought a large Coke Slurpee and a pack of bologna before driving across the Chattahoochee River. After a few miles she turned down a side street, made a series of lefts and rights, went over the railroad tracks and pulled onto the dirt road that dead-ended into the driveway of an old green two-story house with a wrap-around porch and a towering oak in the center of the yard.

A small dog came flying down the steps and bounded across the grass. She knelt and braced herself.

"Hey Mydog!"

He went airborne for the last few feet and landed in her arms, panting and sniffing and squirming and licking. She lost her balance and sat down hard in the dusty driveway, laughing as the little dog attempted to remove her makeup with his tongue.

"Mydog!" her Mema called from the porch. "Mydog, get off the poor girl."

He immediately hopped off her and sprinted toward the house, skidding to a stop halfway across the grass. He looked back at Rayla and whined. Then he darted back over to where she sat in the driveway and barked impatiently. *Let's go,* she imagined him saying. *What's the holdup?*

"Okay, okay," she said, struggling to her feet and brushing the dirt from her uniform pants.

"Damn dog ain't got no sense," said Mema as she opened the screen door and waited.

Rayla grabbed the Slurpee and bologna from the car and made her way across the lawn as Mydog yipped and jumped excitedly by her side at the sight of the familiar round package in her hand.

She remembered when the original Mydog first joined the family. A tiny squirming bundle wrapped in a warm blanket and presented to her Auntie in the outstretched arms of Preacher Lamb's handsome son, Mitchell.

Auntie was her Mema's older sister. She was already in the late stages of dementia when she came to live with them, but she fell in love with the puppy immediately and named him "My Dog" before he ever crossed the threshold of the house. And he was *her dog*. There was no doubt in Rayla's mind that Mydog intuitively understood that Auntie was special and required extra care and supervision. They were inseparable until the day she died. The little puppy now barking at her heels was actually the grandson of the original Mydog but he shared the namesake of his patriarch.

"Come on, boy," she said as they walked up the steps to the porch.

Mema eyed the cup in her hand as Rayla squeezed by and settled into a rocking chair. "Is that for me?" she asked.

Rayla smiled and passed her the cup. Mema loved Coke Slurpees. Rayla's earliest memory was walking the mile-and-a-half to the nearest convenience store in the hot Florida sun with her Mema to buy Coke Slurpees. She learned how to walk on those afternoon trips.

"Where's yours?" asked Mema, removing the lid and dipping the shovel-straw down into the icy concoction.

"They don't make Diet Coke Slurpees, Mema," said Rayla.

"Thank God for that," said the old woman, wrinkling her nose.

Rayla laughed as she bit a hole in the package of bologna and dug out a thin slice, tossing it over Mydog's head. He leaped, twisted and snatched it from the air, inhaling it whole before landing. Then he immediately sat motionless, awaiting round two. Focused.

They turned at the sound of an approaching engine. The mailman arrived in a cloud of dust and braked at the mailbox. Mr. Cummings had been driving the same mail route since her mother was a girl.

"Hey Hellfire!" he called. "'Bout time you came to visit your Mema."

Hellfire was the nickname he gave her when she was a shy little girl. It was meant as a joke, like calling a fat guy tiny or a tall guy shorty. There was nothing volatile about her. Nothing crazy. The craziest thing she ever did was marry Lance Broxson.

They waved as he pulled off.

"Why are you on a diet anyway?" asked Mema. "You're thin enough as it is."

"Not as thin as you," said Rayla. "I hope I've got your genes."

"I'd rather you have my good sense," said the old woman. "I always thought you did until–"

"Mema please don't start," said Rayla. "He's a good man."

"Oh, he's good all right," said her grandmother, shoveling a pile of colafied slush into her mouth. "Good for nothing."

"Mema!" said Rayla.

Mydog finally lost his patience and barked. Just once. Enough to remind Rayla that another piece of bologna was in order. She tossed a piece without looking.

"Rayla, I've never lied to you. Not about Santa Claus, not about where babies come from, not even about your own mom and dad. My gut tells me he's bad news. Hell, Mydog won't even go near him, and that damn dog would play fetch with the devil if a slice of bologna was involved."

Mydog barked at the mention of his name. Rayla absently flipped him another piece of meat. She wished Mema would accept Lance, but her grandmother was as stubborn as they come. To be fair, Lance wasn't exactly working overtime to be her BFF either.

"I know you don't like him," said Rayla. "I just wish you could…"

"Lie?" Mema volunteered.

"No," said Rayla, slumping in her chair, "I don't want you to lie. I just wish you could … conceal your feelings. Sometimes."

"That's lying," said Mema.

"Barely," said Rayla, staring at the oak tree she used to climb as a little girl. "It's just that if ya'll got along better, I'd be able to see you more."

"If you moved back home, you'd be able to see me more."

Rayla exhaled. "He's my husband Mema. I can't leave him." She glanced over at the woman who raised her. "And anyway, I wouldn't want to. I love him."

Mema reached over and patted her hand. "Baby, you don't love that asshole. You just made an impulsive decision. It happens to everybody."

Rayla stiffened. "It wasn't impulsive. We've been married a year and dated for six months before that."

"And before you started dating?" her grandmother asked innocently. "How'd you feel about him then? What was your initial impression? Your gut feeling?"

Rayla was silent.

"Listen," Mema said, "it doesn't matter what I say. How old were you when you stopped listening to me? Six? Seven? Climbing that God-forsaken oak tree over there, climbing and falling and crying and climbing some more. I swear I almost took a chain saw to the damn thing."

Rayla suddenly remembered the terror of falling, the rush of air, the blur of descent, the unforgiving ground knocking the breath from her lungs, the spinning sky above the tree branches.

"You were a stubborn child," said Mema. "You still are, but I realized a long time ago that I can't go around taking a chainsaw to everything that could hurt you. Even though I'd love to gas it up for that husband of yours," she laughed. "Sometimes the only way to learn is to fall."

Rayla tossed another slice to Mydog.

"Before I married your grandfather," said Mema, "I dated a few men. I was even engaged once. I spent a lot of time wondering if each was *the one*. But when Ray came along, I just knew. People say we have only one true love in a lifetime, a twin soul that fits like a missing puzzle piece. Your grandfather was mine. I think yours is still waiting in the wings."

"How do you know mine isn't Lance?"

Mema smiled. "Because I know you."

7

Stranger on the Couch

It was almost dark by the time she pulled onto her street. The sun was a dying bonfire that barely glowed over the distant jagged tree line to the west. A crossing cat paused in the middle of the road and stared into her headlights before sprinting to the safety of a neighbor's porch. The stench of the nearby landfill, dense and pungent, carried in the night air.

The lights in the trailer were out. She was relieved to see Lance's Silverado in the driveway. She turned off her car engine and grabbed the pizza from the passenger seat.

As she walked up the drive she could see the flickering light of the television through the curtains. She hoped he was over the incident in the parking lot that morning. She didn't feel like arguing. She had spent the entire day arguing first with Inspector Fretwell then with Mema. Arguing in his defense. *Always arguing in his defense.* Even when she was alone and the only voice arguing back was in her head.

There were dirty water coolers on the top step of the deck, blocking her passage. She was almost positive they didn't belong to Lance; she would have seen them before. She frowned and balanced the pizza box on the railing while she bent to move them out of the way.

"Lance," she called out.

There was no response.

She turned the knob and the door creaked open. She peeked her head inside. He was smoking in the dark. The flashing black and white images of the Andy Griffith show reflected against his face. The volume was turned all the way down.

"What are you doing silly?" she asked, closing the door behind her. "I got us a pizza for dinner."

He continued to stare at the TV.

Rayla chewed on her bottom lip. "It's Meatlovers, your favorite."

Nothing.

She set the box on the counter and walked over to the couch. "Lance? Baby? What is it?"

He was barefoot and shirtless. White ash was smeared into the brown material of his unbuttoned uniform pants. His chest rose and fell with his breath. Rayla reached for the end table lamp.

"Don't," he growled.

She froze. "What's wrong?"

Suddenly a raucous burst of laughter exploded from his mouth causing his head to rock back against the couch cushion. "What's *wrong?*" he asked, wiping his eyes. "Seriously?"

She turned on the light anyway.

He stopped laughing and looked at her for the first time. His stare was cold.

"Hell, nothing's wrong, Rayla. Nothing at all. I just love catching my wife flirting with other men."

Suddenly she understood. *He was pouting.* She sat down next to him and touched his shoulder, trying not to smile. "Is that what this is all about?"

He swatted her hand away. "I just love having my friends call and tell me about your little secret meetings with Hollis Fretwell in tower three."

"Secret meetings?" she sputtered. "He was interrogating me!" Rayla had heard enough. She jumped to her feet and was about to storm off when his hand clamped around her wrist and snatched her back down to the couch.

He shoved a finger against her nose, pressing it sideways. Hard. The blue in his eyes was gone, overtaken by dilated obsidian. One eyeball twitched spasmodically as he glared down at her.

"You're hurting me," she said, pushing his hand from her face and struggling to get up.

He pinned her to the couch with a massive forearm against her throat. "Listen to me."

She continued to struggle.

He slapped her.

It was neither loud nor hard. It wasn't even in her face. He got her just above the ear on the left side of her head. It was more of a *cuff* than a slap. But it didn't matter. It was the first time he ever hit her. She was stunned.

Her lip began to quiver and tears welled in her eyes. She didn't want to cry. Didn't want to give him the pleasure of knowing he was hurting her. The tears spilled over anyway. It was the way he smacked her. Like she was a disobedient dog.

He held her chin between his thumb and index finger. "I don't give a fuck what you say about me to that wrinkled old bitch across the river," he said, "but if I ever hear about you running your mouth to Fretwell again, I'll personally hand-deliver your resignation to the warden."

Rayla had never seen this side of him. At least not directed at her. "Lance, I don't even–"

He smashed a finger against her lips. "And if I ever catch you flirting with another man again," he leaned forward, pressed his mouth against her ear and breathed, "I'll knock your fucking teeth out."

8

A Tale of Two Bunkies

A line of twenty-seven men marched through center gate carrying their property and bedrolls. The newcocks were easy to spot: wide-eyed and stiff, with rumpled brown bags containing their few personal items. Most of the vets were toward the back of the line, grim-faced men who struggled beneath the weight of years of accumulated property.

The legal work was the worst. A decade's worth of denied motions, court transcripts, depositions, and stacks of case law could easily exceed a hundred pounds. Lugging it from prison to prison was like carrying around a boulder. Literally and figuratively.

Kevin Freeman stared at the twin bulging mesh bags slung over the shoulder of the man in front of him. They were stuffed with files the size of phone books.

He remembered those days – *the direct appeal, the 3.850, the First D.C.A., the State Supreme Court, the Federal Remedies* – each level, a bigger long shot than the last. Each denial, more debilitating. He spent his first five years in the law library researching case law, filing motions and watching the legal mail callout like a junkie watching the road for the headlights of his dealer's car. Hope is addictive like that.

But there's a freedom in saying *fuck it*, in accepting one's fate, in staring at the release date on that gain time slip and bowing to the inevitable. Four years earlier, after the Federal District Court of Appeals in Atlanta denied him without an opinion, Kevin ripped every legal document in his property into tiny little pieces and dumped them in the trash. Once the last stack was shredded and removed, he sat on his bed and gazed into his suddenly spacious foot locker. Gone was the possibility of ever getting a new trial, but so too was the heavy weight of hope…

Literally and figuratively.

As the line moved down the sidewalk, the rest of the prison paused and turned their eyes to the newcomers. Inside grounds men leaned on rakes and shovels. Conversations under the pavilion went silent. Shadows gathered in the dormitory windows.

Some men scanned the passing faces for old comrades from other prisons; others watched for the arrival of old enemies. Christians looked for new souls to win, sissies looked for new daddies, gangbangers looked for sheep to exploit.

Kevin kept his face hard and his eyes forward.

The line slowed to a stop.

"Freeman! Wessel! Step out!" called the guard who was escorting them.

Kevin stepped out of line. A skinny kid with thick glasses and a shaved sunburned head joined him.

"Freeman, huh?" drawled the guard. He was black with bloodshot eyes. The sides of his Stetson were rolled up and the front tilted slightly forward. "Ain't that some shit? A prisoner named Free man?"

Kevin shrugged.

"Ya'll two are going to Alpha Dormitory, low side. See Officer Broxson when you go in. She'll tell you your bunk numbers." He turned to the other inmates still in line. "Rest of ya'll, follow me."

Kevin slung his property over his shoulder and walked up the sidewalk to Alpha Dorm.

"Hey man, you been in prison awhile?" came a shaky voice from behind him.

He glanced over his shoulder. It was the skinny kid with the Coke bottle glasses. Wessel.

Kevin ignored him.

Wessel rushed to catch up. "I'm Eddie," he said, "Eddie Wessel, but everybody calls me Weasel. Do you know if they have a band room here? I heard some prisons have them is why I'm asking. I'm a bass player. Do you play? I'm kinda picking up that musician vibe off you. Star aura, I call it…"

Kevin stopped walking and glared at him. Weasel's words trailed off and his eyes, magnified by the powerful lenses of his glasses, blinked repeatedly.

"Oh," he said, "I'm talking too much. I always do that when I'm nervous. My friends say–"

"Are you gay?" Kevin interrupted.

Weasel frowned. "Am I … no."

"Do you want to be?" Kevin asked.

"Not particularly," said Weasel. "But if you are I won't hold it against you. I mean, lots of musicians–"

"Shut up," Kevin growled.

Weasel opened his mouth then shut it.

Kevin glanced behind them to see if anyone was listening. "Look," he said, his voice harsh, "I'm not friendly. You shouldn't be either. People in here see that as a weakness. Maybe you were too busy running your mouth on the way in to notice all the razor wire and gun towers, but this is a fucking prison."

Weasel swallowed hard and blinked some more.

Kevin exhaled and shook his head. "How long do you have?"

Weasel stared at the ground. "I… uh … life."

Kevin's face hardened again. "You're not a child molester are you?"

"No!" said Weasel.

Kevin looked down at his high water blues, his lanky awkward frame, the thick chomo glasses, his peeling sunbaked head. "Well you look like one," he said. "Listen Weasel, you're going to have a hard enough time as it is. There are probably people sizing you up through that window right now."

Kevin watched and waited as Weasel's eyes darted nervously toward the dormitory window. It was crowded with silhouettes. Predatory faces swam into view then disappeared just as quickly like sharks in the glass tank at SeaWorld.

"The less you speak, the longer it will take them to figure you out. That'll at least delay the inevitable."

He reached for the door handle.

"What should I do then?" Weasel asked from behind him.

The door buzzed. Kevin pulled it open and glanced back at him. "Get a big knife."

They stepped into the foyer. The door slammed shut behind them. Weasel winced. Kevin smirked. The universal clamor of an open-bay prison dorm enveloped them – running showers, flushing toilets, slamming dominoes, blaring television, high-pitched laughter, off-key singing, and the sustained crescendo of voices competing to be heard over the roar.

Kevin walked up to the officers' station, set his property down, and removed his ID tag from his shirt. Weasel followed. The guard in the bubble ignored them.

While waiting to be acknowledged, Kevin surveyed the living area of his new dorm. Hard faces stared back. Some smiled. Some scowled. He saw tattooed foreheads, nasty knife scars, arched eyebrows, burnt flesh, missing teeth, and the occasional normal face peering over the cover of a book or playing solitaire. But like any other prison, normalcy was the rare exception. Hostility was the rule.

"That guy just waved at me," said Weasel.

Kevin turned back to the officers' station. "Maybe he knows you," he said, watching the woman in the booth.

She must have felt his eyes on her because she held up a finger without looking. Kevin continued to study her through the glass. Her brown hair was pulled back in a braid. She sat with one leg folded under her as she leaned over the desk and wrote something in a folder. Her head was cocked to one side and she was biting her bottom lip. Her boots were small. Her eyelashes were long, and gold hoops dangled from her ears. His eyes traced over the delicate line of her throat, the gentle swell of her breasts, the feminine flare of her hip, the soft round curve of her ass.

After ten years in prison, it would be so easy for him to be swept up in longing, to let torturous desire wash over him like a desert monsoon. He felt the stirring deep within, but it flickered and died before it ever had a chance.

It was her uniform that did it. Hideous as a cluster of warts on the tip of her nose, more repulsive than a black tooth grin, her DOC brown and the abuse it represented reduced her to a grizzled hag in Kevin's opinion.

Not that she would ever give a flip about Kevin's opinion. She was trained to hate, to snuff out dignity, to belittle, to demean.

"Okay," she said, closing the folder and smiling as she walked over to the window where they waited. "Sorry about that, Wessel and Freeman, right?"

Weasel nodded dumbly while Kevin held his prisoner ID against the glass.

"Wessel, you're in bunk one-twelve upper. It's in the back left corner of the dorm," she said. "Freeman, you're in one-twelve lower."

He nodded and grabbed his property from the floor.

"We're bunkies!" said Weasel as they walked down the trash-littered aisle to the back of the dorm.

Conversations stopped and card games paused; one hundred fifty eyes tracked their movement.

"Lucky me," said Kevin.

9

By the Banks of the Chattahoochee

Rayla stood in front of the control room window, waiting to be let out. A group of her coworkers were babbling behind her but she didn't pay any attention. She rattled the gate impatiently and glanced up at the tower.

The locking mechanism released and the gate buzzed as she swung it open and headed for the parking lot. The voices of her coworkers trailed off as she made a beeline for her car.

"See you tomorrow, Rayla," somebody called behind her.

She pretended not to hear. A lot of officers enjoyed hanging around after the shift was over, gossiping. Not Rayla. She preferred to be the first one out of the parking lot. Eight hours a day in a prison were more than enough for her.

She dug in her bag for her keys as she walked down the row of cars and trucks. She could see the back bumper of her Accord peeking from behind a mud splattered 4-by-4 on jacked up tires. When she rounded it, she froze. Lance was sitting on the hood of her car.

"We need to talk," he said.

Rayla glared at him but said nothing. All day, the scene from the night before had been on auto-load in her head. His behavior was so strange, so uncharacteristic, so scary that she was still trying to process what happened and what she should do. A violent inmate was one thing. She could deal with that. An abusive husband was something altogether different.

She was in unchartered waters and there was nowhere to turn for guidance. Mema was out of the question; she already hated Lance and if she knew he had hit her and threatened her, she would go through the roof. It felt funny keeping anything from her grandmother, but she had no choice. Mema worried enough about her without any help. There were no friends to confide in either. Her few friends were also Lance's friends. She was on her own.

Lance slid off the hood of her car. His blue eyes were downcast and contrite. Muscles rippled beneath his shirt and his boots crunched against the loose rocks on the asphalt.

"Can we go for a drive?" he asked.

A car honked as it passed. Rayla stared at its brake lights. "I don't know," she said. "Are you gonna knock my teeth out?"

Lance blinked. His lashes touched then parted slowly. "I would never do that."

"That's not what you told me last night," she said, feeling the tears brim in her eyes, hating them. "I can't believe you hit me."

"I didn't hit you, Rayla," he said, reaching out and touching her face.

She brushed his hand away as the tears spilled over. "Well you slapped me!" she said. "Same shit, Lance."

"I didn't slap you. It was more of a push than anything. A hard push."

Rayla had heard enough. She forced her way past him, not caring if he hit her again, silently daring him to. Her fist was balled and her keys extended out from between each finger. He caught her off guard last night. That would never happen again.

"Rayla, please..." he begged as she got in her car and slammed the door.

The rest of his words were drowned out by the engine roaring to life and the loud country music on her radio. She threw the car in reverse and almost ran him over as she backed out.

She knew she was making a scene. The tower was watching, the control room was watching, her coworkers stood open-mouthed beside their cars. Her tires squealed as she shot out of the parking lot like Junior on a restart at Daytona.

The main road was empty. She barely even slowed to pull out. The landscape blurred as she accelerated. To her left were endless acres of brush and pine; to her right, a sea of grass and the prison parking lot.

Lance was sitting on a concrete yellow bumper with his head in his hands.

She stiffened her resolve and floored the Honda, reaching for the radio and cranking it even louder. The road wound its way around curves and sloped over rolling hills until she could no longer see the towers.

Her own eyes stared back at her accusingly as she slowed to a stop on the side of the road. *You're weak,* said a voice in her head. She slammed her palm against the steering column. Then she took a deep breath and made a U-turn, heading back to the prison.

Lance was still sitting in the parking lot, looking pitiful when she pulled up. She reached over and unlocked the door.

Her eyes were aimed straight ahead, trained on a splattered love-bug stuck to the windshield. She turned the radio off. Lance opened the door and slid in beside her.

"Thanks," he said.

They rode in silence, each wondering what the other was thinking. Rayla turned off on Highway 20 and drove until she reached Main Street. The boarded windows of local shops were everywhere, wilted under the grim shadow of the new Super Walmart. It made Rayla sad to see the empty parking lots and crumbling buildings.

Lance must have been thinking the same thing.

"Fuckin' Walmart's choking the life out of the town," he said.

Rayla didn't respond.

He shifted in his seat, trying to get comfortable. "It's a good thing they're not in the prison business. We're about the only thing they *haven't* shut down."

Rayla drove down a side street and cut over to a two-lane road. The town disappeared behind them and gave way to miles of endless flat farmland. She didn't really pay attention to where she was going until she saw the familiar orange clay of the cut-off up ahead.

Lance glanced over at her as she braked and turned off on the dirt road. The way was bumpy and the going was slow but after a series of narrow twists and a fork, they finally came to a bluff overlooking the river, the place where they made love for the first time. Rayla shut off the car.

"Talk," she said.

Lance exhaled. "I'm … I'm so sorry."

Rayla watched the river as he haltingly continued to grope for words.

"Rayla, you have to know I would never hurt you–"

"But you did, Lance," she interrupted. "You hurt me and you scared me. I don't want to be one of those women trapped in an abusive marriage." She paused and looked at him. "I refuse to be."

He grabbed her hand. "You think I want that for us? Come on Rayla, you know me better than that."

She pulled away. "I thought I did. Last night I had no idea who you were."

"Why did you choose this place?"

"Don't change the subject."

He sighed and looked out the window.

"You were a stranger last night," she said. "Your eyes were black and empty. You accused me of holding secret meetings with Fretwell. You threatened me!"

She shivered involuntarily at the memory.

"Why *were* you meeting with him?" Lance asked.

Rayla appraised him coldly. "He was asking about the inmate who assaulted me. He thinks you beat him up."

Lance visibly stiffened. "What did you tell him?"

"Nothing."

He relaxed. "You're right in calling me a stranger. I wasn't myself last night. I was tired and took something to help me make it through the shift and it made me a little crazy. By the time you came home I was completely out of it."

The memory brought hot tears to her eyes; the confusion, the powerlessness, the fear. She blinked them away. "You made a scene in the parking lot yesterday."

Lance smiled. "Well I guess we're even there 'cuz you made another one today, almost running me over and leaving me standing there like a fool."

Rayla didn't smile back. "We're not *even*, Lance. You accused me of cheating."

"No, I didn't."

"Well you accused me of wanting to," she snapped, "and you hit me."

He shook his head. "I did not hit you, Rayla, but," he stuck out his stubbled jaw, "if it'll make you feel better, go ahead, hit me back."

She knew he was only trying to be cute, but for a moment she imagined herself rearing back and knocking the shit out of him.

"I want this to be over," he said quietly. "I made a mistake, a few of them, but you have to understand this week has been hell on me. I know that's no excuse but it's true. The thought of that scumbag in H-Dorm disrespecting you, Fretwell on my ass, your grandmother hanging up on me, and then that big musclehead leaning over your car like that... It just ..." He took a deep breath. "Rayla, if I lost you it would drive me crazy."

He wrapped his arms around her and buried his face in the crook of her neck, his shoulders racked with sobs. She had never seen him cry before. Reluctantly, she returned his embrace and felt her resolve loosen, drifting away like a stick on the Chattahoochee.

10

2:16 a.m.

The strange thing about recurring dreams is that one can never be quite sure if the dream is actually recurring, or if familiarity is simply woven into the fabric of the dream, creating a recurring phenomenon.

Rayla awoke from slumber with a gasp, emerging in a spray of sheets and blankets like a marlin exploding through the glassy surface of the deep.

On the verge of hyperventilation, she noticed her hands were, in fact, not bound. Her heart rate began to slow as the nightmare melted away, slithering back into the cave of her subconscious like a python. She fell back against her pillow and glanced over at the alarm clock. It was 2:16 a.m.

Like most occurrences in the dream realm, much of what she experienced was fuzzy and surreal. She seemed to move effortlessly from Mema's kitchen to her own living room to an unfamiliar hotel room as if they were all parts of the same structure.

The odd thing was that she was not herself in the dream. She was her mother. Naked and bound at the wrists, she remembered running through the maze of rooms with a gun in her hand.

Her father's broad back was to her so she couldn't see his face. The chain was on the open door and he was yelling into the crack of daylight coming through.

The first bullet tore a hole in his shoulder blade and knocked him into the door, pressing it shut. The second shot spun him around and he sank to one knee, as if proposing. The next one took off the entire right side of his face.

Then, with trembling hands, she turned the gun on herself … and awoke in her own body, in her own bedroom, both terrified and relieved.

11

Desensitized

Kevin Freeman had nuts in his face. Again. Not exactly *in* his face, they were about a foot away, but close enough to make him feel uncomfortable and a little disrespected. *Three months Kev*, he reminded himself. *Three months, one week and five days. Pick your battles.*

It was hard to read or relax or concentrate with someone standing over him and it seemed like he had someone standing over him every day since he moved into the dorm.

He rolled over and stared at the open page of his library book without reading. The letters and words were a scrolling, nonsensical computer code that his seething brain was unable to process. They were disrespecting him. They thought he was soft. *No they don't,* he told himself. *Don't make this personal. It's not about you.*

The problem was that half the dorm was trying to fuck his bunkie, which meant unnecessary attention. Which meant unwanted company. Which meant nuts in his face. He tried to ignore the voices. Couldn't.

"So why they call you Weasel, man?"

"Well, my name is really Eddie Wessel, but my friends..."

Prison will do one of two things to a man. He will either look upon the other murderers, rapists, thieves, and junkies as kindred spirits and long lost brothers, or he will completely reject their way of life and begin to hate everyone around him. Either path will harden him. Kevin was in that second camp. After almost a decade behind bars, he had come to detest everyone and everything associated with prison life.

"You got a wife out there Weasel?"

"Nope. Had a girlfriend but she left me when all this happened."

The legs and torso to the right of his face shifted and leaned against the bunk above him. The frame squeaked. Kevin gave up trying to read and focused on his breathing. *In serenity… out anxiety.*

"Have you ever imagined yourself with a man?"

"Uh… whatayamean WITH?"

"You know what I mean."

"Like… with WITH? A dude? No way!"

Desensitization is a by-product of prolonged incarceration. The nose becomes tolerant of disturbing smells; the mouth becomes capable of ingesting putrid slop, as does the digestive track. The ears adjust to the noise level while the eyes become accustomed to the frequent sights of violence and exploitation. Callouses grow over the heart and mind to the point where things that were once appalling, frightening or heartbreaking become just another part of the landscape, like the razor wire and the gun towers.

"It's not really gay Weasel. Don't call it that. It's just the desire to try something different."

"Well, uh, I appreciate the … you know … offer or whatever, but … no. I mean, no thanks."

Kevin smirked at the conversation. *'The desire to try something different,'* he silently mimicked. *Why don't you try something different and kill yourself, you piece of shit.*

Intimidation and psychological bullying were part of the prison experience, right along with stabbings, gang violence, rape, riots, abusive guards, overdoses, suicides, and extortion. After ten years, he was numb to it. Aware but separate. Desensitized.

"Listen Weasel, this is how it's gonna go down. I'm going to the bathroom, back stall. And you're gonna come suck my dick. And when you're done, I want you to shave all that hair off your legs. You're my bitch now and I hate hairy bitches. I know this is a big step for you, so you've got about three minutes to get your mind right. I'll be in the bathroom."

Kevin watched him back away from the bunk and saunter down the aisle toward the bathroom. He could tell he'd been down awhile by the way he wore his prison blues, tight and creased with his shirt tucked and his belt cinched. Only the younger generation sagged.

Weasel was peering down at him from over the side of the bed. His eyes wide with terror, magnified to the size of ping pong balls behind his thick glasses. He gulped.

"W-w-what do I do?"

Kevin reopened his book and pretended not to hear. He had three months left. It was none of his business.

"Please," Weasel begged, his voice trembling. "Help me."

Kevin continued to stare blankly at a random page in his book. "I warned you about that friendly shit," he said without looking up. "This is not a Star Trek convention."

"He... he's going to kill me," said Weasel.

Kevin lay down his book on his chest and glanced up at him. His head was almost purple from hanging upside down off the side of the bunk. His eyes bulged from his face and looked ready to explode from their sockets. "He's not gonna kill you," said Kevin. "Well... most likely, he's not. He's just *sizing* you. Testing you."

"Testing me?" said Weasel, his voice becoming shrill. "How do I pass?"

"You fight," said Kevin. "Show him you're not scared."

"But I *can't* fight and I *am* scared!"

"Well then go shave your legs," said Kevin. "Fight or fuck. Those are your choices." He picked up his book and pretended to read. He knew he sounded harsh but the kid had an *elbow*, a natural life sentence. He'd have to learn sooner or later.

Suddenly, in a whoosh, Weasel leapt from the top bunk and landed cat-like in a crouch.

"Impressive," said Kevin.

Weasel snatched his state-issued brogans from under the bunk and slid them on unsteadily. "Okay damn it," he muttered. "If it's a fight he wants…"

Kevin watched him storm down the aisle then stop halfway and march back to the bunk.

He removed his glasses and handed them to Kevin. "Hold these for me."

"But you're blind without them."

"Doesn't matter," said Weasel. "I couldn't win if I had twenty-twenty vision. I suck at fighting. But these glasses are irreplaceable. My grandfather gave them to me."

It's not your problem he reminded himself as he watched Weasel's lanky frame disappear into the bathroom. He twirled the thick glasses between his fingers, then sat up and reluctantly reached for his boots.

12

Psycho Nerd

Weasel was under the sinks, squirming helplessly on the dirty floor; his face, a mess of blood. The man standing over him, his would-be wardaddy, gripped the sink edge for balance as he river-danced a torrent of vicious kicks into Weasel's face and ribcage. His tight creased prison blues were speckled with red and whipping over the tiles like polyester blades.

Kevin entered the bathroom just as Weasel blindly and miraculously timed a kick and caught a boot. Tight-pants struggled violently to free himself but Weasel wasn't having it. He twisted and forced the ankle under his armpit, securing it, and then buried his teeth in the man's calf, growling, shaking his head, attempting to rip flesh from bone.

"AGHH!" Tight-pants roared. "Somebody get this crazy bitch! Motherfucka's bitin' me!"

Kevin glanced over at the officers' station. Inside the thick glass booth a third shift relief officer was talking animatedly on the phone. Oblivious. A few heads peered around the corner and rubbernecked from the bathroom stalls but for the most part the fight went unnoticed.

Tight-pants reached down and dug a thumb into Weasel's eye socket. Kevin found it odd that the man's shirt was still tucked neatly into his pants despite the brutality he was engaged in. The top three quarters of his body said *compliance, obedience, role-model inmate* – clean shaven, regulation haircut, prisoner ID clipped on pocket, shirt tucked, clothes pressed, belt fastened. It was the bottom fourth where things got weird. That's where the flecks of blood were. And where Weasel was locked on his calf like a rabid pit.

"That's enough," said Kevin.

Tight-pants glared at him while still attempting to gouge Weasel's eye.

Kevin reached down and knocked his hand away. "Break it up," he said. "They're about to change shifts."

The man shook his leg vigorously, trying in vain to dislodge it from Weasel's teeth. "Make him let go, then!"

Kevin glanced down at his bunkmate, purple-faced, eyes squeezed shut, head shaking, growling unintelligibly through the spit-soaked material of his predator's pants leg. Two words popped into his mind as he looked at Weasel's contorted face: *psycho nerd.*

He shook his head, almost smiled, then said, "Weasel, let him go."

Weasel ignored him.

"Come on, dammit!" the man snarled.

Kevin reached down and patted his shoulder. "It's over, man. Let him go."

Weasel opened his eyes and looked up at Kevin, his teeth still firmly sunk into the meat of the man's calf.

Kevin nodded.

Slowly, he let go.

Once free, he reared back to deliver a final kick. Kevin stepped between them. The blow never came.

"This ain't over," said tight-pants.

Kevin shrugged but didn't look away, watching him turn and limp out of the bathroom until he was gone from sight.

He heard moaning behind him and turned to see Weasel lying on his back. He knelt beside him and assessed the damage. His eye was split and swollen, his nose looked broken and a stream of blood ran from his fat lip down the side of his face.

"Did I win?" he asked.

Kevin smiled. *Psycho nerd.*

"Damn right," he said.

13

The Color Red

Bullet-sized drops of horizontal rain blew east to west across the compound drenching the first shift as they splashed and trudged through center gate to their assigned posts.

Rayla held her umbrella forward like a Viking shield and rushed through the wall of water, already tasting the steaming cup of coffee that awaited her in Alpha Dorm.

Lance was waiting under the pavilion as she passed, his FSU bag was slung over his shoulder, his brown DOC cap was turned backwards on his head. Behind him Jarvis and two other officers she didn't know sat and smoked. Their thermoses and lunch bags were piled on the concrete table between them.

Her husband smiled as she stepped under the cascade at the edge of the pavilion and set her umbrella down.

"Hey baby," he said, leaning over to kiss her.

She met him on her tiptoes.

"Where do they have you assigned today?" he asked.

"Alpha," she said, smiling politely at Jarvis and the other men at the table.

He reached out and pushed a wet strand of hair from her face. "No tower duty, huh?"

She smiled. He knew her too well. "Unfortunately not."

Thunder cracked above them. She jumped.

Lance shook his head. "I wouldn't call that unfortunate. Least not today I wouldn't." He paused and glanced out at the downpour. "I doubt I'd be able to sleep knowing you were up there in this weather."

Rayla went warm from his concern. The thought of him tossing and turning with worry was reassuring. Especially after *the incident*. Lance had ripped the world from under her feet that night. Caused her to question all the things she took for granted. Never mind fidelity, honesty, and happiness; his single act of aggression had cast doubt on the very structural elements of their marriage. Little things like being able to disagree without the threat of being slapped, having her teeth knocked out or something worse. But in his defense (there's that word again) *the incident* was an isolated occurrence and he *was* obviously out of it that night.

A thought struck her as she glanced again at the strangers at the table with Jarvis. "Lance," she whispered, "are those the ones who gave you the…"

"Speed?" he finished. "Nah, are you still thinking about that?"

"Not really," she lied.

Lance sighed and shook a Marlboro from his pack. His hands looked huge as he cupped the lighter flame from the wind and puffed his cigarette to life.

"I left your breakfast on the stove," she said.

"Thanks baby," he exhaled, inadvertently blowing smoke in her face.

She reached for her umbrella. "Well, I guess I need to go. I'm late already. I'll see you when I get home."

"I'll be there."

"Love you," she said, raising her umbrella and turning toward Alpha Dorm.

"You too," he said, slapping her on the butt as she stepped out in to the rain.

She heard laughter behind her as she cut across the grass and headed for her post. She hated when Lance did things like that. Especially at work or in front of his friends. It made her feel cheap.

When she reached the overhang at the entrance to Alpha Dorm she looked back across the compound at the pavilion while she wrestled with her umbrella. Jarvis and the other two officers were halfway to center gate. Lance waved once then bolted out into the heavy rain, following. The door buzzed behind her. She pushed it open. It was time to go to work.

There is nothing like the smell of a prison dorm at 8 a.m. It always took her a minute to get acclimated, even after six years in corrections. The contrast between the fresh air and green grass on one side of the door and the stench of sweat, urine, and overflowing trash cans on the other was staggering. She held her breath as she stepped into the foyer.

The moisture from the rain had crept under the door and through the dormitory windows. The floor was slippery and the walls were damp with condensation. A line of sugar ants had a convoy going along the baseboards and up the side of the trash can. Inmates argued in the bunk area and walked back and forth to the bathroom.

"Hey Ms. B," smiled a familiar passing face whose name she didn't know.

"Good morning," she replied.

The graveyard officer stood in the booth wearing a poncho and holding a set of keys. He dropped them in the sliding metal drawer and pushed it toward Rayla. She opened it and grabbed them. Their jingling worked like magic to silence the dorm. Over her shoulder, in the bunk area, conversations and card games froze for a moment as the inmates paused to see who was working, then slowly sputtered back to life, layering, overlapping, competing to be heard, until within seconds the noise level was back at its normal setting – *thunderous*.

She turned and walked through the bathroom to the steel mesh door of the laundry room, averting her eyes from the showers out of habit although no one was bathing anyway. She laid her umbrella on the laundry flap while she rifled through the assortment of keys on the key ring, thumbing through the myriad of lookalikes until she found the one marked "18" and aimed it at the lock. Then, out of the corner of her eye, she saw the blood.

The color red is alien to the prison landscape, a world of steel grey, puke green, inmate blue and officer brown. The somnambulant lull of the same drab colors day in and day out represent routine and status quo. But a splash of crimson is like a slap to the brain. Blood! Violence! Danger!

Rayla spun and examined the bathroom. A small puddle of red seeped across the tiles, trickling into the cracks of grout and networking toward the soap and hair-clogged drain. Tiny droplets marked a blood trail around the island of sinks and urinals. The midnight shift officer stood at the booth window with his belongings slung over his shoulder. It was already five minutes past eight. He gave her an impatient look as she held up a finger and followed the splotches to the far side of the bathroom.

Two men were at the last sink. She recognized them. She was working the day they moved into the dorm. She remembered assigning them bunks but didn't remember their names. The blood was coming from the skinny one's face which was swollen and split in numerous places. He winced as the other one dabbed a wet rag over his wounds. She observed them for a moment before clearing her throat.

"Ahem."

They both turned toward her. The one with the facial lacerations looked embarrassed while the other man fixed her with a blank expression, his bottle-green eyes assessing her.

"What's going on in here?" she asked.

"Nothing, ma'am," mumbled the skinny one through swollen lips.

She glanced back and forth between them and raised an eyebrow. "It looks like you've been fighting."

The tall one with green eyes crossed his arms and leaned against the sink while the other one slowly shook his head. "No ma'am," he said, looking down at the floor. "I… I fell."

She rolled her eyes. "It seems like everybody's always falling around here." She paused and considered them both carefully. "Is whatever this was about over?"

"Yes ma'am," said fat lip while the other continued to brood.

"I need both of your assurances on this," she said. "Otherwise, I'll have to radio security and get somebody down here to escort you to confinement."

Green eyes stared at her in icy silence before finally nodding his head.

She frowned as a stubborn drop of blood crept from the skinny one's nostril and dangled from the tip of his nose. "Who did this to you?" she asked, her eyes darting quickly to the quiet one and back. "Was it him?"

"No!" said fat-lip defensively. The drop of blood broke free from his nose and splatted on the toe of his boot. His battered and swollen face was suddenly desperate and imploring. "He… He's my friend. He was helping me."

"I thought you said you *fell*."

"I did fall," he said, unable to look her in the eye. "I meant he was helping me clean my face. I can't see without my glasses."

Rayla glanced back toward the booth. The relief officer had his poncho-covered arms raised in the universal pose for *what the hell?* She turned back toward the inmates. "I want this bathroom cleaned and I don't want to hear or see either of you for the rest of my shift. The only reason you're not going to the box is because it's raining and I don't feel like doing the paperwork, but if there's another problem and I have to call for backup, I promise you won't see the compound again for the rest of this year. Get to work."

She left them standing by the sinks and walked quickly to the laundry room door, lifting slightly as she turned the key and pushed it open. The laundry room was really more of a hallway with wooden cubby holes lining the walls on either side, each filled with mesh bags and clothing. A staff bathroom was at one end of the hall and the officers' station entrance was at the other.

The midnight officer was holding the door open with his belongings tucked under his arm. "Comin' down hard out there, ain't it?"

"It is," said Rayla, sliding past him and walking up the steps into the bubble. "Sorry I held you up."

"No problem," he said. "Is everything okay?"

"Yeah," she said, heading for the coffee maker. "There might have been a little disagreement in the bathroom earlier this morning, but whatever it was, it's over now."

An image of the one with green eyes popped into her mind, leaning against the sink, arms crossed, brow furrowed, the hard lines and chiseled features of his face smoldering in barely concealed hostility, as if it was taking all the energy he could summon to keep from exploding into *Fuck you!* But why? What had she done besides letting them both off the hook? *Ungrateful bastard.*

"Officer Broxson, I need the keys."

"Oh, I'm sorry," she said, tossing him the ring. "They're going to have to give you overtime if I hold you up any longer."

He smiled and shut the door behind him.

She waited at the window as he locked the laundry room door and walked around to the flap. He dropped the keys in the drawer and slammed it home giving her a final wave as she reached inside to retrieve them.

"Drive safe," she said, pressing a button and buzzing him out. She caught a quick glimpse of the still pouring rain before the door swung shut behind him.

The log book lay open on the counter. The last entry was at 8 a.m. where the previous officer signed off for the day. She glanced up at the clock as she reached for her pen. It was almost 8:20 and her dorm sergeant was still a no-show. She shook her head. She was paired with Sergeant Ron Billingsley, a twenty-year veteran of the department, chronic womanizer and functional alcoholic. It was going to be a long day.

She tapped the pen on the log book and looked over her shoulder toward the bathroom. The ceiling fan whirred above her head. Her radio squawked. She pushed back her chair then stood, stretched and walked casually over to the window.

The bathroom had been swept and mopped. There was no sign of blood anywhere. The trash had been removed from the can and the bag was tied and sitting next to it, a new bag had been inserted.

They were still at the back sink. The skinny one held his head back while the one with green eyes continued to dab a wet rag over his wounds. There was a gentleness in his movements that contradicted his hardened convict exterior. There was kindness in the way he cleaned the smaller inmate's cuts, a tenderness uncommon in the world of prison; uncommon, even in her own home.

When they noticed her watching, she turned away.

14

The Convict and the Bass Player

High hats, keyboards, strings. The falsetto wail of Usher. Music filled the sleeping dorm via a symphony of radios that hung from various bunks. A gentle breeze blew through the windows, the smell of rain still rode the air.

"Hey Freeman," called Weasel in a hoarse whisper. "Are you awake?"

Kevin lay on his back, hands locked behind his head as he stared at the top bunk. "What's up?"

Weasel's face appeared above him, a swollen misshapen silhouette in the opaque glow of the night light. "Why doesn't anyone mess with you?" he asked.

"They did," said Kevin.

"But they don't anymore."

"Nah, not much."

"Why not?"

"Because I did what you did this morning."

Weasel stared down at him considering his explanation. "You mean you bit them in the leg?"

They both cracked up laughing.

"Hold that shit down back there!" a voice grumbled from across the dorm.

They were quiet for a while. The radios played on. Crickets chirped outside the window. Just as Kevin shut his eyes, Weasel spoke again. "Yeah," he whispered, "but you're new here. Just like me. Nobody knows about your fights at other prisons, but they still don't mess with you. Why not?"

Kevin thought about his question. "I guess," he said with a yawn, "when you first come to prison, you stick out. You may not realize you do, but you do. You talk different. You walk different. You think different. I did and so do you. People see that as a weakness and try to exploit it. For money, for ass, sometimes for no reason at all. Because they can. But after a while the street wears off and you change from an inmate into a convict. When that happens the wolves start looking elsewhere for sheep."

Weasel continued to stare down at him from the top bunk. His left eye was swollen shut. His right blinked rapidly. "What are you in prison for?"

Kevin shook his head and smiled. "See what I mean? A convict would never ask a question like that."

"Sorry," said Weasel. "You're right. It's none of my business."

"DUI Manslaughter," said Kevin. "Try to keep it to yourself."

"Manslaughter?" Weasel whispered. "You killed somebody? That's what I'm in here for … except mine is first degree."

These were the exact type of conversations Kevin tried to avoid. "Yeah, I kind of figured that when you said you had an elbow. Let's get some sleep man."

Kevin rolled over and stared out the window. The bright search light from tower two was trolling the compound in a cylinder of neon white. The harrowing memory of squealing tires and shattered glass echoed in his mind. He squeezed his eyes shut until his head throbbed.

"What's an elbow?" asked Weasel.

Kevin groaned and looked over his shoulder. The uneven outline of Weasel's head still hung over the side of the bunk. "An elbow is a life sentence."

"Why do they call it an–"

"I don't know!" Kevin snapped before taking a deep breath. "Maybe it's because life starts with the letter L."

"Elbow is spelled with an E."

"Okay, then I don't know."

"I killed my father," said Weasel, his words spiraling down toward Kevin in the darkness. "Murdered him. That's what my … elbow is for."

Kevin focused on a slow-turning ceiling fan across the dorm. *Why?* He wondered without asking.

"I was eight the first time he raped me," said Weasel. "He left my little brother with the neighbor's daughter and told my mom he was taking me fishing. He took me to the woods instead."

Nausea, insidious and churning, crept into Kevin's stomach as he listened to the monotone, trance-like confession coming from the top bunk.

"On the way home he told me he'd kill my mother if I ever talked about what we did. It wouldn't have taken much. She was already blind and bedridden from her first stroke. I almost told her anyway … snuck up to her room when he was gone one day. But even at that age I understood that she was already in tremendous pain. Half of her face drooped, one arm and leg were useless, and she couldn't talk good, just grunted and moaned a lot. I couldn't hurt her more. No way.

"My dad was unemployed and we lived off my mother's disability checks and whatever extra he could make by selling her pain pills to the junkies in our neighborhood. Every few weeks he'd get drunk and take me on another *fishing trip.*

"My mother had had two more strokes by the time I was twelve and was obviously close to death. I knew my father was only keeping her around for the checks and the pills. Our afternoons in the woods got more violent. And scary. Like he hated *me* for what he was doing. I was just … ashamed. It's hard to feel like a man when something like that is happening to you."

Kevin thought of Bobby at that age. His eyes swelled with tears. He blinked them away.

"When mom finally passed, my grandfather came down for the funeral. I ended up going home with him. I was surprised my father didn't forbid it but looking back now I think he was relieved to get rid of me. Seattle was thousands of miles away from Ocala. We took an Amtrak. That was the happiest time of my life." He paused and squinted with his lone functioning eye. "I'm not rambling you to sleep am I? I know I talk too much … nervous habit."

"It's cool," said Kevin.

"Well, anyway, long story short, Seattle was awesome. People in the northwest are different than Floridians. Nicer. My grandfather's neighbors were musicians and they let me hang out at their house when they practiced. That's where I learned to play bass.

"They gave me an old Fender Jazz that was covered with Chiquita Banana stickers – those little blue ones – and these gigantic rusted tuning pegs on the headstock. It was the most beautiful thing I ever owned. If I wasn't in school, I was plugged into the auxiliary jack of my grandfather's old stereo studying the masters… John Paul Jones, Les Claypool, Geddy Lee, Bootsy Collins. But my idol was Flea. Do you like Red Hot Chili Peppers?"

"Yeah," said Kevin.

"Do you know the song *Soul to Squeeze?*"

"I'm not sure."

"Come on man, you *have* to know that one. It's one of their more radio-friendly songs. The first lyrics are, *I've got a bad disease...*" Weasel did his best Anthony Kiedis impression.

"Oh yeah," said Kevin, more to make him stop singing than anything else. "Sure."

Weasel's voice took on a wistful, faraway tone. "I love that song. Killer bass line, pure Flea. So anyway, music and that Fender bass guitar became my best friends. They got me high for the first time, got me laid for the first time. Well ... I mean the first time by someone other than..." His words trailed off.

Kevin cringed at the evil of his implied statement.

"The bass gave me an identity," he said. "It transformed me from spineless, motherless victim to bad ass musician. I was no longer Eddie Wessel. I was Weasel, man. Capital fucking letters."

The front door buzzed. Keys jingled. Footsteps. They listened for the metallic slam of the laundry room door before Weasel began again.

"But the problem was, no matter how high I got, how hard I rocked, or how loud I played, my thoughts always returned to Ocala. To Andy."

Kevin frowned. "Who's Andy?"

"My little brother," said Weasel, "seven years younger. My mom had him the same year she had her first stroke. He never knew her as a mother, only as the scary lady locked in the upstairs bedroom. He was five when I took off for Seattle. Leaving him behind was the most cowardly, selfish thing I've ever done."

"Weasel, you were only twelve," said Kevin.

"Doesn't matter," he whispered, his good eye burning behind the thick lens of his glasses. "You don't leave defenseless little kids in a snake pit like that. I should have at least told someone. The sad thing is that it wasn't fear that kept me from spilling the beans. It was shame. I was embarrassed by what happened to me.

"Anyway, three years ago, right after I turned eighteen, I stole Grandpa's 38 and hitchhiked down to Portland where I met some travelers who showed me how to jump freight trains. After three weeks of walking, hitching, and hoboing, I finally made it to the Florida line. It took me another two days to get to Ocala.

"Leonard Street was just like I left it. Rusted cars on cinderblocks in overgrown grass, American flags hanging from porches, dogs in the middle of the road. Our mailbox still said Wessel on it.

"The front door was unlocked. The living room was full of strangers. Most of them were nodding. There were needles everywhere. A girl was sucking some guy off in the corner while he sucked on a crack pipe. I ignored it all and walked up the stairs to his room."

Kevin dug his thumbnail into the side of his index finger as he listened, an old nervous habit.

"He was shaving when I pushed the door open. Andy was naked in his bed. I pulled the pistol from the front of my pants and aimed it at his back. I could see his eyes in the mirror. He was … smirking at me. He turned to say something, but I shot him before he could get it out. I didn't mean to kill him. I don't even remember pulling the trigger. I just wanted to get my brother out of there.

"When I wrapped Andy in a blanket and lifted him from the bed, he weighed about as much as my Fender Jazz and there was no recognition in his eyes. My father was barely alive when we left. I could feel him staring up at us as I stepped over his face and carried Andy down to the front porch to wait on the cops. That's how I got here. That's how I got this *elbow*."

Kevin sat up in his bunk. "And they gave you life? For that? They should have given you a fucking medal!"

"I fought it for almost three years. Well, my attorney did. He represented me for free. But in the end there was no getting around first degree premeditated murder."

Kevin shook his head and laid back. "What happened to Andy?"

Weasel's voice was quiet. "Child services, I guess. Foster care. He turned fourteen last Tuesday. I'm hoping he'll write me one of these days."

Kevin thought of his own experiences with DCF and foster homes growing up. "I'm sure he'll find you when he's old enough," he said, thinking of Bobby at that age. "You're the only family he's got."

"Yeah," said Weasel, "me and Grandpa. That's where I hope he's living. Seattle. A million miles away from Leonard Street and Ocala."

"Maybe he is," said Kevin. "Have you written up there?"

"Five times," said Weasel. "I think Grandpa's still pissed or dead."

Kevin looked at the clock at the front of the dorm. It was almost two in the morning. A car dealership commercial blared from the radios, *"Do YOU have a job? Do YOU have ninety-nine dollars?"*

Weasel's head was no longer hanging over the side of the bunk. Scattershot snoring rumbled across the dorm in metronomic waves. He shut his eyes.

"Hey Kevin?" Weasel whispered.

"Yeah," he answered without opening his eyes.

"Will you teach me how to be a convict?"

15

Alaska

Dry leaves crackled beneath their boots. Squirrels darted high above their heads, moving from oak to pine to cypress with boundless frantic energy. Swaths of blue sky and sunlight shone through the tangled, dark green forest ceiling in vivid bursts and slashes. Blue jays and robins trilled. The crisp morning air was rich with the heady scent of earth and pine.

Lance and Jarvis walked side by side, clad in camo, with hunting rifles slung over their shoulders along with their backpacks. Jarvis also carried a shovel. They moved nimbly for men of their stature and communicated mostly with their eyes, a habit forged over twenty years of hunting together, first with slingshots then with pellet guns, and now with crossbows and bolt action rifles.

They knew the forest as well as they knew their hometown and barely acknowledged the landmarks as they passed them – a twisted pine, a deep knife-slash across the trunk of an oak, a piece of cloth tied to a limb. They ducked under branches and sidestepped spider webs and patches of poison oak before finally crossing the dry, sun-cracked creek bed and following a narrow game trail to the clearing.

The tree stand was across the meadow, just visible in the swaying pines. They paused at the edge of the wood and surveyed the field. The twelve-point buck in Jarvis's den – a record kill for the Pine Grove/Wildfork area – was shot along the western tree line. They were standing on hallowed ground.

Jarvis thumped his can of Kodiak and twisted off the lid. "Well," he said, looking around, "whatcha think?"

Lance gazed across the field at the tree stand. "I think we're good," he said. "I didn't see any tracks."

"Naw," said Jarvis, sticking a plug of tobacco in his mouth, "weren't none."

"Let's go," said Lance.

Jarvis picked up the shovel and followed.

A gentle breeze blew through the meadow. The tall grass bent and rippled. Jarvis spit a brown glob of dip-juice on an ant pile. "You seen the new girl?"

"The nurse?" asked Lance over his shoulder.

"Mm hmm."

"Saw her for the first time last night. Pretty little thing."

"Yeah, I guess she's all right," said Jarvis.

Lance smiled to himself as they reached the tree stand. "Are you thinking about asking her out?"

"Hell no," said Jarvis, removing his cap and wiping the sweat from his brow with a massive forearm. "What the hell would she want with a big ugly redneck like me? I was just ... making conversation."

Lance hung his backpack and rifle on the first step of the tree stand. "Making conversation, huh?"

Jarvis nodded.

Lance turned and faced him. "You are so full of shit, Clayton Jarvis. You've got a crush on that damn girl, don't you?"

"No."

"Yes, hell you do," Lance laughed.

Jarvis kicked at the ground. "Naw, man, really. I mean she's nice and all, but ... way out of my league."

Lance's smile faded and his voice became grave as he stared at his best friend. "She'd be lucky to have you, Jarvis. Don't sell yourself short."

Ten years earlier Jarvis's high school sweetheart and wife of a few months decided she didn't want to be married anymore and ran off to Birmingham with a roofer from Graceville. He never dated again.

Jarvis changed the subject. "Do you really think it worked?"

Lance shrugged as he reached in his pocket for gloves and slipped them on.

"Cuz you gotta admit it seems a little farfetched," said Jarvis, his teeth caked with tobacco. "I mean ammonia, charcoal, fishin' line and gunblue, and a month later you magically pull up four ounces of ice. I still think that little bastard is blowin' smoke up your arse."

"We're about to find out," said Lance. "Hand me that shovel."

The *little bastard* Jarvis spoke of was an inmate named Festus "Methlab" Mulgrew from Polk County. His name said it all. Methlab had been cooking high octane dope since the late 80s. From bathtub to anhydrous to shake and bake and phosphorus, the man was a veritable master chemist and a legend among the inmates who dabbled in the crystal trade. Lance had been exchanging favors for recipes. Nothing major, a bunk change here, a *Penthouse* magazine there, a water bottle full of vodka, all very small prices to pay for the information he was receiving.

If the information was worth a fuck.

Lance turned and walked into the thicket using the shovel to hack his way through the dense green wall of brush and thorn. At the bottom of the hillock, he spotted the stone. Gray and flat, it lay undisturbed in the shadow of a river birch right where he left it.

He kicked the stone aside and drove the spade into the earth, coming away with a shovelful of dirt. He flipped it over by the tree trunk and repeated the process. After a few reps his muscles warmed to the task. It felt good to dig. This was man's work.

A small rabbit crashed through the undergrowth. A curious bumblebee circled his head once then buzzed lazily away. Jarvis watched him work from a nearby cypress stump. "Lance, if it didn't work this time, can't we just take it as a sign from the good Lord and forget about it?"

"Sure," said Lance without looking up. He knew Jarvis was uncomfortable with this. Any deviation from Jarvis's normal routine of working, hunting, and drinking was always met with grumbling hesitation. Hell, Jarvis probably didn't even like the high from smoking crystal. But where Lance led, Jarvis followed. It had been that way since middle school and would probably never change.

"Good," said Jarvis, "cuz you gotta admit, takin' advice from inmates ain't exactly the smartest thing in the world. I mean, seems like they wouldn't be in prison if they knew much about anything. 'Cept of course, for the kinds of things that can lead a man to prison. I'm sure they know plenty about that."

Lance smiled and continued to dig. "There's over ten grand down in this hole, Jarvis. Imagine that," he said as he flipped a shovelful of dirt over by the tree, "ten thousand dollars."

Jarvis snorted. "Ten thousand dollars from an old fish tank and a bunch of cleanin' supplies from Walmart?" He paused and spat in the brush. "I'll believe it when I see it."

Two feet down, the shovel made contact with something hard. Gently, Lance scooped the remaining dirt from the top of it before reaching down and working it free from the hole. Black dirt rained down like water as he lifted the cooler and set it on the ground.

He only half heard Jarvis rambling from the stump. "I mean seems like if ice or crank or crystal was that easy and cheap to make, the damn Mexican drug cartels would be out of business. Why do they call it 'ice' anyway? Shit burns my damn nostrils."

Lance ignored him and flipped the top of the cooler. The aquarium rested inside it. Twenty strings of fishing line hung down into the tank over an inch and a half of thick chemical paste. In theory, during the twenty-eight days of cooking, a chemical reaction was supposed to occur sending thick shards of ice up the dangling strings. *If Mulgrew knew his shit.*

"Well," asked Jarvis, "whatcha' see?"

Lance slowly pried the lid from the aquarium and waited a few moments before peeking inside. His eyes widened and a smile crept slowly across his face.

"I see … Alaska."

16

Emerald Lightning

Rayla leaned back in the chair and propped her feet on the desk. Outside the tower windows the sky was a dazzling blue. Fifty feet below her the rec yard was a giant ant farm swarming with activity. The frequent rumble of pounding feet and the rise and fall of hundreds of voices could almost pass for the sound of an elementary school recess were it not for the occasional burst of profanity that rose above the crowd noise. She reached in her pocket for her cell phone to see if Lance had texted her. He hadn't. She snapped it shut and stuck it back in her pocket.

He had been so sweet lately – messages, dinner, flowers. She stretched lazily and glanced at her watch. Two more hours. Things were almost back to how they were when they first started dating. When there was passion and magic and laughter. She knew he felt guilty for his recent actions and was merely trying to atone for his explosion, but the attention was nice and the fact that he cared enough to try made her feel loved.

Suddenly the cold voice of reality forced its way through her thoughts. It belonged to her Mema.

Really? Is that what passes for love these days? That a person cares enough to try?

Rayla stared out at the distant water tower. The words *Town of Pine Grove* were painted on the front. The voice was persistent.

Or is it the fact that he hasn't slapped you or threatened you lately that lets you know he loves you?

"It only happened once," Rayla said aloud, "and he was out of his mind on drugs that night."

Oh, said the Mema voice in a tone soaked with sarcasm, *well that explains everything. He's a good man except for when he gets whacked out on drugs and threatens to knock your teeth out. And they say chivalry is dead. Sounds just like your grandfather.*

Rayla pushed back her chair and stood, banishing the voice back into the depths of her subconscious. She grabbed a file and fanned herself while glaring malevolently at the pigeon who had made its new home atop the broken AC window unit. She flipped the power switch, willing it to rumble to life but was met with stubborn silence. The pigeon stared back coldly through the window, its round unblinking yellow eye assessing her threat level. After determining it to be minimal, it turned away. She rolled her eyes and reached for the cord dangling from the ceiling fan.

"Rec yard to tower three, Officer Broxson."

She grabbed her radio. "Tower three, go ahead."

There was a burst of static, then, "When you're not ten-six, see if you can get a visual on those ten-fifteens over by the northeast fence. I think they're up to something."

"Ten-four," said Rayla, "hang on a sec."

She smiled as she reached for the binoculars. Officer Fleming relished writing disciplinary reports but at well over three hundred pounds and wearing a brown corrections uniform he was about as subtle as a heard of buffalo. He counted on Rayla to do his reconnaissance.

She focused her binoculars on the north fence and scanned the inmates in the area. Most were in motion, walking and jogging along the track. A young Hispanic was skillfully juggling a soccer ball with his feet, legs, and head. Two older men tossed a Frisbee back and forth. But the inmates that Officer Fleming was suspicious of were in the far corner of what used to be the softball outfield, right along the left field foul line. She recognized them immediately. Freeman and Wessel from Alpha Dorm.

Wessel was in a push-up position, his thin arms shaking as he struggled to raise himself from the ground. Freeman was standing over him, shirtless, with hands ready to spot.

She reached for her radio. "Tower three to rec yard, Officer Fleming."

"Rec yard, go ahead," Fleming's voice came back.

"Looks like they're just exercising, sir."

"Ten-four, Officer Broxson," his voice crackled. "Thanks."

She stared out the tower window for a moment before again lifting the binoculars to her eyes.

They were both standing, hands on hips. The cuts and bruises on Wessel's face were fading. He was all bones, so thin she could almost see his heartbeat. His eyes blinked and bulged behind the fogged lenses of his thick glasses. Freeman was saying something to him, she focused on his lips but couldn't decipher his words.

He was a bronze statue next to the small Wessel, not musclebound but lean and cut with strong looking shoulders and a six-pack that disappeared down the front of his pants in a chiseled V. His skin was tan and unblemished. A silver chain and medallion hung from his neck. She focused the binoculars. Freeman had the eyes, the build, and the quiet confidence of someone who had served multiple years in prison. The two men certainly made an odd couple. One looked like an athlete while the other looked like he played Dungeons and Dragons.

She continued to watch them as Wessel crawled to the ground and laid on his back. Freeman then knelt and grasped his ankles, obviously urging him on as he attempted the most pitiful sit-ups she had ever seen in her life. She felt the corners of her mouth curl upward in a smile.

She thought back to the scene in the bathroom, the blood on the floor and the way Freeman was cleaning the smaller Wessel's swollen knuckle-split face. She initially thought she had happened upon the aftermath of an altercation between them, possibly a lovers' quarrel. That would explain the combination of violence and gentleness.

Now, through the tower three binoculars, she saw things clearly. Freeman was no bully and certainly didn't fit the mold of an enraged homosexual. From her vantage point it appeared that he was trying to help the bookish Wessel. What she was watching looked more like survival training than anything else.

As Wessel continued to rock violently upward, struggling to touch elbow to knee, she realized Freeman was staring up at her, his green eyes flashing in the sun.

Although she was a hundred yards away, fifty feet up in the air, and behind tinted glass, she knew he could see her. She made a show of slowly surveying the entire yard before lowering the binoculars from her face.

She could still feel his gaze like flashing emerald lightning as she stepped away from the window and sank back in her chair. Outside the window, the pigeon cocked its head and stared at her accusingly.

17

Shadows in the Portals

Festus Mulgrew had a mouthful of rotten teeth, acne-pocked cheeks, and small coal-black eyes that were constantly narrowing and darting about distrustfully. He had a "D" before his six-digit prison number which usually signified an inmate's fifth time in prison, but two of his five commitments were for stabbings that occurred while he was in custody, so technically he was really only a three-time loser.

Lance stood in the open doorway of his cell watching him feed a moth to his pet spider. Above them a fluorescent light convulsed in spastic intervals. His bed was tightly made with hospital corners and a perfect six-inch collar. The floor was clean and swept although a visible track had been worn into the concrete from pacing. The sink and toilet were polished steel and a pen barrel had been fastened to the faucet for better water flow.

His eyes touched Lance's then darted away instantly, as if repelled. A smile touched his thin lips as he focused on his spider. "So," he said softly, "it appears our little venture was successful. How many days have you been up?"

His arrogant professorial tone irked Lance. *What was up with all these fucking prisoners trying to sound like nuclear physicists and rocket scientists?* "Three," he said. "Almost three days."

"Uh oh," said Methlab. "Shadow people time."

Lance shivered. *How did he know about the shadow people?*

"You have to be careful," Methlab warned. "After three days the portals begin to open."

Lance raked his tongue violently against his upper teeth, something he'd been unable to stop doing since he and Jarvis smoked that first shard in the woods. "Portals?" he whispered.

"Portals," Methlab echoed, inspecting a slender tattooed hand in the flickering light as the spider scurried across his palm, over his knuckles, and between his fingers. "To other dimensions. Parallel universes. Alternate realities. They say weed is a gateway drug, but they're full of shit. Crystal is the gateway." He paused and glanced at Lance. "The gateway for demons."

Lance frowned and looked over his shoulder to see if anyone was listening. It was that time in the morning between breakfast and work-call where the inmates stole a few more hours of sleep before shift change. One old man was reading the newspaper in the dayroom. The rest of H-Dorm slept.

He dug in his pocket for the cellophane bag and tossed it on the bunk. "We're even."

Methlab reached for the baggy and held it up to the light. "Looks good," he said before shaking a small shard into his palm and sticking it in his mouth. He grimaced. "Whoa, that brings back memories."

Lance watched him for a moment. "If any of this ever gets out, you're dead."

"That's quite an incentive," said Methlab, still studying the bag and its contents. "How much did you get?"

"About what you said I would," said Lance. "A little over four."

"I assume you plan on selling some?"

"That's none of your fucking business."

"What's a gram go for up here in the armpit of Florida? One bill? One-fifty tops, right?"

Lance's tongue continued to whip around the inside of his mouth uncontrollably.

"You know you really should get that under control," said Methlab without looking. "It's a dead giveaway."

Lance watched him suspiciously. "What's a dead giveaway?"

"Your jaw," he said. "It's been sliding from side to side since you've been standing there."

Lance realized he was right. He was scraping his tongue with his teeth and his jaw had shifted so far to the left that his molars were cutting into his gums. He willed his face to be still.

"Get some bubble gum," he said. "It'll give your mouth something to do besides chewing your tongue to shreds."

Lance nodded. This was good advice. He was lucky Rayla hadn't noticed it already. It was hard enough to hide seventy-two hours of sleep deprivation, but with his face muscles going rogue, it was damn near impossible.

Methlab stood and put his spider on the window sill. Dawn was breaking outside. He continued to face the window as he spoke. "The most you can get for a gram is one-fifty, no matter how good the quality is."

"So what?"

"So at one-fifty a pop, the most you can make on an ounce is forty-two hundred." He paused for effect. "I, on the other hand, can get three hundred a gram. You do the math."

Lance studied his back. "How? There's no cash in here."

"There's everything in here," said Methlab with a smile in his voice. "And now there's crystal, too."

He looked down the cell block toward the glass enclosed control room. His officers were gathering their belongings and preparing for the next shift. "I'll think on it," he said, turning to leave.

"You do that," said Methlab.

Shadows peeked from behind railings, gathered in cells, and swung from the rafters as he exited the wing. Unable to be seen head on, they danced on the edges of his peripheral, dark fluid blurs of motion swimming through the portals.

He didn't see Rayla on his way out but he wasn't looking either. He walked past inmates and officers with his sunglasses shielding his bloodshot, dilated eyes, nodding occasionally and trying his damnedest not to chew on his tongue. The line between real and imaginary was gone. He could hear people's thoughts. He needed to get home and get some sleep, preferably before he saw his wife. But sleep had been elusive lately. Maybe Jess had a Xanax. She loved those damned things.

He spotted Fretwell too late. His khaki pants, white shirt, and pale complexion blended with the dull beige paint of the administration building, cloaking him in shadows. He held his cigarette between his thumb and index finger like he was smoking a joint. When he exhaled, he didn't just blow out smoke, he spat it. Forcefully. *Pfft*. Lance considered turning back, but to where? His shift was over. He could see his coworkers filing out to their cars on the other side of the fences.

Hollis Fretwell was a small man, smaller even than Festus Mulgrew. His scalp was visible through his thinning hair and his pinched facial expression always reminded Lance of a rodent. It was humiliating to fear such a piss ant, a man he could probably kill with a single punch.

Suddenly a rat peeked its tiny head from the cuff of his pants leg, twitched its nose, then shot across the grass, followed by another, and another, until the small animals were flowing from his pants legs like rain through a drainpipe. Fretwell's tiny body swelled and constricted with every breath. His eyes were bright orange and his lips were pulled back revealing razor-sharp teeth.

Lance blinked. The rats vanished. Fretwell's teeth were small and yellow; his eyes, their normal color. Only the shadow people remained, looking back at him, pointing and laughing and whispering as they climbed the fences and disappeared over the rooftops.

Fretwell rolled the cherry from his cigarette and spat a final stream of smoke, tossing the butt in a can by the door. "Sergeant Broxson," he said, "you're a hard man to run down."

Lance watched him push off the wall, slither out of the shadows and move into the sunlight like a snake from under a rock. "Inspector Fretwell," he mumbled.

A final rat shot from the hem of his Dockers and broke for the safety of the hedges. Lance blinked hard behind his Oakleys, thankful for the mirrored sanctuary.

"Spoke to your wife a few weeks ago, but I'm sure you know that already." He paused and took a sip of coffee. "Nice girl. Very pretty."

Lance nodded and swallowed back the acrid bile that shot up his throat as a pornographic scene exploded across the screen of his mind, a detailed visual of Fretwell fucking Rayla. Her naked body was writhing on a desk as he arched his back and slammed into her hungrily. Lance felt himself growing hard in his pants even as his fists clenched in murderous rage.

Then, just as quickly as it came, the scene evaporated. His anger melted into confusion then wilted and died, as did his erection.

Fretwell watched him curiously. "Are you feeling okay?"

Lance realized he was chewing on his tongue again and silently cursed himself. "I'm fine," he said. His voice sounded odd in his head, like he was speaking through a tin can. "I just need some sleep. It's been a long night."

"I'm sure it was," said Fretwell, momentarily distracted by a passing nurse. "Listen, Lance, can I call you Lance?"

Lance shrugged.

"I know all about you and Officer Jarvis's little episode back in Y-Dorm a few weeks ago."

"I don't know what you're–"

"Save it," said the Inspector, waving him off. "I know what that piece of shit did to your wife. I probably would have done the same thing. Sick bastard's already serving life for raping a grandmother."

"Well then," said Lance stepping around him, "if I'm not in any trouble, I really need to get home."

"I had to file a report with the Inspector General's Office," Fretwell called from behind as Lance walked toward the gate.

He paused and turned around.

The inspector smiled coldly and shrugged his bony shoulders. "Procedure," he said in mock regret. "No getting around it."

"So what's that mean?"

The tiny inspector's face hardened. "It *means* that you are now on a short leash, Sergeant Broxson. Violent and unruly inmates are not the only people around that need to be ... *subjugated* as your wife likes to say. Walk light. I'll be watching you."

He turned and strolled across the sidewalk to his office. Lance watched him go as he waited to be buzzed through the front gate. A rat leaped from the back of his pants leg and scrambled across the asphalt. A shadow darted around the corner leaving a trail of snickering laughter in its wake. When the gate finally popped and he slammed it shut behind him, it felt like he was being released from prison.

18

Finger Ballet

The water fountain clicked and sputtered to life, shaking violently from where it hung on the wall just inside the dayroom. Five aluminum benches faced a mounted television so old that the channels were changed manually by twisting a knob. A coat of dust, thick as carpet, lay undisturbed atop its ancient faux wood body. Under it were three steel tables, each with four seats welded to the frames.

It was a weekday morning so the dayroom was quiet. The television didn't come on until 4 p.m. and most of the other inmates in Alpha Dorm were either at rec or at work. Kevin and Weasel had finished their assigned duties as housemen and were sitting at the middle table drinking coffee.

"I don't see what this has to do with being a convict," said Weasel.

"You never do," said Kevin. "Start with the *A* again." He paused to make a fist, thumb upturned. "Good, now *B*, palm out, fingers together. Mm hmm. *C*, crescent hand, fingers curled, do you remember the *D*?"

Weasel frowned as he attempted the letter.

"Just the index," said Kevin.

"I've never seen anybody else doing this," said Weasel.

"You've only been in prison three months," said Kevin. "You're still shitting Burger King. You haven't seen anything yet."

"I've seen the *Shawshank Redemption*," said Weasel, "and *Lockup* with Stallone, and nobody was walking around doing sign language in those prisons."

"Nope," said Kevin. "Know what else they weren't doing? Shooting Oxys on the rec yard with dirty needles stolen from medical, jackin' off in the mashed potatoes–"

"Yuk!"

"–raping handicapped old men, breaking into lockers with soda cans, smearing shit on their faces and running naked across the yard. This isn't Hollywood, man. This is the real deal. Now show me the *E*."

Weasel held out his palm and bent his fingers. "I just don't see why it's important."

"It's not *important*," said Kevin, "until you need it. It's just a way of communicating that the guards can't understand. And you're right, a lot of inmates *don't* know how to sign, but convicts do. Imagine, if during count, you see two dudes signing back and forth across the dorm about their plans to jump the skinny kid with the Coke-bottle glasses. It would be really helpful to know then, right?"

Weasel grudgingly attempted an *F*.

"Or that guard, what if she had locked us up that morning?" He nodded in the direction of the officers' station. "The only way you can communicate with other cells in confinement is through hand signals and sign language. You may never need it, but you never know. Think of it as another tool in your toolbox."

"Do they really whack off in the mashed potatoes? That's disgusting," said Weasel. "No wonder you gave me yours."

Kevin smiled. "Come on," he said, "first the *G*, one finger. Good. Now the *H*, two …"

Suddenly a hand slammed against the thick glass of the officers' station window. They both jumped. Officer Broxson pointed at Kevin and made a "come here" gesture with her hand.

"I'll be right back," said Kevin.

She watched his approach with an amused expression. He paused at the fountain for a sip of tepid water before rounding the corner and standing at the flap.

She was wearing reading glasses. Her liquid brown eyes touched his own. For a moment, he thought he saw warmth. Something long dead stirred within him like a leaf spinning in the first wind of an approaching storm. Then, her face hardened and the glare from an overhead light ricocheted off her silver DOC name tag. He silently berated himself for being weak.

She is not a woman. She's a prison guard. A shit eater. Probably third or fourth generation with an ex-husband on every shift and a trailer full of mean kids at home just chomping at the bit to take their GEDs so they can get certified to carry on the brutal tradition of mom, dad, grandma and grandpa.

"What's going on in there?" she asked.

The gyrating water fountain roared back to life making it impossible to hear. "I didn't hear you," said Kevin through the round metal talk-space in the glass.

"What's going on in there?"

He watched her enunciate each word. Her mouth was small and pouty. A pink tongue darted between her lips, moistening them. He swallowed hard. She had that little groove that ran in a straight line from the bottom of her nose to the center of her top lip.

He considered her question. *What's going on in where? In here? Like ... inside of me? What's going on inside of me? Is that what she's asking?*

"I'm not sure I understand the question, ma'am."

She tilted her head to the side, her expression equal parts impatience and skepticism. Slowly she raised a hand in front of his face and began to make strange gestures with her fingers. He stared transfixed through the glass as they gracefully dove and twisted in some sort of finger ballet. He had always wondered if hypnosis was a scam. Now, as he submitted to her painfully beautiful hand with its clear half-moon nails, smooth skin and delicate wrist, he knew the truth.

Suddenly her lovely palm reared back and slapped the glass in front of his face. He blinked. The water fountain went quiet.

"Gang signs," she said. "Are you teaching him gang signs in there?"

"Gang signs?" Kevin stammered, feeling as if he'd been ripped from a dream. "I don't ... how would I know any gang signs?"

"Nice," she said, "very convincing. Is that the voice you used on the police at the scene of your crime? Your *DUI Manslaughter*?" She added smugly, "Alcohol? Me? No sir, I *never* drink and drive."

Her words were like a brass-knuckle sucker punch. His knees buckled from the blow. Was it only a second ago that he was lusting over her stubby little fingers? For a moment he imagined himself testing the durability of the Plexiglas by smashing it with his fist. Maybe head-butting it.

Three months, he reminded himself. *Three months six days and it's over. All of it. Don't fuck up now.*

When he was six years old he stuck a paper clip into a wall socket out of curiosity. The high voltage current zapped straight up his arm in a blinding flash clutching his tiny body in its electrical grip, shaking him relentlessly before finally tossing him across the room in a pitiful smoking heap. Her comment had a similar effect.

"Look," she said, "I don't really mind. But if you see my supervisor walk through that door, I need you to stop what you're doing, grab a broom and look busy, okay?"

He nodded and began to walk away feeling as if she had just ripped away an old scab with her teeth and spat it in his face.

"Hey Freeman," she called through the window.

He turned and raised his chin.

"What *are* ya'll doing in there?"

"Sign language," he said, wishing he could show her the universal symbol for *fuck off*.

19

Bubblegum and Marlboros

The moon shone down through the trees like a gun tower searchlight bathing the packed orange clay in its opaque glow. The dirt road was barely a road at all, more like a trail. A turnoff from a two-lane highway in the middle of nowhere that wound its way through a thousand acres of woodland, skirting the southwestern tip of Diamondhead Lake before finally dead-ending back into the same two-lane highway a mile and a half down.

Lance's Silverado was parked in the brush with the windows up and the headlights off. Brad Paisley's *Whiskey Lullaby* played faintly on the radio, seeping through the mesh speaker panels like syrup through a strainer.

He pressed a button on the butane torch and a six-inch flame shot from the nozzle illuminating the smoky truck cab in roaring blue fire. He grabbed the glass pipe from his lap.

Next to him, in the passenger seat, Jessica Maldonado was looking up through the windshield at the full yellow moon. Her skirt had ridden up around her thighs and the top two buttons of her shirt were undone. "The moon is not like the sun," she announced. "It can't shine light on its own. It can only reflect light."

The small shard of crystal liquefied and crawled around the glass as he twisted it slowly in the air, chasing it with the torch. When the bowl was full of billowing smoke he brought it to his lips and pulled deeply.

"My turn," said Jessica, as he blew a tornadic stream at the windshield. The thick cloud spread across the glass like a wave breaking on the shoreline. Slowly he passed her the pipe.

She hit it once, exhaled, glanced over at him, then hit it again before setting it on the center console and stretching lazily. "Mmm," she purred, "it makes me tingle."

He could feel himself hardening in his jeans as he stared at her. Moonlight splashed across the tops of her breasts. "Really?" he asked throatily. "Where?"

She ran a finger down the center of the white triangle of material nestled between her thighs. "Here," she said.

He leaned over and slid his hand inside her bra, finding her swollen nipple and rolling it between his fingertips. Her mouth was warm and her lips were soft. She tasted like bubblegum and Marlboros. She climbed over the console and straddled him, holding his face in her hands, smiling wickedly.

The thought of Rayla at home in their bed flashed across his mind as he freed Jessica's breasts from the confines of her bra and began sucking them. He should have been home hours ago. She pulled his mouth back up to hers and moaned softly as they kissed. He moved his hand down between her thighs and slid his fingers inside her soaked panties.

She pulled back from the kiss. "I want another hit."

He reached for the pipe and torch. She leaned back against the steering wheel as he again ignited the blue flame. Her naked breasts swelled and plummeted in its eerie glow. They both stared trance-like at the glass bowl as he twisted it in the fire. A tendril of smoke appeared, then two, swimming along the stem and back, twirling twining expanding combining until the pipe was brimming with rolling storm clouds. He passed it to her.

She closed her eyes and took a deep pull then released the smoke slowly. It trickled from her nostrils and escaped from between her teeth, sliding up her face, covering it in a dense vaporous mask. She giggled. A wisp of smoke curled into the shape of a skull. He shivered.

"Your turn," she said.

As he brought the pipe to his lips he felt her unzipping his pants and clutching his erection. Suddenly he was engulfed in warmth. He exhaled and tossed the pipe in the passenger seat.

She rode him slowly, touching her forehead against his, holding his shoulders as she ground in slow agonizing circles, her feminine scent permeating the truck, her breath hot in his face.

He gripped her ass in both hands, kneading her silky flesh as she cried out and began to move with more urgency. He buried his face in her heaving chest and found a nipple with his tongue, sucking it hard as he pulled her down onto him and pushed deeper into her.

Her breath quickened as she slid up and down the length of him, the tempo gradually increasing with every thrust until she was slamming against him with wild abandon.

She threw her head back and her body convulsed, rocked by a powerful orgasm. He studied her face in the moonlight. Her red lips stretched wide across her face like a knife slash. Her teeth were sharp and gleaming white. Her eyes bore down on him with a cold unbridled malevolence. She looked *demonic*. Then her face melted, disappearing into a molten pool of bubbling flesh. Slowly, a new face emerged. It was Rayla. He lost his erection.

"Rayla!" he blurted. "I'm–I'm so sorry for cheating on you with that whore. It was a huge mistake." He hurried to explain.

"I only wanted a Xanax to help me sleep and you know what a pill head she is. She talked me into giving her a ride up to the Tom Thumb and one thing led to another and … I'm so sorry. It wasn't even that good."

Rayla blinked back into Jessica. Her face showed confusion, then shock, then twisted in hatred for a brief moment before going slack. She hurried to button her shirt before climbing back across the console to the passenger seat. She squirmed uncomfortably and reached beneath her, coming away with the pipe. She set it in the ashtray.

When she finally spoke, her tone was brisk. "I think you better take me home."

He nodded and grabbed his cigarettes, lighting one with the torch before turning the key in the ignition. The truck roared to life.

She lit one of her own and glanced over at him, blowing a dismissive stream of smoke at his lap. "You better put that away before you go home."

He looked down at his shriveled manhood, pink and innocuous, lying flaccid against his unzipped jeans.

"Wouldn't want Rayla to know you've been out whoring in the woods with a pill head," she said icily.

He shoved himself back in his pants before pulling out on the dirt road and heading home.

They rode in silence. Tree limbs slapped at the hood of the truck and bent against the windshield before sling-shotting behind them as they forced their way through the overgrown trail. Shadows moved across the orange clay, dark streaking objects that sprinted and flew through the foggy white halogen beam of his headlights. Beside him, Jessica ignited the torch and was heating the pipe.

Clay eventually gave way to gravel and the blacktop of Route 18 cut through the forest like a narrow winding river.

Tires spun rocks as he pulled out onto the empty highway. The blue crackle of flame danced in his peripheral and cast the inside of the truck in its flickering light. He glanced in the rearview.

The torch went silent and Jessica sucked the smoke from the pipe, coughing as she exhaled, and then bringing it back to her lips for another hit. Lance cracked his window. She propped her bare feet on the dash and relit the torch.

"Jessie," he said, "I'm sorry for what I said back there. I've been up a few days now and my head ain't on real straight. I keep ... seeing things."

He looked over at her. She was staring at the flame, mesmerized. Her wide glassy eyes were black and haunted. She took another hit, oblivious to the fact that her skirt was around her waist. His eyes fell to the soft cotton mound of her panties. The memory of her riding him flashed across his mind. He swallowed and looked back at the road. The faded yellow lines whipped by as they hurtled through the darkness toward the empty streets and blinking caution lights of town.

She started to cry, first a sniffle, then a whimper, then a choke-sobbing downpour. He watched her in the rearview, pipe in one hand, torch in the other, shoulders shaking as tears streamed down her face and fell from her chin.

He glanced at his watch. "Please, Jess, I didn't mean it."

She wiped her eyes on the back of her hand. "I know. It's not you. It's ... this town. This job. This life. Not exactly what I imagined growing up."

"You probably shouldn't smoke anymore. You're gonna be up a few days as it is."

She took a last hit before setting the pipe in the ashtray. "I'm glad the kids are gone for the summer," she said, inspecting herself in the visor mirror. "I'd hate for them to see me like this."

"You look fine," he lied, as he reached over and patted her leg. Her flesh was smooth and warm. He left his hand there.

"You didn't finish."

"Finish what?"

"Back there in the woods," she said, "we stopped before you…"

He stroked her thigh absently. "Yeah, I know. It's the dope. Strong."

Suddenly her head was on his shoulder. "I had a good time tonight, Lance," she said, rubbing his chest.

He felt himself straining against the material of his jeans as she kissed his neck and ran her hand down his stomach.

"Me, too," he whispered, guiding her head down toward his lap. He felt his zipper slide down and her wet mouth cover him.

He couldn't tell if she was crying again or gagging as he grabbed her hair and forced her lower. *Rayla would never do this,* he thought, *especially not riding through town.* He braked a half-mile from the entrance to the trailer park.

When he released her, she sat up and smiled at him. Her mascara was running.

"I need to drop you off here," he said.

She nodded and grabbed her purse from the floorboard. "Will I see you tomorrow?"

He lit a cigarette and exhaled. "Stop by after Rayla goes to work."

She opened the door and pulled her skirt around her legs before stepping down onto the asphalt. He checked his mirrors for witnesses. The road was empty.

"Bye," she said, slamming the door.

He left her in the red glow of his taillights and drove slowly, using the overhead light to scan the truck for any evidence of her presence. He spotted a few lipstick printed cigarette butts in the ashtray and tossed them out the window. He adjusted the rearview to check his face and smooth his hair. Black hollow eyes, bloodshot and etched with crow's-feet, stared back at him from a thin, sallow face. The face of a stranger. A fly scurried across his cheek. He slapped at it. It circled his head once then disappeared into his ear. He shook his head frantically but it never came back out. He looked back at the mirror. The stranger's eyes were smiling cruelly. He swatted the rearview out of his sight and turned off on his street.

Weather-battered trailers, yellow porch lights, and empty lots lined the quiet street. He pulled into the cracked driveway and cut off the engine. A dog barked. The darkened front windows of his doublewide stared back at him in silent contempt. He shoved the glass pipe and torch under the seat and stepped out of the truck.

The front door was unlocked. The bedroom light was spilling into the hallway. He went straight to the fridge and grabbed a Bud Light. The beer worked like a magic elixir, cool to his parched throat and warm in his belly. It calmed him at once. He crushed the can and tossed it in the trash, then walked down the hall to the bedroom.

Rayla was lying in bed reading a book. "Where were you?" she asked without looking at him.

"With Jarvis," he lied, "over at The Spur."

"Mmm," she said. "Holland called. He wanted to know if you could come in early tonight."

Lance glanced at his watch. He had forgotten all about work. "Did he say what time?"

"Eleven," she yawned.

"Damn," he said, secretly relieved. "I guess I need to get a move on. I'm gonna grab a quick shower before I go."

"Okay," she said, entrenched in her book.

He paused at the door. "What's that you're reading?"

She turned the cover so he could see the front. His twitching pupils focused on the bold yellow letters of the title. He frowned as he removed his shirt and walked in the bathroom.

Sign Language for Dummies?

20

Proverbs 26

"He's cheating on you," said Mema. She paused and took a noisy sip of her Slurpee. "That son of a bitch."

Rayla tossed Mydog a slice of bologna. A pair of blue jays fluttered around the bird feeder in the yard. "Your grass needs cutting."

"You act like you don't care, girl."

"About your grass?"

Mema shot her a look.

Rayla sighed. "I don't know for sure that he's cheating. I just know he wasn't at The Spur with Jarvis."

"Well, I know for sure," said Mema, rocking back in her chair. "Proverbs 26, *As a dog returneth to his vomit, so a fool returneth to his folly.*"

Rayla smiled and tossed Mydog another slice.

"And Lance Broxson is both dog and fool." She took another sip of Slurpee. "And asshole."

"He's my husband Mema."

"Stiff-necked," said the old woman. "Just like your momma. And tough as a two-dollar steak." She shook her head. "But baby, sometimes you've just gotta admit you made a mistake and move on. It's better than wasting your life trying to justify a bad decision."

Rayla began to cry. Mydog barked once and leaped up in her lap.

"What is it girl?"

Rayla shook her head and wiped away the tears.

The old woman stopped rocking. "He's hitting you ain't he?"

Rayla didn't respond.

"Dear God, he is," cried Mema. "Does he know about your mom and dad?" She answered her own question. "Of course he doesn't. When have you ever discussed that with anyone? Rayla, you need to get out of this ... this toxic marriage now."

"It only happened once," said Rayla. "And it was more like a push than anything."

"Don't you dare make excuses for that bully, Rayla Marie Adams."

"Broxson," she quietly corrected.

"You more than anyone should know how dangerous domestic violence is."

Mydog looked up from her lap and barked in agreement. Rayla gave him another slice. "He's not violent," she said. "One shove in almost two years does not make him violent."

Mema stared stoically out at the road.

"But you were right about one thing," said Rayla. "I don't think I love him."

A smile lit the old woman's face. She took a final drink of the Slurpee before setting the empty cup on the table.

"Well hallelujah."

21

Gold Dust

Weasel's face was purple. His ribcage protruded from the thin skin of his torso as he struggled to push his own weight. His palms were flat against the concrete floor and his untied boots were high above his head, toes touching the wall for balance.

Kevin counted the reps from his bunk. He was up to five a set. Impressive, considering the degree of difficulty and the fact that when they started working out he was averaging around negative one per set.

He came off the wall like a falling tree and struggled to his knees.

"Good set, Psycho," said Kevin.

"Stop calling me that," said Weasel.

Kevin fought back a smile. "You wanna be a hardcore convict, you can't call yourself Weasel. Never in the history of prisons has there been a badass named Weasel. A weasel is a shifty-eyed rodent. A rat. We need something more intimidating."

"Yeah," Weasel rolled his eyes, "well *psycho nerd* isn't exactly scary either."

Kevin laughed. "Only I know about the nerd part. To everybody else, you're just plain psycho." He watched him process the information. Weasel would make the world's worst poker player; completely incapable of shielding his thoughts, they paraded across his face in a series of animated expressions. He may as well have had a jumbotron mounted to his forehead.

"Well," said Weasel, gesturing toward the wall, "it's your turn."

"I think that's enough for today," said Kevin.

His voice sounded unnaturally loud even though it was somewhere just above a murmur. There were ten other housemen in charge of cleaning the dorm aside from Kevin and Weasel; most of them had already completed their duties and were back in their bunks. The silence was palpable.

"I love it when everyone's gone," said Weasel, putting on his glasses. "It's peaceful."

Kevin nodded thinking of his friend's life sentence. Peaceful moments would be rare for him.

Suddenly a muffled thud came from the front of the dorm. Weasel adjusted his glasses and looked over the row of top bunks in the direction of the officers' station. He pointed at himself once then frowned and pointed at himself again; finally, he pointed down at Kevin then shook his head. "I think Ms. Broxson wants you."

Kevin scowled and grabbed his t-shirt. "I'll be right back."

She was waiting at the window, arms crossed, chewing on her bottom lip. Her hair was pulled back in a severe bun and tiny gold hoops dangled from her ears. Her long lashes blinked behind black-framed reading glasses.

He approached the flap. "Yes, ma'am?"

"I need the laundry room swept," she said, her voice flat, her eyes dull.

He nodded and grabbed a push-broom that was leaning against the wall before walking through the bathroom to the laundry door. Keys jingled, metal creaked and suddenly it swung open. He stepped inside.

She stood in the doorway of the officers' station and watched as he swept. "I owe you an apology."

He glanced up at her. "Me? For what?"

"For what I said the other day. About your DUI." She looked away uncomfortably. "Your manslaughter."

He tried not to react. He kept sweeping. But inside he was reeling. Officers didn't *apologize*. Not after they handcuffed you and stomped you, not after they stripped you and sprayed you with gas, not after they spit tobacco juice in your legal work, and certainly not after something as routine as an insensitive comment. "You don't owe me an apology for that," he said. "How'd you know anyway? Is my charge on my contact card?" He already knew it wasn't. She shook her head. "I looked you up on the internet."

"Oh," he said. "Well it's all good. I'm at peace with it and I'm just about through paying my debt to society." Acrimony burned in his tone, sharpening the edges of his words. What he intended to sound loose and light came out terse and clipped.

If she noticed, she gave no sign of it. "Has the family tried to contact you?"

He frowned. "Which family is that?"

"The family of the deceased," she said as she looked at her feet. "I'm sorry I'm being nosy. You said you had made peace, I thought maybe you had written a letter or…" She paused and bit her bottom lip again. "I don't know what I thought. Sorry."

He folded his hands over the top of the broom and rested his chin on his knuckles. "I *am* the family of the deceased."

Her brow knitted in confusion. "I'm not sure I understand."

A toilet flushed on the other side of the laundry room door. He watched her in silence, measuring his words. "Ten years ago, me and my little brother were out shooting pool at a neighborhood bar. He was pretty sloshed on Jägermeister. I had two beers over the course of an hour and a half. I've never been big on the hard stuff and anyway, I was driving."

She looked over her shoulder into the empty officers' station as if concerned that someone else might be listening. "Freeman, you don't have to tell me—"

"We decided to head over to New Orleans, to check out Bourbon Street and hit the casino. It's only a three hour drive from Pensacola."

"I've been there," she said.

Kevin continued to lean on the broom, lost in the memory of that tragic night. The night his world changed. He reached inside his shirt and removed the chain. "Bobby had just given me this for my birthday. I miss him."

"I'm sorry for bringing this up."

"We were heading up 29 to the I-10 on-ramp when an SUV pulled out in front of me. I tried to slam on the brakes, but it was too late. Bobby went through the windshield. Everyone else had minor injuries. He died at the scene."

"My God."

"A cop smelled alcohol on Bobby and before I know it, I'm blowing into a tube. The legal limit is point zero eight. I blew a point zero seven-seven, but they arrested me anyway, because of the severity of the accident and loss of life.

"The state offered me three years but there was no way I was pleading guilty to killing my brother. I wasn't even buzzed. That idiot pulled out in front of me. So I took it to trial and lost. They gave me twelve years."

The words flowed from his mouth like water from a rushing faucet. The outpouring was so sudden, the memory so powerful, that even he was held captive by his own words as if he, too, were listener instead of narrator. He hadn't mentioned Bobby's name once over the last ten years. Not even to Weasel,

111

who was becoming more like a brother with each passing day. Yet here he was, baring his soul to a stranger. To a guard. To the enemy.

"Bobby was the only family I had. Sometimes I think we both died in that car wreck. That I'm not even alive. That this is hell."

He looked into her eyes. They were warm and soft. He watched her hand move slowly from her side, reaching across the space between them to caress his face. Her palm was smooth. The scent on her wrist was feminine sweet. He leaned into her touch, soaking it in.

A decade had passed since the last time a woman's fingertips were on his skin. Ten calendars. Her hand was hot. He closed his eyes and swallowed. He could feel her energy vibrating through him, pure and revitalizing. He imagined it as gold dust swirling in his mouth, surging down his windpipe, filling his lungs, circling his heart, warming it, until the hard shell that had formed around it cracked and fell away. He could hear it pounding wildly in his ears.

When he opened his eyes, she was smiling.

PART II
September

22

Patriot Games

The Sandpiper Lodge was a long brown one-story structure of seedy motel rooms on a flat stretch of highway just west of Pine Grove, between a boarded-up gas station and the old Trailways bus depot. Owned by an Indian couple, it did most of its business with out-of-towners coming to visit loved ones at the prison and local crackheads needing a place to trick.

Lance peeked through the blinds at the passing cars on the highway, their headlights left white streaks in the dark. They all looked like feds. *Every fucking one of them. Slimy bastards. With their suits and their sunglasses and their directional microphones and their damned Patriot Act.*

If there was one thing in this world that Lance Broxson hated with every cell in his body, it was that worthless piece of Yankee communist legislation called the Patriot Act.

True, he had only recently learned of its existence while listening to late night AM talk radio and yes, the bill *was* almost eight years old, but he didn't give a fuck. Wrong was wrong. America was supposed to be the land of the free and now the government was spying on its own citizens?

A truck pulled into the motel parking lot, its rumbling engine sounded more like a Harley than a pickup. Headlights flooded across his window as it pulled to a stop in front of his room.

"Who's that?" Jessica whispered from the bed behind him.

Lance ignored her and fired up a cigarette. Outside, a door slammed followed by footsteps, whistling, then a soft knock on the door.

He opened it and Jarvis ducked into the room.

"Well look what the cat dragged in," he said. "Happy birthday man."

"I don't know about all this," said Jarvis, looking around. "First you call me way out here to this lovers' motel, then you answer the door in your underwear. You all right man?" He paused and squinted at the bed. "Is that Rayla?"

Lance shook his head. "Clayton Jarvis meet Jessica Maldonado."

"Hey," said Jessica, reaching for the glass pipe on the nightstand.

"Oh yeah," said Jarvis. "I know you. Third shift, tower one, right?"

"That's me."

Jarvis glanced at his watch. "You ain't working tonight Lance?"

"Yeah," he said, sitting down next to Jessica and holding his hand out for the pipe. "Uniform's in the truck."

Jarvis frowned. "Where is your truck?"

Lance took a deep hit and exhaled. "Out back." He reached under the mattress for the cellophane bag, fished out a chunk of crystal and dropped it in the bowl. He held out his hand without looking, like a doctor performing surgery. The torch was placed in his palm by his busty, if bedraggled, assistant. "Thanks baby."

The pipe danced in the flame. They watched in silence as it twisted and hovered in the crackling blue fire. The threefold transition from solid to liquid to vapor happened quickly. Soon the pipe was swirling with thick white smoke. Lance passed it to Jarvis. "Here you go man. Happy birthday."

Jarvis didn't move. "My birthday was last Tuesday."

Lance's face hardened. "Well, we're celebrating it now. Come on."

Jarvis looked at the pipe. "I 'preciate it Lance, really, but I can't sleep on that stuff and I–"

"Clayton Jarvis, if you don't hit this fucking pipe right now, I'm gonna tell Jessie here all about the time you shit in your overalls in the second grade…"

Jessica giggled.

"…or about the time your mom caught you whackin' to a Sears catalog."

Jarvis looked at Jessica. "That's a lie."

"Or about when you–"

"Okay," said Jarvis, snatching the pipe from his hand, "you win."

Lance watched as his friend took a deep pull and exhaled. He attempted to pass it back but Lance waved him off. "Hit it again."

Jarvis reluctantly obeyed.

Lance then smiled and held out his hand. "All right! Now it's a fuckin' party." He sucked the remaining smoke from the pipe as Jessica watched with hollow, hungry eyes. He ignored her and focused on Jarvis. "You ever heard of the Patriot Act, man?"

"The what?" asked Jarvis, thumping the tin lid of his dip can before twisting it off and shoving a fat pinch in his mouth.

Lance grabbed a Styrofoam cup off the table, half-full of watered-down Mountain Dew. "The Patriot Act," he said, walking over to the bathroom and dumping it in the toilet. He reached for the toilet paper and wrapped it around his hand a few times before sticking it inside the cup. "Here," he said, tossing it to Jarvis as he walked out of the bathroom and peeked through the blinds.

Jarvis held it up to his mouth and spat. "Thanks."

Lance twirled the pipe between his fingers as he watched the highway. "Back in the nineties," he began, "right after the Oklahoma City bombing, a few people in Congress tried to pass this law giving the feds permission to basically do whatever the fuck they wanted."

"They needed permission?" asked Jarvis. "I thought they already had that power."

Although they were both born and raised in Conrad County, Jarvis had the thicker accent by a country mile. Power sounded more like "pire" coming out of his mouth.

"Really?" asked Lance. "You thought they could spy on Americans? Tap our phones, read our e-mails, dig through our trash, all without a warrant?" He shook his head. "This ain't China, Jarvis."

"Yeah, I guess you're right."

"So as you can imagine, Congress voted hell no on that one."

"Thank you, Jesus," said Jarvis.

"But then a few years later those Arabs hijacked the planes and flew 'em into the towers and that changed everything. Congress dusted off that same bill from after Oklahoma City, renamed it the *Patriot Act* and pushed it right on through." He paused and glanced out at the night sky, looking for choppers. "I mean, come on, you remember how you felt after nine-eleven. The whole damn country was emotional. How could any politician vote against something as American-sounding as the *Patriot Act* at a time like that? Slick fuckers."

Lance turned and caught Jarvis staring at Jessica's breasts. He smiled and walked over to the bed. Jessica squirmed to see around him, looking longingly at the pipe he left on the table. Suddenly he reached inside her tank top and scooped out a massive breast.

"Lance Broxson!" she cried, but didn't resist.

"Nice, ain't it?" he said to Jarvis, weighing it in his hand. He stared down at the pale tan line and the large areola.

Jarvis blushed and looked away. "Aw, hell, Lance…"

Lance looked at his watch. "Damn, it's getting late." He grabbed Jessica's hand and helped her out of bed. "I need to talk to you before I go." He winked over at Jarvis. "We'll just be a minute."

He pulled her roughly toward the tiny bathroom. She staggered behind him in her panties. Once inside, he slammed the door and lifted her up on the sink, kissing her hard, crushing her mouth with his, forcing her back against the dirty mirror.

He pulled away and lifted her tank top over her breasts, caressing them. "I need a favor, baby."

She raised an eyebrow.

"Jarvis is gonna drive you home," he said, "but … you don't have to leave right away. The room's paid for and I'll give you a little dope to make it through the night."

"Okay," she said, placing her arms around his neck. "What's the favor?"

The vent rattled above them. Dim yellow lighting made the tiny room appear as if everything in it was covered in a greasy film. Maybe it was.

He kissed her again. "I want you to show Jarvis a good time."

"Okay," she said, then, "Wait, what do you mean by a good time?"

Lance stopped kissing her. They were nose to nose. "I mean I want you to fuck him."

She blinked. "Seriously? Are you crazy, Lance? Absolutely not."

"Shh, hold your voice down," he said, attempting to kiss her again.

She pushed him away. "I can't believe you just asked me that."

"Come on," said Lance. "Just once. For me."

"No!" she whispered. "I ain't your whore."

"You're not?" Lance growled. "What the fuck are you then?"

Her eyes searched his. "You're scaring me."

He softened his voice and touched her face. "Listen, I need you to do this. I'll give you an eightball, okay? And I'll leave you the pipe. Whatever. It's his birthday, Jess. Have a heart."

"Uh uh," she shook her head. "I'm not like that."

"I know you're not," said Lance. "This'll just be a one-shot deal, okay? Baby it's been ten years since Dana left him. Ten years since he's been with a woman. It'll probably be over in two minutes."

"Why don't you get Rayla to fuck him?"

The backhand came lightning quick, as if someone else reached between them and slapped her. There was no thought, no message from brain to hand saying *Go!* The blow was spontaneous. Reflexive.

"Don't you ever mention my wife again."

Her head was knocked sideways. When she turned back toward him, long sweaty strands of hair were plastered across her face.

"Now you're going to do what I tell you," he said.

"I will not!" she shot back, struggling frantically to get away from him. "He's disgusting and fat and ugly!" She attempted to launch a kick. "If you want him to get laid so bad, then you fuck him."

Lance clamped his hand over her mouth and drove her head back into the glass, pressing all his weight against her, pinning her to the mirror. His right hand reached between them and found her swollen nipple. He twisted it violently.

"Listen to me," he whispered, leaning into her. His mouth brushed against her earlobe. His own sour breath mixed with her faint perfume and filled his nostrils. "You have three kids, two boys and a girl, right?"

She stopped struggling and stared back at him.

"I will tie cinderblocks to their dirty little feet and use them as gator bait. Do you understand me?"

She mumbled something into his palm.

"Is that a yes?" he growled, removing his hand.

Her bottom lip was quivering. "You ... you shouldn't say things like that."

He wanted to spit in her face. "Should and shouldn't," he said, "two useless fucking words. *Is!* That's all I give a fuck about, *what is,* nothing else matters."

Like the backhand, he had no idea where the words came from, they leapt from his mouth without consideration or forethought. They tasted foreign on his lips, dark and full of power. The fight went out of her. He smiled.

"Look, it's not gonna be that bad. You'll see. Jarvis is a big teddy bear, okay?"

She nodded slowly.

He leaned forward and kissed her. "I gotta get to work," he said. "I'll leave you some dope on the table."

He glanced over her trembling shoulder into the mirror. A stranger with dark circles under bloodshot eyes and sallow pasty skin was staring back at him. He fixed his hair before reaching for the door.

She watched him from her seat on the sink.

"Smile," he said. "It'll be over before you know it."

23

The Handoff

Rayla knelt and dug a stack of request forms from a slot in the cabinet. Someone had mixed them with the 303s and property sheets. She set them on the desk and ran a damp rag over the dusty wood. It came away filthy. She shook her head.

Sergeant Billingsley had his feet up on the desk and his hat pulled low. A thick salt and pepper mustache covered most of his mouth. "So how's Lance been?" he asked. "I haven't seen him in a while." His voice was gruff, the product of a lifetime of cigarettes, hard liquor, and yelling at inmates.

"He's doing good," said Rayla, "still working midnights, hunting with Jarvis. Same old Lance, really."

"Clayton Jarvis," he said. "Good man. Those two have been best friends for as long as I can remember."

Rayla nodded and continued to wipe the dust from the cabinet, anxious to get off the subject of her husband. Lance had been acting weird lately. Erratic. Whenever he bothered coming home, that is. The thing was, she didn't even care anymore. She spent most nights hoping he *wouldn't* come home. She was sick of pretending to sleep while he tiptoed around in the dark, peeking through the blinds, sick of the static crackle of AM radio coming from the living room, and God forbid if he wanted to have sex.

"Ya'll have been together for a while now," he said.

"A year, Monday," said Rayla.

"That's good. I know a lot of people round here thought it wouldn't last. Lance has always had a wild hair. Hard to imagine him settling down."

Rayla concentrated on separating the forms above the cabinet.

"I guess all it took was a good woman," he said, "but then ain't that how it always is?"

The low-side door buzzed. She could see the massive frame of Officer Redmon through the scratched Plexiglas of the dormitory entrance. She reached over and hit the green button on the control board.

Sergeant Billingsley cocked his head and squinted toward the window from under the bill of his cap. Then, seeing it was just the rookie, he settled back in his chair and folded his hands over his belt buckle.

Rayla smiled and walked to the flap. "Hey!" she said through the glass. "I haven't seen you in a while."

"I've been working the perimeter," he said without making eye contact. He fumbled through a stack of memos and slid one in the drawer.

She noticed his nametag. "Well I guess training is over, huh? We'll probably be calling you *Captain* Redmon in a few years."

He nodded once before turning and hurrying out the door. Rayla watched him go as she retrieved the memo from the flap. She glanced down at it, an interoffice memorandum regarding policy for mental health emergencies.

"Well he's just bubbling over with personality, ain't he?" cracked the Sarge.

Rayla stuck the memo in a binder full of identical papers. She had been wanting to apologize to Redmon for Lance's behavior ever since that embarrassing morning in the parking lot but she never had the chance.

"Wasn't he the one you were training over in H-Dorm when that inmate attacked you?"

"Mm hmm."

He shook his head. "Damned predators and sex offenders. Seems like that's all that's getting off the bus these days. I don't blame Lance for going back there and whuppin' that boy like he did. I would've given him *three* black eyes."

Rayla considered his words as she stacked the forms on the desk. *How can you give a person three black eyes?*

"Two on his face and one on his ass!" said the old man, as he stood and grabbed his radio.

Rayla smiled.

"I'm hungry," he said. "You want anything from the canteen?"

"No, thanks."

"I'll be back in a while," he said, closing the officers' station door firmly behind him.

Rayla listened for the laundry grill gate to slam and watched him walk out into the bedding area. "Hey!" his voice thundered. "It's too damned loud in here!"

The dorm outside the glass bubble collectively paused and every head swiveled in the direction of the old sergeant. He stared down seventy-five inmates for a long moment before turning and heading toward the dormitory exit. He winked at Rayla on his way out.

She hit the button to buzz him out then surveyed the station with her hands on her hips. There was nothing left to do.

Even after six years of working in corrections she was still amazed by the starkness of the officers' stations. They were relics from the 70s, frozen in time, complete with bulky metal file cabinets, broken PA systems and archaic control panels with limited capabilities.

She had heard of new prisons being built with computers and cameras and other technological advancements, but she had never seen one. Everywhere she had been, whether for training or transport, was exactly the same. She was surprised there were no rotary phones and telegraph machines.

"Excuse me, ma'am," came a voice from the talk-space. "Can I have some medication please?"

She smiled and turned toward the window. "What do you need?"

"What do you have?" asked Kevin Freeman.

She rolled her eyes. Every inmate who had been in prison for more than a week knew what was in the medicine box. Ibuprofen, Alamag and Thorets. Anything else had to be administered by a nurse.

"What hurts?" she asked.

"My heart."

"Hmm ... sounds like indigestion," she diagnosed, reaching for an Alamag tablet.

"No," he said. "I think it's broken. Do you have anything for pain?"

"Stop," she mouthed, opening the flap and handing him a packet of Ibuprofen.

He pressed a folded piece of paper into her palm, tugging gently on her finger before releasing it.

She chewed on her bottom lip as he walked away. The note was warm against her fingertips, humming, pulsating as if it were a living thing she held.

She slid it in her pocket, sat down at the desk, then decided that her panties might be a safer hiding place. She made the fumbling switch with a trembling hand, hoping no inmate would choose that moment to stroll up to the window and ask for a request form.

The sharp edges of the folded paper bit into her skin. She sank lower in her chair and stared out into the dayroom. Across the bustling dorm, through the card games and arguments and inmate traffic, her eyes touched his. A smile flashed across his face, then faded just as quickly.

24

Escaping Within

The trailer was dark. Lance's Silverado was backed in the driveway. The front grill looked sinister in her headlights, like snarling metal teeth.

She shut off the car and reached down the front of her pants for the note, watching the silent trailer as she unfolded it in her lap.

The words were written in small block letters. She read them with a pounding heart.

Hi,
I know I'm way out of bounds by writing this and the last thing I want to do is get you in trouble, but I'll be out of here soon and I don't want to regret not telling you how I feel for the rest of my life. You are the most beautiful woman I have ever seen. It hurts to look at you yet I can't make myself do anything else when you're around. And even when you're not around, you dominate my thoughts. My face still burns from your touch. I've analyzed that day over and over since it happened and I can't figure it out. Were you just being nice? Was it pity? Or something more? I walked into that room wanting to hate you and walked out wondering if my whole life was building

toward that one moment... if you were the reason why destiny brought me to this specific place at this specific time. Even after 10 years in prison, I can't imagine freedom feeling any better than your fingertips on my skin. I don't want to complicate your life. I know we live in different worlds and I'm guessing that gold band on your finger is more than just a friendship ring. But if he, or this town, or this world has forgotten to tell you how perfect you are – I wanted you to know the truth.

You are beautiful,
Love, Me

His words were like a surge of warmth rushing over her. She looked up. A curtain swayed. She quickly refolded the note and stuck it back down her pants. Her car door dinged annoyingly as she grabbed her bag and stepped onto the driveway, slamming the door behind her.

She didn't bother locking the car. She never did. Any thief with balls enough to select a trailer park full of correctional officers to commit his crime, especially one that was built in the shadow of a prison gun tower, deserved the few pennies and paperclips in her ashtray.

She walked up the steps to the front door and tried the knob. It turned easily. She pushed it open expecting to be met with darkness. Instead, the living room flickered in the low light of a solitary candle burning on the kitchen table.

Lance looked back at her from the stove. His sleeves were rolled up around his forearms like a politician on a tour of a disaster area. A dimpled smile lit his face.

"You're late," he said.

"Wow," said Rayla. "What's all this?"

"Happy anniversary," he smiled. "Sit down."

She set her bag on the counter and pulled a chair back from the table, not bothering to tell him that their anniversary was two days ago.

He spooned some spaghetti on her plate and sat down across from her. "I hope this is the first of many happy years together."

"Me too," she lied, focusing on her food.

"So what was your post today?"

"Alpha," she said.

"Alpha ... you're working there a lot lately."

She nodded.

"Who'd they have in there with you?"

"Billingsley," she said, wiping her mouth.

His eyes narrowed. "That horny old bastard wasn't trying to put the moves on you, was he?"

"No," she said, wrapping her fork with noodles. *Was it only recently that she had taken comfort in his jealousy?*

He filled her glass with wine then held up his beer for a toast. Her glass clinked against his bottle.

"Me and you, baby," he said, "forever."

She took a sip. "This is good. Where'd you get it?"

"Walmart," he said. "Hey pass me a piece of that garlic bread."

She reached for the bowl of toast and noticed the black velvet box inside.

Lance was smiling at her. "Open it."

She looked at him as she flipped the top. Gold sparkled in the candlelight. A cursive letter *L* hung from a herringbone chain. She wondered whether he had bought it at a pawn shop or a flea market booth.

"Like it?"

"It's beautiful," she lied.

"Know what the *L* stands for?" he asked, rising and walking behind her chair.

Loser? Liar? Low life?

"It stands for Lance," he said, kissing the top of her head, "cuz you belong to me. Let's see how it looks on you."

She instantly thought of Mydog's collar. *If found return to ...*

He removed the chain from the box. She stared at the wall as he lowered it over her face and fastened the clasp behind her neck. Suddenly his lips, dry and cracked, were on her throat while his rough hands squeezed her breasts. Dirt was caked under his fingernails.

She tried not to cringe as he groped her, focusing on the flame as he unbuttoned her uniform shirt. Her marriage was over. It was obvious now. The last bastion of hope was melting away like the wax sliding down the candle.

His hands were icicles on her skin. She closed her eyes. Leaving him was not going to be easy. He was stubborn and possessive and volatile. Although she would never admit it to Mema, she felt like a fool for entrapping herself. Like a teenage runaway who gets two thousand miles from home before discovering that the nice sweet boy she ran off with is not really all that nice, or all that sweet.

Lance was dangerous. More so on whatever drug he was doing. She sure as hell didn't want her *fucking teeth knocked out*, or something even worse to happen. She'd have to be careful. She'd need to take her time and think things out. She needed a plan. An exit strategy.

He was grunting and fumbling with her uniform belt when she realized what he was doing.

She pushed back her chair and stood. "Wait!" she said, walking through the living room toward the hall, "Let me wash first."

He picked her up from behind, laughing, "Aw baby, I don't care about that."

She struggled against his iron grip as he dumped her on the couch and held her down. "Please, Lance, I–"

He silenced her with a brutal kiss. His beard stubble scratched her face. She kicked and squirmed but it was no use. The more frantically she struggled, the more aroused he became.

The candle cast a shadowy yellow glow over the living room as she scanned the end table for a weapon. His putrid breath was rank on her skin.

He pulled back and smiled down at her, half of his face was concealed in darkness. Suddenly she knew what she had to do. She willed her body to relax and looked directly into the vacant black pools of his eyes. She moistened her lips with her tongue and raised her head to kiss him.

He met her halfway, crushing her mouth with his, driving her back into the couch cushion but gradually loosening his grip. She wrapped her arms around his neck and moaned softly as he squeezed her breasts and ground against her.

Slowly, she worked her way out from under him, nudging, pressing, turning, until finally their positions were reversed and his back was against the cushion. By the time he succeeded in unfastening her belt, she was already on her knees in the small space between the couch and the coffee table.

He groaned as she unbuttoned his jeans. His breathing was ragged against the hushed backdrop of the trailer. He grabbed a handful of hair and pulled her face toward his crotch.

In the darkness below, hidden from view, her left hand slid down the front of her pants and removed the note. She pushed it as far back under the couch as she could, then tried turning off her mind and escaping within.

25

Ixia and Jeux

"Come on," said Weasel. *"Qi?* Seriously? No way."

Kevin pushed the Scrabble Dictionary across the table. "Are you challenging?"

Weasel glanced down at the book then back at him. His magnified eyes blinked behind the thick lenses. "Nah," he said finally. "You *want* me to challenge. I can tell by the way you're looking at me."

"Good move, Psycho," said Kevin, smiling. "You would've lost again."

"Stop calling me that," said Weasel. "What's the score anyway?"

"A lot to a little."

"Qi," Weasel grumbled. "I don't care what the book says, that's not a word. And neither is qat. You can't have a Q without a U, it's un-American."

Kevin laughed. "Un-American?"

"I just wish we could use the Webster's Dictionary," he said as he shuffled his tiles. "I think it would be a little more fair."

Kevin stopped listening and stared over his shoulder into the officers' station.

"I mean what the hell is an ixia?" Weasel complained, "or a jeux? Who uses words like that?"

She glanced at him through the glass as she set down her bag and said something to the relief officer who was gathering his things to leave.

"And you call *me* a nerd," Weasel continued to ramble. "I'm pretty sure Scrabble is like the signature game for nerds and you seem to be a master at it, so what does that mean? Hmmm … I'm not sayin' … I'm just sayin'."

He heard the door buzz and slam behind the other officer as he departed the dorm. She looked right and left and then smiled at him and slowly raised her hand. She first pointed two fingers like a gun before lifting a pinkie, making the letters H and I.

He frowned and slowly lifted his chin in response.

She squinted at the ceiling for a moment before raising her hand again. "B-r-o-o-m," she haltingly spelled out.

"I'll be right back," he said to Weasel, grabbing the push broom off the wall.

His heart was pounding as the laundry room grill-gate swung open. The air was sweet with the scent of her perfume. Her eyes sparkled. Her skin glowed. She leaned against the frame of the officers' station door and watched him as he pretended to sweep.

"Where did you learn to sign?" he asked.

"A book," she said. *"Sign Language for Dummies."*

He laughed. "Are you a dummy?"

"I don't know," she said. "I never thought so before, but this is pretty stupid."

"What is?"

"This," she said, holding his gaze for a moment before looking away. "I could get in a lot of trouble. I could lose my job."

He nodded. "The note was probably a bad move."

"No," she said. "It was really sweet, you're really sweet. This is just ... dangerous."

"You don't have to be scared," he said. "We're not doing anything but talking."

"I know," she said before softly adding, "it's what I want to do that scares me."

He stopped sweeping and contemplated her face, heart-shaped and radiant with long black lashes and Bambi eyes. He ached to run his finger along the delicate line of her jaw, to bury his face in the graceful hollow of her throat, to kiss her tender lips.

His heart thumped in his chest. The sound of blood rushing through his veins roared like the ocean in his ears, as if a biological volume knob within him had been ratcheted to maximum level.

The floors could have split open. The walls could have crumbled. Chunks of ceiling could have crashed all around him. He wouldn't have blinked. He was drunk off proximity, lost in the details of her face. He shook his head.

"What?" she asked, shifting her weight from one foot to the other.

He wanted to tell her that he loved her, that he had loved her for a thousand lifetimes and would love her for a thousand more. That she made him believe in reincarnation, in angels, in God. But instead he just said, "I can't believe you know sign language."

"I had a good incentive to learn."

"What's that?"

"I'm nosy," she said, smiling. "I wanted to know what the hell you were talking about."

His eyes dropped to her hand, to the wedding ring on her finger. "Can I be nosy?"

"Depends," she said.

"Is he good to you?"

A pregnant silence ensued. She stared at the floor. He dug his index nail into the side of his thumb. *Good job, idiot,* the scornful voice in his head remarked, *why don't you ask her how much she makes while you're at it? Hell, don't stop there, get her address, ask what size bra she wears, find out what brand of toilet paper she uses...*

"No," she said, "he isn't."

He studied her pretty face. "Well I know the polite thing to say is 'I'm sorry to hear that,' but I'm not gonna lie to you. I'm glad. Because if he doesn't adore you like I do, if he doesn't treasure you and worship you and crave you like me, then it'll be that much easier to steal you from him."

"You don't crave me."

"You have no idea."

"You've been in prison too long."

"I'm free right now."

He leaned in to kiss her. She didn't turn away. Her eyes closed and her head tilted back as he stroked her face and tasted her lips.

Suddenly a spark appeared in the dark cavern of his soul, a glimmer of light in the cold ashes of a long abandoned campfire.

Her lips parted and her tongue, slippery sweet, tentatively touched his. Her warm body was pressed against him, filling his senses, intoxicating him. The spark exploded into a raging fire as he drank ravenously from her lips. He pulled her closer. He couldn't get enough. She moaned softly as he devoured her mouth, feasted on her scent, binged on the feel of her body in his hands. Then she was pushing him away.

He opened his eyes. His ears were ringing. His knees were trembling. He reached for the broom to steady himself. She ducked her head into the officers' station and surveyed the windows before turning back to him. "If someone walked in on us right now," she said, "all it would take is one look at your face and you'd be in handcuffs."

He took stock of himself. She was right. He could feel the corners of his mouth pulling upward in what he could only imagine was a goofy grin. His face felt warm. His vision was blurry. His brain was fuzzy.

"What about you? Would you be in handcuffs too?"

She shook her head. "Worse. I'd be in Fretwell's office."

He pursed his lips and narrowed his eyes, summoning his most ferocious scowl. "Better?"

She laughed quietly. "Ooohh, I remember that face."

"Oh yeah?" he said, sweeping again. "From when?"

"That first morning, in the bathroom. You were cleaning your friend's cuts."

"Was I intimidating?"

"No," she said. "I just thought you were an asshole."

"I was hiding my feelings," he said. "It was love at first sight for me."

Her eyes softened. "Really?"

"Hell no," he laughed. "I hated you."

"Why?"

"Your uniform. It wasn't personal. I just can't stand correctional officers."

"So what changed your mind?"

"I'm not sure," he said. "I think it was your ass."

"Shut up."

"Nah," he said, looking into her eyes, "it was your touch that got me. It was healing."

"You've been in prison too long."

"You said that before. And you're right. I have been locked up too long. But I've never felt this way, even before I came to prison."

Her radio crackled. She reached down to silence it. "Is anyone waiting on you out there?"

He shook his head. "You mean like a girl?"

"Anyone," she said. "Where are your parents?"

"Gone. I can barely remember them. I grew up in foster care. Bobby was my only family. We were state babies."

She bit her bottom lip. "I barely knew my parents either. My grandmother raised me."

Her eyes were faraway. He wanted to pull her close, to kiss her again, to let his touch attempt to relate what his words could not.

She took a deep breath and nodded, as if agreeing with a voice in her head. "Nobody knows this," she said, "not even my husband. My mother killed my father, and then herself." She paused and looked down at her boots. "He used to beat her."

He reached out to touch her but drew his hand back sharply as a loud banging came from the front of the dorm.

"Go," she whispered.

He slid through the laundry door and she locked it behind him. He hurried to the back of the bathroom and began sweeping furiously.

The front door buzzed and slammed shut. He heard the clamor of jingling keys and a squawking radio in the hall, then a hulk of a guard with sergeant stripes emerged and pressed two giant hands against the officers' station glass.

"Hey baby," he said.

Kevin watched as she came to the window and said something before dropping her keys in the flap.

"Uh uh," he said, removing them. "Holland needed me to pull a double."

Kevin stared at his nametag as he swaggered over to the laundry room door. *L. Broxson.*

"What the fuck are you looking at?" he growled.

Kevin averted his eyes and continued to sweep. "Nothing sir."

26

Festus and Junior

Lance strode down the long row of cell doors shining his flashlight in each window as he passed. An industrial-sized fan rattled pointlessly from the front of the wing, barely circulating the stale hot air. He could feel the sweat from his armpits trickling down his sides while his uniform shirt clung adhesively to his back. Even his hair was slick with humidity.

Halfway down the wing he paused and glanced up at a cell number while reaching for his radio. He removed it from his belt with the practiced spin of a gunfighter drawing his six shooter.

"Roll 3107," he said.

After a few moments the door creaked and slid open a few inches. He grabbed the handle and pulled it back. Festus Methlab Mulgrew was smoking in the dark.

"Sarge," mumbled the bony inmate, squinting as his eyes adjusted to the light.

"Don't fucking *Sarge* me you scrawny piece of shit. I want my money."

"Take it easy," said Methlab, reaching across his bunk. "I've got it right here."

Lance could see the bones protruding from his back as he dug under his mat for the money. "It'd better all be there."

Methlab turned and tossed a roll of bills across the cell. Lance snatched it out of the air, glancing down the wing at the officers' station as he stuck it in his pocket.

"It is," said Methlab, quickly averting his eyes when Lance turned back toward him, "plus five hundred. I need some more."

"Tomorrow," said Lance.

Methlab stared at the wall. "You don't have anything on you now?"

"I said tomorrow," Lance growled.

"Okay. Tomorrow's fine."

Lance backed out of the doorway and reached for the handle.

"One more thing," said Methlab, pausing to take a drag from his cigarette, his rodent face illuminated in the orange cherry at the end.

"What?" asked Lance.

"I need to move."

"Where?"

"Anywhere," he said. "Out of this dorm."

"Why?"

Methlab stared at the floor. "Gang members. Jits. They've been making little sideways comments. Nothing direct. Just innuendo. But I've been doing this a while. I know what tension smells like."

Lance frowned. *What the fuck is innuendo?* He shook his head. "It's the ice. Makes me paranoid too."

Methlab's eyes touched his then quickly darted away. "No, they broke into my locker yesterday. Stole my radio and a few packs of rip. I doubt that's what they were looking for."

Lance studied him from across the smoky cell. His pale skin was stretched tight over his knobby shoulders and his head trembled slightly. "What, are you scared or something?"

A flicker of a smile touched his gaunt face as he crossed his skinny arms and leaned back on his locker. "No," he said, "but killing is such an inconvenience. I'd have to go to lockdown. Then the county jail. Our little business venture would be over, and worse, I'd be estranged from Junior. Probably never see him again."

Disgust twisted Lance's face. "Who's Junior? Your faggot lover?"

Methlab stood. The light from his cell window slashed across his concave chest. He extended a skeletal hand toward the ledge. A dark shape scurried across the Plexiglas and climbed onto his slender finger. "Very funny, Sergeant Broxson," he said, lifting his hand to his face. The spider leapt to his chin and crawled over his fleshy lips, moving slowly up his cheek before crossing his nose. "But no, Junior here is my son. My only begotten son."

Lance shivered despite the heat.

Methlab tilted his head back and spoke to the spider as if it was a small child. "You're my little baby, aren't you? Yes you are. Now tell the big strong officer we're ready for a dorm change, Junior."

The furry black spider crawled across his eye and sat on his forehead.

"I'll see what I can do," said Lance before slamming the cell door.

27

Plexiglas

"Nice necklace," said Kevin.

Her hand flew to her throat. She almost offered an explanation but decided against it, just as the words were forming on her lips. She shook her head in wonder. Nothing got past him. A change of perfume, a different shade of eye shadow, a new flavor of lip balm, a subtle shift in her mood. He noticed everything.

He stood at the glass smiling with his eyes. Behind him the circus that was Alpha Dorm paraded back and forth to the bathroom, telephones, and dayroom in its usual boisterous clamor. She tucked a strand of hair behind her ear and rifled through the box of medication.

"So how long do you have now?" she asked, afraid to look in his smoldering green eyes, afraid that another inmate would see the feelings she was fighting so hard to conceal. A rumor would be catastrophic at this point for her and for him.

"I think I'm exactly one day closer than the last time you asked," he said with a straight face. "But every time you remind me of it, the clock starts to drag."

"Sorry," she said.

He leaned against the talk-space and lowered his voice. "I was thinking about something last night."

She raised an eyebrow as she filled out his information on the medication check sheet. She knew his DC number by heart.

"I don't know your first name. I've kissed you, held you, told you my secrets and listened to yours. I think about you every hour of every day, but I have no idea what your first name is. That's a little strange, don't you think?"

She tapped her pen on the clipboard.

"I mean, it's gonna be a little awkward when you run away with me and we finally make love for the first time. *Oh! Yes Officer Broxson, right there ma'am!* Not very sexy, right? Unless you're into role playing."

She laughed and handed him a packet of ibuprofen. "It's Rayla."

"Rayla," he repeated, testing it on his lips with a glazed look in his eyes. As usual he held on to her finger for a moment before releasing it. "It's … beautiful."

"It was my mother's name," she said, attempting to look busy by shuffling papers. "My grandfather was named Ray. He wanted a boy."

She watched his Adam's apple move up and down in his throat as he swallowed. He looked longingly back at her through the glass. Beneath her swirling emotions and her pounding heart, an alarm bell was sounding. *How many stupid naïve women had she seen being escorted off the compound for having a relationship with an inmate?* Fretwell seemed to relish not just firing them but ensuring that they were made social pariahs, scorned by the entire town.

"That thing you told me the other day, about your parents," he said. "I didn't have time to tell you then, but, well, I just wanted you to know that I will die with that secret in my heart.

The fact that you thought enough of me to share such an intimate detail of your life is... I'm honored."

She was about to tell him that she felt the same way – that *he* honored *her* by talking about his brother and growing up in foster care – when a loud banging at the front door caused them both to turn.

She was relieved to see an inmate's blue uniform waiting outside the scratched window of the dormitory entrance. Lance had been working a lot of doubles lately. She pressed the button to buzz him in. The lock popped and a sallow-faced, shifty-eyed, child-molester type shuffled through the door and dropped his property in the hallway.

Kevin stepped aside as he approached the flap, displaying his inmate ID card. His eyes darted from her face to her nametag to the floor.

"Festus Mulgrew, ma'am. I'm coming from H-Dormitory. I should be on the move sheet."

28

Jessica's Gauntlet

The lake was flat as a mirror and just as reflective. Overhanging trees and drifting clouds shone clearly on its surface. Jessica Maldonado was sitting between Clayton Jarvis's legs, leaning against his ample belly. The smell of Stetson cologne and Kodiak dip enveloped her.

His breathing was deep and calm as he leaned against a pine. His arms folded protectively around her. She stared down at his massive hands, calloused, knuckle-scarred and reddened. The hands of a country boy.

She wriggled her fingers between his and twisted her body so that her cheek was pressed against his chest.

"Clayton?" she murmured in a little girl's voice.

"Yeah," he said.

"Have you told him yet?"

"Told who what?"

She rolled her eyes. "Lance. Have you told Lance about me and you?"

"Naw…"

She raised her head to look in his eyes. They were wolf-gray and sheepish under unruly reddish-yellow eyebrows. His cheeks were like two apples, his face a sweaty roadmap of laugh lines and creases. "Why not?" she asked.

He shrugged. "Ain't had the chance."

She struggled to her knees then straddled him, his t-shirt was pulled up exposing his fist-sized belly button. "Clayton Eugene Jarvis," she scolded, tugging on the red hair of his beard, "don't you dare lie to me. I saw ya'll come in together last night. I work tower one, remember? Who do you think buzzed you through the gate?"

Jarvis closed his eyes. "Please don't start in on me. It's too pretty a day."

"What are you afraid of?"

His eyes snapped open. "I ain't afraid of nothin'."

"Well then tell him, Clayton. Tell him I'm your girl."

He looked out at the lake. "I just don't see why it's any of his concern."

She leaned forward and breathed in his ear. "*Am* I your girl?"

She heard him swallow. "Course you are," he said, his voice thick and throaty.

"Do you love me?" she asked, running a fingernail down his plump red face.

"Aw come on, Jess, you know I love you." His hands were on her butt.

She stiffened and looked coldly into his eyes. "Then you tell him that, Clayton. Tell him I'm your girl. Tell him you love me and tell him to stay the hell away from my trailer."

29

The Janitor

Rayla squirted a glob of lotion into her palm and rubbed her hands together as Mydog watched impassively from his worn spot on the hardwood floor.

"You don't have to do this, you know," said Mema into the couch cushion.

"I know," said Rayla.

"Stiff-necked girl," mumbled the old woman. "Stiff-necked and willful, just like your momma."

Rayla sat on the couch and moved her grandmother's knees across her lap. Slowly, deliberately, she began working the lotion into her swollen feet, massaging the cracked heels and varicose ankles, the bruised arches and calloused balls, the gnarled toes.

Rayla had been rubbing her Mema's feet since she was four years old. There was a brief period during high school when she thought she was too cool and too grown up to perform such a menial task, but then a friend's grandmother passed away and Rayla attended the funeral. Afterwards she came straight home, ordered Mema to the couch and rubbed her feet until the old woman was snoring.

She did it lovingly. The older she grew, the more she cherished the moment. Rubbing Mema's feet was an honor to Rayla. A tradition. Like Coke Slurpees and rocking chairs. It felt like family. Like home.

"What are you smiling about?" asked Mema.

"I'm not smiling," said Rayla.

"You're not *now*," the old woman rasped, "but you were."

Rayla stared at her. "How do you know?"

"Because I know you."

Rayla rolled her eyes.

"Don't roll your eyes at me girl."

Rayla frowned and slowly shook her head while continuing to massage her feet. Suddenly the old woman's tiny shoulders began to convulse and a cackle erupted from her end of the couch.

"What's so funny?" Rayla asked.

"Do you remember what you gave me for Christmas last year?"

Rayla glanced at the golden-framed mirror hanging over the fireplace. Her grandmother's eyes twinkled in the glass.

"Gotcha," said Mema.

Rayla smiled sweetly and aimed a middle finger at the reflection.

"That's not very ladylike," Mema scolded. "Not too long ago that would've earned you a spanking."

Rayla reached for the lotion on the coffee table. They both knew she was full of shit. Mema had spanked her once in her life, for kicking a boy in her kindergarten class. After the punishment was delivered, Rayla ran to her room crying and refused to speak to her for a week. Numerous peace offerings were turned down flat – brownies, a new doll, Coke Slurpees, a trip to the river – until finally a deal was struck: No more spankings. Ever.

"So what was that smile for?" asked Mema. "Oh Lord, please don't tell me the asshole snookered you with a nice anniversary gift. You didn't renew your vows, did you?"

"No," Rayla laughed, reaching in her collar for the necklace. "He gave me this."

Mema squinted. "Cheap."

Rayla nodded. "And late."

"But there's that smile again," said Mema. Suddenly she was squirming and rocking. "Help me up."

Rayla gently assisted her into an upright position. Mema smoothed out her dress while watching her suspiciously. After a long moment she nodded to herself and asked, "What's his name?"

Rayla stared at her hands. "Kevin."

"Ha!" the old woman exclaimed. "I knew it!" She turned so that their knees were touching. "What's he look like?"

Rayla smiled. "Tall. Green eyes. He's … amazing."

Mema touched her arm and her voice dropped a notch. "Does he have those six pack abs?"

Rayla laughed. "Is that important?"

Her grandmother shrugged innocently.

"Well," said Rayla, "not that it makes any difference... But yes, he's very muscular."

"Ooh!" Mema clapped. "What's he do for a living? He ain't another prison guard is he?"

"No," said Rayla, an image of Kevin sweeping the laundry room rippled through her mind. "He's a … actually he's a janitor."

"A janitor?"

Rayla nodded.

"Well nobody can ever accuse you of being a gold digger, can they?"

Rayla continued to stare down at her hands. At her wedding ring.

"Does Lance have any idea?" asked Mema.

"No," said Rayla. "He's been off in his own little world lately."

"Good," said Mema. "Leave him there. Your old room's just like you left it. You can move back in tonight."

Mydog barked once, seconding the motion.

Rayla shook her head. "I wish it was that easy."

"It is," said Mema.

Rayla chewed on her bottom lip. "He's not going to let me go without a fight." *And if I ever catch you with another man again, I'll knock your fuckin' teeth out.*

"Then we'll have to get one of those restraining orders," said Mema.

"I don't know if that would stop him."

"Well if it didn't," said Mema, "your grandfather's shotgun sure would."

Rayla shook her head again. "I just need some time to think. I'll come up with something."

30

The Lookout

Weasel was trying his damnedest not to be nosy, to just ignore the grinding rasp of metal on concrete, to mind his own business, to be a convict.

Scrrrp. Scrrrp. Scrrrp.

He looked out the window at the yellow lines painted on the sidewalk and the single-file inmates moving between them. He looked at the officers' station where Ms. Broxson sat at the desk doing paperwork. He looked at the empty bunks in the front of the dorm, white six-inch collars against dark wool blankets. He looked everywhere *but* the opposite corner of the dorm, the direction from where the grinding came.

Scrrrp. Scrrrp. Scrrrp.

It was a sunny day and the yard was open. Most of the other housemen had finished their jobs and were outside. Kevin had a classification call-out to meet with the pre-release specialist. Weasel tried to imagine the awesome feeling of sitting in an office signing papers that said he was going home. *Home. Andy.* He wondered where his brother was.

"Hey man," a voice called in a sandpaper tone that almost rivaled the grinding.

Weasel turned toward the voice. It was the new guy in twenty-three lower. He was pale and thin with faded blue, amateurish-looking tats and greasy hair. He hadn't bathed since he moved into the dorm. Or slept. At least not that Weasel had seen. Not that he was paying that much attention. He was a convict. And convicts minded their own business. However, there was nothing wrong with being aware of one's surroundings. Even a hardliner like Kevin would agree with that.

"Yeah?" said Weasel.

"Check this out," said the stranger.

Weasel slid off the side of his bunk and landed in a half-crouch before slipping on his boots and sauntering across the dorm. He stopped short when he realized the man was holding a knife.

"I need you to do me a favor," said the man.

Weasel took a gulp of air and stared at the knife.

The man smiled without making eye contact. "I need you to look out for me while I do this. I'm almost done but I wouldn't want the lady in the booth to get curious and call for backup, you know?"

Weasel glanced at the officers' station and nodded.

"Sit down," ordered the man.

Weasel reluctantly sat at the foot of his bunk.

Scrrrp. Scrrrp. Scrrrp.

He dragged the shank over a rough patch of concrete on the floor.

"Who's that for?" Weasel asked. Kevin's disapproving voice was automatic in his head: *A convict would never ask that question.*

"Whoever fucks with me," hissed the stranger.

A black shape scurried across his sweat-stained pillowcase. Weasel stiffened. "Dude, there's a really big spider on your bed!" He looked around for something to kill it with. He reached beneath the bunk and found a shower slide.

When he sat back up, the man was pointing the knife at him. "Drop it," he ordered, his shifty eyes moving around the dorm in rapid ticks.

Weasel frowned as he dropped the flip-flop to the floor.

Slowly, the man turned the knife from Weasel and extended it toward the pillow. In short jerky bursts of movement that were oddly synchronized with the stranger's darting eyes, the spider approached the blade.

"This is Junior," said the man, a faint smile on his lips. "We've been bunkies for quite a while now."

"Oh," said Weasel. "He's your pet."

"You could say that," said the man, helping the spider back onto the pillow before holding up the blade and inspecting it. "Pet, best friend, son … yeah."

Weasel tried to split his concentration between knife and spider, wanting neither to get too close.

"I'm Methlab, by the way," he said, reaching behind his locker for a cup. "My real name's Festus but only the guards call me that."

Weasel watched as he dipped the shank in the cup and spun it in slow circles. When he finally removed it, a dark sludge covered the blade. He held it upside down and it dripped back into the cup.

Suddenly a wall of stench, thick and foul, was bearing down on Weasel. He gagged. "Oh man. What is that? It smells like–"

"Feces?" offered Methlab. "Shit? It is. I can tolerate the smell because I produced it. I've always found it fascinating that a man can be driven to nausea by the reek of another man's bowels, yet remain unmoved by the scent of his own."

"Yeah," said Weasel, cringing. "That's a um … that's a huge mystery."

Methlab grinned, revealing jagged yellow teeth that were black around the gum line.

"Well I know I'm being nosy," said Weasel, "but why are you dipping your knife in shit?"

"Bacteria," said Methlab. "I want the blade to be saturated with it. That way if the puncture wounds don't kill you, the gangrene will at least compound your misery."

Weasel resisted the urge to shiver. *A convict should never show weakness or fear.*

Methlab's eyes darted toward the window. "Oh shit, time to roll up the tents. The natives are coming home."

Weasel glanced over his shoulder at the long line of inmates returning from the rec yard. He stood.

"Wait a minute," said Methlab, digging under his blanket and coming away with a small cellophane baggy. He extended it to Weasel. "For your trouble."

Weasel accepted it reluctantly. "What is it?"

"Rocket fuel," said Methlab, his eyes touching Weasel's for a moment before pinballing around the dorm.

Weasel shrugged and stuck it in his pocket. "Thanks."

"What do they call you?" asked Methlab.

Weasel glanced over at Kevin's bunk before answering. "Psycho," he said. "They call me Psycho."

31
Vero Zay and Tampa Black

A hard thin stream of lukewarm water rained down on Kevin's head, trickling over his shoulders and down his back. Seven other men were showering alongside him, their voices echoing off the mildewed tiles. He kept his eyes forward and his back to the wall.

"Excuse me," muttered a fat Hispanic man as he exited the shower, his spot immediately seized by the next man waiting.

Although he was accustomed to living in close quarters with seventy-five other men from every walk of life, the community shower was something he could never get completely used to. Even after ten years, there was something unsettling about being naked in a room full of killers and rapists. He looked forward to the day when he could shower alone. *Fifty six and a wake up*, he thought.

Snippets of a conversation at the other end of the shower broke into his consciousness like an overlapping radio wave.

"I wouldn't give a fuck if there was thirty muthafuckas in this shower. If a bitch walks in that officers' station, I gotta have her... real talk."

"Straight up," agreed a high-pitched nasal voice.

"Best thing I can tell a muthafucka is don't look. Either that or get missin' while I handle my business, know what I'm sayin'?"

"I feel you."

Kevin knew the voices. The first belonged to Vero Zay, so named because he was from Vero Beach. His real name was Isaiah Banks. Light skinned and ripped from a lifetime on the blacktop, the rumor was he had a full scholarship to play basketball at one of the big ACC schools, but caught a robbery/kidnapping charge in the summer before enrollment. He was now close to forty with a collection of scars and dents marring the clean shaven topography of his head, souvenirs from past battles with combination locks and other makeshift prison yard weapons of war.

The second voice was Tampa Black, an ironic name for a skinny white kid, he was crackhead thin with a dollar sign tattooed beneath his left eye and tiny ears that jutted from his head like batwings. The only time he left his bunk was when a female was in the officers' station.

Both were notorious gunners.

Of all the twisted characters in the circus sideshow that was the Florida prison system, Kevin hated gunners the most. They were worse than thieves, worse than chomos, worse than snitches. Punks, wardaddies, jits, even gung-ho guards, none of them were as disrespectful as gunners.

"You seen that new bitch in D-Dorm?"

"Nah, I heard about her though."

"Aw, man, straight animal."

"That's what they say."

"Yeah, I had to duck off in there at lunch and break her in."

Public masturbation had become a fad in prison. Whacking off to unsuspecting female guards – many of them grandmothers – was the accepted norm. These weren't sex offenders either, these were drug dealers and jack boys who came to prison and picked up a new past-time. *Coming soon to a supermarket in your neighborhood,* thought Kevin.

"Where's Ms. Thompson been at?"

"I don't know. Vacation maybe."

"Damn, I miss that big ass."

"Is she down with it?"

"You better believe it."

"Not like Maldonado, though?"

"Oh hell nah. They know better than to let that freaky bitch on the pound."

"What about Ms. B? I wanna test that shit so bad."

Kevin felt his jaw tighten at the mention of her name. He realized he was clenching his washcloth so hard that his knuckles were a bloodless pale. He studied the tiny drops of water dotting the tight skin of his hands as he fought for calm. Getting into a fight with fifty-six days left would be stupid. Getting into a *naked* fistfight in a prison shower would be the most boneheaded move in his already questionable history of choice-making.

"You talkin' 'bout Ms. Broxson? On day shift?"

"Mm hmm."

"You gotta catch her when she workin' the tower. She likes to watch through binoculars."

"Man, Vero, you're shot out! That woman ain't on that. Remember she locked up crazy-ass Re-Rock a while back in H-Dorm? Sprayed him too."

"That shit was a publicity stunt. I'm tellin' you she's 'bout it. All you gotta do is find you a spot out in the grass and ... "

Kevin had heard enough. He grabbed his towel and quickly dried off before stepping into his boxers and exiting the shower.

He knew it was bullshit. He'd heard different variations of the same conversation a thousand times over the last ten years. Most gunners were not only delusional but also compulsive liars regarding their conquests. It was part of the sickness.

As he walked by he *accidentally* knocked their towels and underwear onto the filthy wet shower floor.

"Hey cracker! Watch where the fuck you goin'!" said Vero Zay.

"My bad," said Kevin, hoping the towels landed in piss.

32

The Master Knifeman

The dirt road curved around the back side of Diamondhead Lake like a dusty orange frown. A stubborn strip of grass persisted between the tire tracks. Jarvis took his foot off the accelerator and let the truck coast.

"It's just up ahead," said Lance, turning down the radio, "on the left."

Jarvis grabbed the spotlight, a million-candle power, and rolled down the window. He took a deep breath. "Hey Lance. I … there's something I need to tell you."

"Tell me after you cut that light on," Lance snapped, aiming his Mini 14 out the passenger side window and looking through the 70mm scope.

Jarvis hated shining. Not only was it illegal, but it was cowardly in his opinion. Paralyzing deer with a spotlight in the dark and picking them off was too easy, like shooting fish in a barrel. But he went along with Lance as always. The pattern was etched firmly in his character like the worn groove on a vinyl record. Where Lance Broxson led, Clayton Jarvis followed, forever and ever, amen. It had been that way since elementary school.

Jarvis lay the spotlight over the cab of the truck with one hand while steering with the other. He pulled the yellow rubber trigger. Suddenly the forest was illuminated in dazzling white light.

"Now what did you want to tell me?" asked Lance, scanning the tree line with his rifle scope.

"Well, it's about Jessica."

"Hold on," Lance hissed as they rounded a turn and came to a clearing. "There," he whispered.

A small family of deer in a field of clover had paused and were staring mesmerically into the spotlight. Their eyes shimmered like dimes. Jarvis counted three, an eight-point buck, a large doe, and a young velvet spike.

He heard Lance release the safety then, *BOOM!* the roar of the rifle filled the forest. The deer broke for the trees, bounding across the meadow at a frantic, desperate pace.

"Come on," said Lance, opening his door.

Jarvis put the truck in park and followed with the spotlight. He noticed the baby deer had collapsed twenty feet from the edge of the wood.

"What were you saying about Jessica?" Lance asked over his shoulder.

Jarvis was already out of breath and struggling to keep up. The forest bounced in the spotlight as he stumbled across the meadow. "She's ... my ... girl."

Lance burst out laughing as he arrived at the spot where the young deer lay panting in the field. "Your girl?"

Jarvis nodded and removed his cap, wiping the sweat from his brow on his forearm. He saw that the little deer had a hole in his shoulder.

Lance slung his rifle over his back, reached down and lifted the young spike by a small antler. He then drew his knife and slit its throat. "Jess is a whore, Jarvis," he said, hefting the small deer by its legs and turning back toward the truck. "She's everybody's girl."

Jarvis stared at the dark puddle of blood as it soaked through the flattened grass and was absorbed by the earth. Then he smashed his cap back on his head and followed his best friend.

Lance was already skinning the deer on the bed of the pickup when he reached the truck. It was messy work but he had always been a natural at it. Efficient. Lance Broxson was a master knifeman. There was nothing he was more skilled at, except maybe for women. Jarvis reached for his dip can as he watched him work.

"I told her to fuck you, you know," said Lance, removing the backstrap with a long straight incision, "at the motel that night. For your birthday."

Jarvis knew that. *She* told him. Nothing happened though. Not that night. He just held her while she cried and promised to never tell Lance. "I know," he said. "I 'preciate it. We had a good time."

Lance tossed a wet strip of blood-matted fur over the side of the truck. "Yeah, well there's a difference between a good time and a girlfriend."

Jarvis spat in the clay. "I know."

"I just don't want you to become the laughingstock of the prison," said Lance. "Hell, of the whole town."

Jarvis stared out at the tree line and continued to squeeze the power trigger on the spotlight as if it were an AK47. Suddenly, incredibly, the doe appeared at the edge of the forest, her head low, sniffing the ground where her offspring had fallen. He admired her courage and felt small for his own cowardly actions.

If Lance saw her, she'd be dead in a matter of seconds. He subtly moved the spotlight a few feet back to the left, allowing her to grieve under the protective cover of darkness.

"All right, we're good," said Lance, tossing the small carcass in the dirt, hopping off the bed of the truck and wiping his hands on the grass.

Jarvis released the trigger and allowed the light to dim as he walked around the driver's side door. The shocks groaned and squeaked as he wedged his massive body behind the wheel.

Lance was already heating up his pipe in the passenger seat, the blue flame exposing the remaining blood on his hands. "Don't worry, buddy," he said. "We'll find you a *real* girlfriend."

33

Te Adoro

The laundry cart was piled with damp, unsorted clothes. The broom, their ever present prop, was leaning against the garbage can. She could feel the pulsating heat from his strong hands through her uniform shirt, just above her waist. Never groping, always pulling, drawing her to him, close against him, unwilling to allow even an inch of space to exist between them.

His eyes were shut and his lashes fluttered as if he were on the verge of waking from a dream. His mouth was soft and warm against hers but his kiss was dire. Urgent. She could almost taste the longing on his lips and feel it in the gravitational pull of his touch. Ten years of no human contact, of emotional solitude, of loneliness and isolation. It was all there in his kiss, in his ravenous desperate kiss, vibrating through him like a billion supercharged electromagnetic pulses. Out of him and into her. He didn't just kiss her, he *drank* from her lips like she was water. Oxygen. Freedom.

Her radio crackled. She reluctantly placed her hands on his chest and pushed him away. He took a step back and licked his lips. His post-kiss facial expression was identical to yesterday's and the day before: lost, dazed, disheveled.

"I'm doing it again, aren't I?" he asked.

She nodded.

He stood up straight and blinked, the features of his face transformed into a brooding, pouty scowl. "Better?"

She crossed her arms and leaned against the wall, studying him. "A little," she said. "Above the neck you're fine. But below the belt you're as guilty as hell."

His eyes widened as he glanced down at the jutting projectile in the front of his pants. "Damn," he said, "just, um, just try to ignore him – *It!* I meant to say 'it.' Sorry. *It* will go back to sleep in a second."

He was blushing. She tried not to laugh. "So how many days do you have left?"

"Fifty-five."

"Liar," she shot back, "you have forty-nine."

"If you already know then why are you asking?"

Rayla deliberately let her eyes fall to the diminishing tent in the front of his pants. "I was trying to divert your attention from other things."

He shook his head. "I can't believe I found you hidden away in a prison."

She smiled. "You make it sound like you knew me from before, like you were looking for me."

He smiled back mysteriously. "Maybe I was."

She snorted, "You're so full of shit."

His face grew serious. "What made you wanna work at a prison? I mean, you're so beautiful and smart. Why this?"

"I don't know." It was her turn to blush. "I was working at a supermarket and I heard a commercial on the radio. The money and the benefits were better than anything else around here so I signed up for the course and went back to community college to get certified."

"Wow, college," he said. "And here I was thinking that you only needed a sixth-grade education to work here."

"Very funny."

"What other courses did you take in college?"

"Last time, just the corrections certification stuff," she said, "but I was also in the dual enrollment program in high school. I took a Spanish course and a few semesters of graphic design. Why?"

He shrugged. "I was thinking about going to college when I get out."

She tried to imagine him as free, with a haircut other than the standard regulation prison buzz and clothes of a different color than blue. It was hard to picture, like imagining his eyes as brown or his body as flabby and slumped. This was the only version of him she knew.

"Hablas Espanol?" he asked.

Rayla frowned. "Huh?"

"Tu me dijiste que tomaste clases Espanol en colegio. Can you speak it?"

"Oh, no," she said. "That was a long time ago. I forgot most of what I learned, never had a chance to use it. Where did you learn to speak it?"

"In here. From cellmates, library books, soccer games."

Rayla was impressed. "And you're fluent?"

"I can communicate."

"But you don't know *all* the words, do you?"

He cocked his head and smiled. "I don't know all the words in English."

He had a point. "Well, I'm impressed. Is there anything else that I don't know about you?"

"Volumes," he said, grinning.

"Really? Like what?"

"I'll tell you in bed," he said, "pillow talk."

A scene of them lying together flashed through her mind. White sheets, a darkened room, her head on his chest, his fingers in her hair. "I'm sure my husband would love that."

How ironic that a mere two months ago she was consumed by the thought of Lance cheating. Now she was the cheater. Guilty of what Lance would see as the ultimate betrayal, an affair with an inmate.

"Do you feel guilty?" Kevin asked, his green eyes piercing her soul.

"No," she said, suddenly hyperaware of the web in which she was tangled, the intoxicating allure of forbidden desire, the thrill of risk, the threat of danger, the heart-pounding promise of new love.

A toilet flushed on the other side of the laundry room door. He grabbed the broom and pretended to sweep. "Listen," he said, his voice quiet and serious, "I don't want to scare you away, but this needs to be said."

Rayla watched his face and waited while he formed the words.

"I think you know that we're playing with fire here." He glanced at the door. "Someone could walk in on us or even *think* they saw something, and the rumors would spread until they reached the right ears and then all this would come crashing down around us."

Rayla stabbed an incisor into her bottom lip.

"If that happens, and I go to the box, they're gonna tell you that I broke, that I sold you out and told them everything. If it ever comes to that – and I pray it won't – I want you to remember this conversation and know that I would die before I betrayed you. Do you believe me?"

"Yes," she whispered.

"Good," he said, reaching out to stroke her face, "don't forget."

"I won't," she said, aching for him.

"Forty-nine days."

She nodded.

"You know you're going to have to give me a way of contacting you, right? A phone number or something. I'll flush it once I have it memorized. Promise."

"Do you want it now?"

"Whenever," he said, reaching for the door.

"Okay," she said, following him with her eyes.

He paused before opening it. "When you were studying Spanish, did you notice how some words seem to carry more weight in that language?"

She considered his question. "Not really," she said, "but the only words I can remember are 'que hora es'."

He stared at the metal door. "In English the word 'love' has been so watered down that we use it for anything. A song, a car, a hat." He shook his head. "Even the phrase 'I love you' has been diluted to a definition closer to 'see you later' than anything else. People use it when they're hanging up a phone."

His words made her soul tingle. A rush of warmth swept through her as she stared at his broad shoulders and the tan skin at the nape of his neck. She had never met an inmate who spoke like he did. She had never met *anyone* who spoke like he did – with depth and passion and intensity. He was the anti-Lance, one hundred eighty degrees from any semblance to the man she shared her bed with.

"Do you hunt?" she blurted.

He turned and smiled. "Well that was random. Do I hunt? No. Why? Are you into the hunter/gatherer type? I don't think convicted felons are allowed to hunt," he said, "but hey, if killing a wild hog or moose or even a grizzly bear is the way to your heart, I'll do it with my bare hands." He pantomimed a vicious neck snap.

"No, I ... You're right, that was random. Finish what you were saying."

"What was I saying?"

"Spanish," she prompted.

"Oh yeah," he said, smiling, "Spanish."

"Well? Say something. Give me an example."

He pulled the door open. "Te adoro."

"What's it mean?"

The smile disappeared from his face as he stared into her eyes. "It means 'I adore you'."

She paused in the doorway as he pushed the broom over the damp tiles of the bathroom floor and vanished around the corner. *Te adoro,* she sighed, watching him go.

A sniffle yanked her from her reverie. She frowned and stood on her toes, surveying the bathroom. The hollow sound of a single drop of water carried across the latrine. She leaned around the doorframe and peered beyond the row of rusty scratched mirrors that were mounted over the stainless island of porcelain sinks. She flinched. Suspicious, close-set eyes stared back at her for a moment before quickly darting away.

He was leaning over a sink, holding the sides, his skeletal fingers as white as the porcelain he gripped. Ugly tattoos blotted the sallow skin of his arms in a meandering scribble of faded blue shapes and letters. Black hairs sprang forth from the loose yellow collar of his dingy t-shirt. Pock marks littered his face.

"What are you doing in here?" she asked.

"Life, with twenty mandatory," he said, tapping a disposable razor against the sink.

She twisted her face into a practiced fearless glare and pointed her radio at him. "Don't get slick with me. You know what I mean. What are you doing in the dorm? You're supposed to be at rec."

"I'm a bathroom houseman," he said.

"On my shift? Since when?"

"Almost two weeks now." His eyes were everywhere but on hers. "Since I moved in this dorm."

Nervous energy both sinister and repulsive emanated from his scrawny body in fits and tics as he dragged a razor over the pitted flesh of his stubbled cheek. He made her skin crawl. "I'm going to check the roster," she said, "and if you're not a day-shift houseman, I'm going to write you a disciplinary report."

"Okay," he said, again tapping the razor against the porcelain, cleaning it.

She could see the clumps of facial hair clinging to the side of the sink. She imagined the microscopic fragments of his mottled skin mixed with the shavings, imagined she could smell them, a sickening blend of feta cheese and wet carpet. "What's your name?" she asked, her nose wrinkling in disgust.

"Mulgrew," he said. "Festus Mulgrew."

34

Wiretaps

Lance Broxson was tweaking. Sweat poured down his face as he knelt by the living room wall and unscrewed the beige cover plate of the final electrical socket in the trailer. He tossed it into a pile of wires, converters and screws on the coffee table and inspected the rectangular hole in the wall panel for electronic listening devices.

Tweaking is a by-product of meth life, just like tooth decay, scab-picking and sleep deprivation. The act itself is a potent mix of extreme paranoia, aural and visual hallucination, and pin-point laser focus.

Lance was certain he was being spied upon by the government, by Hollis Fretwell, or some other shadowy force. He could feel the tiny camera lenses tracking him as he moved throughout the trailer. He could hear the static hiss of microphones recording his every footstep, every cough, every fart.

It was hard for him to do anything without feeling the prickly sensation of someone looking over his shoulder. He couldn't even make love to his wife without looking around the bedroom wondering about camera angles. The thought of a couple of fat guys in suits counting the pimples on his ass severely affected his performance in bed. *Not that Rayla gave a damn about his performance.* Lately it seemed like she was just staring up at the popcorn ceiling the whole time, waiting for it to be over.

Fucking cold fish, he thought. Sometimes he wondered if Rayla was a part of the conspiracy. There were definitely some gaping holes in her life. No family aside from the old bitch across the river and always so vague about her parents. He was beginning to question whether they really died in a car wreck, whether they were even dead at all. For all he knew Rayla could be the daughter of KGB agents.

He crawled across the living room floor and grabbed his pipe from the coffee table, then leaned against the couch and ignited the torch. He spun the glass in the flame until it filled with smoke then sucked it greedily into his lungs.

After a second hit, he set down the pipe and gazed around the room at the gutted wall sockets and light switches. He imagined the men who were monitoring the cameras laughing at him. His eyes narrowed as he examined the room for other possible hiding spots.

The problem was technology. Gone were the days of the bulky camera hidden away in an AC vent or FBI agents listening to a reel-to-reel in a nearby van. This new generation of nosy spying Patriot Act motherfuckers had somehow managed to reduce a camera to the size of a pinhead. *It could be anywhere.*

He hopped to his feet and peered down into the lampshade on the end table then sent it crashing to the floor with a backhand as he turned and surveyed the quiet room. The clock on the mantel ticked loudly. He spun and charged it, grabbing it with both hands and shaking it violently.

"Leave me the fuck alone!" he roared into the glass before slamming it face down and storming toward the coffee table. He flipped it end over end, scattering the pile of loose wires and screws all over the carpet. It landed on its back, the four wooden legs pointed skyward like a dead animal.

He leaned forward and stared into the dark blank screen of the television. His distorted reflection stared back at him, wild-eyed and winded. He reared back his fist to smash it then thought better of it.

Out of the corner of his eye he noticed the couch. It sat serenely in the middle of the tossed living room like a Buddha in a warzone. He kicked a light switch fragment as he approached it, sending the broken cover plate tumbling over the carpet and skidding across the kitchen floor.

He ripped a maroon cushion from the sofa and flung it Frisbee-style toward the kitchen where it crash-landed on the counter, knocking over the canister set. He tossed the other cushion over his shoulder as he stared down at the filthy underbelly of the couch.

Among the pretzels and pennies, paperclips and bottle tops, he noticed the white buttons of the remote jammed into the side. He reached down and dislodged it, holding it limply between thumb and index like a dead rat.

"Testing one two three," he said, as if speaking into a microphone, before dropping the remote into a glass of water on the end table. "Record that, motherfuckers."

He leapt onto the couch and placed a boot on the back, leaning his weight forward and rocking until it finally tipped. He rode it to the floor then hopped off, searching for the next thing to destroy.

It felt good to rage. Therapeutic. If the bastards were going to spy on him anyway, he might as well give 'em a show. He jumped back over the couch.

And froze.

There was a folded white piece of paper lying on the carpet centered between the four round indentations left by the sofa legs. He bent down and plucked it from the floor, wondering what it was and how it got there.

He unfolded it as he walked to the kitchen, taking care not to trip over anything in the ransacked living room. His cigarettes were on the counter. He shook one out and fired it up before smoothing out the paper on the table and beginning to read.

His head was pounding after the first sentence and his hands were trembling by the time he reached the end. An ash fell from his cigarette to the page. He slapped it away. He didn't know whether to laugh or cry or throw the table through the wall. In the end, he pulled out a chair and sat down to think.

35

Hydroponic Popcorn

Kevin lay in his bunk with his pillow doubled over and his fingers interlocked behind his head. Clusters of tiny bugs moved lethargically across the window screen unable to enter yet unable to break free, pinned to the metal by the powerful suck of the exhaust fans.

Beyond the window, a lone guard made his way to the center gate saluting the tower as he walked by. Then another strolled into view, his hat low and his bag slung over his shoulder, followed by a group of three, laughing and backslapping as they made their way across the square television screen of his window. The sidewalk was a river of brown as the day-shift officers sauntered, limped and waddled toward the front of the prison and the outlying parking lot.

He sat up in his bunk when he spotted her. Although it hadn't been five minutes since she gathered her belongings and exited the officers' station, he still felt a rush of excitement at the sight of her. He followed her across the sidewalk with his eyes, absorbing every trace of her fading presence like a junkie scraping a bag of dope. His old mantra of counting the days until he got out had been replaced by counting the hours until she returned. *Sixteen.*

She looked alien against the shambling procession that surrounded her, a princess in a parade of trolls. She was smiling. He knew that she knew he was watching. Her hand moved slowly across her shoulder to adjust the strap on her bag. She cryptically extended a pinkie from her closed fist, *I*, then thumb and index like an imaginary pistol, *L*, then thumb and pinky like a surfer's 'hang ten', *Y*.

He deciphered the letters as she walked through the gate, repeating them in his head as he stared at her retreating backside. *I-L-Y, I-L-Y*. When she faded into the distance, he lay back in his bunk and licked his lips, still tasting her afternoon kiss.

"Hey Kevin," said Weasel, his head popping over the side of the top bunk. "You know what I really miss?"

"What's that?" he responded, imagining he could still smell her lingering perfume in the air.

"You know when you cook microwave popcorn and you get those little half-popped seeds in the bottom of the bag?"

"Mm hmm," he mumbled. *I-L-Y*.

Weasel inched further over the side of the bunk. "Not the hard kernels. I'm talking about the ones that are splitting open, like right on the verge of exploding into a fully realized piece of popcorn."

"Right," said Kevin.

"I miss those. I wonder why no one has tried to market them as their own snack like peanuts or cashews."

"I don't know."

"I bet we could make a lot of money off that," said Weasel. "We could call them half-pops."

Kevin looked at his friend's upside down face. His glasses had slid to his forehead and his eyes were dilated and twitchy. "You all right, man?"

"Yeah," said Weasel. "The problem would be producing them. You know, *mass* producing them."

Kevin nodded. It was hard to listen to Weasel ramble on about business ideas when there was a ten-thousand-pound elephant in the room named *Life Sentence*.

"They kinda happen by accident," he was saying. "Sometimes there's only three or four in the bag, sometimes there's more than ten. The logistics would be a bitch, especially if there was like a great demand for them."

"Definitely," said Kevin. Weasel was acting weird. Even weirder than his normal level of weirdity which was, well, *weird*.

"Ooh," he said suddenly, "I know. We could do it hydroponically." His dilated black eyes grew from pennies to quarters. "Hydroponic popcorn. Hydroponic half-popped popcorn seeds."

"It could work."

"Hell yeah, it could," said Weasel, disappearing back over the side of the bunk.

Kevin glanced at the sidewalk beyond his barred window. A few pigeons had landed and were pecking at the cracks in the concrete; otherwise, the compound was empty. Over a thousand inmates were locked in their dorms awaiting count.

"You can tell, can't you?" asked Weasel.

Kevin followed the sound of his voice to the right side of the bunk, the opposite side from where his head just hung moments before. "What are you talking about?"

"You really can't tell?"

Kevin observed his owl-like face, eyes blinking rapidly behind the thick glasses. "Your eyes are dilated. Are you high or something?"

Weasel leaned close and whispered. "I've been awake two days, man. You haven't felt me tossing and turning all night?"

"What are you doing? Coke?"

Weasel shook his head. "Ice."

A strange mix of guilt and embarrassment washed over him. He had been so caught up in *her* that everything else had diminished in importance. If he wasn't with her in the laundry room then he was at the window pretending to need medication or discreetly signing to her in the dayroom, smiling at her, watching her, daydreaming of her. Somewhere over the last month, his razor-sharp awareness had plummeted to love-sick oblivion. If he was so distracted that he couldn't even pick up on the fact that his best friend and bunk-mate was wired on crystal, what else had he missed?

"Where in the hell did you get ice from?"

Weasel shrugged. "Some dude."

"Some dude," said Kevin. "How'd you pay for it? You're broke."

"He gave it to me."

Kevin sat up in his bunk. "Somebody gave you some dope, for free, in a level-seven prison, and it never crossed your mind that there may be a hidden agenda?"

"Like what?"

"Like enslaving your green ass with an addiction you can't support and then pimping you to their homeboys. Come on, Weasel. That's a sucker move. I thought you wanted to be a convict."

"It wasn't like that," he said.

"Well then, what's it like?" Kevin shot back, annoyed by his reckless naïveté.

"It was given to me in exchange for a favor," he explained, "for looking out for somebody while they sharpened a knife."

"Oh, well then never mind," said Kevin, unable to resist the sarcasm, "at least you're making some new friends."

The metallic clang of the laundry door slamming and the sound of jingling keys instantly quieted the raucous dormitory. An obese officer with a stack of letters and newspapers rounded the corner and glared at the inmates of Alpha Dorm until the last voice trailed off into silence.

"Mail call!" he bellowed. "Bring your IDs. I need Paxton, Simmons, Wessel."

Weasel looked sharply at Kevin. Neither of them were ever called for mail. His face burst into a beaming smile. "I bet it's Andy!" he said, jumping to his feet and snatching his ID off the top bunk.

Kevin shook his head as he watched him tear off down the aisle toward the waiting officer.

Crystal meth, he thought, *why would anyone in prison wanna do a drug that kept them awake for days and weeks at a time? Especially when sleep is the only escape.*

But Weasel had a point. He wasn't a short-timer. He was a lifer. Unless a miracle occurred, this was his last stop before the grave. Prison. There was no incentive for good behavior. No gain time. No parole. His gain-time sheet cited a tentative release date of 99/98/9999. Translation: Never.

Who am I to judge? Kevin thought. *He's doing a lot better than I'd be doing in his situation.*

Weasel slunk back down the aisle clutching the open letter, disappointment evident in his body language. "It wasn't Andy."

"Oh," said Kevin. "Who was it?"

"My attorney," said Weasel, stepping on the edge of Kevin's bunk and hopping up into his own. "He's gonna try to get my case back in front of a judge."

Kevin smiled at the creaking overhead bunk. "For about a hundred thousand other prisoners in the state of Florida, that would be a reason to celebrate. But you look like somebody ran over your dog."

Weasel's response was barely audible. "I was just hoping it was Andy."

36

Cellmates

Rayla braked at her cul-de-sac and flipped on the blinker. She drummed her fingers on the steering wheel as she waited for the oncoming traffic to pass. The afternoon sun in the western sky blasted around her down-turned visor, exposing the tiny flecks of lint and dust particles that swam in the air.

An SUV zipped past, followed by a car full of screaming high school kids. Rayla smiled as she turned down her street. In her rearview, the familiar vehicles of her neighbors and coworkers formed a snaking convoy of pickups and family sedans, each turning off into their respective driveways.

The sight of Lance's truck was deflating. She was hoping to have the trailer to herself for the night without him peeking through the curtains, mumbling incoherently, launching into wild-eyed drug-induced paranoid anti-government rants, or worse, touching her with his clammy, jittery, nicotine-stained hands.

It dawned on her that her marriage had in many ways become a prison sentence; her double wide, a cell, and the man she once thought she loved had become a psychotic cellmate prone to bouts of rage and erratic behavior. How ironic that the only time she felt free was when she went to work. In a prison.

When she exited the car and slammed the door behind her, she noticed Jessica Maldonado two lots down checking her mailbox. She was dressed in her standard slutty off-work attire of cutoff shorts and a halter top. When their eyes met, there was no sign of the haughty arrogance Rayla was expecting. Instead she saw kindness, warmth, sympathy. She frowned as she walked up the steps to the front door. An electrical socket was laying on the deck.

She reached for the door knob. It wouldn't turn. She bit her bottom lip. Even when the door was locked, the knob still turned a few inches to the left and right. It was almost as if someone was holding it stationary, not allowing it to budge. She flipped through her keys until she found the one for the trailer then wiggled it into the keyhole. Nothing. She looked around, unsure of what to do.

Had Lance super glued the door in one of his paranoid fits? Maybe he thought the president had sent agents to confiscate his guns and force him into gay marriage with an illegal immigrant. She almost smiled.

Suddenly the door was ripped open and her shirtless husband was towering over her. "Hey baby," he said with a big phony smile. "How was your day?"

She fought the urge to take a step backward. Instead she just stood there staring transfixed at this stranger who was glowering through Lance's eyes, inhabiting his body like a demonic possession. Her husband. *Her cellmate.*

"Long," she said, finally breaking eye contact and looking behind him into the trailer. "Is the power out again?"

"What?" He glanced over his shoulder. "Oh, uh-uh." He stepped aside to allow her in.

She walked past him, dropping her bag on the recliner as she headed for the kitchen. She paused when she saw the light switch. It was new. The cover plate was white, instead of the stock beige that came with the trailer, and there was an ornamental gold seashell attached to the top of it. She thought of the electrical socket on the deck as she looked around the living room. All the outlets and switches had been replaced.

"This is nice," she said, flipping on the light.

"Yeah," said Lance, closing the door. "It was overdue."

His tongue was doing that crazy thing again. Even though his mouth was closed she could see it sliding over the front of his teeth, darting from cheek to cheek in recurring protrusions as if it were a living thing, independent of his body, trapped in his mouth and frantically seeking escape from its cage of flesh.

She looked away. The trailer was clean. She wondered if Lance had company over while she was at work. *Jessica Maldonado?* She thought about the way she looked at her in the driveway. Crazy that only a few months ago she was tortured by the thought of her husband cheating and now she could only hope he was. Over and over, preferably. Until he was so sated and spent from his extracurricular exploits that he wouldn't even consider touching her.

She glanced down at the floor. He had even vacuumed. There were barely visible lines in the carpet. Straight and precise, they traversed the length of the living room like the faint stripes left by a lawnmower on freshly cut grass. She stared at them a moment, nagged by something undiscernible and far off. She frowned as she mentally reached for it, fumbling in the distant corners of her memory for a piece of thread to unravel. Lance was not into housecleaning. She learned early in the relationship that he expected her to maintain the upkeep of the trailer.

Suddenly, the vague and far off thought came hurtling into her mind like a rock through a glass window. Her knees buckled as her eyes darted to the couch. *The note!* She had been meaning to move it to a safer place, to possibly even flush it, but each day had melted into the next and she simply hadn't gotten around to it. She knew it was safe under the couch. The low-slung monstrosity of corduroy and oak hadn't been moved an inch in the last year-and-a-half. There was no reason to move it, unless someone wanted to vacuum beneath it.

Lance clamped a massive hand over her shoulder. She stared at the gold band on his ring finger and the black hair that shot from either side of it. His nails were gnawed and the skin between his index and middle fingers were nicotine-brown.

"You look awfully tense, babe," he said. "Think you may need a nice relaxing massage."

She fought to keep the revulsion from her face, suppressing and swallowing it down as she glanced back at the ominous piece of furniture across the room. Had he found it? Was he toying with her?

"Tell you what," he said, his hand falling from her shoulder, sliding down her back and coming to rest on her butt. "I need to take a shit, but how about when I get done, we spend a little quality time together?"

He winked and gave her a squeeze before stepping around her and heading toward the bathroom. The hollow thrum of his heavy footsteps reverberated throughout the trailer.

Rayla waited until the door clicked shut, then ran to the couch. It was heavier than she remembered. She strained against an arm before finally lifting it and moving it a couple feet back. It landed with a dull thunk. She glanced down the hall as she hurried to the other side and did the same thing.

She saw the folded white paper even before lowering the couch. It lay undisturbed in the carpet. Just where she put it.

She breathed a sigh of relief as she worked the heavy sofa back to its normal location, vowing to destroy the incriminating evidence the moment Lance left for his shift.

Adrenaline ebbed and her hammering heart slowed as she sank down on the couch. Though her own safety was at stake, it was Kevin that she was worried about. Lance's hatred for inmates went beyond the job, beyond the training, beyond the pedestrian distaste for those who couldn't abide by the laws of society. Even in the early days of their relationship, when he was gentle and loving with her, his reputation for violence and abuse toward inmates was legendary. She had often wondered if his boundless hatred was rooted in insecurity. If maybe he caught a glimpse of himself in those he cuffed and sprayed and beat unconscious. Maybe he thought he could cleanse himself through his brutalization of them. Whatever his reasons, she knew she could not let him find out about Kevin.

She heard the muffled sound of the flushing toilet followed by the creaking of the bathroom door and footsteps in the hall. Suddenly he was standing over her, smiling.

"Ready?" he asked, rubbing his hands together.

She nodded slowly.

37

Cracker Beach

Methlab had always considered himself a patient man. A virtue forged on the front porch of his ramshackle childhood home, staring out at the road, waiting on a mother who would never return. A skill sharpened like a gleaming blade during hours spent locked in a dark closet with no food, no water, and no bathroom, waiting on his schizophrenic father to open the door. A talent honed in isolation, in Juvie, in the county, in Raiford, in confinement cells and CSUs and TCUs and ICUs. Waiting.

If Methlab had a strong suit, besides cooking the best dope in the state, it would have to be his rock-like, oak-like, monk-like patience. But after a month of waiting, his patience was redlining.

The problem was a slimy little bitch-made fuckboy in B-Dorm named Sip who was late with his money.

Blake Mississippi Burkett, Sip for short, was from a small town called Ocean Springs, two hours west of Pensacola on I-10 just over the Alabama/Mississippi line. He loved to brag about how his family was in the casino business and carried himself with the smug air of a rich kid.

Methlab hated him from the outset but he swallowed his displeasure and kept it tightly concealed in furtherance of the greater good – the advancement of the *People's Republic of Festus Mulgrew. The nation of Methlab.*

Though he never bought into the whole sovereignty bullshit that was sweeping through the system like a central Florida wildfire, he did take something away from his brief flirtation with the movement: A foundation for his personal philosophy.

He was a nation. A nation with enemies and allies and borders like any other country on the globe. He had his own GDP (the money he made from dope), his own national debt (the money he owed for dope), and his own military (the shit-encrusted knife jammed in his waistline). He viewed Sip Burkett the way he imagined China viewed America: He hated him but he needed his money.

Florida boasts the third largest prison system in the U.S. with an inmate population far exceeding a hundred thousand in camps, compounds, and correctional institutions that dot the map at a rate rivaling that of car dealerships and public schools. Out of the thousand or so inmates at any given facility in the state, maybe five hundred got high, and out of those five hundred, maybe fifty had the financial wherewithal to support an ongoing drug habit. Less than five percent.

So as much as Methlab hated him, he realized that his nation's economy was dependent on Sip Burkett. He was his sprawl-mart shopper. His golden goose. His five percent.

But what happens when China wants its money and America turns up her runny, meth-reddened nose like she's too fucking good to pay her debts? What happens after you've tried diplomacy and you've tried sanctions and you've exhausted every peaceful avenue at your disposal? What then?

Military fucking action, that's what.

The pungent smell of reefer floated toward him as he stepped around the backstop of the old softball diamond and made a beeline across the orange sunbaked infield. Some black dudes were gathered around a concrete picnic table beating and rapping. A glance in their direction was met with red-eyed hostility. He quickly looked away, patting the knife on his hip for reassurance.

The pitcher's mound was a tarnished hyphen outlined in black and surrounded by a few stubborn sprigs of grass. He kicked a rock from its rubber surface as he walked by, sending it tumbling over the scorched clay and into the unmowed outfield.

Methlab looked toward deep center in the direction of Cracker Beach, a vibrant swath of glistening green surrounding a muddy PVC faucet. A high-arching spray of water shot out from the pipe and fanned out over the grass as he scanned the area. A faint half-rainbow shimmered translucently in the misty irrigation.

Just beyond the reach of the water, sprawled haphazardly across the grass like grazing farm animals, shirtless bodies dotted the landscape in flesh tones ranging from neon white to violent red. He could hear Avenged Sevenfold coming from someone's headphones as his eyes flitted over the shaven heads and tatted torsos in search of Sip Burkett.

He spotted him by the track, lying on his stomach with his shorts pulled up in his ass. He frowned as he wove his way through the sunbathers and headed toward him.

Methlab could not understand this new generation of prisoners. They shaved their arms and sculpted their eyebrows and cared about shit like getting suntans on their legs. The fact that they were able to act like bitches and roam the compound freely without a wardaddy was an indictment on the overall softness of the twenty-first-century Florida prison system.

He glanced through the razor wire at the slow-moving gun truck on the perimeter road, following it with his eyes until it disappeared around the back side of the prison. Then he removed the knife from his waist and eased down beside Sip Burkett.

He watched him for a long moment, lying in the sun as if he didn't have a care in the world; eyes shut, headphones in, blond hair parted perfectly to the side. A ladybug landed on his shoulder blade. Methlab reached out with the knife and flicked it away.

Sip's eyes snapped open.

"Good afternoon," said Methlab. "It's been awhile. I was beginning to think you were emergency released."

Sip turned down his radio. "I ain't hiding."

Methlab pretended not to notice the curled Elvis-like smirk of his top lip and his cocky confrontational tone. "Right," he said. "Do you have my money?"

"Look man, you need to–" A noticeable inflow of fear melted the arrogance from his eyes as they finally registered the knife.

"Back off?" asked Methlab. "See, I would, but I wasn't fortunate enough to be born with a silver spoon in my ass like some people. I can't just let seven hundred and fifty go. I'm sure you understand my position."

Sip struggled to his side. A tattoo of a naked woman sitting on a pair of dice rippled over the thin skin of his chest.

Methlab glanced back at the tower. "Don't move," he said, shielding the knife with his body until the guard's silhouette disappeared.

"Listen," Sip pleaded in a quivering voice, "I'm gonna pay you man."

"Oh, I know you're gonna pay me," said Methlab, raising the knife to his panic-stricken face and sticking the tip just inside his nostril. "The only question is whether you'll pay in money…"

"Please," Sip whined, squeezing his eyes shut.

Methlab suddenly ripped the blade from his nose, slicing through the cartilage with a power flick of the wrist. "… or blood."

His hands flew to his face as he rolled in the grass. Methlab quickly concealed the knife and jumped to his feet. He scanned Cracker Beach and the yard beyond. No one was paying them any attention. He slid a boot under Sip's stomach and flipped him on his back. Blood flowed between his fingertips.

"Don't stab me man," Sip begged. "My sister's coming this weekend. I'll have the money."

Methlab was disgusted by his whimpering. He resisted the urge to kick him full in the face. "You've got one week," he said, before turning and heading back toward the diamond.

38

Obvious

Kevin sat on an aluminum bench in the crowded dayroom, staring up at the television mounted on the wall. The news anchor's face was caked with makeup and pumped with Botox, both stretched and condensed at once. The effect was a perpetual expression of intense concern.

He couldn't hear the TV over the roar but he didn't need to in order to follow the stories. Car bomb explosion in the Middle East, pirates off the coast of Africa, murders, human trafficking, homelessness, drought. The world outside the razor wire was the same as it ever was.

"It's crazy out there," said Weasel from his place beside him on the bench.

Kevin nodded in agreement as a helicopter tracked a high-speed chase through Los Angeles.

"Sometimes I think it's safer in here," said Weasel.

Kevin looked at him. "You must still be snorting meth."

"No, I'm not," he said, stiffening with indignation. "I just did it that one time. But think about it. In here there's no terrorists, no dirty bombs, no food crisis."

"Nope," said Kevin, "none of that. Just good old-fashioned stabbings and the occasional rape."

"Well, it's almost over for you anyway," said Weasel, his voice barely audible above the noise.

Kevin sank an inch in his seat as a massive wave of guilt swept over him. He knew it was irrational. There was no reason to feel guilty. It wasn't his fault Weasel had life. Still, leaving him behind was going to be hard.

"It's almost over for you too," said Kevin, injecting optimism into his voice. "That life sentence won't hold up. The next time you get a letter from your attorney, I bet there's a court date in it."

"Maybe so," said Weasel, not looking at him.

Kevin glanced over his shoulder into the officers' station.

"She's gone," said Weasel. "Took her bag and everything."

Kevin turned slowly back to his friend. "Who?"

"Ms. Broxson."

"What makes you think I was looking for her?"

"Who else would you be looking for?"

They both stared at the TV. The world news had ended and the local news was leading off with the weather. Kevin watched the pretty meteorologist walk back and forth across the screen. A storm was coming. She relayed the information with a dazzling smile, accentuating the map with all the hand gestures and facial expressions of a *Price is Right* showcase model.

"Don't get mad at me," said Weasel, "you're the one who taught me that a convict should always be aware of his surroundings."

"Yeah, well, I didn't say anything about being nosy."

"I don't need to be nosy," said Weasel, "not when you're being obvious."

There was a commotion on the row behind them as two men forced their way through the narrow walk space to an open spot on the bench. He heard a piece of their conversation as they walked by. He didn't have to look to know who it was. Vero Zay and Tampa Black.

"*You full of shit, Zay.*"

"*Man, I'm tellin' you, Ms. Broxson is 'bout it. You see how she stay cuttin' her eyes over here. What you think she's lookin' for?*"

"*I don't know. She acts pretty strict.*"

"*For real? Come on, Tampa! That's the throw off.*"

Kevin felt his face flush with heat as they moved behind him. He tried to focus on the images flashing across the TV screen, on the sound of dominoes slamming against a steel table, on Weasel's boot swaying back and forth in his peripheral.

"*I'd like to catch her on the turf. Get her good and strung out on that glass dick and put her ass on the stroll...*"

An elbow grazed the back of his head as they squeezed by. Suddenly the fury was boiling over. He spun off the bench in a blur, knocking Weasel to the side as he reached for them. Either would do. He was beyond making choices. Reason and sensibility had been drowned out in the white noise of rage. In the spinning dayroom he found Vero's collar and ripped him sideways over the bench.

His stammering protest was silenced with three rapid blows to the face followed by a crushing elbow that splashed blood over the aluminum. The release was intoxicating. The give of flesh and crack of bone beneath him was incremental freedom. The violence was liberating.

He raised his elbow again and stopped. The crowded dayroom had gone quiet. Vero's limp body was leveraged over the bench. His eyes were unblinking and blood trickled from his mouth to the floor. Kevin glanced coldly at Tampa Black before releasing his friend, allowing him to slump over the backrest of the bench.

"See what I mean?" said Weasel as the dayroom murmured back to life. "Obvious."

Kevin forced his way through the row feeling every eye on him as he headed for the bathroom. The remaining adrenaline caused his hands to shake and his knees to tremble. He glanced in the officers' station as he passed. The only guard in the booth was flipping through a magazine. He silently thanked God.

What am I doing? he thought as he entered the bathroom. It had been years since he had a fight and even longer since he'd been written a disciplinary report. He prided himself on control, on restraint, on making sound decisions. How ironic that now, with the finish line in sight, on the very doorstep of freedom, that he would suddenly become this emotional powder keg.

He turned on the water at the first sink and stared into his distorted reflection in the scratched mirror. *You're slipping,* he whispered. Friend or not, Weasel was the greenest, least perceptive, most oblivious man in the dorm. If *even he* was aware of what was going on, who else knew?

"Psst. Hey, man."

He looked over his shoulder. It was the weirdo who slept in twenty-three lower. His close-set eyes ticked rapidly around the bathroom, skirting the edges of Kevin's, but never meeting them head on. A flicker of a smile twitched weakly across his strange mouth, dark fleshy lips stretched wide over his narrow, pock-marked face like two purple gummy worms.

"That was incredible," he said. "You completely humbled that loudmouth in there. He deserved every bit of that."

Kevin studied his hands. The middle knuckle on his right fist was split and gushing blood. He stuck it under the cold running water.

"Well, anyway," said the weirdo, "I thought you might want this as a souvenir. A trophy. I found it on the floor."

He extended an upturned tattooed arm and unfolded his fingers one at a time while his eyes darted nervously in every direction. Kevin glanced at his outstretched palm. In the center of the myriad of intersecting lines, dull and caked with dried blood, was a single gold tooth.

39

Broken Glass

Jessica Maldonado stared up at the massive deer head mounted on the wall as Jarvis kissed her neck and fumbled with the clasp of her bra. His beard felt like a scouring pad against her skin. His breath was hot and ragged. The sickly sweet scent of his chewing tobacco combined with the rich aromas of leather upholstery, polished hardwood, and beer to conjure an ambience of potent masculinity. She scanned the Spartan living room for any trace of a woman–a flower vase, the color pink, a photograph – there was nothing remotely feminine. His house was a man cave.

"Clayton?" she said, wiggling free from his embrace. "When did your wife leave?"

"Aw hell, Jess, I don't know. A long time ago." He reached for her again.

She slapped his hand away. "Yes you do. Tell me."

He sank back against the couch. "What's the date?"

"September the nineteenth."

He stared at the wall. "Ten years. Ten years, two months, fifteen days."

"You miss her don't you?"

"Sometimes," he said, then looked quickly at her, "but not when I'm with you."

A loud knock on the front door caused them both to turn. After a few seconds it flew open and Lance Broxson staggered inside. His jeans and shirt were dirty and rumpled. A cigarette hung from his mouth and a half-bottle of Jack swished in his hand.

"Hey Jarvis, what the fuck? I thought we were going to The Spur tonight." He slammed the door behind him and swayed drunkenly in the dim light of the foyer.

He seemed smaller than the last time she saw him. The clothes that once hugged his muscular body now hung from his shrinking frame. His eyes bulged from his skull. There was a scab on the side of his face that he picked at distractedly.

She inched closer to Jarvis who in turn wrapped a protective arm around her. "I left a message on your voice mail," he said.

Lance plopped down in the La-Z-Boy and took a swig of whiskey before grimacing. "Lost my phone. Probably out in the woods somewhere." He dug in his pocket and produced a charred glass pipe. "Who wants a blast?"

Jessica was embarrassed by the familiar need that ballooned within her at the sight of the paraphernalia. Her mouth went dry as she watched him seductively roll the pipe between his fingers.

She glanced at Jarvis. He shook his head once. The movement was barely perceptible but it was enough. A gentle nudge back to reality. Lance held misery in his hand. Enslavement. Insanity. No person in her right mind would ever sign up for that again. Not after escaping it once.

"No thanks," said Jarvis, patting her back. "The last time I did that I couldn't sleep for three days."

"Jessica?" offered Lance.

She shook her head.

He gulped down the remainder of his whiskey then dropped his cigarette in the bottle and set it on the table. "Suit yourselves," he said as he ignited the flame to heat the pipe.

"I'd appreciate it if you didn't do that in my house," said Jarvis.

The flame died. Lance glared at them from across the living room, his suspicious eyes flicking back and forth between them. "What the fuck is going on here?"

She looked away.

"What do you mean?" asked Jarvis.

"Don't play stupid," said Lance. "I'm sick of the big dumb redneck act. Who are you working for?"

"I think you need some sleep," said Jarvis.

"I'll sleep when I'm dead," said Lance. "Now who turned you? Was it this ... this prostitute?"

Jarvis shot to his feet. His enormous frame cast a giant shadow over Lance. "I think you need to leave."

Lance sprang from the La-Z-Boy, grabbing the neck of the whiskey bottle and smashing it on the table. Glass rained over the hardwood floor as he held out the broken bottle with one hand and made a *come on* gesture with the other.

Jessica sat glued to the couch, unable to move or even speak, as the two friends faced off. A minor chord sounded deep in her stomach and resonated throughout her body.

Jarvis snatched a flannel shirt from the back of a chair and wrapped it around his fist.

"It's been awhile since I kicked your ass," said Lance. "When was the last time? Eighth grade?"

Jarvis held his fists up and circled him warily. "Seventh," he said. "You gonna cut me with that bottle?"

"I should," said Lance, wobbling a little. "I should carve you up good for being a goddamn traitor!"

"I ain't never betrayed you," said Jarvis. "You're the only family I got."

Lance's prominent chin appeared to bubble over with emotion. His lips quivered. His eyes shut. He took a clumsy step back and sat down hard in the broken glass.

Jessica was surprised by the first tear. It dove down the side of his face and swam straight through the cracked scab on his cheek. A moment later he was blubbering like a small child.

"What's happening to me?" he wailed.

Jarvis reached down and carefully extracted the broken bottle from his clenched fist. "You're destroying yourself," he said, "little by little, day by day. And for the people who love you, it's hell to watch."

Lance wiped a tear on the back of his hand. "Rayla's cheating," he said. "She's gonna leave me."

"I'm sorry to hear that," said Jarvis, "but if you keep on the way you're going, you stand to lose a whole lot more than Rayla."

Jarvis's boots reverberated throughout the house as he walked into the kitchen and tossed the broken bottle in the trash.

Lance watched him for a moment then turned to her and mouthed the words *I need to talk to you.*

An icy wind rocketed up her spine as his hollow eyes moved over her body. His teeth were almost a caramel hue and caked with yesterday's food. His ashen lips were thin and cracked. His head dropped back to his chest as Jarvis returned.

"Come on man," he said, holding out a hand, "you need some sleep. I'll drive you home."

Lance allowed Jarvis to pull him to his feet. As he stood, broken glass fell from his jeans to the floor.

"Jess," Jarvis turned to her, "do you mind following in my truck?"

She shook her head.

"The keys are on the counter," he said.

When they reached the foyer, she heard Jarvis mumble something to Lance who paused and stared back at her from the doorway. She imagined storm clouds in his gaze, racing across a steel-gray sky. When he spoke his voice was contrite, belying the secret sneer on his face.

"Sorry for calling you a prostitute, Jessica."

40

Reckless

She knew she was being foolish. Reckless even. Especially after the close call with the note, which she finally, grudgingly, burned and flushed the ashes. Each night she'd resolve to be more cautious, to take fewer chances, yet each morning she'd see him and freefall right back into the same pattern. It was unsustainable. They were going to be found out if they kept it up.

She leaned in the doorway of the officers' station and watched him sweep. His smooth muscular forearms flexed as he pushed the broom. It was her own lack of control that scared her. Even as she attempted to think rationally, the responsible thoughts and nervous words in her head were drowned by the aching need to be wrapped in those arms.

He stopped sweeping and smiled at her. "So how was your weekend?"

"Long," she said, feeling the familiar subtle change of the molecules in the quiet room as the space between them slowly diminished.

"Most people look forward to time off from work."

She shrugged, watching him. His words were filler, meaningless collections of vowels and consonants. Random sounds.

She recognized this as part of the dance. The real conversation was taking place below the surface. His pheromonal energy was a tangible thing; his eyes, equal parts velvet and steel. She imagined a paperclip sliding across a table, helpless in the invisible pull of a magnet.

"But I know what you mean," he said, "times a thousand actually. Your *long* is my eternity. I keep staring at the door hoping you'll appear with your little bag."

"Don't exaggerate," she said, desperately wanting his arms around her, his hands all over her. "It's just forty-eight hours."

"Sixty," he corrected her. "You leave at 4 p.m. every Friday and return at 8 a.m. on Monday. That's sixty hours. Believe me, I know."

He leaned the broom against the wall and reached for her. Linear time seemed to dissolve as he wrapped her in his powerful embrace. There was lightning in his fingertips. Every cell in her body sprang to life and vibrated in harmony beneath his touch. He was a conductor and her flesh an orchestra, responding eagerly to the direction of his skilled hands. When he stroked her back, the violins awakened, when he caressed her face, the cellos, then his hands were on her breasts, her stomach, her hips, until her entire body was singing with the symphonic power of desire.

She forced him back against the wall, cradling his face in her hands and kissing him with untamed fire. The only noise in the quiet room was the faint whisper of their uniforms brushing and the soft wet clicking of their lips separating and rejoining. His body was warm and hard against hers. She could feel his heartbeat drumming in his chest, pulsating in his embrace. She imagined it synchronized with her own, beating in unison.

The timeless thrill of a private moment in the arms of a lover worked its special magic as shimmering waves of heat rippled upward through her trembling body. She slid her hands down his sinewy arms and laced her fingers between his.

He flinched and stiffened.

"What is it?" she whispered.

He shook his head and pulled his hand away grimacing. The roaring passion ebbed to a trickle before the last spark died, leaving her breathless and hollow. She slumped against the wall, studying him, then she saw the gash across his swollen middle knuckle.

"Let me see it," she said.

He slowly lifted his hand for her to inspect.

"What happened?" she asked, gently holding it in her own.

"Nothing."

She looked into his troubled green eyes. "Oh, I see," she said, "you're gonna play righteous convict with me now. Are you worried about snitching? Disciplinary reports? I think what we were just doing in the corner is a much more serious violation. Don't you trust me Kevin?"

"Of course."

"Then tell me what happened."

"It was no big deal," he said. "Someone disrespected me and I couldn't let it slide."

She pressed the area around the scab with a fingernail. "It looks infected."

"It's not," he said. "I cleaned it out with bleach."

"Is it broken?"

"Fractured," he said. "It happens every time I fight."

"Do you fight a lot?"

He stared at her. "I used to."

"Well, it looks like you won," she said, forcing a smile.

He took a deep breath and exhaled heavily. "Rayla what are we gonna do?"

"About what?"

"About us. I'm getting close to a month left. I don't even have a way of contacting you."

She grabbed her pen and searched her pockets for something to write on. "Here," she said, scribbling on a stick of Juicy Fruit, "this number will never change. It's a landline. Throw it away after you've memorized it."

"Can I eat the gum?" he asked.

"No," she said, finally getting a smile out of him.

"What about your husband?"

She stared at her boots. "It's complicated."

"Why? Do you love him?"

"I thought I did," she said, "until I met you. The problem is that he's just unstable. Like scary unstable."

"Does he hit you?"

"Once," she admitted, "but that's not what worries me. I think he's going crazy. I'm scared he might do something worse than just hit me if I try to leave."

"Tell you what," he said, sliding the gum in his pocket, "why don't you wait it out 'til I'm released, then we can handle it together. Can you hang on a month?"

She shook her head. "For what? You to come galloping through the prison gate on a white horse? I'm a big girl, Kevin. I don't need a bodyguard."

He looked away. "I didn't mean it like that."

She instantly softened. The stress was getting to her; the danger, the risks, the secrets, the lies, the close calls, the lack of control, the yawning black chasm of an unknown future. She felt trapped, but it wasn't his fault.

"I know," she said, aching to be in his arms again, to let him melt away the fear and the stress with his touch. "Sorry. I just don't want you involved. You've done enough time in prison. It would destroy me if you came back because of my psycho husband. Because of me. I don't want you to be enemies with him."

She leaned against the doorframe and gazed at the chiseled features of his handsome face. His jaw was set stubbornly and those pretty green eyes that normally radiated confidence and intelligence had narrowed to a malevolence so dark that she had to resist the urge to take a step back.

"If he's hitting you," he said, "then we already are enemies."

She noticed he was digging his index fingernail into the side of his thumb, something he had a habit of doing when he was nervous or uncomfortable. She marveled at how well she knew him after such a short amount of time. And how well he knew her. She had never felt so close to anyone in her life. He even knew her darker secrets, like what happened to her parents and only seemed to love her more for them.

"I'll be waiting for you Kevin," she said softly.

He moistened his lips with his tongue and was about to respond when the laundry door swung open. Inspector Hollis Fretwell paused in the doorway and looked first at Kevin, then at her. His face morphed from surprised to suspicious as he processed the scene.

Busted! Her mind screamed as a tsunami of fear washed over her, crippling her mental faculties and causing her knees to knock.

It was Kevin who broke the silence, lifting his swollen hand and displaying the angry red scab on the knuckle.

"I swear I wasn't fighting, Ms. B," he pleaded. "It happened on the basketball court. Honest. You can ask anybody."

She seized her cue without hesitation. "Well it sure looked like a tooth mark from the window."

"It *is* a tooth mark," Kevin continued in a performance worthy of an Oscar, "but I wasn't fighting, I was going up for a rebound and accidentally caught somebody in the mouth."

"Hmmph," Fretwell interrupted with a knowing smirk, "the old basketball defense. I've heard that one about a million times. So who was this flagrant foul victim? I'd like to get a look at his knuckles too. For shits and giggles."

"I don't know who he is," said Kevin. "Some black dude out of D-Dorm, or E, I'm not sure."

She glanced over at Fretwell. "It looks at least a day old, maybe two. What do you think?"

Kevin held out his hand for the inspector to examine. He scrutinized it carefully before making his prognosis.

"Twenty-four hours minimum." He frowned as he continued to study it. "As for the cause, it's hard to tell. If I had to guess, I'd say he was fighting, but I'll concede that there's an outside chance he's telling the truth. I'll defer to you on this one, Officer."

She shielded her relief with a scowl and turned her gaze back to Kevin. After an adequate amount of deliberation she cleared her throat. "Go get a toothbrush and scrub the bathroom floor. Every tile."

"Yes, ma'am," he said, averting his eyes as he moved past Fretwell through the door.

"Hold it!" said the inspector.

Kevin froze. Rayla was hyperaware of the stick of gum in his pocket with her phone number on it.

"What's your name?" Fretwell demanded.

"Freeman, sir," he answered without turning. "P18722."

41

A Minor Favor

For the first time in a long time Lance Broxson wasn't high. It had nothing to do with turning over a new leaf. He had a quarter-ounce in his boot. He just wanted a clear mind for the mission, then he'd reward himself with a fat bump later on.

"Hey Sarge," called a voice above him.

He shielded his eyes from the spotlight and looked up at the tower. Blond locks fell from the open window. He couldn't remember her name. She was young and new.

"See anything interesting from up there?" he asked.

"I sure do," she said, blowing a pink bubble.

He lit a cigarette and sent a cloud of smoke up into the illuminated night air. "Maybe I need to come up there and make a security check later on so you can show me."

"I'll be here," she said with a girlish giggle as he turned up the crosswalk and headed for Alpha Dorm.

He noticed the captain and a few other white-shirts sitting under the pavilion drinking coffee. He gave a quick wave as he passed, grateful that they didn't call him over, but suspicious of what they were saying behind his back. His mind quickly offered up a few possibilities: *Wow, that Sergeant Broxson sure is huge, I bet he gets more than his share of ass around here. I heard a rumor that he was smoking meth. They say his wife is fucking an inmate.*

He felt his face harden as he imagined their words. He wanted to turn and yell, *Say it to my face!* but thought better of it. He had to respect his superiors, at least during his shift. The parking lot after work was a different story. There were no captains and majors outside the fence. Only men. He cracked his knuckles.

A swarm of gnats circled the plastic, covered light over the low-side entrance of Alpha Dorm. He dropped his cigarette in the butt can by the door and signaled the officer inside with his flashlight. He reached for the handle and shook it until it buzzed, then pulled it open and stepped inside.

A pale, bleary-eyed guard appeared at the window of the darkened officers' station.

Lance quickly waved him off. "Just a walk through."

The guard nodded and returned to his chair. Lance felt a heavy swell of disgust rise within him as he watched him lay his head on the desk. It wasn't the fact that he was catching a little shut-eye, most of the shift did that. Napping on the job was the biggest perk of working graveyards. It was his slight build, his pimpled face, the peach fuzz on his nonexistent chin. *What the fuck was he gonna do if a riot popped off?* Lance smirked as he answered the voice in his head. *Nothing.*

He twirled his flashlight as he strolled down the row of bunks. The random sounds of snoring and softly playing radios came at him from every direction. Exhaust fans rattled overhead. He hit the button on his flashlight and dragged its beam over the sleeping faces in search of Rayla's Romeo. Although he had no idea what to look for, he figured he'd know it when he saw it. Probably someone similar to him – tall, handsome, muscular, intense.

The sight of his own bicep temporarily distracted him. He flexed and admired its smooth curvature before returning to his search.

He used the process of elimination, casually dismissing each bunk as he passed, mostly on the grounds of missing teeth, tattooed faces, obesity and plain old ugliness. He knew his wife well. If she was going to cheat with an inmate, it'd have to be with someone who stood out, someone who separated himself from the rank and file of losers that populated the prison.

When he reached the end of the row he could feel a draft of cool air coming through the window. The scumbag in twelve-lower had his blanket over his head. He held the flashlight on him for a moment before moving to the top bunk. Huge eyes blinked back at him from behind thick glasses. He kept the bright beam on the face as he stepped between the bunks.

"What's your name?" he asked, keeping his voice low.

"Wessel, sir," said the inmate.

"Who's this under you?"

His Adam's apple moved up and down his skinny throat. "I'm not, uh ... I ... Freeman, sir."

Lance nodded at the bottom bunk. "He look anything like you?"

"Like me?" he asked in a shaky voice.

"What is there a fuckin' echo in here? Yeah, like you. Like a skinny, ugly, child molester. Does he?"

"Yes, sir," said the inmate.

He aimed the beam down at the bottom bunk for a few more seconds before finally turning and moving down the aisle. The circle of light bounced off gold teeth, eye patches, and wrinkled weatherworn faces. He smirked at a known homosexual as he walked past.

Each bunk number was stenciled in black spray paint. He paused when he got to twenty-three lower. A stained yellowish towel hung from the rail at the foot of the bunk. He shined the light toward the pillow. Mulgrew was smiling. His twitchy eyes darted about while his spider scurried across the loose, pocked skin of his face.

"He's not a sandbox ranger, you know," said Methlab.

Lance frowned. "Huh?" *What the fuck was this freak talking about?*

"A chomo, a baby raper, a diaper sniper," said Methlab. "He's not in here for that. The kid with the glasses in twelve-upper. He's doing life. Murder."

"I don't give a fuck," said Lance, surveying the surrounding bunks with the flashlight before returning to his face, bathing it in the harsh white glow. "Now put your little friend away and get dressed."

Methlab glanced nervously left and right. "For what, Sarge?"

"Urinalysis."

He waited while the skeletal inmate slipped on his blues and put his pet spider away, then escorted him past the dozing guard in the booth and into the empty bathroom.

"Do you have my money?" he asked.

"I'll have it next week," said Methlab.

"You said that last week."

"I know. I apologize. Circumstances beyond my control."

"I don't want to hear it," said Lance, putting an edge in his tone.

"Sarge, you know my word is iron," he whined, his eyes frantically dancing around the walls. "How many times has this happened?"

Lance leaned forward imposing his physical dominion over the spindly inmate. He scowled down at him and let him dangle and twist in the silence for a few long moments before finally relenting. "One week."

"Thank you, sir."

"Now I need a favor."

"Name it," Methlab whispered.

"I need to borrow your eyes," he said. "Do you know who my wife is?"

Methlab nodded. "Day shift. She works in here sometimes."

Lance folded his arms over his chest and glanced over at the officers' station. In a few hours she would be in there; polished red fingernails clicking against the desk, her uniform pants hugging her thighs, smiling a secret smile while looking out across the dorm, her eyes touching her lover's. *When did she start wearing nail polish anyway? Cheating fucking whore.*

"Can you watch her for me?"

Methlab frowned. "I can. But it would be helpful to know what I'm looking for."

"I wanna know who you see hanging around the window. Who you see her talking to the most."

"An inmate, I assume?"

Lance nodded.

A smile played on the corners of his wide, fleshy lips as he clasped his hands together and gave a slight bow. "Say no more."

42

The Cantonment Crowhop

"I smell wine," said Weasel as they walked into the empty bathroom.

"Ignore it," said Kevin, glancing down the long row of toilets to ensure they were alone.

"But how are they making it?" he pressed, inquisitive eyes blinking behind thick, slightly fogged lenses.

"Rotten fruit and sugar," said Kevin. "Why? Are you thinking about giving up meth for booze?"

"I did meth one time for Christsake! You make it sound like I'm a junkie."

Kevin could feel him following as he stepped around the shower wall, a four-foot tiled partition that separated that area from the rest of the bathroom. He turned and studied his friend in the fluorescent yellow light. His shirtless chest was still bony and concave, but it looked like all the pushups were beginning to have an effect on his shoulders, and there were thick rope-like veins visible beneath the skin of his arms.

"All right, let me see your set," said Kevin.

Weasel slowly raised his fists.

"What happened? Did you become left-handed overnight?"

Weasel shook his head.

"Then why are you leading with your right foot? Your left is your jab hand. Come on man, you know all this, left foot forward. Let's go."

He held up his palm as a target and moved in a slow semi-circle as Weasel clumsily attempted off-balance jabs. Every punch was accompanied by a sharp hiss of air.

"Stop with that noise," Kevin said.

"Sssp." Weasel continued to jab. "Sssp, sssp … what noise?"

"You know what I'm talkin' about, cut it out!"

"But it's a boxing sound," Weasel protested. "You can't throw a jab without it. Not a proper one at least. Sssp, sssp."

"According to who?"

"Oh no one special," said Weasel. "Just every single *Rocky* movie plus *Raging Bull* and *Cinderella Man*."

Kevin smiled and shook his head. "You watch way too much television. Now jab."

"Sssp."

"Again!"

"Sssp."

"Two more."

"Sssp sssp."

"Good, now, right hand. Hard. Come on!"

Weasel threw a floundering hook which Kevin easily stepped under, driving him forcibly into the wall and locking his arms around his neck.

"Get me off you," he commanded.

Weasel grunted and contorted his body, trying desperately to break free of the hold.

"Who's your enemy?" Kevin whispered, keeping an eye on the officers' station as he controlled his squirming, panting, purple-faced friend.

"Not my opponent," Weasel croaked, attempting unsuccessfully to spin away.

"Who then?" Kevin demanded.

"Fear, panic, rage, doubt, eragghh!" he grunted, finally breaking free.

"Good," said Kevin, holding up his hand again. "Jab!"

"Sssp."

"Remember this," said Kevin, "the opposite of fear isn't courage. The opposite of fear is faith."

Weasel stopped moving. "Faith as in God?"

Kevin shrugged. "In God, in yourself, in your training, whatever it takes."

Weasel stared at him for a moment before responding. "But how do you make yourself believe when you don't?"

"Repetition," said Kevin. "Now jab."

Weasel ignored his palm. "I'm serious, man."

"Me too," said Kevin, dropping his hand and leaning against the shower wall. "Look, you've seen a lot of movies, right? Do you remember any of the old Kung Fu flicks where there's a group of people and they're all throwing the same punch over and over again?"

"Like on *Enter the Dragon* when they first get to the island?"

"Exactly," said Kevin, "or even in a real karate class. Have you ever seen them repeating the same kick ten, twenty, fifty times and thought, 'that's nice but how does it help in a real fight?'"

Weasel nodded.

"Repetition, that's how. After hours and weeks of jab after jab, roundhouse after roundhouse, the motion becomes so imprinted on the brain that it becomes a reflex."

Weasel attempted a slow jab. "But what does that have to do with faith?"

"It's the same shit," said Kevin, "except that instead of punches and kicks, you're reppin' your thoughts, over and over, replacing fear and doubt with strength and confidence, reprogramming that big fat computer sitting on your neck until it believes."

"Is that what you did?"

"Yep," said Kevin, raising his fists, "now come on. We need to finish up. The yard's gonna be closing in a few minutes."

Weasel shifted into his stance then paused, looking at the officers' station. "Ms. Broxson is watching us."

Kevin glanced at the window. She was smiling. "Don't worry about her."

Weasel jabbed at his palm. "You really do like Ms. Broxson, don't you?"

"A convict would never ask a question like that," Kevin growled. "Jab."

"Sssp."

They circled each other warily, their boots squeaking on the shower floor as they pivoted, ducked and weaved.

"Are you gonna come back and find her when you get out?"

Kevin suddenly dropped and swept his leg, knocking his friend off balance and causing him to sit down hard on the floor. "Ooph."

"Listen," he hissed, getting in his face, "you need to quit talking about shit like that. I know you don't mean any harm, but there's too much at stake for a rumor to get started because somebody overheard you talking about us in the bathroom."

"I wasn't talking about you in the bathroom!" Weasel whispered.

Kevin resisted the urge to choke him. "You just were," he said, looking up at the ceiling and exhaling. "Weasel, I need to be able to trust you on this. Can I?" He stared hard into the thick foggy lenses of his glasses, boring his point home with his eyes.

After a moment of contemplation, Weasel finally nodded.

"Good," said Kevin, "I knew I could count on you."

"Is that your signature move?" Weasel asked.

He frowned. "What?"

"The leg sweep. Is that your signature move?"

He shook his head. "This isn't MMA, Weasel."

"You don't have to be into MMA to have a signature move," Weasel said, rolling his eyes.

"Well, what's yours then?"

"I don't have one. I was hoping you could teach me one. I've got the jabs and the overhands down pat."

Kevin raised an eyebrow.

"Okay," Weasel conceded. "I've got them as down pat as I can get them considering how uncoordinated I am."

Kevin climbed to his feet. "The only reason you're uncoordinated is because you *think* you are."

"I know," said Weasel, "affirmation, visualization. I'm familiar with the concept."

"Repetition," Kevin interjected.

"I get it, I do, but it would be a major confidence builder if I had a *go to* move in my repertoire. Something to work on between all the jabs and hooks."

He was still sitting on the floor with his arms resting on his kneecaps. Kevin thought about the last time he saw Weasel on the bathroom floor. He was under the sinks with his teeth sunk in somebody's calf. Kevin smiled as he held out his hand. "Hmm," he said, helping him up. "A go to move, huh? Well this may not qualify but…"

Weasel rubbed his hands together. "What is it?"

"It's called the Cantonment Crowhop," he said. "I learned it in high school. It's really more of a sucker punch than an actual move but what you do is get a running start, hop, and swing."

He demonstrated the technique a few times before leaning against the wall and allowing Weasel enough room to attempt it.

"What's Cantonment?" Weasel asked.

"A little town north of Pensacola."

"Oh," said Weasel. "What's a crow hop?"

"I just showed you," said Kevin. "Now are you gonna try it or what?"

Weasel took a deep breath then burst into a five step sprint, leaping in the air and swinging clumsily at an imaginary target.

"Not bad," said Kevin. "Do it again."

His second try was worse than his first and he even tripped on his third, but after every attempt he turned and walked back to his starting point to begin again. Within minutes he had the basics down.

Kevin looked over his shoulder at the officers' station window. She hadn't moved. Slowly she raised her hand and began to sign. The words made him smile.

"T-e a-d-o-r-o."

43

Chair Aerobics

Rayla was on her hands and knees searching for the phone jack behind the bookshelf. She'd been close on a couple of tries but Mydog was making the most of her compromised position by using it as an opportunity to lick her face.

She scrunched her nose, shut her eyes and turned her head from side to side. It was no use. He only mistook her squirming resistance and ticklish outbursts as a willingness to play. She was reduced to stabbing blindly with the cord, hoping for a lucky click.

"Mydog, stop it!" she laughed, falling to the floor and covering her face.

He went into one of his frenzied, manic, breathing/licking/yelping episodes, attacking her with unbridled love.

"See," said Mema, "Mydog don't want that damn thing neither."

Rayla abandoned the unconnected cord and crawled from under the desk escaping the aggressive adoration of the hyperactive little dog. "Mema, everybody's got a computer," she said. "This is the twenty-first century."

"Not everybody," the old woman sniffed. "There's not a single soul in my aerobics class that has one. Reverend Lamb says they're the next step in the new world order."

Rayla smiled. Mema's chair aerobics class was a group of seniors in their eighties and nineties who met at the community center three times a week. On the few occasions that she attended, she sat between Mema and a blind ninety-three-year-old named Myrtle who repeatedly touched each hand to the opposite knee while the instructor shouted encouragement over a scratchy old phonograph blaring *76 Trombones*.

"You're gonna love it," said Rayla.

"No, I'm not," said Mema. "I ain't even turning the damn thing on!"

Rayla laughed. "You said the same thing about the cell phone and the DVD player."

"Well this is different," the old woman said.

Mydog barked.

"Whatever you say," said Rayla, reaching down to scratch behind his ear. "Can you hold him while I go back under the desk?"

Mema shook her head. "He's got just as much a right to that space as you do."

"Fine," she said, rolling her eyes.

She walked quickly back to the desk and ducked into the crawl space. She did her best to block Mydog's access to her face while she grabbed the cord and slid her hand behind the bookcase. She could feel his cold nose pressing against her elbow and hear his paws tapping the hardwood as he frantically sought an angle to her face. She found the square hole with her finger and maneuvered the cord toward it. Mydog whined.

"Hang on buddy," she said, pushing the plastic tip into the jack, forcing it with her thumb until she heard it click. "Here we go." She slowly backed out of the crawl space, allowing

Mydog to get in a few licks, then got up and brushed her hands on her jeans.

Earlier that week, she had arranged for internet access with the cable company. The computer was an older model Dell she had found at a yard sale. The monitor was gray and dusty with a thick bubble screen and there were brown cigarette burns on top of the tower. She grabbed the keyboard and mouse from the chair and attached them to the setup, then turned to her scowling grandmother.

"Wanna see how to use it?"

"Absolutely not," said Mema.

"Come on, it'll be fun. We could look at gardens."

"I look at my own enough. I don't need to see other people's."

Rayla smiled. "And you call me bull-headed?"

"I've never called you that," said Mema. "Your grandfather was bull-headed. You're just stiff-necked."

"We could look up some of your friends from high school."

"I don't need no computer for that," Mema scoffed. "I see 'em every Sunday in church."

Rayla affected an air of defeat. "Okay. You win. I just wanted you to see his picture."

Mema's eyes lit up. "The janitor?"

Rayla nodded.

"Uncle!" exclaimed Mema, coming to stand beside her.

"Okay," said Rayla, "first thing we're gonna do is press this button over here, then this one on the monitor." She knew her grandmother was focusing on her every move. She imagined a blinking red recording light in her steel gray eyes as she stood by and watched impassively. Her advanced age meant nothing. Mema had a mind like a straight razor.

"Then we're gonna take this thing here, it's called a mouse, and–"

"Why do they call it a mouse?"

"I'm not really sure," Rayla admitted, "but do you see that little arrow on the screen? See how I can move it around? So I'm gonna steer it over here to Internet Explorer and click."

Rayla went to the Department of Corrections homepage, clicked on the inmate locater and typed in Kevin's information. Suddenly his brooding face appeared on the screen. The penetrating green eyes over high cheekbones, that strong jaw, that slightly crooked nose and lips she was well acquainted with. His blue uniform shirt was tight against his shoulders and chest.

Mema frowned. "Is he in...?"

Rayla nodded. "He's an inmate. But he is a good guy. You'd like him." She glanced over at the old woman, attempting to read her. "Do you remember telling me about Grandpa, true love, and missing puzzle pieces? How you thought mine was still waiting in the wings? You were right." She tapped the computer screen. "This is him."

She wanted to say more, but before she could continue, Mema threw her head back and cackled mischievously. "Oh the asshole's going to love this!"

44

Crystal, Jack and the Bedside Nine

The trailer appeared to be breathing, swelling to the brink of explosion then collapsing inward and folding over as if a belt were being cinched around its midsection. Lance took a deep hit from the glass pipe and chased it with a swig of Jack.

The windshield of his truck was like a movie screen. He had no idea how long he'd been sitting in his darkened driveway watching the show. The crickets seemed to be working in tandem with the trailer, providing the soundtrack. He imagined them scattered in the tall grass chirping their steady Bates Motelish *Reep Reep Reep*, increasing in volume as the trailer ballooned and the windows bulged outward. Then stark silence as it sagged, deflated.

He wished the motherfucker would make up its mind and explode or collapse already. Either would be fine with him. Send the cheating bitch spiraling into orbit or crush her lying ass into the ground. Just do something. But no, he was being teased. Again. It seemed like he'd been being teased since he met her. *Build up. Build up! BUILD UP! Nothing.*

He was suddenly horny. But not for his contaminated wife. Two trailers over, Jessica's porch light was burning bright. The memory of her body flared within him, her tan thighs against the white mini skirt. Her unbuttoned blouse, the scent of her hair.

He opened the door and staggered out of the truck, whistling as he stomped across the neighbor's lawn. A dog barked somewhere down the street. The light from tower one was visible through the pines, glowing like a lighthouse on a rocky shore. He thought about the new girl, Amber, in tower two and wondered if she was working. She had been fun the other night but expensive as well, helping him snort most of his dope before sunrise. Now he was running low. It would be time to take a trip to the woods pretty soon.

He paused by the hedges next to Jessica's trailer and took stock of himself. His jeans looked relatively clean and his shirt was dark enough to conceal the booze he had spilled on it earlier. He ran his fingers through his hair then used a shirt sleeve to wipe his teeth. He checked them with his tongue afterward and they felt smoother, less gritty. He lit a cigarette and walked out into her driveway.

There were two bikes and a tricycle laying at the bottom step of her front porch. He imagined her standing in the doorway, calling her little snot-nosed crumb-snatchers to dinner and them flying up the drive, leaping from the bicycles and running up the steps to stuff their dirty little faces with mac and cheese and whatever other instant bullshit she was serving.

He walked up the steps and looked through her window. The lights were on but he didn't see anyone. He tried the door. Locked. He took a drag from his cigarette and tapped a knuckle against the glass.

She appeared in the hallway wearing a robe with a towel wrapped around her head. She looked pissed. He smiled.

"Lance, it's after midnight!" she whispered through the open window.

"I know. I'm sorry. I just … couldn't get you out of my mind."

"You're drunk."

"A little," he admitted, pulling the pipe from his pocket. "Mostly high though. You wanna hit this?"

She shook her head. "You need to leave."

He dug out his lighter and began heating the glass. "Do you remember that first night in the woods? The way you–"

"Jarvis wouldn't approve of this," she whispered.

"Screw Jarvis," he said, taking a deep pull and blowing the smoke through her screen. "I told you to fuck him, anyway, not marry him."

"Well we're together now," she said, "and I don't think he'd like you standing out on my porch at this hour. Come to think of it, your wife wouldn't appreciate it either. Go home."

She slammed the window and locked it, then lowered the blinds. He thought about kicking out the glass, for no other reason except to show the stupid bitch that she wasn't safe, that her rickety-ass lock couldn't stop him if he really wanted to get to her.

Instead he took another hit, then turned and headed home.

The driver side door to his truck was still open. The overhead lights illuminated the filthy interior. There were empty balled up cigarette packs and soda cans on the sandy floorboard. The open bottle of whiskey was propped against the ripped upholstery of the passenger seat. He grabbed it and pushed the door shut.

The trailer was no longer gasping and pulsating but the crickets were going stronger than ever. There was an accusation in their ominous harmony that he didn't catch before. He imagined them pointing up at him from the grass, chanting *freak freak freak* as he hurried toward the front porch. He ran his hand over the hood of Rayla's car on the way. It was cool against his palm. She'd been home for a while.

The front door was unlocked. He pushed it open and slid inside. The trailer was so eerily quiet, so deathly still, that every sound was magnified. The tick of the clock on the mantle, the creak of the floor when he walked, even the sound of his heartbeat.

He took a final swig from the bottle and set it down on the coffee table. A beam of light from his neighbor's backyard was coming through the window and reflecting against a silver picture frame. He picked it up and inspected it. It was their wedding photo. Jarvis had taken it outside the courthouse. He'd seen it a million times since Rayla first set it on the table, but for some reason it was now painful to look at.

He felt tears streaming down his face as he traced a finger over her body. How had he gotten from there to here? From then to now, his past stretched out behind him like a grid of a thousand crossroads. Every thoughtless, impulsive decision was another wrong turn leading further away from the moment captured in the photograph. His whiskey and amphetamine soaked brain recounted every crazy risk, every stranger's bed, every new batch of dope.

Who gives a shit? a voice in his head screamed. *She's fucking an inmate!*

He set the picture down. It was that tiny little truth that nullified his own indiscretions. No amount of stupid impulsive acts on his behalf could match her betrayal.

He glanced at the couch and thought about the folded piece of notebook paper it concealed. He was suddenly overcome by the urge to read it again. He reached down and lifted the heavy piece of furniture, easily tilting it back. The letter was gone. He smirked as he lowered it back down to the carpet. *Too late for that, you silly bitch.* It didn't matter. He had copies.

The hallway seemed longer as he walked to their bedroom. Huddled shadows were pointing and snickering. He knew it was just the dope toying with his mind but that didn't weaken the hallucinations. A spider dangled from the ceiling. "Portals," it whispered as he ducked beneath it. "Portals for Demons."

He immediately thought of Mulgrew and wondered if the strange rodent-faced inmate had gathered any information yet. He was tired of pretending. He needed to hurt something, to punish, to crush.

Rayla's bedside lamp was on. Beneath it on the nightstand he noticed her reading glasses sitting atop a textbook. He leaned forward and read the title: *Introduction to Spanish*.

He imagined her in the arms of some Latino inmate, giggling as he whispered his dirty thoughts against her ear in a foreign tongue. He wanted to spit in her face.

He tiptoed over to his side of the bed and removed his loaded 9-millimeter from the drawer. It was sleek and black and heavy in his sweaty palm. The trigger beckoned like the soft flesh of a lover. He flipped off the safety and walked back around the bed to where she lay tangled in the sheets and breathing softly.

He stood over her and pointed the gun at her head then slowly moved it across her face, down her throat, between her breasts, circling her belly button and finally stopping in the area of her vagina.

"Bang," he whispered, before bringing the pistol to his lips and blowing the imaginary smoke from the barrel.

She mumbled something unintelligible and rolled over. He stood there watching her for a while, then turned and walked back to his side of the bed, replacing the gun and sliding in next to her. Shadows gathered in the corner of the room. He crossed his arms over his chest and focused on the slow turning ceiling fan.

45

Poker Face

Breakfast generally lasted from 4 a.m. until dawn. Each dorm was lined up on the sidewalk and escorted to the chow hall by hustling guards who hurried up and down the lines shouting instructions and warnings. The inmates were herded through the gates like cattle to a feeding trough while the tower light illuminated their sleepy, staggering progress. The experience always made Weasel want to throw back his head and bellow his best Elsie imitation.

Mooooo, he thought as he walked through the center gate.

The chow hall was a drab beige structure made of cinderblocks, surrounded by box-like hedges that were meticulously maintained by the inside grounds crew. Light emanated from the windows as the line of hungry inmates wrapped around the side of the building.

"Shut the fuck up!" a voice thundered from inside.

Weasel could see the rows of tables filled with blue uniforms and the scowling guards that paced between them. A blast of warm air that reeked of garbage blew in his face as he stepped through the door.

The inside of the chow hall was a far cry from the stereotypical prison cafeterias in the movies. He was still a little disappointed that there wasn't a line of hard-looking convicts in hairnets standing over stainless inserts of gruel, ladles ready, behind a shield of Plexiglas. He wanted to growl at someone for shaking the spoon, at least in his imagination. Instead there was only a dirty tiled wall with a window at the end and a sallow-faced guard inspecting each tray as it came out. He grabbed his food and followed the old man in front of him to an empty table toward the back.

He stared down at his tray, careful not to make eye contact with any of the passing faces on either side of the aisle. Breakfast consisted of two crumbling biscuits, an orange blob of sweet potatoes that were grown in the prison garden and served three times a day, a quivering slice of grits that resembled white Jell-O, and a frozen ball of margarine that rolled around the tray like a marble.

Weasel hated prison food. He could have easily slept in and missed breakfast like Kevin and so many others did, but he knew he needed the weight. His metabolism was lightning fast and he had to fight for every pound he could add to his lanky frame. Missing meals was not an option, not if he wanted to survive.

He set his tray on the metal table and slid into the seat across from the old man, thankful that Vero Zay and Tampa Black were nowhere around. The shitty food was hard enough to eat on a good day, but with menacing scowls and hostile vibes radiating toward him from across the chow hall, his appetite didn't stand a chance.

"This seat open?" asked a familiar voice.

He looked up to see Methlab standing in the aisle inspecting the baseboards on the far wall then the ceiling fans.

Weasel shrugged, defrosting the frozen margarine marble in a biscuit. "It's a free prison."

Methlab sat down. "Very funny. Free prison. An oxymoron. I love it."

Weasel thought back to his high school English class and tried to remember the difference between an oxymoron and a metaphor.

"Psycho, right?" asked the twitchy, tattooed Methlab. "I know you told me before. I'm horrible with names."

Weasel nodded. "Psycho's fine."

Methlab shoved a spork full of congealed grits into his mouth as a large female guard walked past their table. Weasel noted the sweat stain on the back of her uniform shirt and her mullet haircut.

"Only on midnights," Methlab remarked without looking up. "That one was built like a sweet potato."

Weasel didn't smile. There was something unsettling about Methlab, something that went beyond his strange appearance and cut-throat reputation. It wasn't even the knife or the dope or his inability to make eye contact. Weasel was sensitive to energy and aura and Methlab's was black as a swarm of flies.

"So how long have you been down?" asked Methlab, sniffing his biscuit before taking a bite.

"Down?"

"Yeah," he said in a spray of crumbs. "How long have you been in prison?"

"Oh," said Weasel, "a few months. I got here in July."

"I heard you had an elbow."

Weasel shrugged. Kevin had taught him that it was bad form to discuss his sentence or to inquire about anyone else's. The fact that an old-school convict like Methlab was unaware of this breach of prison etiquette was a little surprising.

"Don't wanna talk about it, do you?" he said, his eyes briefly scanning Weasel's before darting across the chow hall. "That's understandable."

Weasel focused on his food. It was bland and dry but at least it filled his stomach.

"Are you a musician?" asked Methlab.

His head shot up. "How'd you know that?"

"Uh oh," said Methlab, a smile stretching across his lips. "There's the power button. How did I know? I've seen you playing air guitar across the dorm."

"Actually, it's air bass."

"Ah," Methlab nodded, "a bass player. I should have guessed that. They say most bass players are failed lead guitarists."

"Not me," said Weasel, warming to the conversation. "I started out on bass and never wanted to do anything else. Do you play?"

"Let's go fellas!" shouted a passing guard. "Less talking and more eating!"

Methlab paused and took a bite of sweet potato as the guard moved out of earshot. He wiped his mouth on a skinny tattooed forearm. "I wouldn't say I play guitar. It's more like I play *with* it."

"Right on," said Weasel. "What type of music are you into?"

"Mostly southern rock," said Methlab. "Skynyrd, Molly Hatchet, Blackfoot, stuff like that. You?"

"I'm more into musicians than bands. I like Les Claypool and John Paul Jones but my all-time favorite is Flea from the Chili Peppers."

"Sissy music," Methlab mumbled under his breath.

"Excuse me?"

"Sick," said Methlab. "I said they're sick. Bad ass. Is your buddy a musician too?"

Weasel frowned. "Who?"

"Your homeboy. Freeman."

"Oh, Kevin? Nah. He just likes to read books."

"Boy he sure fucked up that dude in the dayroom the other day."

Weasel nodded and bit into his biscuit.

"What was all that about?"

Weasel shrugged.

"Some people say it was over Ms. Broxson. Is he fucking that lady or something?"

His biscuit was suddenly impossible to swallow, no matter how much he chewed. Slowly, he shook his head.

"Shit," Methlab chuckled. "You wouldn't tell me even if he was. Oh well, none of my concern anyway."

Weasel tried to remain poker-faced as he stared down at his tray. He could feel those skittish eyes dancing across his flesh, attempting to read him. He was relieved when Methlab finally stood and joined the shuffling throng of inmates making their way down the aisle to the trash cans.

46

Catapulting

"How many days?" she asked, watching him move gracefully around the laundry room pretending to straighten stacks of blue uniforms that were already neatly folded on the table.

"Thirty-one," he replied, surveying all of the cubbyholes stuffed with mesh laundry bags and off-white t-shirts and boxers.

"Are you scared?"

He tossed a pair of socks into a cardboard box on the floor. "Of what?"

"I don't know," she said. "I just hear people saying that a lot, especially after they've been in a while."

He gave her a worried look. "I'm terrified. All that steak out there, and pizza, and the beach and beautiful women and amusement parks."

She smiled sweetly and flipped him off.

"Oh yeah, and let's not forget the frightening fact that I'll be out on my own without your loving coworkers telling me when to eat, sleep, and go to the bathroom and dousing me with pepper spray when I'm in need of a little discipline. How will I ever survive?"

She patted the canister of mace on her belt. "You keep up with the sarcasm and I'm going to spray you myself."

He raised an eyebrow then moved quickly across the room. Before she had time to react, he was on her, pressing her against the wall. When he spoke, his lips brushed the side of her face. "I didn't hear you, Officer Broxson," he whispered. "Did you say you needed the staff bathroom cleaned?"

Her heart began to race as he held her. His arms were warm and strong. His lean body meshed perfectly with hers. She opened her mouth to speak but no sound came out. Suddenly he was pulling her by the hand.

"Come on," he urged.

She looked over her shoulder toward the empty officers' station as he opened the door to the tiny bathroom. Her sergeant could come walking through the door at any moment, or the captain, or the warden, or the inspector. "You're gonna get me in trouble," she said.

Then he was kissing her and nothing else mattered.

The bathroom smelled of disinfectant. A single light bulb hung from the ceiling beside a slow turning vent. A paint-flecked mirror presided over a porcelain sink next to the toilet. He led her inside and left the door open as he began unbuttoning her uniform shirt.

She pushed his hands away. "Are you crazy?" she whispered.

He silenced her with another kiss and went right back to work. Suddenly his mouth was on the hollow of her throat, then the tops of her breasts. She shivered as he tugged on her bra and his tongue found her pink upturned nipple. The wet warmth of his hungry mouth melted what little resistance remained. She stroked his hair and held him as he sucked her breasts.

Staring back at her from the mirror was her reflection, panting, eyes glazed over, pinned against the wall. The heady thrill of danger mixed with pleasure caused goose bumps to rocket up and down her tingling flesh. She explored the contour of his muscled back with her fingertips. His body was chiseled and warm, like a statue in the sun.

The image in the mirror was otherworldly and surreal. It was as if she was watching a sweeping love scene in a Hollywood movie while simultaneously experiencing every sensation and emotion felt by the leading lady as she was taken by her lover.

She brought his face back up to hers and tasted his lips. He returned the kiss passionately. She felt her belt being unfastened then her uniform pants sliding down her legs. Her knees were shaking. A flash flood of desire and need gushed throughout her body as he moved his strong hands over her hips. His fingers, though gentle, crackled with electricity. She steadied herself against the wall as his tongue danced circles around hers.

Suddenly his hard erection was inside the elastic of her panties, pressing against the sensitive folds of aching flesh. She reached down to guide him into her and gasped as their bodies became one.

He lifted her from the floor and she shook off a pants' leg, wrapping her calf around his lower back as they fell into a slow grinding rhythm. His hands were hot on her ass, squeezing her, as he bit her bottom lip and made love to her in long, agonizing strokes.

"Kevin," she whispered, "we've got to stop." *Don't stop, don't stop, please don't stop.*

"Okay," he breathed.

She held on tight as the outer bands of a powerful orgasm crashed against the shore of her trembling body. In the spinning bathroom, she again found her eyes in the mirror and witnessed herself in the throes of passion. In spite of the setting, there was nothing cheap about what was taking place. It was beautiful. Spiritual. She clung desperately to his back as the climactic storm moved through her, causing her to convulse and cry out. He silenced her with a kiss.

In the midst of soaring pleasure, a bolt of revelation hit her, sending a surge of understanding throughout her entire body. In that one ecstatic moment, she knew wholeness, tasted nirvana that seeped through the cracks of consciousness.

As her own climax ebbed and his continued to build she reached for that elusive thought that had seconds ago consumed her. The closest she could get to it was a vague and hazy idea, random streams of syntax attempting to explain the unexplainable. Something about everyone being halves, about lovemaking expanding beyond physical union and sensual pleasure. *Expanding? No. Ascending, escalating, catapulting ...* about the joining of two souls. About finally finding home.

She held him tight as he shuddered, then collapsed against her, still inside her as he stroked her face and kissed her lips.

"We have to stop," she said, not wanting the moment to end.

He bent down to kiss her breast once more before nodding and taking a step back. He glanced helplessly around the small bathroom as she stepped into her uniform and began pulling her pants leg over her boot.

"Do you need me to... I mean, I could help clean you up. I don't mind, I ... sorry. It's been forever since I've, you know. I'm not sure what I'm supposed to do."

His face reddened. He looked more like a nervous teenage boy than a hardened prisoner in his thirties. "It's okay," she said, trying not to smile. "Just give me a second."

He leaned against the sink and watched her.

"Alone!" she whispered.

She shook her head and turned on the faucet as the door clicked shut behind him. The toilet seat was cold against her skin. She noticed her knees were still trembling as she dampened a piece of toilet paper and dabbed it between her thighs.

Had they really just made love or was she asleep in her trailer, dreaming? She wondered if, at any second, a static blast of AM radio would snatch her from this parallel universe. If her eyes would suddenly open to find Lance masturbating in bed beside her.

She stood quickly and pulled up her pants, pausing to check her hair before reaching for the door. In spite of her still-pounding heart, she looked fine. Her makeup was good, her uniform was unwrinkled, her shirt was buttoned, her belt was fastened. The reflection in the mirror was smiling as she stepped through the doorway into the laundry room.

He was sitting on the table, legs swinging.

"They'll be back from the yard any minute," she said.

He nodded and dropped to his feet, brushing against her as he headed for the door.

She wanted to kiss him once more before her shift was over, to feel his strong hands caressing her body, stroking her face. Instead she let the moment pass and simply whispered his own words to his back, the words he had taught her.

"Te adoro."

He turned and smiled, tapping his chest twice before pushing open the laundry room door and disappearing into the dormitory beyond.

She realized she was humming as she stepped into the officers' station. Even when she stopped, the incessant melody persisted in her head. *What was it from?*

A fist pounded against the scratched window on the lowside door. She could see the portly silhouette of Sergeant Billingsley peering through the fuzzy Plexiglas. She reached over the control console and pressed a button that released the lock.

Daylight filled the hallway as he held the door open and a long line of sweat-soaked inmates came shuffling in. The quiet dorm was instantly transformed into an echo chamber of competing voices as they lined the sinks and urinals in the bathroom and stomped past the officers' station into the bedding area.

After the last few men trickled through the door, Sergeant Billingsley slammed it shut. "It's entirely too loud in here," his voice boomed. "Take it down a notch, gentlemen."

Rayla dropped her key ring in the flap and he winked at her as he retrieved it. She saw Kevin across the dorm. He was standing in front of his bunk, shirtless. Suddenly she recognized the tune in her head. It was the theme song from *Titanic*. She wondered what brought it to mind, the fact that it was a love story, or the fact that it ended in tragedy.

"Just like a bunch of zoo animals," said the sergeant as he walked through the officers' station door, "give 'em a damn ball and they're happy."

Rayla watched as he removed the radio from his belt and plugged it into the charger. Every time she blinked, a flashback of Kevin making love to her against the bathroom wall ripped through her mind. She was suddenly aware of his scent on her skin, of her trembling knees and flushed face. She felt exposed. Naked.

"Fair'll be here pretty soon," he said.

Rayla frowned. "I'm sorry?"

"The county fair," said Sergeant Billingsley. "It'll be here pretty soon."

"Oh yeah," she said, straightening files to do something with her hands. "October, right?"

"That's right," he said, pouring a cup of coffee.

His eyes narrowed as he stared at her. She was immediately self-conscious. *Oh God, what is it?* she thought. *Smeared lipstick?*

She touched her throat. She couldn't remember him giving her a hickey. He wouldn't do that. Would he?

"Your eyes are better than mine," said Billingsley, "can you see the back of the dorm? What's all that commotion about?"

Rayla glanced over her shoulder, relieved from surviving yet another close call. Then a siren wailed inside of her as her eyes widened and she raced to the low-side window and stood on her tiptoes to see over the gathering crowd.

"No!" she screamed.

Kevin's face was covered in blood. He staggered drunkenly in a halting circle, fists raised, while another inmate swung a belt looped through two combination locks at his head. The weapon was a black and silver blur that helicoptered sideways through the air and tore into the flesh of Kevin's face with a sickening *thwack!* that she could hear through the Plexiglas. Her own knees buckled as he fell to the floor.

Sergeant Billingsley was already on his feet and running for the door. "Call medical," he commanded as he snatched his radio from the charger.

She felt like she was underwater. It was impossible to move with any speed. She reached for the phone in slow motion as the laundry room door slammed and Billingsley flew by the window and waded into the bloodthirsty crowd. "Everyone on their fucking bunks!" he shouted. "Move!"

She could see Kevin's limp body through the legs of the disbursing inmates. His opponent stood over him launching kick after kick into his head and abdomen without response. Backup arrived at the front door. She buzzed them in just as Sergeant Billingsley was emptying a can of pepper spray into the face of Kevin's attacker. She recognized him as Isaiah Banks or *Vero* as the other inmates called him. He howled and attempted to escape the blinding chemical pain by crawling under a bunk. Rayla was too heartbroken to rejoice in his suffering. She picked up the phone and dialed the extension for the triage. After four rings, a disgruntled, raspy voice filled the receiver. "Medical."

"We have an emergency in Alpha Dorm!" said Rayla.

"Seizure, stabbing, or fight?" the bored nurse responded.

"It was … it was a lock," said Rayla, glancing back across the dorm.

"I'll send the stretcher."

PART III
October

47

The Letter T

The cell was a claustrophobic nightmare, an eight-foot-by-ten-foot sarcophagus of concrete blocks with bunk beds bolted to the wall and a stainless toilet/sink by the door.

Kevin stared through the swollen reflection of his face in the small confinement window and out into the dense morning fog. The a.m. shift gradually appeared, trudging to their posts like apparitions of soldiers haunting an ancient battlefield.

The center gate tower rose up from the ground and vanished into a thick blanket of white. Headless, powerless and blind, the only evidence of its existence was the murky outline of its titanic stalk and the metallic clacking of the gate it controlled.

She emerged from the fog like a ray of sunlight. He swallowed as he watched her move gracefully down the sidewalk toward tower three. His bandaged head throbbed with every step she took. A howling gust of need swept through him, distracting him from the other pain. His fingers found the line of stitches that were temporarily supplanting his right eyebrow. Tiny stubbles of hair had finally surfaced overnight. He was relieved by their arrival, a sign that things were slowly returning to normal. He pressed his hand against the glass as she faded back into the fog and disappeared from view.

Knuckles rapped against his cell door. He turned. The chaplain was filling his window slat with his phony televangelical smile. He held up a tattered green book that said *The Living Word* across the front.

"Bible?" his muted voice offered through the door.

"Already got one," said Kevin, turning back to the foggy scene outside his window.

Prison chaplains were glorified guards to him. Worse in some cases. They didn't wear the DOC brown or carry cuffs and pepper spray, but they still abused their positions as God's representatives. Of course there were exceptions. He'd met a few over the years that were sincere and kind, but the majority were paramilitary types that used their pulpit to push their own intolerant brand of religion while discriminating against other less popular walks of faith.

He remembered the chaplain's speech from orientation: a bunch of high-minded, dogmatic drivel about how an imprisoned man could know soaring freedom while a free man could know crushing imprisonment. How freedom was a state of mind. Kevin always scoffed when some chain-gang holy man trotted out that tired-ass sermon. It was easy to toss around lofty philosophies and sanctimonious ideas when you got to walk through the gate and go home to your family every night. But anyone who ever lived in a razor wire cage knew that freedom was not and never could be a state of mind. Unless *distant memory* or *unattainable dream* qualified as states of mind.

He smirked at his own reflection. *Judgmental dick*, he thought. The chaplain wasn't the problem. The problem had gauze wrapped around his hard-knotted head and was staring back at him in the Plexiglas. All this jaw-jacking to Weasel about survival and being a convict, yet he was so love-stoned that he allowed Vero Zay to walk right up on him with that lock.

For the hundredth time that week, his hand shot to his throat in a panic, groping for Bobby's chain. It was gone. Ripped from his neck in the fight.

Again, knuckles rapped against his cell door.

"I said I've already got one," he half shouted, not bothering to turn.

"What you got, boy?" a deep voice responded through the door. "A black eye? A broken nose? You're about to get a lot worse than that if you don't get your ass over here."

He looked over his shoulder. Sergeant Broxson was scowling at him through the glass, arms crossed and face twitching. Beside him a tired looking nurse in heavy makeup and pink scrubs held a small white cup.

Keys jingled and the rectangular tray flap on his door fell forward. The drone of the industrial sized fan at the end of the hall grew louder. The nurse assessed him through the glass. Kevin stuck his hand through the slot.

"How are you feeling today?" she asked, emptying the cup in his palm. Her voice had the nasal twang of a fly buzzing against a window.

"Fine," he said, glancing at the meds before popping them in his mouth. He reached over and pressed the button on the sink and took a few gulps of warm water, then turned back to the window and opened his mouth wide.

The nurse gave him a cursory inspection and nodded. "Any blood in your urine this morning?"

He shook his head.

"Dizziness? Vertigo? Lightheadedness?"

"No, ma'am."

"The doctor will see you on Monday then." She smiled at Sergeant Broxson before turning to leave.

Kevin was vaguely aware of the crocodilian eyes of gunners in the windows of the adjacent cells tracking her movement as she disappeared down the wing.

"Looks like somebody gave you a good old-fashioned country ass-whuppin' boy," said the sergeant, leaning on the open flap of his cell door.

Kevin glanced at the ring on his left hand, a dull gold nondescript band nestled in a thatch of black hair. He imagined that same hand touching Rayla. His stomach churned.

"I'm Sergeant Broxson. I'm here to investigate your disciplinary report."

"Disciplinary report?"

"You're being charged with two-dash-four, fighting. It carries thirty days in confinement and thirty days loss of gain time."

"Fighting?" Kevin stammered. "I wasn't–"

"Save it!" he snarled. "I don't give a fuck. If you want to make a statement, fill out this form." He slapped a paper on the flap. "Otherwise, just write 'refused' and sign on the bottom."

Kevin grabbed the form. "I need something to write with." He studied the sergeant as he rifled through the pockets of his uniform pants, muttering and cursing as he searched for a pen.

A disciplinary report meant Kangaroo Court. In ten years, he had never heard of anyone being found not guilty. He was going to do thirty days in the hole and, worse, his release date was going to be pushed back thirty days. Writing a statement in his own defense was really a waste of time. Still, he had to try. The idea of Rayla spending thirty more days with the twitchy scab-faced monster on the other side of his cell door was unbearable. And anyway he wasn't *fighting* anyone. Not this time at least. He was blindsided with a lock in a sock.

"Here," said Sergeant Broxson, tossing a flex-pen through the open flap, "you got three minutes."

Kevin retrieved the pen from under the toilet. It was clear and rubber and bendable, designed to be useless as a weapon. *Genius,* Kevin thought as he flipped back his mat to write on the steel. *How many countless wretched lives had been spared since the advent of the flex-pen?* Problem was, it was useless as a writing instrument as well.

He wrote his statement as quickly as possible, all the while wrestling with the schizophrenic pen. Every word was an adventure. One moment the ink poured forth in messy blots and smudges, the next he was carving dry lines into the page.

"Time's up," growled the sergeant.

Kevin hurried to finish the final sentence and sign the bottom.

He rapped on the steel door with an oversized cell key. "I said time's up, jackass!"

Sidestepping bullies and aggressive types was a survival skill Kevin perfected during his first year in prison. Things like respect, logic and reasoning were foreign to the average knucklehead. The only language brutes understood was brutality. But there were still ways to outthink them, especially the ones in brown with more to lose than just gain time. Navigating these volatile overlords required a Tao-like effort of balance. Too much deference would be taken as weakness and exploited, yet too much confidence would be seen as a challenge and invite more attention. It was the middle way that kept them wondering.

He forced himself to breathe, calmly placing the statement and flex-pen in the outstretched hand on the other side of the door.

"You know this ain't gonna make a lick of difference, right?" said Sergeant Broxson, smirking down at the paper. Then his eyes narrowed as he studied it. His Adams apple climbed slowly from his uniform collar then slid back down his throat. The right side of his mouth flinched and flickered like a neon tavern sign at dusk. When he looked up, the arrogance had vanished from his eyes, replaced by something cold and appraising. "Nice handwriting," he said. "I like the way you make your T's ... very girly ... very sweet."

Kevin shrugged. *Whatever, psycho.*

He turned to walk off, then paused. "What dorm were you in?" he asked. His jaw was clenched, his face ashen.

"Alpha," said Kevin, "low side."

48

The Ascending Pitch of Focus

Methlab sat hunched in the back stall with a canteen mirror balanced on his leg and a small pile of ice dumped in the center. A stream of water trickled from the toilet beneath him and raced toward the tarnished drain. Surrounding his feet were crumpled yellow tobacco pouches, waterlogged magazine tear-outs of naked women, and discarded strips of toilet paper.

He watched a fat black fly round the wall and circle his ankles in a lethargic figure eight.

The kid began to whistle.

Methlab sat up straight and peered over the wall. "What is it?"

"Mellowship Slinky," said Weasel. "Chili Peppers."

Methlab pinched the bridge of his nose. Whistling was supposed to be the signal that the guard was exiting the officers' station. "Is the man coming out?"

Large owl-like eyes blinked behind thick glasses. "What? Oh ... no."

"Then why the hell are you whistling?" he hissed.

"My bad."

Methlab shook his head and got back down to business. He first laid his inmate ID flat over the dope and ground it into the mirror, then he used the edge to chop it into fine talc.

The fly levitated lazily between his legs and landed on his kneecap. He watched it sink back and raise its tiny front legs, rubbing them together as if anticipating a meal.

Glancing over the stall wall again, he reached down the front of his pants and removed his tools. The spoon was plastic with the back end chewed off. The needle was from medical, cuffed by a diabetic at insulin call and purchased for a half gram. He could feel the kid looking at him from the front of the bathroom. He nodded him over.

"Where?" asked Weasel.

"Just duck down," said Methlab, shoveling a little less than half the dope into the spoon. The kid obediently crouched by his feet causing the fly to panic and take off.

There were twenty cc's of water in the syringe. He emptied it into the spoon then pulled the small plunger from the back of the needle and used it to stir the toxic concoction before licking it clean and reinserting it.

The fly returned to his kneecap. He could feel its tiny legs tickling him. He stuck the needle in the spoon and drew up the water. The gauge read forty cc's. He smiled. *Fire.*

"Let me see your arm," he said.

The kid eagerly obeyed. He was a cinch to hit, a junkie's dream, ropey mounds of squiggly vein under taut thin skin. The needle sank into his flesh with barely any pressure, as if the sharp tip had found a microscopic alley between follicle and pore. There was no stab or prick. It *whispered* in, penetrating both flesh and vein like a knife through warm butter. A solitary droplet of deep crimson appeared at the point of entry serving as a checkered flag. He mashed the orange plunger like a fuel injection throttle. The kid's eyes fluttered. Then he coughed.

Methlab watched for a moment as he sank back against the dirty tiles. There was dark power in shooting someone up for the first time, in revealing a new world to the green and uninitiated. A sheen of sweat covered the kid's forehead. Methlab knew exactly what he was experiencing. The swell of exhilaration, of creeping warmth and pounding heart, the ascending pitch of focus. He quickly scooped the remaining dope in the spoon and reached behind him to flush the toilet.

The water disappeared down the dirty streaked hole with a powerful roar then began to rise incrementally. Methlab stuck the needle down between his legs and drew toilet water up into the syringe. He checked the amount, leveled it off at twenty cc's, then emptied it into the spoon. The dope dissolved like ice caps in the North Atlantic.

The kid blinked rapidly. "You're … you're gonna shoot up with toilet water?"

"Why not?" said Methlab, flexing his forearm. "You did."

The fly relocated to the mirror in his lap. He watched it dance atop its own reflection as needle met pulsing vein. "One of the luxuries of having *from now on* in this shithole is not having to worry about things like that. What's the worst that could happen? AIDS? Hep C? Bird Flu? I'm not running from death. I'm running *toward* it, full speed." He pressed the fast forward button. Meth amphetamine surged into his body, racing through his bloodstream like quicksilver. His heart rate accelerated to a Death Metal drum solo. The acrid taste of dope flooded his saliva. He gagged, then smiled.

Suddenly the laundry room door rattled and swung open, banging against the wall. Panic filled the kid's eyes. "It's cool," whispered Methlab, the needle still hanging from his arm. "Just stay down."

"Inmate Mulgrew, bunk twenty-three lower," the officer called out into the dorm, "Festus Mulgrew."

He recognized the voice. It was Ms. Broxson. He raised his head over the stall wall. "I'm using the bathroom, ma'am."

She frowned at him from the doorway. He tried to hold her stare. Couldn't. "Inspector Fretwell wants to see you," she said in a robotic monotone. "Do you know where his office is?"

Methlab nodded.

"Hurry up," she said, slamming the door.

He removed the needle from his arm and looked over at the officers' station. She was already back inside. There was no doubt she had something going on with the pretty boy. Ever since he was beat down with the lock and moved out of the dorm she had that dazed lovesick look about her. He was almost positive he saw her crying the other morning.

The kid was crouched on the wet floor, bony elbows resting atop bony knees. Methlab glanced at him. "Is it me or has she been acting a little pissy lately?"

The response was barely a shrug.

Methlab sighed and spat in the toilet. Then he went straight for the throat. The kid squirmed and kicked but he couldn't break free. His eyeballs bulged from his purple face, almost touching the thick lenses of his bifocals. "Do you think I'm a snitch?" Methlab hissed. "Do you?"

The kid shook his head frantically.

He released his throat but kept him forced against the tiles by the collar of his shirt. "Listen to me you sniveling little fuckstick. I'm sick of you lookin' at me like I'm a cop every time I mention your faggot ass buddy and his shiteater girlfriend, okay? If I was five-oh do you think I'd be back here shooting dope?"

"No," the kid croaked.

"Fuck no," Methlab echoed, "and anyway everybody knows your homeboy was taggin' Ms. Broxson in the laundry room. It wasn't exactly a military secret, right?"

His shoulders slumped. "Yeah."

Bingo, thought Methlab. "Good. Now I wonder why the investigator wants to chat with me. I haven't broken any rules lately. At least none that I'm aware of anyway." He smiled and held out the needle, spoon and mirror. "Hang on to these for me, will you?"

The kid's hand was shaking as he reached out and accepted the contraband.

Suddenly the fly sailed between them in a sluggish arc toward the stall wall. Methlab plucked it from the air without looking then shook it in his cupped palm for a moment before hurling it to the floor where it lay stunned. When he picked it up, he watched until the tiny legs began to kick and convulse with life, then he ripped off a wing.

"Would you mind feeding Junior while I'm gone?"

49

Ommatophobia

Fretwell's office was tucked between the law library and GED classroom in a rectangular beige structure about the length of a city block. A Saints' fleur-de-lis was plastered to the window and the dust-covered blinds were arranged so that he could see out but never the inverse. A rain-rusted butt can sat just outside a door so plain it could easily have been mistaken for a janitor's closet were it not for the ominous reputation of the man behind it.

Methlab knocked, acutely aware of the sidelong suspicious glances from passing inmates and guards. Fair or not, the common belief was that any man who entered Fretwell's inner sanctum was, for all intents and purposes, a snitch.

He stepped inside and shut the door. The unmistakable scent of Lemon Pledge filled his nostrils. The inspector was standing by the window in his socks, launching darts at the far wall of his office.

"Mulgrew?" he asked.

"Yes sir," said Methlab.

Thwack. A dart hit the particle board. The inspector smiled. "Or should I call you Methlab?"

Methlab shrugged, still zinging from the monster shot in the bathroom. He scanned the certificates and plaques that hung from the wall. "Technically my name is seven five one nine eight four. Why don't you call me that?"

Fretwell walked behind his desk and plopped down into the chair. The springs creaked as he made himself comfortable. "I'm going to give you a pass on that insolent mouth just this once since our conversation hasn't even started yet. But you should choose your next words carefully because if I don't like them, you're going to end up on the short wing of Y-Dorm for a hundred and eighty days, understand?"

Methlab nodded.

"Have a seat," said Fretwell, kicking his feet up. "I was looking over your file this morning. Stabbings, possession, extortion. Quite a resume. It's a wonder our paths haven't already crossed." He lowered his brow and smiled. "Welcome to my radar."

Methlab sat in the small chair in front of his desk. He glanced at the darkened balls and heels of the inspector's white socks before looking quickly away. He could sense Fretwell's face morphing into a frown in his peripheral.

"Are you high?" asked the inspector.

"No sir," said Methlab, finding the corners of the ceiling.

"Look at me," he demanded.

Methlab tried to hold his gaze but his eyes slid from the man's face as if being repelled by some magnetic polarity.

"You know," said Fretwell, swinging his feet from the desk and rifling through a drawer. "Let's see, I know there's one in here somewhere. Ah, yes. Here we are." He tossed the dull gray package on the desk. "Know what that is?"

"Piss test," said Methlab. *Lovely.*

"That's right," said the inspector with a wink. "Multi-panel. Thing picks up every drug known to man. Weed, benzos, opiates, narcotics. But I doubt that's necessary for you. If your name's any indication, there's only one thing I need to test you for."

"I don't do drugs. Quit a long time ago."

Fretwell resettled in his chair and smirked. "My father taught me to never trust a man who can't look me in the eye."

"Yeah, well, your dad and my dad would've never been bowling partners then, because nothing enraged my father more than eye contact. Especially from me."

The inspector stared at him while absently gnawing on a pen cap.

Methlab glanced at the thick folder on his desk. "Is my psych history in that file? Check it out. You'll see words like ommatophobia, psychoneurosis, and post-traumatic stress disorder. Every prison shrink in the state has weighed in on my ... condition. All I can tell you is that for me eye contact is the visual equivalent of fingernails on a blackboard."

Fretwell sighed and shook his head. "Heart-wrenching. Really it is. Yet somehow I'm having trouble feeling sorry for you."

"I don't need your sympathy."

"And I may still piss test you–"

"Just show me to the toilet."

"–depending on the outcome of this meeting." Fretwell reached over and grabbed a notepad. "Now, down to business. Do you know Blake Burkett?"

Sip thought Methlab, overcome by a sudden sinking feeling. "Never heard of him."

The inspector glared across the desk. "You've never heard of Blake Sip Burkett?"

"Doesn't ring a bell."

He paused to light a cigarette. "Oh come on man. Everybody knows good ol' Sip. Rich kid. About your height. Pretty boy, at least he used to be pretty 'til somebody disfigured his face with a shank." He leered at Methlab. "Well he checked into protective custody this morning."

Methlab cringed. *Seven hundred and fifty dollars. Gone.*

Fretwell spat a cloud of smoke over his head. "Said he feared for his life. Apparently his family got tired of supporting his dope habit and decided to give him a little dose of tough love."

"Good for his family," said Methlab, wondering how he was going to pay his own debt now that Sip was gone.

"He checked in under your name," said the inspector, leaning forward, the overhead fluorescent revealing white streaks of scalp beneath his thinning hair.

Methlab shrugged. "Well then he should receive an 'F' for originality. Using my name to get a free transfer has been going on for twenty years. It's almost a cliché at this point."

"A cliché," said Fretwell, ashing in a Mountain Dew bottle on his desk. "I'll tell you what's cliché. You. You and your shifty eyes and your ugly tattoos and your knife and your dope and your slick mouth."

Methlab squirmed in his chair as the inspector took another harsh drag from his cigarette and exhaled forcefully.

"Burkett claims you're pushin' dope," said Fretwell. "Ice. Says he owes you a decent chunk of change that he can't pay. He's terrified, thinks you're gonna kill him. By the way, that was a nice little piece of reconstructive surgery you performed on his nose."

Panic and paranoia screamed through his veins, whipped onward by the amphetamines, gathering momentum. *What if he was put in the box? His house would be thoroughly searched and scrutinized. His remaining dope and works were safe, the kid was holding them down, but his knife was stashed behind his locker and more importantly, he left Junior on his bunk.*

Fretwell produced a set of handcuffs and began clicking them. The grating roll of their chattering metal teeth sounded like a rattlesnake to Methlab. "Well," he said, "this has been a huge waste of time. You obviously don't feel like talking and I'm already tired of looking at your ugly face. Let's get you an apartment over in administrative lock-down and see if a few months of sleeping on steel will change your tune."

The inspector pushed his chair back and stood. "Get up and put your hands behind your back."

"But I didn't do anything!" Methlab protested.

"Shut up," said Fretwell, extinguishing his cigarette on the way around the desk.

"I didn't say I wouldn't cooperate," Methlab pleaded, already imagining Junior searching for him on an empty bunk, wasting away from having to find his own food, being crushed under a brogan.

"That ship has sailed," said the inspector.

Methlab felt the first cuff tighten around his left wrist. "Wait! I have concrete information regarding an officer inmate relationship."

Fretwell paused. "What type of relationship?"

"Romantic … sexual."

"Who's the officer?"

He wavered for a moment at the precipice before shutting his eyes and stepping into the abyss. "Ms. Broxson."

The inspector went still behind him. A silence fell over the smoky lemon-scented office. Suddenly his wrist was being uncuffed.

"Sit down," said Fretwell.

50

Baby Bumblebee

Rayla's eyes fluttered open, the familiar shapes of her bedroom materializing in the dark like rocky outcrops in an ocean cove. The dresser emerged, then the ironing board. She glanced over her shoulder. The alarm clock glowed *3:11*. She shut her eyes and willed herself back into the murky void of the dream realm. Her breathing slowed, her body relaxed. Her head sank deeper into the pillow. Then suddenly, *AWAKE!*

A hand was stroking her hair. *His* hand. A foreign yet familiar chemical scent twined with the aroma of stale tobacco wafting from his fingertips like tendrils of poisonous gas. He lightly caressed her face, tracing jawline to chin before moving on to her throat. Panic began to swallow her as his fingertips and thumb crept around the sides of her neck, flirting with asphyxiation.

The beginnings of a scream stirred deep within her but died on the way to her vocal chords as his hands fell to her breasts. Through squinted lashes she could see the silhouette of his body in the dark, elbow propped on pillow, hand supporting head. She feigned sleep, hoping unresponsiveness would derail his lust.

He lifted her shirt. She rolled over. The trailer creaked and groaned in the heavy waiting silence.

She pretended to snore. A collection of words bubbled to the surface of her subconscious. A nonsensical nursery rhyme from her childhood. She clung to it desperately like the fervent prayer of the devout, repeating it over and over with her hands clasped and her eyes squeezed shut.

I'm picking up a baby bumblebee
Won't my momma be so proud of me?

He snuggled behind her, nuzzling her neck, his prodding erection smashed up against her, evidence of his intentions. She remained still. Her only movement the words scuttling across her mind.

I'm squishing up a baby bumblebee
Won't my momma be so proud of me?

His hand danced down her ribs and over her hip, sliding beneath her shorts, breeching the waistband of her panties.

She clamped her fingers over his wrist. "Lance … no."

She could feel his muscles tense. "What the fuck do you mean, no?"

"I can't," she said, hating her own fear.

"What's the problem?" His tone was equal parts ice and steel. "You being faithful to somebody?"

"*What?*" she said, the darkness concealing her guilt. *Where did that come from?* "Lance, you know it's the end of the month." She was actually a few days late, but the dates lined up. Thankfully. Lance knew her menstrual cycle. In the old days they used to plan around it. She was as predictable as the cable bill.

"That never stopped you before," said Lance.

She yawned. "In the shower, maybe. Not the bed."

"Then let's go take a shower," he growled.

She forced a laugh that came off sounding nervous and echoed in her mind. "It's three-twenty in the morning. Don't be silly."

A foreboding silence hung over the room, blanketing it in tension. She shut her eyes and resettled into the bed, willing him away.

I'm squishing up a baby bumblebee
Won't my momma –

He yanked her head back with a fistful of hair and clamped a hand over her mouth. "Silly? There's only one silly little bitch in this trailer and it ain't me." His face loomed over hers. "You're lucky this room is infested with cameras," he whispered before releasing her.

She hugged herself in the darkness, refusing to cry.

Suddenly his foot slammed into the small of her back forcing her over the side of the bed. She landed with a thump.

"If you're not going to fulfill your wifely duties," he said, "then you can sleep on the floor."

51
Synthesis

Inspector Fretwell saluted the shadowy outline in tower one as he walked through the interior gate of the prison entrance. A response was neither expected nor received. He smiled and stuck his cigarette in the side of his mouth, biting on the filter.

A couple of nurses in floral print scrubs, pasty skinned and plump from working graveyard too long, waddled toward him. He held open the gate as they passed. "Morning, ladies."

They stopped bickering for a moment. One gave him a curt nod while the other ignored him altogether. He released the buzzing gate allowing it to swing shut behind them. The crack of the bolt slamming home was like a gunshot.

He took a deep satisfying drag and surveyed the activity before him. Inside grounds crews were already hard at work edging, clipping, weeding and raking. They were scattered along both sides of the road that ran through the heart of the prison.

He nodded at the work squad supervisor, a cocky punk whose name he couldn't recall but was instantly recognizable with his Stetson hat, mirrored sunglasses and blade of grass jutting from his mouth.

"Good morning, sir," the officer responded, surprising him.

He flicked his cigarette into the grass and switched his briefcase to his left hand. Out of the corner of his eye he noted an alarmed looking inmate striding toward the plume of smoke in order to quickly remove the eyesore from the otherwise pristine expanse of lawn.

Orderlies were standing outside the chapel door clutching their King James and NIVs. Further down, the rattle of a convoy of laundry carts sent pigeons darting for the roof of the chow hall. Officers sipped coffee outside the staff canteen. A line of inmates was waiting to be admitted to the library.

He barely glanced at the darkened window of his office as he passed. He had business to attend to first. The information Mulgrew had given him regarding Rayla Broxson was a potential bombshell. *If* it turned out to be true. Ten years with the Inspectors Office and almost twenty in Alabama law enforcement had taught him that junkies and dope fiends would say anything to wiggle out of trouble. He'd even assisted prosecutors in coaching a few of them to hit all the right notes when testifying against a bigger fish. But this was different than some crackhead rolling on his connection. This was about Lance Broxson's haughty little wife fucking an inmate. His blood pressure rose at the tease of escorting Rayla Broxson out of the prison. This was going to be huge. *If* it turned out to be true.

He needed concrete evidence. Something a little more substantial than the word of an inmate named Methlab. That was the reason he was heading over to see Candace and Blanche Marie, to set a trap.

The mailroom was in the warehouse across the perimeter road. He sidestepped the pallets of shrink-wrapped junk food and soda that were awaiting delivery to the inmate canteens, maneuvering his way around carts and forklifts until he came to the cracked door tucked away in the back corner of the building.

He peeked inside. A bag of mail was scattered over a table while two obese women sat reading with glasses perched on their noses.

"Looks like Cummings' wife is finally gonna leave him for that attorney fella down in Sarasota," said Blanche Marie. "I knew that was comin' soon as she took that job."

Across the table, Candace sniffled.

"What is it?" asked Blanche Marie.

"Paxton's daddy's got Alzheimer's," said Candace.

Both women were so absorbed in the inmate mail that neither noticed him in the doorway. He studied their pudgy faces. The similarities were striking, the highlighted hair, the identical frown lines, the way they moved their heads from left to right while they silently mouthed the words they were reading. Though not related, Blanche Marie and Candace had spent so many years isolated from the world in this stuffy little windowless mailroom that it was almost as if a gradual form of synthesis was occurring beneath the harsh fluorescent lighting. A process that was slowly morphing them into middle-aged twins.

He cleared his throat, startling them.

Candace recovered first. "Well look what the cat dragged in," she said. "We ain't under investigation are we?"

His smile felt phony on his face. Social banter was never his strong suit. "Not that I know of."

She refolded the letter she was reading and slipped it back into the envelope. "Haven't seen you in a while, Hollis. I was beginning to think you got transferred."

"I've been busy."

"Too busy for church?"

He shrugged.

It was Blanche Marie who finally broke the uncomfortable silence. "Well, Inspector," she paused and glanced nervously at Candace, "what can we do for you this morning?"

"I need to red flag an inmate's outgoing and incoming mail."

Blanche Marie grabbed a pen and a sticky note. "Name?"

"Kevin Freeman."

52

Dancing in the Dark

It was hard to tell what time it was. He was certain it was sometime after midnight because his cell light was off and the officers had already changed shifts but beyond that, he had no idea. If his stomach was any indication, it was approaching breakfast time but his stomach was not trustworthy. When he was awake he was hungry. After fifteen days in the box he was used to it. Hunger had become another annoyance to be tolerated. An aggravating companion. *Like Weasel.*

Somewhere down the wing a cell door slammed. He shut his eyes and allowed his thoughts to drift ... *to her.* Unlike any other memory that he attempted to draw from the murky depths of the mind where memories swam, Rayla emerged in shimmering Technicolor. He pulled the thin pillow from beneath his head and wrapped his arms around it as he recalled her soft lips, her warm brown eyes, the faint scent of her perfume, the lull of her voice, the way light seemed to attach itself to her skin.

Keys jingled outside his cell. Voices. Rayla disintegrated, replaced by the dark. He sat up in his bunk. The steel door rocked in its frame as the flap was unlocked. A rectangle of light spilled through the opening.

"Freeman, cuff up," a familiar voice drawled.

WITH ARMS UNBOUND

He knew who it was without seeing. He swung his legs over the side of the bunk and stood.

"Let's go asshole," said her husband. "I ain't got all night."

As Kevin walked over to the door he could see him through the window slat, facial muscles twitching, wincing, lurching. Beside him, in cuffs, was an inmate Kevin didn't recognize. A hard-faced man with a shovel jaw and tattoos from his neck to his knuckles. Sergeant Broxson leaned over and said something to him. He nodded once, eyes straight ahead.

Kevin was overdue for a cellmate. He'd been lucky to skate since they found him guilty in Kangaroo Court, but confinement was too overcrowded to expect to do a thirty-day bid alone. At least he was assigned to the bottom bunk.

He turned and put his back against the door, ducking slightly so that his hands were even with the flap. The cuffs were slapped on his wrists with violent precision, grating against the bone and cutting off his circulation. Kevin looked back over his shoulder through the window.

The sergeant was glaring at him. "Problem?"

Kevin shook his head.

"Didn't think so," he said. "Now go catch the wall."

Kevin walked to the back of the cell and stared out the window. The tower light crept slowly over dormitory rooftops and reflected off the gleaming razor teeth of the fence line. He followed its beam as he attempted to adjust the handcuffs.

"Roll eighteen," said the sergeant into his radio.

The locking mechanism released and the door rolled open. Again, Kevin glanced over his shoulder. What little light there was on the catwalk shone against the sergeant's back, darkening his twitchy face, covering him in shadow.

"Face. The fucking. Wall," he ordered.

Kevin turned away. He had done enough box time in the early years of his sentence to know that it was institutional policy, whenever a confinement door was rolled, that the cell occupants be cuffed and facing the rear wall. He'd also crossed paths with countless abusive guards along the journey, enough to know the personality type he was dealing with. Still, there was something in the sergeant's baleful sneer that gave him pause, something that went beyond security and standard dickheadery.

Did he know something? Could he?

Kevin heard his new cellmate step in. The door slammed behind him. He turned and squinted in the dark as the man held his wrists to the flap to be uncuffed. The click and whir of metal sounded like the spin of a revolver. Then his hands were free and it was Kevin's turn.

"Get over here," said the sergeant, jingling his keys impatiently.

He slid past the shape of the stranger and turned his back to the door, anxious for his aching wrists to be unbound. He felt a gloved hand brush against his forearm, then seize the link of chain between the cuffs, forcing them an impossible click tighter, holding him steady, pinning him to the door.

Suddenly a tattooed fist shot out of the darkness and smashed into his face. The room burst into a cascade of color and light. Another blow followed, the iron taste of blood filled his mouth.

He struggled to break free from the sergeant's grip but it was no use. His wrists were leveraged against the flap, bending him forward, restricting his ability to move. Even if he could break free, what difference would it make? He was handcuffed, behind his back, in the dark.

He tried to shield his face by bringing chin to chest and giving his attacker his head to hit, but an uppercut with enough force to lift him to his toes rocked his head straight back against the door, loosening his front teeth.

He imagined the circuitry in his brain popping and emitting sparks as his body went limp. The already black cell sank to ocean floor darkness as he submitted to the barrage of heavy fists driving him down.

He awoke to the sound of his cell door rolling and shower slides shuffling by his face, leaving. His entire body throbbed like a caution light, blinking bright pain in steady intervals. He groaned and attempted to sit up. His wrists and forearms had become so numb from the handcuffs that he'd forgotten they were still there.

Carefully, he rolled over onto his stomach and used his forehead and knees to assist him in getting up. His cell door slammed.

A flashlight beam came down through the flap, blinding him. When he squeezed his eyes shut, the unmistakable afterimage of a pool of blood rippled on the concrete beneath him. He struggled to his feet and leaned against the wall.

"Come here," said Sergeant Broxson. "Let's get those cuffs off."

Kevin blinked and attempted to right his blurred vision. Even in his addled drunken state, it seemed important to stand up straight and look her husband in the eye. *Her husband* ...

He staggered to the cell door. Through the window slat he could see the stranger who attacked him. He was handcuffed again and staring straight ahead. There was no lingering trace of violence on his stoic face. His eyes were flat and emotionless. He looked bored.

"Turn around," said the sergeant.

Kevin obeyed.

The cuffs rattled as they were removed. His arms fell to his sides. The feeling returned in prickly waves. He opened and closed his hands.

Sergeant Broxson squatted outside the door, resting his chin on the flap. Conflicting emotions chased each other across his face – a raised eyebrow, a sneer, a smile – the expressions churned and morphed so fluidly that his flesh began to resemble a bubbling sheet of molten lava.

"You sure like getting your ass whupped," he said. "You must be one of them masochistic freaks I've heard people talk about. Is that it, boy? You like pain?"

Kevin leaned over and spat a glob of blood in the toilet, not bothering to answer.

The sergeant continued to stare at him through the flap. "Tell me," he said, "what's more exciting for you? Getting your face beat in … or fucking my wife?"

The cell began to tilt.

"I read your little note. Very sweet. The only thing that was missing were the *do you love me? Check yes or no* boxes at the end." He shook his head derisively. "You're not man enough for Rayla."

"I have no idea what you're talking about," said Kevin.

"Yes you do," he said through clenched teeth. He paused and glanced at the tattooed stranger beside him. "Hey, go stand over there somewhere." When he turned back to Kevin, the face that filled the flap was an evil thing, a mask of unbridled hatred.

"Did you really believe that you could take my wife from me? I'd die before I let that happen. *She'd* die before I let that happen." The weight of his threat hung in the silence between them.

Kevin pressed his thumb against his two front teeth, forcing them back up into the gum. "I think you've got the wrong cell."

"Oh, I don't think so," he said. "Your handwriting on the witness statement matches up perfect with that love note. I've compared 'em. Plus you live in Alpha Dorm. Plus you're pretty enough." His face stretched into something resembling a smile. "'Least you used to be."

Kevin shut his eyes and breathed through his nose. *The note. The only note he'd ever written her. The lone piece of incriminating evidence in existence and this psychopath had somehow found it.* He couldn't blame Rayla though. Being covert and underhanded were simply not in her DNA. He shook his head, marveling at the bottomless depths of his own terrible luck.

Suddenly a voice from the past rang out in his groggy, punch-drunk mind. *"Man my luck is so bad, it could be rainin' pussy and I'd get hit in the head with a dick!"* Bobby. A surge of laughter welled within him. He tried to stifle it or at least reduce it to more of a muffled snort. Instead it racked his shoulders and exploded from his lungs like a sonic geyser, echoing down the wing.

"What the fuck is so funny?" the sergeant hissed.

Kevin's laughter trailed off as he wiped his eyes. It was difficult to see in the dark but he thought his hand came away smeared with blood. "Oh, I just think you're delusional. Tweakers always make me laugh."

A burst of static erupted from the sergeant's radio. He reached down to silence it. "I'll tell you what I think is funny," he said. "I went down to records yesterday and checked you out. Now all this time I was expecting you to be some Latino Casanova type or at least a badass. That's what these local girls usually get in trouble over. So imagine my surprise when I learned that Rayla was screwing a drunk. A drunk that killed his own brother. 'Round here, even the weakest men can handle their liquor."

Kevin's muscles tensed. "Fuck you."

The sergeant glanced over his shoulder then squeezed his face into the four-inch flap. His skin was pulled tight, his eyes bulged, his teeth were bared. "I don't think so," he said. "You're the one who's fucked."

Maybe it was the memory of his brother that did it, or maybe it was the beat-down that he had just endured, or that cocky condescending tone, or the thought of Rayla being pushed around by him. Maybe it was the cumulative effect of everything, of ten years of tongue-biting and pride-swallowing and eye-averting. Whatever it was, it was enough.

"Why don't you roll that door and come on in?" said Kevin. "We can settle this right now."

"I'd love that," her husband said, "problem is, I'm still under investigation for the last inmate I stomped over my wife in a confinement cell."

"Did *you* really stomp him? Or did you just hold him by the handcuffs while someone else did your dirty work?"

He stared at Kevin through the flap, taking his time to respond. His twitchy face sent rumbling tremors through the door. "Good one," he finally said. "That was a good one. I bet Rayla really loves your ... your wit."

Kevin was astonished to see the glassy whites of his eyes brim with tears. He blinked them away before continuing.

"Now shut up and listen. When I leave, you're gonna wash up and you're gonna clean this cell as good as you can in the dark. Then you're gonna get in your bunk, go to sleep and forget this ever happened."

Kevin leaned against the sink. "How could I ever forget the warmth and kindness you've shown me this evening?" He paused and spat another glob of blood into the toilet. "I only hope I can someday repay you–"

"And if anyone asks you about your little bumps and bruises," the sergeant continued, "you're gonna blame them on your first fight, the one that got you put back here. Just say you're a slow healer."

"Spoken like a true professional," said Kevin. "No wonder you're wearing those sergeant stripes. But I think I'll pass on doing things your way."

"I'm not asking."

"I know," Kevin said. "I get it. You're threatening me. But see, the thing about threats is they're usually delivered *before* the beating. Otherwise they kinda lose their magic."

"You haven't even begun to suffer," the sergeant said quietly.

"Even if you take all my gain time and gas me every day, my max date is nineteen months away. That's the absolute most I will do." Kevin bent forward and stared hard into his eyes. "You can't break me."

A smile crept over his face. "I could break her fingers. Have you noticed how pretty they are? How delicate and graceful and smooth? With those little dark creases runnin' across the joints? 'Course you have, you mentioned her wedding ring in your note … *our* wedding ring." He paused and nodded to himself. "Yeah, I could easily break her fingers. Or I could break her nose, never liked her nose, or snap her fuckin' neck."

A sinking feeling fell over Kevin as he listened, like an invisible net tightening, suffocating, choking.

"Or I could take a copy of your note to the inspector or even the sheriff's office, tell 'em all about ya'll's little fling. Inmate-lovers are worse than lepers in this town. She'd be prosecuted to the fullest extent of the law. I'd hate to have to testify against my own wife, but …" His words trailed off into a shrug.

"Okay," said Kevin, desperate to banish the parade of terrifying images that were streaking across his mind. Images of her fingers being snapped sickly backwards, his fist pounding her face, his hands around her throat, her crying in the back of a police car. "Okay, you have my word. I'll do whatever you say."

He smirked and shook his head. "You know the difference between me and you? I mean, besides the fact that you're a piece of shit criminal who murdered your own brother." He paused and waited for a reaction. "The difference is that, unlike you, I didn't *fall* in love with Rayla. I selected her. She was chosen. You think about that," he said, before slamming the flap and walking away.

Kevin went to the door and pressed his face against the window. He caught a glimpse of him escorting the tattooed stranger back down the wing before they disappeared from view.

When he stepped away he noticed the Plexiglas was smeared with his blood and breath.

53

Radical Change

There is peace in decisiveness. Rayla felt a calm that she hadn't known in months as she walked down the dirt driveway to Mema's house.

Dry leaves crackled beneath her shoes. The yard was full of them, a rustic blanket of orange and red that stretched right up to the porch and wrapped around the house.

The porch light was on even though there was plenty of daylight left. Rayla kept expecting Mydog to come bounding down the steps or flying around the side of the house, but the only sound she heard was the whisper of the wind through the trees and the creaking of the boards on the porch.

The screen door was open. She glanced in the living room window while bending to remove her tennis shoes. Although the "no shoes in the house" rule was no longer enforced, it was a habit that was firmly embedded in Rayla's psyche. You flushed the toilet when you used the bathroom, you turned off the light when you left a room, and you removed your shoes before entering the house. These three non-negotiable rules were instilled in her before she hit kindergarten and were as second-nature as looking both ways before crossing the street.

The door was unlocked.

"Mema," she said as she stepped inside. "Hello?"

"In the den," her grandmother called.

Rayla shut the door and turned down the hall. The den was just outside the kitchen. She smiled when she saw Mema sitting at the desk, her face bathed in the soft glow of the computer. "Well look who finally decided to join the twenty-first century," said Rayla. "Are you having fun?"

Mema raised and dropped her shoulder. "Fun? I don't know, but I'm learning a lot."

Rayla kissed her on the side of the head. The faint, familiar smell of jasmine tickled her nose. "Oh yeah, like what?"

She glanced at Rayla, then back at the screen. When she spoke, her words were solemn and grave. "Never google barnyard animals, child."

Rayla swallowed her smile. "Okay."

"Disgusting," Mema whispered.

"Where's Mydog?" Rayla asked, looking around.

"Down here slobberin' on my toes."

Rayla looked beneath the chair. She had to squint to see but there, under the desk, she could vaguely make out the dark panting shape of Mydog. "Is he okay?"

Mema nodded. "A little touch of dog flu is all. Poor baby. He's had the trots since Tuesday. I think he's finally coming around."

"But how do you know it's not something serious?"

Mema tapped a fingernail against the computer screen. "I googled the symptoms."

Rayla smiled and shook her head. "Can I borrow your computer for a few minutes?"

"What's wrong with yours?"

"Nothing. I just need to type a letter and–"

"And you don't want the asshole to know," Mema finished. "You do know that you can delete a Word file, right?"

Rayla rolled her eyes. "I know, Mema. I'd just rather do it this way."

"Well, hang on," grumbled the old woman, muttering to herself as she punched a few more keys. "I still don't see what all the waiting's about. Why can't you just leave him and be done with it?"

"I've been meaning to talk to you about that," Rayla said. "Do you think I can move back in for a while?"

Mema's eyes widened as she spun in her chair. "When?"

Rayla realized she was biting her bottom lip. "Next weekend."

The old woman clapped her hands and shot to her feet like a teenager.

"Careful," said Rayla.

Suddenly Mema's arms were around her. "I'm so proud of you, girl!" Then, she was off. "I'll need to dust your room first and change the sheets. There's probably something over here I can…" Her voice became muddled as she moved down the hall. The sounds of closet and cabinet doors opening and shutting followed her, mixing with her footsteps, drowning her words.

Mydog was snoring softly under the desk. Careful not to wake him, she eased into the warm chair and opened a Word document on the computer. After staring at the blank screen for a while, she placed her fingers on the keyboard and began to type.

> Dear Kevin,
> By the time you receive this letter my life will be undergoing some radical changes. I have decided to leave my husband …

54

The Long Shot

The outer gate buzzed. Lance pushed it open and let it slam behind him.

"You're late, Sarge," a voice called down from the tower.

He raised a middle finger without looking as he waited at the interior gate.

"Does that mean I'm number one?" the voice playfully asked.

He looked up at the tower. The face was familiar but he couldn't recall the name. Some punk kid from the evening shift pulling a double. "No," said Lance. "It means open this fucking gate before I come up there and open it with your face."

The interior gate buzzed.

Lance was livid. It had nothing to do with disrespectful little turds or being late to work or even his cheating whore of a wife. Lance was pissed because he was stone cold sober for the second night in a row.

He couldn't understand it. He'd done everything exactly the same. The gun blue, the non-scented ammonia, the charcoal, the clear fishing line. He'd sat on his hands for the full twenty-eight days, even though he wanted to dig it up early. But when he did dig it up, nothing. No dope. *Was it possible that he had forgotten a key ingredient? He'd been up close to a week when he dropped the last batch.* He slammed his fist into his palm. *Could Jarvis be sabotaging him? The area surrounding the river birch was undisturbed...*

And on raged the monologue, spinning in his head, examining and re-examining as he walked down the road to center gate and the compound beyond. When he reached tower two, he waved. The gates immediately popped open. He cut straight across the grass and headed for the dim lights of Alpha Dorm, snatching the radio from his belt as he approached the door.

"Security nine to Alpha Dorm," he said.

The response came in a burst of static. "Alpha, go ahead sir."

Lance tried to see through the scratched Plexiglas. "Pop your low side door."

"Ten-four," said the voice.

He spun his radio once before jamming it back down on his belt. Then he yanked the door open.

The foyer reeked of piss and tuna. Inmate telephones dangled from the wall on fraying cords. An overflowing trash can, splattered with mustard and dried clumps of food, sat in the corner. He shook his head. *Fucking animals.*

He knew the officer in the bubble from the firing range, a tight-assed, by-the-book type who was a little too ambitious to be trusted. He was hoping for the chinless wonder whom he'd found sleeping at the desk last month. Instead he got Robocop. He cursed his luck. *First the bad batch of dope and now this.*

"How's it going Hurst?" he asked through the talk-space. He immediately noticed the Florida Administrative Code lying open by the glowing lights of the control panel.

Officer Hurst stood ramrod straight with his hands locked behind his back. "Outstanding, Sergeant. What can I do for you?"

"I need to borrow one of your inmates," Lance said. "Twenty-three lower, Mulgrew."

Hurst frowned and glanced up at the clock. "At one in the morning?"

Lance swallowed his anger in gulps, forcing it down like acid reflux bile. Nothing pissed him off more than having his authority questioned by an underling. When he trusted himself to speak, he leaned against the glass and whispered into the round metal talk-space, "He's my snitch."

"He's your ... Oh," said Hurst, a conspiratorial expression settling over the craggy features of his face. "I see, well, next count is in half an hour. Is the dayroom private enough or would you prefer that I unlock the laundry room?"

"Dayroom's fine," said Lance, turning and removing his flashlight.

It was still relatively early by prison standards. He could feel eyes all over him as he walked down the aisle. He knew he was hated by pretty much every inmate in the dorm and every inmate in the compound. But they only hated because they feared and with that fear came respect and obedience. There was something intoxicating about silencing a roomful of murderers and carjackers with your mere presence. He slapped the flashlight against his palm as he strode between the bunks.

Twenty-three lower was halfway down the aisle. He spotted Methlab's dirty rumpled towel hanging from the end of the bunk like a pirate flag on a death ship. The raw onion smell of body odor intensified as he drew near. He breathed through his mouth.

There was no one living in twenty-three upper. A gray plastic mat lay rolled at one end and various laundry hung from the sides, swaying in the breeze of a nearby ceiling fan.

"Mulgrew!" he hissed, shining the flashlight on the bottom bunk.

Suddenly a head sprung from beneath the wool blanket and two close-set eyes with dark half-moon bags beneath them squinted into the beam before darting across the dorm. His hair was mussed and there was a bemused expression on his ugly freak-show face, as if there was some private joke going on that only he knew. "Evening, Sarge."

Lance was about to let loose a mini-tirade of whispered insults and threats when he noticed the extra bulk beneath the blanket. "Who is that?" he asked. "And don't tell me it's your fucking spider."

Methlab sighed and lowered the blanket enough to reveal the face of a skinny trembling kid with Coke-bottle glasses.

"Aw what the fuck," said Lance, almost gagging. He switched off the flashlight and took a step back. Out of the corner of his eye he could see Hurst standing with his hands on his hips in the officers' station window. "Get up. Get dressed and get in the dayroom," he growled before turning back down the aisle and heading for the front of the dorm.

He gave Hurst a thumbs-up as he walked by and took a seat at one of the metal card tables, his skin still crawling from the scene he'd just encountered. He needed a cigarette. He *needed* a blast, but a cigarette would at least take the edge off.

The tower light crept across the windows, inching over his fidgety hands, illuminating the gold band on his ring finger before sliding beyond the wall, leaving him to the darkness. The only light remaining was the dim overhead bulb that shone down on Hurst's salt and pepper flattop in the officers' station window.

He straightened at the approaching sound of shower slides slapping the linoleum. Methlab rounded the corner, his jerky avian-like head movements and slippery eyes filling the room with nervous energy. His sallow unwashed skin was still slick with sweat. The stench of him pulsated outward in rank waves.

"Sit down," said Lance, glancing over at the officers' station, wondering if Hurst was listening through the P.A.

Methlab slid into the metal seat across from him.

Lance spoke through his teeth. "What the hell was that back there?"

Methlab opened his mouth to answer.

"You know what? Don't even answer that," said Lance. "Just gimme my money and you can get back to whatever you were doing."

"I don't have it."

The water fountain clicked and rumbled to life, rattling and gyrating like a go-kart engine bolted to the wall. Lance was glad for the cover of noise. "What do you mean you don't have it? Go get it!"

Methlab's eyes were ricocheting around the room. "I don't have any money."

Lance leaned across the table. "You said one week, damn it. I gave you three."

"It's not my fault," Methlab pleaded. "Sip Burkett checked in ... protective custody. He owed me seven-fifty, a grand with tax."

"Then you're a jackass for letting him get that far in the hole," said Lance, imagining ripping his throat out.

"He's paid it before," said Methlab. "His sister brings it to Vizo and he brings it back in his ass. Usually along with a half-ounce of hydro. I never saw this coming."

Lance massaged his temples and exhaled heavily. "Do you have anything left?"

Methlab's eyes slid quickly across his. "What? Dope? Yeah, I've got a little, but–"

"Go get it!" said Lance, his pace quickening at this long-shot Hail Mary development.

"Okay, but ... it's the end of the month, sir. By my calendar you should be sitting on four zips right now."

Lance's heart was racing. The things that were so important a second ago all dissolved, eclipsed by a blinding need. In that single, sparkling instant the only thing that mattered was the promise of dope. "Yeah, I fucked up the last batch," he confided. "I haven't even got anything in the ground right now. I was gonna use that seven-fifty to get something to hold me over."

Methlab smiled. "I can show you how to make it faster if you don't want to wait."

The water fountain went silent. Lance cut his eyes at the officers' station. He could see the bald spot in the center of Hurst's flattop as he leaned over the rulebook. "How fast?"

"Depends," said Methlab, "for high speed chicken feed, a few days. For shake and bake, a few hours."

A few hours!?! thought Lance, mystified. He could feel the momentum swinging, the upper hand shifting. He forced a scowl. "You're lying."

Methlab shook his head. "It's true."

"Your word means shit to me. Didn't you give me your word you'd keep an eye on my wife? What happened there? I'll tell you what happened, you were blowing smoke up my ass."

"I haven't *seen* you," Methlab stammered, his indignity driving his facial tics into warp speed, "but his name is Kevin Freeman."

Lance yawned. "Old news."

Methlab crossed his arms and stared at the ceiling. "Yeah, well it wasn't old two weeks ago."

Lance chuckled and shook his head. Then he reached out and grabbed the spindly inmate by the uniform collar, snatching him forward. "Is that impatience I hear in your tone? Am I pissing you off? Stressing you out? Maybe it's just bad timing.

Should I come back when you don't have a faggot waiting under your blanket?"

"I didn't mean to disrespect you sir," Methlab stated in a blank, monotone voice.

"Fuck what you meant. Everything about you is disrespectful, all the way down to your breath and your armpits."

"Yes sir," Methlab agreed.

Lance released his collar with a shove and glanced again at the officers' station. Hurst quickly looked away.

"Here's how you're gonna make things right," said Lance. "First you're gonna bring me whatever dope you've got left."

"Okay."

"Then you're gonna stay up all night and write out a detailed recipe for this three-hour shake and bake. Put it in your shirt pocket when you go to breakfast. I'll pat you down at center gate and take it off you then."

Methlab nodded.

"If everything goes right, I'll forget what you owe me and maybe bring you a little something for the weekend. Sound fair?" He didn't wait for an answer. "Good, now go."

Methlab stood and motioned with his head toward the officers' station window. "What about your coworker over there? He's watching us."

Lance didn't bother looking. "Don't worry about him. Just fold it in a piece of notebook paper and hand it to me like a note. I'll take care of the rest."

"If you say so," said Methlab with a shrug, turning to leave.

"There's one more thing," said Lance.

Methlab paused.

"I'm gonna need your knife."

"Now?"

"No," said Lance. "Soon. I'll let you know."

55

A Fish Named Rayla

Fretwell bounded up the warehouse steps two at a time and walked quickly across the swept concrete floor. A couple of guilty-looking inmate workers froze as he passed but he was in too big of a hurry to investigate. A fish named Rayla was nibbling on his line.

He knew it was only a matter of time. He was almost disappointed. A challenge would be nice every once in a while but he rarely came across one. These stupid prisoners and the naïve women who fell for them repeated the same mistakes over and over. In his Alcoholics Anonymous meetings they called that insanity.

He remembered Inmate Freeman now; remembered him from that afternoon in the Alpha Dorm laundry room. He had the cuts on his knuckles from somebody's teeth and was being counseled by Officer Broxson, *privately*.

His gut told him they were up to something that day but their impromptu acting performance and her solicitation of his professional opinion regarding the teeth marks on Freeman's fist had thrown him off the scent.

Had that minor victory emboldened them? Maybe out-smarting him made them feel clever. Powerful. Untouchable. Were they not aware that pride comes before the fall? He'd show them the difference between winning the battle and winning the war.

He knocked on the mailroom door and pushed it open. Candace and Blanche Marie were sipping coffee at their desks. The day's mail was divided into stacks and separated for each dorm.

"Afternoon ladies," he said.

Blanche Marie smiled behind her coffee and gave a quick nod.

"You sure took your sweet time," Candace rasped.

"Sorry about that," he said, looking around the office.

Candace flipped a dismissive wrist. "On the corner of the table, far side, sittin' by itself."

Fretwell shut the door and walked across the room to where the solitary white envelope lay away from the stacks of sorted mail.

"You'll notice that the return address says Dothan, Alabama, but it was postmarked local," said Candace. "I doubt that's even a real address."

"Probably not," Fretwell agreed, as he raised the envelope to his nose.

"What are you sniffin' for?" Blanche Marie asked. "Drugs?"

Candace shook her head. "Probably the same thing he was sniffin' for the last time, right before he escorted that Sopchoppy gal off the compound. The redhead from Food Service. What was her name? Slaughter?"

Blanche Marie shut one eye and looked up at the ceiling. "Food Service, Food Service … I think it was Slater, wasn't it? Lots of Slaters in Sopchoppy," she frowned. "So he's sniffing for food?"

"Perfume," said Candace, rolling her eyes. "He's sniffin' for perfume."

Fretwell was only half listening to the meandering conversation of Tweedledum and Tweedledumber as he carefully removed the letter from the envelope. He unfolded the paper and studied its contents. No hearts, no flutterbys and no smileys. Just a single typed paragraph in an unobtrusive font, signed "Te Adoro." He read it twice.

"You know," Blanche Marie was saying, "I think she might've been Jacob Slater's daughter. The one that–"

"Can I use your copy machine?" Fretwell interrupted.

The two women looked at him as if they were surprised he was still there. Candace gestured in the direction of a closet door. "Have at it."

The machine was a dinosaur from the eighties. It took him a moment to familiarize himself with the control panel but after a couple of false starts he made a copy of both envelope and letter. He folded them neatly and slid them into the back pocket of his Dockers. Then he placed the original back in its envelope and walked over to Candace's desk.

"Can you make sure this is delivered today?" he asked. "It was postmarked the fifth and any delay might cause suspicion."

Candace tapped the letter on the armrest of her chair. "I'll put it on the top of the stack."

"I appreciate your time ladies," he said, heading for the door.

"So who's the girl?" asked Blanche Marie.

"You know that's classified information," he said.

"Well did you smell any perfume?" she pressed with a nervous giggle.

He turned in the doorway. "I definitely smell something, but it ain't perfume."

56

A Business Decision

Weasel watched the sky. Clouds swam over the horizon and raced across the top of the world like plumes of smoke from the mouth of God. He could almost feel the earth spinning. It was times like these that he was reminded that life was not the static illusion that it sometimes appeared to be, that he was really flying through space, thousands of miles per hour, on a rock with billions of others.

Rather than pass him the joint, Methlab nonchalantly tossed it in the grass between them so as not to arouse the suspicion of the gun tower. Weasel plucked it from the ground and took a deep hit, blowing the smoke between his knees before tossing it back.

It was late morning. The sun was a groggy, yellow smudge that awakened and dozed beyond a stratiform veil of sky. The wind, although still lukewarm from summer, was swirling and hostile and probably the reason the yard was so empty. A lone fat crow sat perched on the pull-up bar, its fidgety head tucked beneath a raven wing. Sporadic debris tumbled end over end across the basketball court and collected against the perimeter fence. The stench of the nearby wastewater plant came in warm thick gusts, hitchhiking the wind.

They sat side by side on the edge of the track, facing the drab beige cinderblock circle of dormitories. As the weed began to work its magic, Weasel's mind began to peddle down side streets and alleys both familiar and foreboding.

Prison is like a little town inside a fence, he thought. *There's a mayor (the Warden) a police force (the guards) a supermarket (the canteen) a library, a laundry mat, a hospital, a school, a church, a playground ... there's even a prison inside the prison for those who break the rules.*

He glanced at the confinement wing where Kevin was being held, just across the dirt lined field of sweet potatoes and turnips.

Kevin ... the best friend he'd ever had. How ashamed would he be of this sickness? How disgusted? The drugs were bad enough but this other stuff. He was seriously beginning to hate himself. No. Hate is too weak of a word. To loathe, to despise, to abhor himself. To puke at the sight of his own reflection. His only excuse – if there was an excuse for being a spineless coward – was that when Methlab leaned on him for the occasional favor, he was back in the woods with his father. Helpless, powerless, trapped.

The joint landed beside him again, halfway gone and sticky with resin. He grabbed it and took another pull. The green glow of THC crept through his bloodstream like warm molasses, softening nerve endings and loosening tensed muscles while simultaneously revving the paranoia bullhorn in his brain.

People in the dorm were beginning to refer to him as Methlab's punk, Methlab's boy, Methlab's personal property. He didn't mind it so much when he was flying on crystal, but in the cold light of day, with no chemical partition to dull the voices, the plastic bag of reality was suffocating.

The hard truth was that no matter how many push-ups he did, how many fighting techniques he learned, no matter how much convict training he engaged in or how far he ran, he would never be a man. That option was taken off the table a decade earlier in the Ocala National Forest and lost forever when he abandoned Andy to the same fate. Even killing the monster that started it all couldn't undo his destiny. In his mind it only reinforced his impotence and cowardice while giving him a new nightmare.

"Did you have fun last night?" Methlab asked, taking a last toke from the J before popping the roach in his mouth.

Weasel shrugged.

"You could show a little gratitude," he said, the weed doing nothing to subdue his ocular breakdancing. "That was a hundred bucks worth of ice you banged in that dainty little arm of yours."

"Thanks," Weasel mumbled, his soul as bleak as the slate gray sky.

He remembered the night before. Remembered it vividly. The night before was still going. It just happened to be daylight now. When he pushed his glasses up the bridge of his nose, he noticed his index finger was stained from all the weed he'd been smoking.

"I hate it when you poke your bottom lip out like that," said Methlab. "Makes you look like a little bitch. Oh wait, you *are* a little bitch," he laughed and reached in his pocket for Junior. "He's our little bitch, isn't he, Junior?"

Things were getting to the point where every time the needle punctured his vein, he hoped the dose was lethal, prayed it busted his heart.

There was movement on the compound side of the fence. Beyond the tilled rows of flapping turnip leaves, an officer held the confinement door open and a line of inmates filed out of the building one by one with their property bags slung over their shoulders.

Weasel sat up straighter and again adjusted his glasses as the last man squeezed past the guard. "Hey!" he pointed. "That's Vero! The guy that attacked Kevin!"

"Attack is a strong word," said Methlab, playing with his spider.

"He beat him with a lock."

"Only after your Kevin knocked his tooth out, possibly in defense of his lover's honor," he smiled. "But that's just speculation."

Weasel changed the subject. "If Vero's getting out of lockdown, shouldn't Kevin be getting out too?"

Methlab sighed and shook his head. "I doubt it."

"Why not?" Weasel blurted, unexpected relief suddenly washing over him. Maybe it was the weed and possibly the sleep deprivation, but he realized he didn't want to face Kevin. Not yet.

"Well," said Methlab, a slender blade of grass sloping from his mouth, "probably because I told the inspector about his little laundry room love affair with Officer Broxson."

Weasel's newfound relief was shot from the sky, disintegrating into a thousand pieces of guilt. "Why would you do that?"

Methlab shrugged. "It was a business decision."

57

Black Jesus

The fluorescent light switched on without preamble, transforming Kevin's cell from pitch black sarcophagus to blinding white tanning bed in a flash. His eyes snapped open. *Four a.m. Breakfast.*

He sat up and wiped the sleep from his eyes, resisting the impulse to nod off again. Bobby's sleepy second-grader voice rang out in his mind. *Just gimme five more minutes, Kev.* He chased it back down the mineshaft of memory.

Five more minutes would result in an empty stomach till lunch. If he wasn't dressed and at his cell door when the chow cart rolled by, it would keep right on rolling to the next cell. No discussion, no sympathy, no quarter.

He brushed his teeth in his boxers, squinting into the rusty steel mirror over the sink. His most recent cuts and bruises were beginning to heal but his face looked thin and even his good eye, the one that wasn't blackened from lock and fist, still sported a purplish crescent beneath it. His neck felt naked where Bobby's chain used to be. He splashed water in his face then grabbed his uniform from the foot of the bunk.

Losing the chain trumped any physical pain he'd endured over the previous month. He was still having nightmares about it being ripped from his neck during the fight, only to wake up panic-stricken and realize that the nightmare was now reality.

He could hear the approaching rumble of the chow cart down the wing, of squeaking wheels and tray flaps being unlocked. He tucked in his shirt on the way to the door.

Breakfast rolled into view like an oasis on wheels. His stomach was a clenched empty fist. He could smell maple syrup through the steel and see sloshed oatmeal oozing from between the trays, dripping down the sides. He was so entrenched in lusting over the promise of food that he didn't see the scowling sergeant pushing the cart. Until his contorted face was filling the window like Nicholson through the ax hole in *The Shining*.

Here's Johnny!

The flap on his door fell forward. "Top of the mornin' asswipe," said her husband. "How's your face?"

Kevin didn't bother to respond.

He was obviously wasted. A stream of sweat trickled out from under a bristly sideburn, his pupils were dilated and vibrating horizontally, and his jaw swung side to side like a carnival funhouse entrance.

"No cellmate yet, I see," he remarked, looking past Kevin at the empty top bunk. "I'll have to look around, see if I can't find a big snoring, farting motherfucker to move in with you. There's gotta be a few horny rapists back here somewhere. You like it in the ass, boy?"

Kevin just breathed, refusing to bite.

"Rayla *loves* it," he said with an exaggerated wink. He paused and glanced at his watch. "Matter of fact, I get off work in a few hours and it's her day off so…" He licked his lips suggestively. "But you don't wanna hear about that."

Kevin watched as he reached over the cart and pulled a tray from the nearest stack. His appetite was gone, sunk by the procession of catastrophic potentialities that backstroked across the pool of his mind, one after the other. *Spit, piss, shit, boogers, pubes, drugs, poison…* There was no way he was eating anything hand-delivered by Lance Broxson. He'd starve first.

Turns out that was never an option in the first place.

"Bon appetite," said the sergeant.

Then he bounced it off the flap.

Suddenly oatmeal and sweet potato gruel were everywhere, splattered on the floor, dripping from the juice keg, streaked across his brown uniform. The tray wobble-spun to a halt and collapsed atop a flat pale pancake in the middle of the catwalk.

The subsequent silence was even louder than the clamor. It carried with it a finality. The reverberating crack of a judge's gavel, of a boulder covering a tomb, of a fate being sealed.

Kevin dug his middle fingernail into the calloused flesh of his thumb. He could see the heads lining the windows across the tier, watching the show.

Sergeant Broxson looked down at his uniform and attempted to brush off some of the food. "So you like throwing trays at officers?" he said. "Not very smart. You just earned two disciplinary reports. One for assault, one for disorderly conduct. That's ninety days right there."

Kevin went and sat on his bunk. He knew checkmate when he saw it.

The sergeant slapped his wedding ring against the metal flap. "Get your ass over here and cuff up."

Kevin exhaled heavily then removed his shirt. "You're not putting handcuffs on me again. Not you."

"Disobeying a verbal order," he said, "that's another thirty."

"Fuck you."

"Disrespect. Thirty more."

A door buzzed down the wing. Sergeant Broxson waved his hand. "Hey Jarvis, you got your pepper spray on you? I got a tough guy in here that's refusing to cuff up."

Kevin rose to his feet and snatched the wool blanket from his bunk. Then he hurried to the toilet and flushed it twice before stuffing the blanket in the bowl.

"That ain't gonna help," her husband smirked.

He let the toilet water saturate the blanket for as long as he could, then quickly pulled it out and dunked his shirt.

A red-bearded giant appeared in his window. "Did you notify the shift commander?"

"We'll notify him afterwards," said her husband.

"That's against policy, Lance."

"Give me your canister, dammit!"

Kevin hurried to tie the shirt around his face like a ninja mask then wrapped himself in the wet blanket.

"He threw a tray at me Jarvis! Look at this mess!" He paused and glanced through the window. "Hell, look at him!"

"I'm looking at you," Kevin heard the big officer say, "and it ain't pretty. Have you looked in a mirror lately?"

"I ain't got time for this," Broxson snarled, slapping his own chest like a zoo primate. "You see these stripes? I'm the ranking officer here. Me!" He then reached down and yanked the pepper spray from the giant's leg harness. "Now you go ahead and radio the OIC if that's what you feel like you need to do." He glanced at Kevin through the oatmeal-speckled window. "I'll deal with this disorderly inmate."

Kevin backed against the rear wall. The waterlogged blanket and shirt were cool against his skin. Through a small crease in his makeshift mask he watched as the sinister eye of the nozzle appeared above the flap, a hissing cobra gathering to strike. His knees began to tremble and knock. The ever-running monologue in his head accelerated in speed and octave. He would have crawled under the bunk but he didn't want to give this bastard the pleasure of seeing him so desperate to evade the coming terror.

... and you don't think it may have tipped him off that you were a little antsy about this coming terror when you doused yourself with toilet water? His inner voice piped up.

Maybe. Probably. But he had good reason to fear. The industrial-sized container in the hand of his enemy was not the standard kitten piss that most COs carried on their belts, or some other garden variety mace. This was Black Jesus, the mother of all pepper sprays.

Why it was called Black Jesus was a mystery to Kevin. Maybe because it made you scream in agony for God or because it burned the flesh like apocalyptic dragon fire. *Black Jesus.* It seemed wrong to him to name something so painful, so horrible, after the most peaceful man in history. Like naming a nuclear warhead Gandhi, or a street sweeper Buddha.

The gas erupted from the nozzle in a long gargling blast. Then her husband slammed the flap, leaving him to marinate in the chemically altered oxygen that was creeping across the cell. He could still hear muffled voices bickering outside the door as he squeezed his eyes shut and tried to breathe in short sips.

He lost track of time as he waited for the pain. Five minutes can feel like thirty when your thoughts are racing and you're swaddled in a sopping wet blanket with a shirt tied around your face.

Was it his imagination or was that a burning sensation between his toes? An unseen flame licked his ankles then spread over his feet like a brush fire. *Definitely not imagined.* Suddenly he was standing on glowing red embers. He tried to alleviate the pain by shifting his weight between each foot but all that seemed to accomplish was to fan the blistering heat up his damp pants legs.

The inside of his mouth tasted like strong licorice. He coughed once then got greedy on his next sip of air and sucked a stream of sparkling gas through the shirt. A swarm of angry wasps zzz'd in his lungs. His eyes snapped open in panic and his eyeballs were instantly covered in fire ants. He staggered sideways and collapsed into the corner of the cell.

The flap on his door bounced open again. Metal hinges squeaked. The aerosol roar of the canister sounded more like the flame on a rocket thruster as it gushed more misery into the room in three consecutive bursts.

Kevin pulled the blanket tight around him and huddled in the corner. His skin was on fire. He twisted and contorted his body trying anything to escape the searing pain. But as the moments passed and his desperation mounted, merely escaping pain evolved into fighting for his life.

He coughed. He gagged. He gasped for air but it seemed as if his lungs would not accept the toxic oxygen in the cell. He shrugged off the blanket and leaped to his feet charging the door like a bull. He crashed into Plexiglas then slid down steel and banged his shirt-covered head against the concrete. An inch of space ran along the bottom of the door. He buried his face in the gap, frantic for relief. He was able to steal a mouthful of air before his throat filled with glowing metal sandspurs, triggering another round of terrifying hacking that overtook his body and sent him thrashing on the floor.

The shirt unraveled from his face in the chaos. It felt as if every cell in his body simultaneously burst into flames. As if every vein, artery and capillary were flowing with sizzling hot grease, scorching his vital organs.

In agony, in desperation, he launched his body at the door again, feet first. Then he rolled to his hands and knees and began mule-kicking it.

You're dying! His mind screamed. *It's over. Give in. Lie down. Quit fighting it.*

He ventured a final weak kick before crumbling to the floor and curling into the fetal position. His face attached to the cold concrete in a sticky paste of vomit, sweat and gas. He submitted to the burning, stopped trying to breathe, and entered into a hypothermia-like state where the apex of pain crossed over into numbness.

He was in the laundry room again. Her eyes were warm and soft. Her hand moved slowly up from her side and reached out to caress his face. Her palm was smooth. The scent on her wrist was feminine sweet. He leaned into her touch, soaking it in. He could feel her energy vibrating through him, pure and revitalizing. He imagined it as gold dust swirling in his mouth, surging down his windpipe, filling his lungs.

Then a single word appeared in his mind like a billboard on the turnpike. *PRANA.* He blinked. *Prana?*

Years ago, around the beginning of his prison odyssey, angry and bitter from losing Bobby and armed with a laundry list of resentments toward the God of his childhood, Kevin turned to eastern religion in search of a new truth. It was in those books that he first heard of prana, an invisible form of energy that moves in air, food, water and sunlight and is a link between the astral and physical bodies. He pictured it as shimmering gold dust. Although he could never fully subscribe to the polytheistic dogma of the east, the idea of prana remained with him. It just *felt* true. He wondered if the prana in his lungs was keeping him alive at that very moment.

A fresh wave of burning coughs racked his shoulders almost lifting him from the floor. It was as if his body was responding to all this talk of prana by screaming *BULLSHIT!*

His door shook and the flap reopened. He squinted up toward the Plexiglas through scalding watery eyes. The faces staring down at him seemed far away, like he was looking through the wrong end of a telescope.

"This is against protocol, Lance," said a gravelly, authoritative voice. "You should have waited."

"I know, Captain. I apologize," he heard her husband say. "When he threw the tray, I was thinking about procedure but when he spat in my face, I just … I lost it."

Fucking liar!

"Can anyone corroborate your version of the events?"

"My version?" her husband said in a defensive tone. "I'm sure Officer Jarvis …"

Kevin's flesh began to sizzle again. He squeezed his eyes shut. His nostrils burned. His armpits burned. Every crack, every orifice, every microscopic pore was set ablaze by invisible chemical fire. He gasped.

"Hey! Inmate! Get up here and cuff up!" ordered the gravelly voice.

Resistance never crossed his mind. He was so overjoyed to be leaving his torture chamber that he almost fell in the toilet while stumbling blindly to his feet. He turned and put his wrists to the flap, still gagging as the manacles tightened. Then his door rolled and he was pulled from the cell.

An unfamiliar officer with a handheld camera walked next to him while the captain nudged him toward the decontamination shower.

"Hey Sarge, grab his ID card off the bunk will ya?" said the cameraman.

The shower was a little bigger than a phone booth, enclosed by bars and mesh. Water dribbled from the nozzle and made tinkling wind chime music as it hit the drain. He was guided inside then the barred door clanged shut behind him and the handcuffs were unlocked and removed.

He felt his way along the slimy wall as he staggered toward the shower head and the cool trickling water. He groped for the metal button to turn it on, desperate for relief from the burning, not even bothering to remove his pants.

It came in a deluge, crashing down on his smoldering flesh, sending him to his knees. The pain was persistent in spite of the downpour, shifting from one area of his body to another, disappearing and resurfacing like a pepper spray version of whack-a-mole. But his vision was returning and the panic was fading. He swished a gulp of water around in his mouth and spat it at the wall. His eyes narrowed as he watched the stream blaze a trail between the mildew and peeling paint. For a moment he thought he saw golden flecks.

"Get those pants off," a voice behind him commanded.

He turned. It was the cameraman. Still filming. He pulled off the pants without leaving the water.

"Come on dude," he said, "boxers too. Don't be shy. Those gotta go in the bio-hazard bag. Just stick 'em over here in the door. We'll get you a new pair."

Kevin stepped out of his boxers and walked over to the bars, stuffing the wet clothes between them. Shyness was not an issue. He'd been lifting his nutsack and bending over and coughing for ten years. It was part of the prison experience, although the camera was a little awkward.

When he glanced over at the open door of his cell he saw her husband emerging from inside, hacking and gagging from the fumes. Hate twisted in his guts like a rope on a limb.

"Here's his ID," he called, holding up the card. "He's going to the strip cell, right? 101 single? Somebody else needs to pack his property. I've got a shitload of paperwork to do."

He winked at Kevin as he walked behind the camera.

"How much property's he got?" asked the red-bearded giant from the front of the wing where he was conferring with the captain.

"I don't know," said her husband, "not much. A bible, a toothbrush, a few letters. The sheets and blankets need to go too."

"I'll take care of it," said the giant, pulling a bandana from his pocket.

Kevin was on fire again. He hurried back to the water and banged his palm against the button. As the burning diminished to an icy-hot throb, he thought about what had transpired over the last couple of hours. He'd been set up, lied on, sprayed with gas and his body had barely recovered from the last beating he'd suffered at the hands of Lance Broxson. But it was not himself he was worried about.

Is he doing the same thing to her? Something worse? Is he beating her? Threatening her? Using me as a pawn in some sick little game?

He wished there was some way to talk to her, to reassure her, to let her know that nothing had changed, that he thought about her nonstop, that he was coming for her, that all the pepper spray in the world couldn't keep him away.

He wondered how much gain time he just lost. He guesstimated the damage to be around five months, depending on how many lies her husband told. His release date was flying backwards. He'd be lucky to make it out by spring.

Suddenly the light coming through the bars dimmed, eclipsed by the hulking frame of the giant guard. He was holding something but Kevin couldn't adjust his eyes in the shadows to make out the shape.

Then light hit the blade and he knew.

The giant's breath was ragged when he spoke. "What the hell is this?"

A nail in my coffin, thought Kevin.

"Where'd you find it?" the cameraman asked, nudging the big man clear of his camera angle.

"Under his bunk."

"Let me see," called the captain from the front of the dorm.

The giant lifted the knife.

"Ooh," said her husband, "looks like sixty more days and loss of all gain time to me."

58

Buried Alive

Rayla sat on a concrete bench beneath the pavilion eating apple slices with Nutella. The compound was secured for count and with the exception of the pigeons that were scouring the sidewalks for food, she had the yard to herself.

Despite the serene setting, her thoughts and emotions were a tangled mess. There was little doubt that Lance was in a freefall. His weight was plummeting, he never slept, and the trailer had taken on the permanent smell of chemicals. Charred glass pipe fragments dotted the living room carpet and strange products – drain crystals, Sudafed boxes, camp fuel – were strewn about the kitchen counter.

He was obviously manufacturing and using dangerous drugs, yet another reason why she should get the hell out of there, *and she planned to.* All she had to do was pack a few suitcases and drive across the river to Mema's house. A move that would take less than an hour. The physical act of leaving was simple, it was what had to follow that made her waver.

Although the idea of a restraining order seemed to her a flimsy line of defense, there was really no other course of action besides Mema's shotgun and the stand-your-ground law.

A chill whispered at her neck as a vivid image of her enraged husband blew through her bones. She imagined him pounding on doors, rattling windows, demanding entrance and *to hell with restraining orders!* flashing in the lightning of his eyes. How ironic that the man she married was a thousand times more terrifying than the ax murderers and rapists she worked around every day.

But it wasn't fear alone that made her dawdle. A restraining order would ruin Lance. And just what would she tell the sheriff when she filed it? That he beat her? She'd seen battered women on Oprah and listened to their horrifying stories. A shove in the face and a kick in the back hardly qualified. So what then? That he threatened her? That he was unstable and she feared what he *might* do? Or was it that she was leaving him for another man, *a prisoner*, and that she knew it would drive him into a murderous rage?

Involving the sheriff could result in Lance being arrested for other things. It wouldn't take much poking around to learn that he was using drugs, making drugs and possibly selling them as well. *Who else was involved? Jarvis? Jessica? The entire graveyard shift?* The repercussions were potentially exponential. She could cause a lot of people a lot of misery and for what? Freedom? Lust? Love? Did she really want to push this domino?

She ate a slice of apple and stared across the compound at the ugly beige confinement unit where Kevin was being held. Every Thursday she watched for his name on the move sheet but it never appeared. A high school friend who worked in the Classification Department told her that he had received thirty days for fighting, but she didn't want to arouse suspicion by asking too many questions. Now a full month had passed and there was still no sign of him.

The same shrill voice in her head that rambled frantically about the ripple effect of the restraining order paused and sniffed the air, then narrowed its inner eye at her hidden fears regarding Kevin and began to hammer away.

You stupid silly gullible little girl. What on earth were you thinking? You could so easily have been caught, fired, arrested! Who would hire you after such a scandal? Who would speak to you? And if you think Kevin is going to magically transform the sorry state of your life, you're delusional. Where's he going to live? Where's he going to work? Do you really think he's going to jump straight into a relationship after being locked up for ten years? You're being selfish to expect such a thing. Do you even love him? Are you sure? What is love? Imagine his face right now. You can't. Seems like if you truly loved someone you'd at least know what they look like ...

She leaned forward on her elbows and massaged her scalp with her fingernails, almost hyperventilating from the pressure. It felt as if the walls in the hole she dug herself were collapsing inward, raining dirt on her head, burying her alive.

"Better watch out for that pigeon," said a voice.

Rayla jumped. The bird flapped up into the rafters.

"He was going for your Nutella," said Officer Redmon, her old trainee, smiling and leaning against the column. A stack of papers was pinned against his torso by a muscular arm. Tribal tattoos peeked from beneath his tight shirt sleeves. "Some of these pigeons are bigger thieves than the inmates."

Rayla forced a smile she didn't feel.

Suddenly a white splat fell from the rafters and exploded on her table.

"I think he's expressing his displeasure," said Redmon, patting his hand against the mace canister on his side. "You want me to spray him?"

Rayla laughed. "It's okay."

He glanced over his shoulder. "Your husband isn't pulling a double today, is he?"

She shook her head. "I've been wanting to apologize to you for his behavior in the parking lot that day."

"It's cool," he said. "If you were mine I'd be overprotective too."

Rayla felt her face flush. She looked away.

"Well," he said, pulling the stack of papers from beneath his arm and straightening it against his stomach. "I probably need to get back to work."

"What's your post?" she asked, more out of politeness than genuine interest.

"Inside security. Posting rule changes in the dormitories. Exactly the kind of excitement I was hoping for when I decided to get into Corrections."

"Where are you heading now?"

"The confinement unit."

Her pulse quickened. "Can I go with you?"

He kicked at a sprig of grass that grew from a crack in the concrete. "I don't know, the last time we walked through H-Dorm together you almost got me fired."

"I did not!" she said, removing the scrunchy from her wrist and pulling her hair back. "I covered for you."

"Yeah," he said, "but that was after you picked a fight with a serial rapist."

"Well the cell doors are locked in confinement," she said, "and I promise not to pick any fights."

"Okay," he said, smiling, "but no wandering off. Matter of fact, I want your finger in my belt loop the whole time."

She stood and brushed off her pants. "Yes sir."

The walk to the confinement unit took less than five minutes. He handed her half the stack of memos to make her visit look official. Over their radios a crackly voice announced that count had cleared as they rounded the H-Dorm fence. Behind them, she could hear the dormitory doors banging open and inmates noisily lining up for chow.

Redmon rambled the whole way over about work squad supervisor openings at the forestry camp and other institutional shop talk. She nodded and chuckled at the appropriate places but it was hard to hear anything over her pounding heart. She hoped she could see him, even if just a passing glimpse, a smile, a wave, something, anything.

"And why did you want to come down here anyway?" Redmon asked as they waited to be buzzed through the door.

"Down here?" Rayla repeated only catching the end of his question.

He rolled his eyes. "Yeah. Down here. Confinement. Why?"

"Oh, I don't know. Something different, I guess. It's been awhile."

The door finally buzzed. He held it open for her. "Well, hold your nose."

The unit was eerily quiet. She was expecting singing, yelling, animal calls; instead, she was met with mausoleum silence. Even the drone of the exhaust fans high above the second tier only seemed to thicken the hush.

An ancient guard with a hearing aid dozed at the desk.

"Ahem," coughed Redmon, winking at Rayla.

Oblivious, the old man scratched his testicles and settled deeper into the chair.

"Hey, Mr. Kyle," Redmon called, tapping a massive knuckle on the desk. "Officer Jeudevine!"

The old man blinked, then bolted upright in the squeaky chair. "Did count clear already?"

"About five minutes ago," said Redmon.

"Shit," he said, reaching for the log book with gnarled arthritic fingers.

"Hey," said Redmon, "I've got a lady here with me. Watch your language."

The old man glanced at Rayla. "Hell, her nametag says Broxson on it. I 'magine she's heard worse at home."

Rayla smiled. "I have."

Redmon caught her eye and spun his finger in circles around his ear as the elderly guard made a trembling entry in the coffee-stained book. When he finished, he pushed it aside and looked at his watch. "The chow cart should be rolling up the sidewalk any minute," he said. "Do me a favor and go fetch it. Damn thing's got a bad wheel on it. I almost flipped it yesterday."

Redmon turned to Rayla and raised his eyebrows. The creases in his forehead deepened. "Will you be all right?"

She shooed him away with her stack of memos, popping him on the arm. "*I* trained *you*, remember?"

"Those memos go on that bulletin board over there," he said as he waved up at the officer in the control room to be buzzed back out. "This will only take a sec."

Rayla glanced over her shoulder at the long row of steel doors that extended down one side of the wing then resumed on the other. There were two levels, forty-eight cells, and Kevin was in one of them. She chewed on her lip.

"Here's the stapler," said the old man, rising to his feet. "You're gonna have to excuse me though. Gotta piss worse than a nine dick dragon."

Rayla grabbed the stapler and walked over to the bulletin board as the bathroom door slammed. She wondered if Kevin was watching her. There were shapes and silhouettes appearing in every cell window but it was difficult to see faces from a distance. Muted whistles and catcalls rang out from behind the doors.

"*Hey Becky, you lost?*"

"Come here. Lemme show you somethin'."

"Work Call!"

She listened for his voice between the insults and lewd remarks but it never came. She wondered if he'd received her letter. Maybe he was having second thoughts too.

Suddenly she wanted out of there. She hurried to separate the memos from the proposed rule notifications, then began attaching them to the bulletin board as fast as she could.

She was almost through when the stapler slipped from her sweaty palm and bounced off the floor in an explosion of tiny silver u's. She dropped on one knee and began to gather them as her anxiety boiled over.

"That's what I'm talkin' 'bout!"

"Hell yeah, bend over bitch!"

"I can't see, turn this way!"

She looked down the wing. Every door was shaking, every window was full, except one. The first cell on the bottom: 101. There were three strips of masking tape on the door with writing on them. She continued to rake the loose staples with her palm as she squinted to read the words.

The first piece of tape said *Loaf.* The management loaf was served three times a day in place of the regular tray. She'd seen it being prepared in the kitchen during her training years ago. A golden-crusted brick that contained a disgusting mix of all three of the previous day's meals: spinach, grits, carrots, oatmeal, onions, beans, cornbread. The management loaf was not supposed to be a punishment, merely a security measure against confinement inmates who threw trays. But from what she remembered it sure smelled like a punishment.

The second piece of tape said *Strip.* Another management tool. An inmate on strip status was denied clothes, sheets, blankets, or a mattress. They were only allowed a single pair of underwear and they slept on the steel. Toilet paper was distributed by the confinement officer on a square-by-square basis to prevent the inmate from making a rope, or covering himself in the frigid cell.

The third piece of tape was more difficult to read. The letters were sloppy and written in magic marker. The handwriting resembled Lance's. She stood and took a few tentative steps toward the door, ignoring the noise that surrounded her. Then the circles and lines separated and swam into focus, forming a name: *FREEMAN*.

The front door buzzed and banged open as Redmon forced the chow cart through the narrow entrance. He abandoned it by the stairwell and stomped past Rayla into the center of the rowdy wing. The cell doors continued to rumble as the inmates behind them shrieked and howled. He removed the whistle from his pocket and released an ear-splitting banshee wail that cut through the roar like a blowtorch.

"Everybody off the doors now!" he bellowed. "Twelve upper, I see you. Don't fuck with me. I will fill your cell with gas. Next head I see is gettin' sprayed, gentlemen. That's a promise!"

Officer Jeudevine emerged from the bathroom and came to stand next to him as he pointed at the top tier and made more threats. While they were busy restoring order Rayla sidled over to Kevin's door and glanced in the window.

He was curled up on his side facing the wall. She could see his vertebrae cutting a line down the middle of his emaciated back like train tracks buried in snow. He was shivering on the steel. She tapped a finger against the Plexiglas. He rolled over and stared blankly at her from two hollow, blackened eyes. Then recognition dawned and for a moment his gaunt face stretched into a dazzling smile. A scab slashed diagonally across the bridge of his nose. His necklace was gone.

Tears threatened to spill over the barricades of her lashes. He shook his head, admonishing her not to cry. Then he raised his right hand and began to sign. He formed each letter slowly, leaving no room for misunderstanding. Her heart sank as she read his words.

"H-e k-n-o-w-s."

59

Rewriting the Code

The first decade of the millennium brought sweeping change to the Florida prison system. Secretaries were appointed and dismissed and indicted. Privatization became the trendy buzz word. Annexes were erected. Yellow lines were put down. Fences were put up. Budgetary shortfalls were overcome by cutting food portions and limiting access to toilet paper and soap. Programs, both vocational and recreational, were slashed. The canteen was outsourced, prices were jacked, and the inmate welfare fund was abolished. Rumors of a coming tobacco prohibition were in the air.

But perhaps the biggest change came in 2008, when all the weights were removed. The reason was that the suits in Tallahassee were concerned that prison weight piles were "manufacturing super-criminals." Once the decree came down, every warden in the state scrambled to comply and almost overnight, every bench and every squat rack were dismantled and loaded on a truck bed full of barbells and dumbbells, then driven off the compound, never to return.

The only exercise equipment they left behind were the pull-up and dip bars that rose from the dirt like hangman's gallows.

Weasel leapt in the air and grabbed the high bar in a reverse grip, exactly the way Kevin had once taught him. The iron felt good in his hands. Familiar. He struggled to pull his chin up over the bar. His lats and biceps burned from the effort. Because his arms were so gangly, the distance for him was almost twice as long as it was for others. His ascent was slow.

When he finally reached the top, he silently counted *one*, then dropped like a rock in an elevator shaft until his elbows snap-buckled into a locked position and he was dangling in the breeze.

"Ouch," said Methlab from his spot in a nearby patch of grass, watching, *always watching*, in his non-watching way. "Do you have to drop so hard? That cannot be good for you. It's hurting my joints just watching."

Weasel ignored him as he kick-pulled his chin back up towards the bar. His face shook from the effort.

Appearances aside, he was not really working out. Although if he were, it would look about the same. He was doing surveillance, and the pull-up bar provided a perfect view of his target.

Across the yard, against the dirty wall of what used to be the weight pile, Vero Zay had Tampa sitting on his shoulders and was doing bucket squats with his weight. Weasel could see the sweat pouring down his scarred bald head while the sun shimmered off the chain hanging from his thick muscled neck. Kevin's chain.

He'd been going hard since the yard opened – squats, lunges, burpies, hammies. His legs were beginning to wobble between sets.

That's right, thought Weasel, his nose touching the iron as he watched. *Push it. Get 'em good and fatigued for me.* Then he dropped his weight again. His elbows jolted from the shock as he hung from the bar.

"Yeah that's real healthy," said Methlab, playing with Junior, "keep going. One of these days your arms are gonna rip right off."

Across the yard, Vero was preparing for another set.

"And you're gonna be lying down here in the dirt with no arms while your hands are still gripping the pull-up bar."

Other inmates around them chuckled at his comments.

"And you know what I'm gonna do, don't you?" Methlab asked, playing to the audience. "I'm gonna jump up there and snatch one of your hands down, then I'm going straight to the back stall!" He simulated masturbation with his hand.

Weasel ignored the laughter and pulled himself up again. He deserved the ridicule. The depths he had sunk to since Kevin went to confinement were the most humiliating of his twenty-one years. Voluntary enslavement, prison within prison, the only thing keeping him from hanging himself was the fact that he didn't want to die a coward. Suicide would be the exclamation point capping a life spent shrinking, bowing, running.

He dropped to the ground and spat in his hands, then reached down and grabbed a fistful of dirt and rubbed it between them. He wasn't sure why he did it, just seemed like the convict thing to do.

"Who's your enemy?" Kevin whispered.

"Not my opponent."

"Who then?"

"Fear, panic, rage, doubt …."

"Remember this – the opposite of fear isn't courage. The opposite of fear is faith."

He glanced across the yard at Vero and figured that his legs were about as stable as two socks full of Jell-O at that point. He removed his glasses and cleaned them on his t-shirt before setting off in his direction.

"Where are you going?" Methlab called from behind him. "I was just joking, man. Don't be like that."

Weasel knew it was time to turn the page. In the last letter from his attorney he was informed that an evidentiary hearing had been set for December, and that he was confident the life sentence would be tossed due to mitigating circumstances. He could be transported back to Ocala any day now. His window of time to act honorably, to redeem himself, to avenge his best friend was sliding shut.

As he made his way across the yard he recalled a late night conversation with Kevin regarding predisposition. It was Kevin's theory that each person's life path was like a computer program set by DNA, environment, and a list of other variables. He thought that most people went through life as prisoners to their scripts, swept along by the familiar impulses and patterns embedded in their own software, never knowing that they had the power to change the narrative, take control of the plot, and override the program.

The past was gone, spilt milk under the bridge. There was nothing he could do about his father or his mother or Andy or anything else that had happened up to the present moment. Those days belonged to unconscious living and walking blindly to the drum of biological computer programs.

He was about to rewrite the code.

Vero's muscles rippled in the sun. His shirtless upper body was covered in scars and ink. The words *UNTAMED GORILLA* dipped across his chest from shoulder to shoulder like a banner. Kevin's Saint Christopher medallion was stuck to the letter *O*, plastered there by sweat. He hobbled back and forth on rubber band legs as Tampa Black smoked in the shade of the rec office.

"Hey 'Ro," said Tampa, pointing at Weasel as he approached, "check it out."

Vero turned and hung his thumbs on the waistband of his pants, flexing his chest. "Whatchu' doin' on the yard by yourself, bitch? You lookin' for a new wardaddy? What's wrong?" he asked, nostrils flaring. "Methlab's dick too little for you?"

Tampa cackled and blew a stream of rip smoke at an overhead wasp nest. Weasel kept coming.

"Why you walkin' like that? Hey Tampa, don't he look like the cop in the Termin–"

Weasel ran the last six steps, leaped in the air, cocked his fist back and Cantonment Crowhopped Vero Zay with impeccable technique. If his eyes weren't shut, he would have seen him spiraling to the ground like a drunk figure skater. Kevin would have been proud.

When he did open his eyes, he caught a glimpse of Tampa disappearing around the corner of the building. Casually, he leaned over Vero and began to maneuver Kevin's chain over his thick neck. There was dirt caked to the side of his sweaty face from the knockout. His eyes fluttered open. He started to struggle. With surreal calm, Weasel drove his fist into Vero's throat, then worked the necklace over his ears, pulling it free.

From the corner of his eye he could see people gathering, pointing. He stood and slid the chain over his head then swung back his foot to kick Vero in the face.

"Hey!" a voice shouted.

He paused and turned.

Lumbering toward him, breathing heavily and sweating profusely, was the rec officer. *Fleming.* "Hold it right there."

Weasel's legs were moving before he even realized what he was doing. He kicked up a cloud of dust as he sprinted across the yard leaving the obese officer fumbling for his radio.

He ran as if his life was at stake, leaping over concrete picnic tables and cutting across the basketball courts. Blurred faces scattered and crowds parted as he blew by. He lost a boot in the sand beneath the volleyball net but he kept running.

He glanced over his shoulder. Two officers were chasing him. Two more were coming through the rec gate. "Stop running!" ordered the guard in the tower through her megaphone. He kicked off his other boot and went turbo.

Although there was nowhere to run, there was still something liberating about tearing across the yard full speed with officers stumbling in tow. He felt aerodynamic as he zigzagged through a game of soccer. The wind in his face was exhilarating. The ground trembled beneath his feet.

Another guard cut across the softball diamond and attempted to head him off. He stutter-stepped left, then bolted right and shook him with ease, leaving him grasping at air. When he looked back, more had joined the chase.

His peers were suddenly cheering him on. "Go, go, go," they shouted, as he pushed himself even faster. From every corner of the yard he saw pumping fists and clapping hands. He had never felt so alive.

He ran until his lungs burned and his side ached; juking, feinting, weaving, sprinting, skipping and reversing, until he finally slowed to a jog then stopped completely by the pull-up bars.

"Man that was awesome!" said Methlab, rushing to meet him with a rotten-teeth grin.

Weasel unleashed a savage right hook that dropped him on his ass. "Sssp!"

The crowd roared.

"What the hell did you do that for?" Methlab howled.

Before he could answer he was tackled from behind his back and cuffed tightly. As he lay there in the dirt, he remembered Methlab's own explanation regarding why he snitched on Kevin.

"It was a business decision."

60
The Patron Saint of Travelers

Kevin was awakened by the putrid smell of his own breath ricocheting off the wall, an inch from his face. The ill effects of his perpetually empty stomach, the lingering traces of his most recent attempt at eating the management loaf and his daily pittance of chalk-flavored state toothpaste were working in concert to produce an aroma not unlike raw sewage.

He rolled off his bunk and pounded out fifty push-ups before staggering to his feet and walking over to the sink. Even in the hazy metal mirror he could still see white flakes of dandruff in his eyebrows. He shook his head as he pressed the button and swished the tepid water in his mouth. He was humiliated that she'd seen him in this pitiful state. The only bright side was that she couldn't *smell* him through the door. At least he hoped she couldn't.

He thought of her letter again, the only letter he had received during the last ten years that wasn't stamped *legal mail* in red ink. Yet her terse, indifferent, business-like tone was even icier than many of the judges and clerks of court that had denied his motions over the years.

She's keeping it cryptic, dumbass. Just like you told her to do. Now is not the time to get all insecure and needy. She's in way worse danger than you are. *The whole point of the letter was to let you know she was leaving him. You should be thrilled.*

Outside his door, he heard the sound of metal chair legs being dragged across the floor. Then Inspector Fretwell appeared in his window.

"We meet again," he said as he unlocked the flap and sat down in the chair. He studied Kevin through the rectangular slot. Slowly the corners of his mouth climbed up the sides of his face revealing two rows of tiny, straight, yellow teeth. The smile stopped before reaching his eyes. "Looks like you've been playing more basketball."

Kevin returned to his bunk and reclined on the steel, leaning against the wall. He kept his expression blank but behind his mask, a panicked voice slashed at his detached façade. *The Inspector!*

"You know," he said, "that day in the laundry room, in Alpha. My gut told me there was something fishy going on. I could see the sparks flying."

"I don't know what you're talking about," said Kevin.

The inspector smirked. "I read her letter."

"What letter?"

"Don't play stupid with me, Freeman."

"The only letter I've received over the past ten years was from an ex in Alabama."

"Right," said Fretwell, "from a bogus address with a local postmark. Let's cut the shit, shall we?"

Kevin shrugged. "Believe what you want."

The inspector tapped his pen on the flap and shook his head. "So she's leaving Lance, huh? How's he taking it?"

Kevin stared at his hands.

"Judging by your condition, I'd say not too well," he snorted. "What was the plan? Happily ever after? A cottage by the sea? Heads Carolina, tails California?"

Kevin wondered what he knew. Rayla's letter alone was nothing. Typed, unsigned and vague. There was no way any court could convict her on such flimsy evidence. But his letter to her was a little more specific. *Had her husband opened his mouth? Was this simply the next phase of his twisted little game?*

"Maddening isn't it?" said the inspector with a smug smile. "Sitting there wondering how much I know, how long I've known, how many of my snitches have been watching your every trip to the laundry room, listening at the door, recording dates and times."

"The only time I was ever in the laundry room was when I was being reprimanded by the dorm officer, which you witnessed, and when I was performing my assigned duty."

"Your *assigned duty?*" he scoffed. "That's putting it eloquently."

Kevin shrugged his shoulders. "That's all I was doing."

Fretwell sighed. "You know what I find ironic?" A potent whiff of stale tobacco floated across the cell with his words. "Your last disciplinary report was in 2002. You've been a role model inmate for eight years. Now all of a sudden, right when you're about to go home, you get locked up for fighting, stripped, sprayed, put on the loaf. You've got five major write-ups pending, one for a knife–"

"That knife wasn't mine."

"–and every disciplinary report was written by Lance Broxson." He rested his chin on his hands. "Hell hath no fury like a husband scorned."

Kevin absently fingered the dry scab that stretched across the bridge of his nose.

"Those cuts and bruises can't be five weeks old either," said Fretwell. "Has he been beating on you, son?"

Kevin shook his head.

"I can help you, you know."

"I don't need any help."

"You sure?" said Fretwell. "I can get you a mattress, a blanket, clothes, food."

In exchange for what? thought Kevin, *my soul?*

After a long uncomfortable silence, Fretwell nodded as if concurring with a voice in his head. "Okay," he said, patting the flap with an air of finality. "We're getting nowhere. Transport will be down here in an hour or two to dress you and shackle you. I'll have you on a van before shift change."

"A van?" said Kevin. "Where am I going?"

"Wherever there's an open bed," said Fretwell. "That's not my concern. But Lance Broxson will kill you if I leave you here. I won't have that on my conscience, or my resume."

Kevin blinked when the flap slammed shut. He listened to the chair being dragged back across the floor to the officer's desk before he rose from the bunk and walked over to the window.

The wing door buzzed loudly and Fretwell pushed it open without a backwards glance. "A transfer," he mumbled, struggling to grasp the implications. He would be further away from Rayla. He may never see Weasel again. Then, slowly, his mind began to warm to the idea. *No more sleeping on steel, no more management loaf, no more strip cells, no more pepper spray, no more Sergeant Broxson, no more bullshit write-ups, no more handcuffed beatings, no more...*

As he stared through the window into the middle distance of the unit, eyes unfocused, mind alive with the sudden and unexpected arrival of hope, his attention was captured by someone frantically waving a hand in the Plexiglas of a second tier cell across the wing.

He leaned forward and squinted, then shook his head in disbelief. *Weasel!*

Kevin watched as his friend pantomimed a fight, excitedly throwing a flurry of jabs and hooks that momentarily carried him out of view. Then he reappeared, tapped his fist against his chest and signed the word "C–o–n–v–i–c-t."

Kevin smiled and gave him a thumbs-up.

Weasel held up a finger before turning and vanishing from the window. When he returned he held something against the glass.

Kevin felt his heart swell as he leaned against the door, distrusting his eyes. *It couldn't be, could it?* There, dangling in the glow of the overhead fluorescents was Bobby's chain.

He began to cry.

61

Benedict Arnold and the Fallen Dictator

Rayla stared at her reflection in the bathroom mirror as she buttoned her uniform shirt. There were faint lines stretching across her forehead that were not there the day before. The stress was getting to her. She wondered why Lance had not yet confronted her about Kevin if he really knew. *To continue torturing him in secret?*

A fresh wave of nausea sent tremors through her body. She leaned over the toilet and retched violently for the second time that morning. Her stomach was already empty. A stream of spittle ran from her lip to the toilet seat. She imagined a herd of microscopic bacteria galloping up the tiny thread of saliva, infiltrating her mouth like foreign invaders as she sputtered to break the connection.

There was still over an hour to kill before her shift started and nothing left to do. All her worldly belongings were stuffed into two Hefty bags and crammed in the trunk of her car. She didn't bother with any of the furniture. *He could have it*, and although she considered withdrawing her half of the fourteen hundred dollars in their joint checking account, in the end she decided to leave it. Seven hundred dollars was a small price to pay for her freedom.

She switched off the bathroom light and walked down the hall to the bedroom, surveying it a final time before she left. There was nothing sentimental about her departure, no pangs of regret for what might have been as she looked around the doublewide. The trailer had never become a home to her. Home had always been across the river. This was just the place where she slept.

She grabbed her purse off the ironing board and headed back down the hall to the front door. She froze when she saw Lance standing in the doorway.

"Going somewhere?" he asked.

"Yeah," she said, looking away. "Work. Why aren't you there?"

He shut the door behind him, leering at her. "Got off early," he said, a cold smile creeping across his face. "Haven't seen you in a minute, and I figured we could get in some quality time before your shift starts."

"Lance, I …" she began to protest, glancing at her watch.

He cut her off. "But then I noticed that your trunk was open and I saw the garbage bags full of your shit."

Rayla took a deep breath, stood up straight and looked him in the eye. "It's over, Lance."

"What's over?"

"Us," she said.

He nodded and stared up at the ceiling. Tears streamed down his face.

A twinge of guilt gnawed at Rayla as she stood there watching her husband cry. *For better or for worse, in sickness and in health, until death do us part.* Images flooded her mind of happier times, earlier times. She realized she was clenching her purse in a death grip.

He shook his head and wiped his tears on his sleeve. "It's not over ... until I say it's over!"

He was across the living room in two steps, reaching for her throat. She flinched. Too late.

"Lance! Stop!" she screamed as he slung her over the coffee table.

She fell backwards. Her head slammed hard against the carpet. She attempted to gain her footing but before she could stand, a vicious backhand sent her flying into the wall. The sharp taste of blood filled her mouth as she dropped to her hands and knees.

"You fucking whore," he growled as a boot thunked against her butt. "You sorry cheating Benedict Arnold no good fucking whore."

The kicks kept coming. She covered her face and balled into a defensive position against the wall. Numbed by adrenaline and shock, she huddled in a dark corner of her mind. The war raged on outside. Each blow was delivered in a brilliant explosion of white that lit up the darkness behind her tightly closed eyes like a flashbulb. And in the pulsing strobe she saw Kevin in his cell, sunken-eyed and cadaverous from malnutrition, bruised and bloody from abuse.

She realized she was clenching her fists. Suddenly she was swept from the floor in a wave of rage.

She spun and launched herself at him, driving her shoulder into his sternum, squeezing his testicles through his pants. His arms flailed as she forced him backwards into the TV, knocking it to the carpet in a loud crash.

"I'm gonna kill you, you fucking bitch!" he bellowed as he went sprawling to the floor like a toppled statue of an overthrown dictator.

She released his balls and bolted for the door. He reached out and grabbed her ankle, reversing her momentum with a savage yank. Her head bounced hard off the floor, disorienting her. She felt herself being reeled back across the carpet to her psychotic husband.

She twisted violently and kicked desperately. It was no use. She was a captured animal, strapped to a conveyor belt, in route to her own slaughter. "Let me go!"

"Shut up," said Lance as he fought to straddle her writhing body.

A hairy arm crossed her face. She seized it with her teeth. With an anguished roar he slammed her head against the floor and ripped it free, her teeth left clenching his torn flesh.

He used his weight to force the air from her lungs as he pinned her wrists to the floor. Veins bulged from his bloated red face as she struggled beneath him.

"Stupid bitch," he hissed.

Panic consumed her. She couldn't breathe. He added even more weight, baring down, pressing harder, crushing her, before finally relenting and raising his hips.

She sucked down hot air in massive gulps, feeling her heartbeat in her eyeballs. Weakly, she raised a knee and drove it into his backside. He didn't budge.

"Want some more?" he asked. "I can do this all day, Rayla. You ain't gonna win."

"I want a divorce," she said. The words hovered in the air between them. They came out sounding petulant to her. Whiny and immature. Like a kid at the playground threatening to take her toys and go home.

He snorted and spat a thick glob of snot in her face, then erupted in maniacal laughter as she attempted to blink the slimy fluid out of her eyelashes. "Why?" he asked. "Did I do something wrong?"

She forced herself to continue staring into the black mineshafts of his eyes. A bead of sweat dripped from his chin and landed on her cheek. Gravity caused his flesh to sag from his face, transforming his crow's-feet into twin roadmaps of deeply etched lines.

A crease appeared between his eyebrows. His jaws tensed. "Or is it that you think your little boyfriend can give you a better life?"

"I think you're insane," she said.

"I heard you went to see him the other day. How'd he look? As cute as you remember?"

"I have no idea what you're talking about."

"No?" he said, releasing her wrist and snatching his wallet from his back pocket. "Maybe this will jog your memory."

Still straddling her, he removed a folded piece of paper and shook it violently until it whipped open, then he clamped it over her face. "Does this look familiar?" he asked as he smashed the incriminating evidence against her eyes, nose and mouth, suffocating her with the truth.

Although it was too close to read, she knew exactly what it was. *But how? She had set it on fire and flushed the ashes.*

He let the paper fall to the side of her face with a final push. "Keep it," he said, "I've got plenty of copies."

She forced her body to relax and softened her voice. "Lance, look what the drugs are doing to you."

"Drugs?" he said with a smirk. "Who told you I was doing drugs? Are you fucking Jarvis too?"

Rolling swells of nausea, frothy with power, crashed against her stomach lining.

"And anyway," he snapped, "it's not what the *drugs* are doing to me. It's what *you* are doing to me."

She shut her eyes and breathed. "What am I doing? Besides being your punching bag?"

"You're cheating on me with an inmate!" he roared. "That's what the fuck you're doing!"

I'm going to die, she thought. *Right here on the floor of this trailer. He's going to kill me.*

He suddenly whipped his head around and squinted up at the corner of the room. "Did you hear that?"

"What?" she asked.

He pressed a nicotine stained finger against her lips and leaned close. "Shh, listen. There! You didn't hear that beeping sound? Bastards are recording me Rayla. See? There it is again."

She was engulfed by the rank smell of his sweat, his breath, then his mouth was on hers, his cracked lips dry and hard, his sore-caked tongue seeking entry. She gagged and turned her head, repulsed.

"It's for the cameras," he whispered in her ear. "I don't like it any more than you. Your mouth tastes like prisoner cock."

She resisted the urge to fire back, *How would you know the taste?*

He scowled as if he heard what she was thinking. Then he reached for her throat, hooking his finger around the necklace he had given her as an anniversary gift. "You don't deserve this," he said, snatching it from her neck like he was rip-starting a lawnmower.

She didn't flinch.

He dangled the gold cursive *L* over her mucus-encrusted lashes. "I'll find someone who does."

An idea began to form in Rayla's mind as she lay there trapped. She forced her eyes to open wide and cocked her head to the side, affecting a listening face.

Lance frowned and glanced over his shoulder in the direction she was looking. "What is it?"

"The beeping," she whispered. "I think I know where it's coming from. I just saw a red light blink."

His eyes were twitching as he turned back to face her. "Where?"

She nodded at the air conditioning vent. "There."

He climbed off her in a trance, shuffling toward the dusty vent with the mesmerized fascination of a fly approaching a bug zapper. "Gonna need a flathead," he mumbled, "or I could just nail something over the damn thing. Fuckin' Patriot Act."

Rayla sprang to her feet, scooping her purse from the carpet in a dead run, hurdling the coffee table as she bolted for the door.

Her car was backed up to the porch steps, trunk wide open, just like she left it. She slammed it shut as she passed, feeling Lance's shadow upon her. She ripped open the driver door and jumped inside, quickly locking it behind her.

She heard his boots on the gravel as she rifled through her pocketbook for her car keys. "Come on, come on, come on," she urged, finally dumping the whole purse in the passenger seat and sifting through its contents.

The shocks on her car creaked and sank a fraction as Lance sat on the hood, just over the left front tire. He smiled his crooked smile as he held up her keys. "These were in the trunk when I pulled up."

Her heart plummeted. Right along with her hope. *You will not cry Rayla.*

He pressed a button on the key fob. The alarm chirped. "Oops," he said before pressing the other button. *Thathunk.* The doors unlocked.

She frantically relocked them.

He smirked and pressed the button again. *Thathunk.*

Again, she relocked them.

Thathunk.

She jumped to lock them yet again but he pressed the button before she could react and relocked them himself. "Gotcha," he said, laughing. "This is fun. Are you having fun? It's been a while since we had any fun together."

She glared at him through the dirty windshield.

He lit a cigarette. "You know that I can snatch you outta there whenever I get good and ready, right?"

She shrugged, hoping to convey indifference. "And I can lay on this horn and scream until the sheriff comes."

His cigarette smoke wafted through the two-inch crack in her window. She wished she could shut it.

"Art Bell was just talkin' about this very same thing on the radio the other night," he said, pausing to take a drag. "The cold war. Mutually assured disasters."

Destruction, she corrected, remembering her high school world history teacher. *Mutually assured destruction.*

As an unfamiliar car passed by, Lance waved without looking. "And basically what that means is that, sure, you could go to the law with some domestic violence sob story, maybe throw in a few other little secrets for good measure, but when Robert Earl comes out here to arrest me, guess what I'm gonna do?"

Rayla didn't bother offering a guess.

"I'm gonna show him that love note from Freeman and explain to him that the reason I kicked your ass is because you were fucking an inmate at the prison. We'll both go to jail. But I'll be the town hero and you'll just be a slut."

Despite her steely resolve, she began to cry.

"It's too late for that," he said.

"I want a divorce!" she shouted through the crack in the window.

"Fine," he growled, his eyes scanning neighborhood porches and lawns. "You were a dead fuck anyway. But I want you to end it with Freeman. *NOW*. I will not have my coworkers snickering behind my back because you're hot in the ass for an inmate. He'll die first. You both will. Are we clear?"

Rayla brushed a tear from her cheek.

"Go fuck the mailman or something," he said, flicking his cigarette butt in the grass. "And remember, irreconcilable differences, right? No abuse, no threats, no drug gossip. America and Russia. Mutually assured devastation. Everybody's got nukes but everybody dies if one is fired. You've got your dirty little secrets," he paused and pulled a glass pipe from his pocket, twirling it between his fingers, "and I've got mine."

In the midst of his rambling tirade a strange warmth crept over her. Her pulse quickened, her heart fluttered, she fought to keep the smile that was swelling within her from reaching her eyes.

Although her head throbbed and there was blood in her mouth and snot in her lashes, a powerful surge of relief flooded her mind. No more agonizing over a way out, no more worrying or wavering, no more living in fear. The door to her cell had rolled open and a crack of daylight appeared on the horizon. She caught a glimpse of what Kevin would soon experience: Freedom. Exhilarating, invigorating freedom.

Her car bobbed slightly when he stood. She readied her finger on the lock and eyed him warily as he approached her door. He stopped at the window and pushed her keys through the crack.

"So we've got a deal," he said. "Now get the fuck out of here and don't ever come back." He turned and sauntered back up the driveway. "I've got shit to do."

She tracked him in the rearview as he climbed the porch steps and disappeared into the trailer, slamming the door behind him. Then she dug out the keys from where they had fallen beside the seat and hurried to crank her car.

She realized that her hands were shaking as she passed the familiar vehicles of neighbors and coworkers for the final time, the rusty trailers, the kiddie pools and the pontoon boats. A season of her life was coming to an end. Yet she felt no nostalgia, only sweet relief, as she pulled out onto the two lane highway that led to the prison.

The parking lot was astir with the bustle of shift change. Country music blared from the open window of a passing pickup. Motorcycles coughed and sputtered to roaring life while the more elegant sedans and SUVs of the administratti pulled into their paint-stenciled reserved spaces. Rayla found a spot between a limo-tinted lowrider and a mud splattered truck with a gun rack and a rebel flag.

She cut the engine and inspected her face in the mirror. It wasn't nearly as bad as she thought. Just a few red marks. The bulk of the damage would be concealed by her shirt. Her ribs began to ache as her adrenaline ebbed. She wiped his drying snot from her eye with a Kleenex, then leaned closer to check her teeth. They were coated in a veneer of blood. She opened the door and spat.

In over six years of employment, Rayla had never taken a sick day. And although Kevin represented a lapse in her professionalism that was difficult to reconcile, she still prided herself on her solid work ethic and dependability, traits that were instilled in her by Mema since she was a girl. *But if there was ever a day to call in ...*

She shook her head as she raked the belongings scattered over the passenger seat back into her purse. There was no way she was giving Lance the pleasure of knowing that he hurt her bad enough to make her call in sick. Plus she felt closer to Kevin when she was on his side of the razor wire.

She hurried to touch up her makeup before grabbing her purse and stepping out of the car. Her alarm hiccupped once behind her as she smoothed out her uniform and headed for the control room.

Midway across the parking lot a fresh wave of nausea blossomed in her abdomen. She slowed and leaned against a light pole, fighting the urge to heave. Tiny beads of perspiration suddenly forced their way through her skin, covering her face in a sheen of cold sweat. It felt like Lance was still kicking her ribs. *Or pulverizing them with a sledgehammer.*

"Easy there, missy," a familiar voice drawled from behind her.

She turned, searching for a face in the kaleidoscopic panorama of streaks and blurs.

"Which'n is it?" the voice asked. "Too much Tequila or one too many turns on the mechanical bull at The Spur?"

Rayla blinked, finally locking in on a brown cap and white whiskers in the surrounding swirl of color. "Both," she lied.

"My kind of woman," said Officer Jeudevine, cackling as he slammed his car door.

Rayla remembered the old man from the confinement unit. A question about Kevin suddenly sprang up from her heart but was forced aside by another attack of violent retching. When the storm subsided she was thankful that her near emotional outburst was vetoed by her body and stillborn on her lips.

"Mighta' shoulda' called in today, girl," he said as he ambled over to where she was standing.

It hurt to breathe. "I'm fine," she said.

"You sure?" he asked. "You're awfully pale."

She nodded, releasing the light pole as if that proved her stability.

"Well, I'll walk you to the gate then," he said, still eyeing her skeptically.

There was something settling about the old man's presence. Something patient and grandfatherly. He smelled like varnish and pipe smoke. She resisted the urge to reach for his hand as they made their way across the parking lot.

"You're Hazel Adams' grandbaby, ain't you?"

"Yes sir," said Rayla.

"Thought so," he said. "I went to grade school with your Mema. You look just like her. I was wonderin' about that the other day after you left the confinement unit."

Again, Rayla thought of Kevin in the strip cell, bruised and emaciated, staring back at her with those haunted eyes.

"Can I ask you something?" said the old man.

Rayla nodded.

"It's none of my business, but what made you wanna marry a man like Lance Broxson?"

"That's a great question," said Rayla.

"He's just mean as a snake," he said, "and nuttier than squirrel shit. Every time I have to work behind him in confinement, some kid is bleedin' outta his ear and coughin' up pepper spray. Especially that poor bastard in the strip cell."

Rayla felt herself getting nauseous again.

"Speaking of squirrel shit," he nodded toward the admin building, "I think the inspector over there is trying to get one of our attentions."

Rayla followed his gaze across the parking lot. Fretwell was motioning her over with a manila file. "He wants me," she said.

"Give him hell then, darlin'," said the old man to her back as she cut across the grass.

The admin building was a square brick structure just across the perimeter road from the control room and tower one. It was encompassed by a thick, waist-high block of hedges that ran level around the back of the building in an unbroken line. At the front entrance was an awning and beneath the awning, smiling through a cloud of cigarette smoke, Hollis Fretwell awaited her arrival.

"Rayla Broxson!" he exclaimed with the enthusiasm of a carnival barker. "Just the gal I was waiting for."

She stopped at the edge of the awning.

He raised an eyebrow and lowered his voice. "It *is* still Broxson, isn't it?"

She lost her patience. "Is there something you need from me? I'm late."

His face hardened to a sneer. "I transferred your boyfriend yesterday."

Her head began to pound.

"You didn't really think I believed your little charade in the laundry room, did you? Please. I've been watching you and Freeman for weeks." He paused and shook his head in disgust. "I didn't even have to lean on him during the interrogation. He opened up to me like I was Dr. Phil. Guess he was desperate to get away. Lance must have really been putting a world of hurt on him back there. But you know that, you saw him."

Suddenly Kevin was standing there, his chin resting on his hands, his hands resting on the broom, staring at her with those intense green eyes. *"They're gonna tell you that I broke, that I sold you out and told them everything. If it ever comes to that, and I pray it won't, I want you to remember this conversation and know that I would die before I betrayed you."*

Rayla blinked away the tears that were gathering in her eyes and smiled.

"Something funny?" Fretwell asked. "We'll see if you're still smiling when the charges are filed. Of course you can make things much easier on yourself by coming clean."

"I have no clue what you're talking about."

Fretwell spat a mouthful of smoke at her. "Remember our little meeting in the tower? Didn't I warn you about that flip attitude? I told you it was going to come back and bite you in the ass."

"Don't talk to me like that."

He smirked. "Forgive me. I forgot you were a good Pentecostal woman."

Rayla glared back at him.

"It's over," he said. "Freeman told me everything. The letters, the gifts, the sex in the laundry room. He even told me about your parents." He shook his head in mock sympathy. "So sad."

His words stung like a slap. Her knees buckled. She almost sat down on the concrete. Instead she straightened, took a rib-rattling breath and turned back for the parking lot.

"Where in the hell do you think you're going?" Fretwell demanded.

She paused in the road. "Am I under arrest?"

If he answered at all, it was spoken too softly to hear.

She headed for her car.

"What about your shift?" he called.

"I quit."

62

Shake and Bake

Lance dropped the remainder of his dope in the glass bowl of his pipe and chased it with the torch while pressing one eye against a crack in the blinds and watching the road. He figured that if Rayla called the law, they'd send a patrol car by the trailer.

He took a deep hit. His senses sharpened. He saw an ant on a blade of grass. He could hear the interstate traffic twenty miles away. Hours passed. Sweat poured. He remained glued to the window, waiting and smoking, milking the pipe until it burned his lips, until the glass was charred and spider-webbed from his torch.

An overflowing ashtray sat next to him on the table. He dug out a butt, blew the ashes off the filter and fired it up. It was almost noon. He'd been at the window since Rayla left that morning.

Maybe his gut was wrong. Maybe he was just being paranoid. Maybe his lying contaminated whore of a wife was telling the truth for once. Maybe she didn't go to the law. Regardless, he knew he needed to pry himself from the window. The dope was gone. It was time to cook.

Reluctantly, he stepped away from the blinds and walked into the kitchen, dropping his cigarette butt in a beer bottle on the way. He opened the cupboard beneath the sink and began removing the necessary items: sodium hydroxide, camp fuel, a box of 30-milligram Sudafed, a pack of Energizer batteries.

He walked over to the fridge and grabbed the cold pack from the second shelf and flipped open his pocket knife. The white pellets in the cold pack were ammonium nitrate, an essential ingredient. He needed them out.

He had just laid the cold pack on the counter and pressed the blade into the casing when the living room AC vent caught his eye. He thought of Rayla's words earlier about the red light. He knew she was lying to try to distract him, but ...

He dropped the knife on the counter and started snatching open drawers until he found the hammer and nails. Then he ripped off a cabinet door and took it with him into the living room.

He pulled the coffee table to the hall and stood on top of it, positioning the small wooden door over the vent. "Show's over, you nosy bitches."

He pounded five nails into the drywall in rapid succession, the hammer banging like gunshots, echoing throughout the trailer. When he finished he hopped down and inspected his handiwork.

Although the cabinet door, complete with handle and hinges, looked slightly out of place on the popcorn ceiling, it served its purpose. It was even sort of artsy in a way. Maybe he'd do the windows next.

With a renewed sense of privacy, he sauntered back into the kitchen and removed Methlab's cooking instructions from a canister by the microwave. He was fairly certain he had the recipe down pat, but he still erred on the side of caution, since any misstep could turn the trailer into a roaring fireball.

He smoothed the rumpled sheet of notebook paper on the counter and got down to business. First, the safety precautions: he went to the pantry and grabbed a bottle of vinegar to neutralize burns, and was looking around for a blanket to dampen when he spotted Rayla's throw draped over the loveseat. He walked back into the living room and yanked it from the cushion. A feminine sweet gust washed over him in the backdraft. He shut his eyes.

The phone rang. He glanced across the room. The sound of Rayla's voice came tumbling through the answering machine speaker.

"You have reached the Broxson residence. Sorry we're missing your call. Please leave your name and number at the tone and we'll get back to you as soon as possible."

Beep.

"Hello, Rayla? Lance? *If you're there pick up, it's Hollis Fretwell. Okay, well I just wanted to apologize for my behavior this morning. I was hoping I could meet with ya'll sometime tomorrow, and talk about this Freeman thing."*

Lance whirled and slammed his fist into the wall. *Fretwell?!?* He grabbed a framed picture of Rayla off the table and smashed his face against it. "Did you hear that you stupid bitch?!? The inspector wants a family meeting to discuss the inmate you're fucking!" He slung the picture across the room. It cut through the air like a buzz saw blade and crash-landed into the side of the television that was still lying face down in the carpet.

He stomped back into the kitchen with the throw over his shoulder, then he pulled it off and dunked it in the murky sink water. *If Fretwell knows, then who else? Was the whole fucking prison snickering behind his back? The whole town?* He reached over the sink and grabbed a bowl, slamming it on the counter. In three hours he'd have a batch of dope ready. He'd figure out his next move after that.

He tore open the Sudafed box and began popping the tiny red pills from the blister pack into the bowl. All ninety-six of them. *Red Hots,* Methlab called them. He crushed them to fine talc. Then he removed the ammonium nitrate from the cold pack. There was a twenty-ounce water bottle on the table. He grabbed it, emptied it in the sink and set the empty bottle on the counter next to the drain crystals. He quickly measured out two cups of camp fuel before moving on to the batteries, carefully peeling off the casing and removing the strips. These were highly flammable, ignited by water or wind. The kitchen began to reek with the egg smell of lithium.

He worked methodically, economically, no wasted motion, no wasted time. He followed the scribbled steps to the letter without shortcut, performing each task in a Zen state of no-mind, lost in the execution of instruction.

He poured camp fuel into the water bottle then made a paper funnel for the crushed Sudafed. Next came the ammonium nitrate pellets, followed by a quarter-cup of drain crystals. Then he tore the lithium strips into smaller pieces and carefully inserted them too. They swirled around the bottle like confetti.

The peroxide was the catalyst, the kick in the ass that ignited the entire process. He unscrewed the cap and filled it with the liquid chemical. "Let's get this party started," he mumbled, emptying the cap into the water bottle.

The reaction was instantaneous. Bubbles began climbing the sides. A blizzard of froth rose up from the center and surged toward the neck in an effervescent belch. He quickly clamped the lid over the top of the bottle and screwed it on tight.

As he watched it continue to bubble violently, he was reminded of a Christmas decoration his mother used to place on the mantle each December. One of those glass globe deals that you could shake like hell and visit a vicious snowstorm on the little picturesque town that was glued to the base.

The bottle began to convulse and swell, bulging grotesquely, its cylindrical shape contorting into some unrecognizable balloon animal. He grabbed the cap and twisted. The burping process was essential during the cooking phase. Pressure needed to be relieved regularly until it was no longer necessary. When the storm was completely calm, the dope was ready to be filtered.

Problem was, he couldn't get the cap off.

He leaned into it, frantically wrenching the bottle top, his bloodless sweaty fingers slipping over the ridges. It wouldn't budge. With rising terror he realized that the coiled thread inside the cap had expanded, locking it in place.

Suddenly it erupted in a deafening thunderclap, exploding in his hands. The cap launched skyward like a champagne cork blasted from the barrel of a sawed-off, drenching his face in camp fuel and lye, peppering him with lithium bits.

He stood stunned in the ensuing silence, his heart thumping wildly. The trailer creaked. A dirty plate shifted in the sink. An insidious hiss was whispering somewhere nearby. He surveyed the settling debris in a daze. A vaporous tendril floated in front of his eye. Hiss became crackle and crackle, sizzle. Electric white searing pain broke through. He realized that his face was cooking in lye.

Seized by horror, he forgot the emergency instructions and acted on instinct, thinking that water would quench the agony. He almost jerked the faucet knob off in a panicked frenzy, desperate to escape the chemical burn, splashing the cold water in his face, which caused the lithium to spark and ignite the camp fuel that was streaming down his chin.

He went up in a blaze, the singed hair shriveled back into his scalp and the flesh dripped from his face like mozzarella. He groped blindly for the sink, burying his head in the overflowing dishwater. His anguished screams were muffled and turned to bubbles.

When he finally came up for air, he saw scattered fire on the countertops and floor. A trail of flames crept across the Formica, incinerating Methlab's recipe on the way, reducing it to a sheet of black ash as it licked a path around the vinegar bottle.

Vinegar! His mind snapped, suddenly remembering Methlab's instructions. *To neutralize chemical burns.* He snatched it up and doused himself with it. The festering hot pink blisters that covered his flesh instantly smoldered in gratitude. He dropped the bottle on the floor and staggered back to the sink. Rayla's throw was still soaking among the dirty plates and glasses. He pulled it free and used it to snuff out the surrounding fires.

When the last flame was extinguished, he gazed at the charred cupboard doors and burnt wallpaper. He kicked the empty vinegar bottle across the trash-strewn floor. All around him was wreckage, devastation, nuclear winter.

"Rayla's gonna be pissed," he mumbled, his words hovering in the stillness for a moment before finally drifting to the floor of the bombed out kitchen with the rest of the dust and ash. *No,* he corrected himself. *Rayla's not gonna be pissed because Rayla doesn't live here anymore.*

He glanced down at his hands. His right was fine but the back of his left was a sticky pool of slimy fluid that oozed and bubbled as he looked on in fascinated horror. The burns extended under the melted plastic of his watchband, almost reaching his elbow.

He swayed. In a flash, the pain skipped from silent movie to surround sound. And it wasn't just his hand. Suddenly a hot iron was being held against his face. He needed something to deaden the siren wail of agony. He stumbled forward, ripping open the blackened door of the liquor cabinet, knocking over bottles in frantic desperation.

When he found the right label, he fumbled with the cap then guzzled down half the bottle before pausing to breathe. "AAGGHH!" he roared, slamming it on the counter and grimacing. When he wiped his mouth on his tattered shirt sleeve, a bloody strip of flesh came away like a sheet of wet tissue. He brushed it off and downed another quarter of the bottle.

As the whiskey spread through his belly, numbing the pain from the inside out, he squinted at his distorted reflection on the stainless faucet. He frowned at the image for a moment, then turned and staggered to the bathroom for a better view.

When he flicked on the light, there was a horror movie starring back at him in the mirror. His right ear was gone, all that remained was a clump of molten flesh with a black hole in the center. The entire right side of his face from cheek to jaw was also missing. He could see his teeth and tongue behind the myriad crosshatched strings of skin.

Seeing the severity of his condition triggered a fresh wave of torment. He was going into shock. The whiskey was no match. He figured that the only reason his body hadn't completely shut down was because he was still hopped up on crystal, even though he didn't *feel* high. But he was going to need something for pain. Something stronger than whiskey. He hurried back down the hall and unlocked the front door.

The wind had picked up and was blowing from the north. The chill was like balm on his melted flesh. He limped across his neighbor's yard to Jessica's trailer. He found her sitting on her porch steps smoking.

She screamed when she saw him.

"Shhh!" he hissed, glancing over his shoulder.

"Oh my God Lance!" she exclaimed, covering her mouth. "What happened to you?"

He wasn't certain whether it was disgust or pity he saw in her eyes. "Long story," he said, flinching as the wind sent a raw strip of skin flapping on his jaw. "I need something for pain."

"No," she said, "you need a burn unit."

"I'm heading to the hospital now," he said, "but I'm scared I'll pass out on the way from shock if I don't numb the pain." He held up the bottle. "This ain't workin'."

She rose to her feet. "Well, I know I've got some Xanax in my purse," she said, "but I think there may be something stronger in the…" The screen door slammed behind her as she disappeared inside the trailer.

Her sweatpants were tight. The word "sweetcakes" was stamped across the ass in pink letters. *Sweetcakes…* His pet name for Rayla a lifetime ago.

The door swung back open and she hurried down the steps clutching her purse. "Here," she said, holding out an orange pill.

"What is it?" he asked, plucking it from her palm.

"It's an Oxy forty," she said. "Chew it if you can, it'll kick in faster."

He chewed up the bitter pill and washed it down with a swig of Jack.

"Give me your keys," she said. "I'll drive you to the hospital."

He dug in his pocket for the key ring and handed it over.

The pain started fading before the truck doors slammed and was a dull throb by the time the engine rumbled to life.

"This stuff works," he said, watching the trailers pass in a blur. "Where'd you get it?"

"My ex came home from Afghanistan with a script." She glanced over at him. "What happened to you Lance?"

He reached up and adjusted the rearview for another look at the puckered oozing flesh of his Freddy Kruger face. "I almost burned my trailer down."

She turned onto the highway. "You were cooking meth, weren't you?"

He nodded, sticking his finger inside the intersecting strands of taut melted skin, touching his teeth through his cheek.

She watched the road. "Why are you so hell bent on destroying yourself like this? Jarvis is worried sick about you."

He took another swig of whiskey, wishing she'd shut the fuck up.

"Did Rayla leave?" she asked.

He turned slowly toward her. "What?"

"Did your wife leave you?" she repeated, fidgeting nervously in the driver's seat as the miles of farmland rolled by behind them.

"She didn't leave me," he croaked. "It was a mutual parting. Irreconcilable differences."

"I heard she quit this morning," said Jessica, glancing over at him. "They say Fretwell was trying to interrogate her and she just turned around and drove off."

His blood began to scald as a thermal wind blew through him. His face grew warm. But not from fire or chemical burns. There was something haughty in her tone, something almost spiteful.

"Everybody's talking about it," she said. "There's a rumor going around that she was having inappropriate relations with an inmate."

He glared at her over the bottle as he took another drink. "You shouldn't spread rumors."

"Should and shouldn't," she said. "I thought you hated those words. Hey would you grab me a cigarette out of my purse?" She slowed when she came to the fork in the road and took the two-lane that led to Interstate 10.

He tightened the cap on the bottle and set it on the floorboard. Then he reached across her body and grabbed the driver's side door handle.

"Lance!" she screamed. "Get off me! What are you–"

When he got the door open, he grabbed the wheel and kicked her from the moving vehicle, sliding over into the empty driver's seat and slamming the door. As he drove away, he glanced in the rearview. She had rolled to a stop and was sitting on the faded yellow line in the center of the road.

He dug a cigarette from her purse and grinned at his hideous reflection in the mirror as he struck the lighter. Then he stepped on the gas and headed for the cut-off that led back to the Chattahoochee River.

63

The Reckoning

There is a saying on the Florida Panhandle: The fair brings the cold. It happens every fall. When the convoy pulls into the fairgrounds and unpacks the midway rides, livestock tents and vending booths, it invariably brings the year's first cold snap with it.

Rayla was trying to read the newspaper but it was difficult to concentrate. Her mind kept reverting to the fight with Lance and the scene with Fretwell in the parking lot. Her hands were still trembling. She glanced outside the kitchen window at the swirling leaves. Mydog bounded into view, attacking the falling foliage with gusto. Mema would be back from her chair aerobics class any minute. Rayla knew she wanted to go to the fair. She had been dropping hints for weeks, but Rayla didn't feel like dealing with the phony smiles and knowing smirks of her former coworkers. And anyway, her body was still aching from Lance's kicks.

The sound of an approaching engine made her pause. She refolded the paper and tossed it on the table. Mydog ceased slapping at leaves and flipped back an ear. Lance's Silverado came screaming around the corner in a cloud of dust. She watched with a sinking feeling as he rumbled down the dirt driveway. Mydog barked. Something told her he wasn't coming to return her Backstreet Boys CDs.

He rolled to a stop at the edge of the grass and shut off the engine. She could barely make out his shape through the windshield as he sat motionless in the truck watching the house. She suddenly regretted not filing a restraining order.

High above, a cloud stretched its fingers over the shining yellow eye of the sun, bathing the ground in creeping shadows. The truck door swung open. A boot hit the driveway. Rayla glanced around for her cell phone. When she looked back up, he was striding across the grass.

Mydog met him halfway, hackles raised and teeth bared, barking viciously. Lance swung back his leg and launched a kick with such violent bone-jarring force that she heard it make impact from inside the house. The little dog went flying through the air and landed in the hedges, broken.

Rayla ripped open the front door and was sprinting down the steps before she even realized what she was doing. "Don't you dare kick my dog, you fucking bas—" She froze.

He raised his lone remaining eyebrow and smiled with half his face as he closed the distance between them. "Don't worry," he said, "it looks worse than it feels."

She tried to turn and run, but his iron grip was clamped around her wrist before her brain could get the message to her feet. She opened her mouth to scream. He silenced it with a fist. The first blow knocked her down. The second knocked her out.

When her eyes fluttered open, she saw tree branches and patches of sky overhead. She realized she was being dragged across the lawn by her hair. He opened the driver's side door of the truck and pushed her inside, then climbed in behind her.

She reached for the passenger door. He crushed her nose with a backhand. "You're only making it worse."

She began to cry, not out of fear, although he was terrifying, and not out of pain, although her face was swollen and bloody, but out of sheer frustration. Dream-crushing, soul-sucking frustration. *Hadn't she just been free a moment ago? Wasn't this part of her life over?* "I thought we made a deal," she mumbled.

"We did," he said, stroking her hand, "and the deal *was* that we were going to split quietly and nobody was going to know about your little boy toy." He grabbed her finger and bent it backwards. "But the problem is that *everybody* knows. So now we're gonna need us a new deal."

She snatched her hand away and glared at him. His eyes were almost as horrible as his melted face. A scary snippet of a Sunday school Bible verse popped in her head, something about weeping and wailing and gnashing of teeth. That's what she saw in his eyes. Shrieking, tormented, demonic hell, and no sign of the Lance she once knew.

He reached into the purse that was sitting in the console and produced a prescription bottle. A few blue football-shaped pills rattled around inside. He twisted off the cap and shook one into his palm. "But first I need you to eat this."

He forced a pill between her lips.

She spit it out on the floorboard, refusing to be drugged.

"Fine," he said, "we'll do it the hard way then."

His elbow slammed into her temple causing her head to bounce against the window. She drunkenly raised her fists in a feeble attempt to protect her face. She felt a ridge-hand straight out of the defense training class drive into the crook of her neck, incapacitating her, before the final punch scrambled her brain.

Consciousness turned to water in her cupped hands, slipping through the cracks. Awareness was a far off flickering light. Somewhere, miles away, she heard the rattle of a pill bottle. She was vaguely aware of being shoved face first into the door panel and her pants being ripped down around her legs. Then his fingers, cold and surgical, were pressing against her anus.

She struggled weakly. He slammed her face against the window.

As the lights went dim she could feel him forcing the pills up into her rectum. They burned as they dissolved. The last thing she heard was the truck engine cranking.

She awoke outside of her body. Back in the trailer, floating against the bedroom ceiling and staring down at the gruesome scene below.

Her hands were locked behind her back in steel restraints. Her clothes had been stripped off and were scattered on the bed. A belt was looped around her neck like a leash, yanking her head back as she was mounted by a monster.

It occurred to her that she was witnessing her own execution, that the body being brutalized on the bed below belonged to her.

Lance grunted and gasped as he violated her from behind. Sweat poured down the remaining strands of bunched and twisted flesh that stretched from his cheekbone to jawbone like a tangled mass of rubber bands. He alternated between muttering incoherently, laughing hysterically and arguing with hallucinations, all the while slamming into her limp body with merciless savagery. It was obvious that any remaining sanity or humanity had melted away with his skin.

She wondered how she had separated from her physical body. Her only guess was that her spirit was expelled due to the trauma, ushered to shelter like scurrying school children when an armed psychopath was rumored to be roaming the halls. It was safe from her vantage point on the ceiling. Heartbreaking, but safe.

Suddenly there was a loud knock at the front door.

"Fuck off," Lance growled, still pounding away, using the leash as leverage.

The knock grew louder, more persistent, causing the trailer walls to tremble. "Lance!" a muffled voice shouted. "I know you're in there. Open this damn door! We need to talk."

"Aw shit, Jarvis," Lance whined, dropping the belt. Her body slumped forward on the bed.

He zipped his pants and was almost to the doorway when he turned and walked back to where she was lying.

Jarvis pummeled the front door with fists of rolling thunder.

"Hang on a fucking minute!" Lance bellowed over a shoulder as he sat down next to her and shoved a hand beneath her breast, presumably searching for a heartbeat. Satisfied, he pulled open her eye and stared at the pupil for a moment before allowing it to blink shut.

"I'll be right back," he whispered in her ear. "Don't go anywhere."

His footsteps faded down the hall. A vast compassion filled her as she considered the pitiful sight splayed below. Dark bruises on pale skin, damp hair matted with blood and sweat, mascara running from the swollen slit of an eye, drugged, handcuffed, trapped, waiting to die.

Then she was falling back toward her body, descending like a waterfall into herself. *No!* Her mind shouted as she settled into the familiar parameters of her skin. *I don't want to! I'm scared.*

Her eyes snapped open. Like it or not, she was back. Back in her terrestrial prison of flesh and bone. *Rayla Broxson Correctional Institution*, she thought. *No, not Broxson, not anymore.*

She could hear his voice reverberating throughout the trailer. "I didn't kick that lying bitch out of no damn truck. I haven't even seen Jessica today."

Her thoughts grew fuzzy and difficult to grasp. They stretched out before her like a field of dandelions. She swiped at them lethargically but they disintegrated on contact. The drugs he forced inside of her were still rolling through her bloodstream in murky waves of vagueness. Her eyelids became heavy.

"…my wife," she heard him say. "She's asleep. Why? Are you banging her too? I think you need to get the hell off my property, Jarvis."

An early memory of Kevin shone on the white wall of her mind, lighting up the darkness like a slide projector. He was gently cleaning Wessel's wounds at the sink. She wished he could clean her wounds.

"By all rights, I can shoot you dead right there on the porch," Lance was ranting. "You ain't never heard of the stand-your-ground law?"

I wish somebody would shoot you, Rayla thought as she slid to the edge of the cliff of consciousness. And stopped.

She opened an eye and glanced over at the nightstand. *Would he be stupid enough to leave her alone in the room with a gun?*

She rolled onto her back and wiggled her butt between her handcuffed wrists then pulled her legs through them so that they were in front of her. When she was able to sit up, her reflection was staring back at her in the dresser mirror. With trembling fingers she removed the belt from her neck.

Down the hall, Lance's psychobabble was rising in both hostility and decibel. "You betrayed me, Jarvis! You're just as guilty as that whore back there and the American government!"

Rayla chewed on her lip as she rose to her feet. The motion seemed to stir the chemicals in her blood. The floor shifted beneath her. She leaned against the bed for balance and reached toward the nightstand. Her legs were as heavy as her mind was groggy.

Hurry! urged a shrill voice in her head. Her naked reflection mimicked her from across the room as she reached for the second drawer and slid it open. She saw the chrome box immediately. She glanced behind her before unsnapping the latches.

The pistol lay snug in the contoured box like a coiled and sleeping viper. She could see the clip protruding slightly from the handle. It was loaded. She grabbed it and flipped off the safety, contorting her bound wrists to chamber a round. Then, clutching it in her hands, she staggered from the bedroom and hobbled down the hall.

The voice grew louder as she neared. He sounded more like a snarling enraged animal than a human being. She raised the gun as she emerged into the living room, as if in a dream.

His back was to her. The chain was on the open door and he was yelling into the crack of daylight coming through.

She took another wobbly step. The floor creaked.

He paused mid-rant and turned the mangled side of his face in her direction. A soulless black eye appraised her.

"Put some fucking clothes on, you contaminated skank!" he bellowed.

She sighted his head in the pistol.

"Oh, you're gonna shoot me, huh?" he chuckled. Then he sucked his teeth. "Well you better make damn sure you kill me because if you miss, I'm gonna drag you back in that bedroom and use that same gun to finish off what we were doing." He turned back to Jarvis. "Before somebody interrupted us–"

The first bullet tore a hole in his shoulder blade and knocked him into the door.

The second shot spun him around and dropped him to his knees.

The last one took off the remainder of his face.

She stumbled forward and tripped over the television, losing the pistol in the process. With her hands bound and her reflexes dulled, there was no way she could break her fall. Her face bounced off the coffee table and she sagged to the floor with the echo of gunshots still clapping in her ears.

The last sound she heard was the approaching wail of sirens.

Epilogue

Seven Months Later

On the first Wednesday of May, after ten years, eleven months and seventeen days in a time capsule, Kevin Freeman sat in the visitation area awaiting his name to be called.

Three other men filled out the row of chairs next to him, talking excitedly about their plans for the first night out. Two of them were wearing the current style of name brand clothing and sneakers sent by loved ones, the other man was dressed like Kevin in the indigent outfit of state supplied Dickies, a white t-shirt, and rubber-soled bobos. A pile of discarded blue uniforms lay rumpled in the corner.

All three of the men were unfamiliar, as were the occasional passing faces of guards and inmate orderlies. Although the compound was an exact replica of every other prison he'd seen over the past eleven years, he never got the chance to experience it firsthand. There was no one to bump fists with or wish him luck, no patronizing officer to wag a finger and tell him not to come back. He had stepped off the van in chains and shackles two hundred and twenty-five days earlier and spent all of winter and most of spring in the hole. It would have been worse if all of Broxson's bullshit disciplinary reports had been processed. Thankfully, they were not.

He clasped his address book in his hand, a faded blue folder with rusty staples given to him by the Lake Butler chaplain years before and filled with names and numbers of former cellmates and bunkies he would never contact. It was the only property he carried.

The door opened and a guard strode in carrying a stack of files. Kevin eyed him warily. Even though freedom was only a few steps away, a part of him was skeptical. He was conditioned to expect trouble, bad luck, setbacks.

"Freeman," the guard called, opening the top file.

"Yes sir," said Kevin.

"Grab your stuff and come here."

Kevin stood and walked across the waxed floor to where the guard was waiting. He wasn't a day over twenty-four. Probably younger. He wore way too much hair gel and even more cologne. He stared back at Kevin over a pair of dark Oakleys.

"Damn dude, you need a suntan," he said. "How long have you been in the box?"

"Since September," said Kevin.

He shook his head and flipped a page back in the file. "Okay, gimme your DC number."

"P18722."

"How old are you?"

"Thirty-five."

"Where were you born?"

"Pensacola, Florida."

"Mother's maiden name?"

"Division of Children and Families."

The guard frowned and looked up from the file.

"I'm an orphan," said Kevin.

"Go stand over there, smart ass," he said as he jerked his head toward the door before calling the next name. "Odom."

Kevin's heart began to pound as he moved another ten steps closer to freedom. He waited by a mural on the wall, a DOC seal with the words "We Never Walk Alone" painted above it.

Once the other men were identified, the officer handed them each a check for fifty dollars and radioed the control room to pop the door. "Come on," he said.

They followed him through a metal detector and down a short hallway to another door which led outside to the sally port. Kevin shielded his eyes and looked up at the gun tower for the final time. An old woman behind the glass in the control room smiled at him. Then the front gate buzzed and he walked across the threshold into the rest of his life.

There were families in the parking lot, smiling, waving, and jumping up and down. He even saw balloons.

"Odom, Trevino," the guard said, "your people are over there." He glanced at Kevin and the remaining releasee. "Ya'll follow me to the van. I'll drop you at the Greyhound station."

The drive took half an hour. Kevin spent it with his face glued to the window. The world seemed more vibrant than when he left. Greener. The lush and verdant regalia of spring, the season of new beginnings and rebirth, was everywhere he looked.

He saw Rayla everywhere too. In passing cars, jogging down the sidewalk, mowing her grass, walking her dog. He knew it was stupid to look for her when she lived one hundred miles away, but he couldn't stop himself. Her memory had been his faithful companion for the last seven months.

He wondered what became of her. He hadn't received a single letter since he'd been transferred. *Not a good sign.* She knew how to find him, why hadn't she? *Maybe she made things right with her husband. Maybe she was so scared that she decided to vanish without a trace and start a new life somewhere safe. Maybe she found someone new.*

The van pulled to the curb in front of a red brick building with a Greyhound sign jutting from over the door.

"All right gentlemen, here's your tickets. Freeman, the Pensacola bus leaves in twenty minutes. Eblen, your bus leaves in an hour. Try not to get arrested before you make it home," the officer said as they climbed out. "We'll leave a light on for you."

Yeah, Kevin thought, *well, you are gonna have a high power bill then because I'm never going back.* He knew the odds were against him. The recidivism rate was high, the economy was down, and prisons were the lifeblood of every struggling small town in the state. He was now job security, a commodity in the prison industrial complex. And it wasn't just Florida. The U.S. made up five percent of the world's population, yet twenty-five percent of the world's prisoners resided in the U.S. How ironic that planet Earth's freest country was also her most voracious incarcerator. *And it wasn't even close.*

He wondered if Rayla was still working at the prison. The inspector seemed hell-bent on firing her. But a single unsigned typed letter was not nearly enough evidence. It was probably for the best that she never wrote again.

He walked through the depot. A grizzled man in a camo jacket and VFW hat dozed by the door. He looked homeless. An Hispanic woman with tired eyes was scolding a hyperactive little boy. He also saw other ex-cons sprinkled in among the faces. He would have recognized them even if they weren't wearing the same indigent Walmart getup as he was. They had that lean predatory rec yard look that was universal to prisoners.

A row of buses was parked in the terminal. He found the one headed to Pensacola and presented his ticket to the man by the door.

"Watch your step," he cautioned.

Kevin found a seat near the back. He thumbed through his address book out of boredom, remembering the faces that matched the names. He touched the Saint Christopher medallion that hung from his neck when he came to Weasel's Seattle info, hoping that his friend got some love on his appeal. He wasn't built for prison.

He flipped to the back and looked longingly at the seven bogus names and phone numbers scrawled across the page. The last digit of each number moving vertically from bottom to top equaled the number she had given him, copied from a stick of Juicy Fruit and encrypted should Fretwell ever confiscate the book.

Maybe he would call her after a few months at the halfway house. After he gained some weight and got a tan and some decent clothes and a job and a ride. Maybe one day.

He shut his eyes and leaned back in the seat. She was smiling at him through the officers' station glass, reaching out to touch his face. He was kissing her in the laundry room, holding her in his arms, making love to her against the wall.

He jumped to his feet and hurried down the aisle.

"The bus is departing in seven minutes," called the driver behind him as he leaped down the steps and bolted for the double doors.

The woman at the desk resembled a bulldog with pink hair. "Can I help you?"

"Do you have a phone I can use?"

She shook her head. "I'm sorry. It's against company policy. There's a pay phone right over there."

Kevin glanced in the direction she was pointing. He heard pay phones had gone extinct while he was away. He reached in his pocket and removed the fifty dollar check. "Can I cash this here?"

She smiled. "You're just getting out of prison aren't you?"

He nodded.

"My dad's in prison," she confided. "I used to visit him once a month back when he was at A.C.I. Then they shipped him way down south." Her eyes widened. "Hey, you never ran across a John Phillips in there did you? Everybody calls him Bulldog."

Kevin shook his head and looked out the glass double doors into the terminal. His bus was pulling out.

"Here," she said, looking right and left before sliding her cell phone across the counter. "I've got unlimited minutes anyway."

"Thank you," he said as he picked it up. It was flat and black and looked like something that fell out of a UFO. There were no buttons on it.

"You don't remember how to use a cell phone, do you?"

"I've never seen one like this," he said, turning it over in his hand.

"How long were you in there?"

"Eleven years."

She held out her hand. "Tell me the number. I'll dial."

He opened his address book to the last page and read off the number.

She passed him back the phone. "It's ringing."

He held it to his ear.

"Hello," said the voice on the other end.

"May I speak to Rayla please?"

After a long pause the voice asked, "Is this the janitor?"

"No ma'am," he said, "this is Kevin. Freeman. I'm a friend of hers."

"I know who you are!" the woman snapped. "They turn you loose today?"

"This morning," he said.

There was another long pause punctuated by the sound of something crunching. *Was she eating a carrot?*

"Jury's still deliberating," she said. "Court's supposed to reconvene at two. Where are you?"

"Tallahassee," he said. *Jury? Court?* "I'm at the Greyhound station."

"I'll be there in an hour." *Crunch.* "Wait out front."

The city street was alive with exhaust fumes, horns and car stereos. The sleek body styles of late model vehicles looked like spaceships interwoven between the taxis and police cruisers. He watched life unfold like a documentary. The fast food drive thru, the bickering couple at the red light, the pigeons on the power line, the cyclists, the pedestrians, the garbage trucks, the city buses, and the babies strapped into car seats of passing minivans – taking it all in with the same "what the hell is all this?" facial expression that he'd been catching in his own reflection since the gun towers dropped over the horizon.

He knew the maroon Accord was his ride even before it stopped. He first noticed it hugging the white line of the northbound lane, moving much slower than the passing traffic. An elderly lady in black sunglasses was holding the wheel with both hands, while on the passenger side, a little dog had its head stuck out the window, ears flapping.

He watched it fade to a distant speck before floating across the road in a U-turn and puttering back toward him.

The old woman pulled up to the curb. The dog greeted him with a bark. "Kevin?" she asked.

"Yes, ma'am," he said, holding out his hand for the little dog to sniff.

She opened her door into the oncoming traffic and walked around the car, tossing him the keys.

"I don't have a license," he said.

"Neither do I."

"I haven't driven in eleven years."

"I haven't driven in forty."

The dog barked once, declaring the winner.

He wanted to tell her that his license was suspended for life, that the last time he was behind the wheel he killed his own brother, but he could tell by the stubborn set of her jaw that she wasn't going to argue.

She opened the passenger side door and got in, slamming it behind her. The dog climbed in her lap. "Rayla's on trial for second degree murder," she said. "I'm sure you know what that carries. Now are you going to shilly-shally around on that sidewalk all afternoon, or can we get to the courthouse before the verdict?"

Kevin hustled around to the driver's side. He adjusted the seat, cranked the engine, and nosed slowly out into traffic. After a few red lights he saw the on-ramp and within minutes they were headed west on Interstate 10.

Driving is a metaphor for life. On the surface, it seems there's so much to do: check the mirrors, use the blinkers, brake, accelerate, turn, pass. Lots going on simultaneously. Yet after a while, all those little things become second nature, and driving, like living, becomes an unconscious act. The miles, like years, can tick away while you're not paying attention.

"I told her not to marry that asshole," she was saying. "Her daddy used to beat on her momma the same way. Stiff-necked girl. I guess we all are."

"When did it happen?" Kevin asked.

"Right around the same time that miserable inspector had you shipped off. Can you believe he told Rayla that you threw her under the bus? He even mentioned her momma, said you told him all about that too," she glanced over at him. "I told her I thought Fretwell was lying through his teeth."

"Thank you."

"I don't know what that man's problem is," she said. "He was pushing so hard to use you as the motive, I'm surprised he didn't get a hernia! But the judge wouldn't allow it, called his testimony 'speculative and circumstantial.' That's probably why you never got subpoenaed."

A passing sign read *Panama City 87 miles, Pensacola 175 miles.* "Let me know which exit," he said.

She nodded. "So the prosecutor dropped it down to second degree, which is more like heat of the moment than premeditated."

"I'm amazed they charged her with *anything*," he said. "What about self-defense? Or stand your ground? If there was ever a case that qualified—"

"Oh, you don't know the half of it," she said, petting the dog's head. "That bastard beat Rayla bloody, drugged her, kidnapped her, raped her, not to mention he almost killed Mydog and kicked some poor girl from a moving vehicle."

Kevin flinched at the image of Rayla being brutalized by her husband, knowing firsthand his boundless cruelty.

"But," her grandmother continued, "there were drugs in both of their systems. The kitchen was destroyed by some type of meth lab explosion and the prosecution's star witness, a forensics expert, is saying that she shot him in the back." She began to cry. "That he was trying to get away, that it wasn't self-defense."

The little dog licked at her tears. Kevin reached over and patted her hand. "Everything's going to be all right."

She dug in her purse for a tissue. "It's the next exit."

"Why didn't you contact me before?"

She sniffled and dabbed at her eyes. "Rayla asked me not to."

The courthouse in Pine Grove resembled a skull with its domed roof head, black tinted window-eyes and dirty gray steps as teeth. Like many small-town Panhandle courthouses, the county jail was connected to the back. When he parked the car and got out, Kevin could hear the basketballs bouncing in the rec cages.

Mema had a quick heart-to-heart with Mydog, then lowered the windows halfway before slamming the door.

"He won't run off?"

The old woman shot him a funny look. "What? And miss the news about Rayla? He's more worried about her than we are."

He heard the little dog bark once in agreement as they walked up the steps to the side entrance.

The courtroom was packed. He saw familiar faces everywhere. Most of them were scowling, some whispered and nodded in his direction. His Dickies, t-shirt, and bobos might as well have been a blue prison uniform.

"Piss on 'em," said Mema, leading him to a pair of empty seats on the back row.

He had just sat down when a door opened and the bailiff escorted Rayla in. The crowd began to murmur as she slowly made her way across the carpet. He could hear her leg irons rattling in the hum of voices. Her hair was seven months longer and spilled over her small shoulders in dark sheets of silk. Her face, untouched by makeup, was flush with a radiant glow. And although her frame was swallowed by the orange jumpsuit, he could see her swollen expectant belly stretching the elastic waistband.

He looked sharply at the old woman sitting next to him.

A smile played at the corners of her mouth but she kept her eyes straight ahead. "Didn't I mention that?" she asked innocently. "Well it's a wonder she didn't miscarry. She was unconscious when they found her. Cracked ribs, broken jaw, head trauma. The doctors in the ER said it was a miracle. Baby's as stubborn as her momma." She glanced at him. "It's a girl, by the way."

"A girl," he repeated as he watched Rayla settle into her chair. She was chewing on her bottom lip the way she always did when she was nervous. He had never seen her more beautiful, or more vulnerable.

"Her lawyer had DNA tests done," Mema whispered. "Lance ain't the father."

He was overcome by the urge to run to her, to sprint down the aisle, leap the wooden gate, fall to his knees and kiss her swollen belly.

There was a defiant look in her eyes as she scanned the gallery. He remembered the torment of waiting for his own verdict to be handed down. He wished he could somehow comfort her.

Her eyes softened when she saw her grandmother, then passed over him indifferently before stopping and doubling back with dawning recognition.

He tapped his fingers against his heart and smiled.

Her eyes brimmed with tears.

"All rise," the Bailiff commanded. "The Honorable Judge Mattson presiding."

The courtroom stood as a distracted looking man in a black robe whisked through the side door and took his position behind the massive oak bench. "Be seated," he said without looking up.

Kevin disliked him on sight. Disliked his bowtie, disliked his comb-over, disliked his mustache, disliked the arrogant manner in which he licked his thumbs and scanned through paperwork while lives hung in the balance. Innocent lives.

He glanced at the exits, wondering if he could somehow get her out. *There had to be a way.* As he surveyed the courtroom in desperation he noticed Inspector Fretwell two rows down, staring back at him with a smirk. Mema patted his hand.

"Bailiff would you lead in the jury?" the judge finally said.

The elderly court officer stepped outside the door and returned with a line of six people. Four males and two females. They all appeared to be worn down by the process. One woman looked angry.

"Has the jury reached a verdict?" the judge asked, once they were settled into the jury box.

"We have, Your Honor," said the foreman.

A hush fell over the courtroom.

"Proceed," ordered the judge.

Kevin clutched Bobby's Saint Christopher medallion in his fist. He could hear Mema whispering a prayer next to him.

"As to the single count of second degree murder, the jury finds Rayla Broxson…"

He shut his eyes and waited.

"Not guilty."

The crowd reacted in outrage and exultation. Some leapt to their feet, others slumped in their chairs. There was laughing and crying and heated arguing as they headed for the exits like moviegoers from a matinee. The judge banged his gavel in vain.

Kevin remained in his seat, gazing across the courtroom at the beautiful girl in the orange jumpsuit.

People were passing through their line of vision. Mema was still praying next to him. Tears were streaming down her face. Rayla's attorney was talking animatedly to someone in the first row.

She lifted her hand and began to sign.

Hope and joy filled him as he read each halting letter from her pretty fingers with a growing smile.

"T-e a-d-o-r-o."

Lagniappe

I was a songwriter before I was a book writer. Music has always consumed me. I held onto the bars of my crib and bounced to the Lawrence Welk Show. (Unfortunately, holding onto bars would become a theme in my life.) I danced with my father to Chuck Berry and Buddy Holly, wanted to be a rapper when I first heard Rakim, and fell in love with the guitar as a teenager in prison, back when prisons supported that type of thing.

Although the callouses on my fingertips faded years ago, I still consider myself an estranged musician and long for the curved and contoured feel of my old acoustic like the body of a distant lover. One day…

I know books don't have soundtracks but these are some of the songs that inspired the characters and scenes in this novel.

- Prologue: *Into the Mystic* by Van Morrison – beautiful and subtle, a love song to my city by the bay, Pensacola, Florida.
- Chapter 8: *I Hear Them All* by Old Crow Medicine Show – I can hear this as the scene opens. Music for the traveler, the prisoner, and the seeker.
- Chapter 21: *First Day of My Life* by Bright Eyes – "When he opened his eyes, she was smiling."
- Chapter 25: *Hold You in My Arms* by Ray Lamontagne – the first kiss.

- Chapter 37: *Let Me Out* by Future Leaders of the World – Ladies and Gentlemen, Festus Methlab Mulgrew.
- Chapter 46: *Empire* by Shakira – Rayla catapulting.
- Chapter 48: *Put Your Lights On* by Santana (Featuring Everlast) – a dark song for a tragic scene.
- Chapter 58: *Only One* by Yellowcard – Rayla sees Kevin in confinement.
- Chapter 59: *Change* by Blind Melon – Weasel rewrites the code.
- Chapter 62: *Bat Country* by Avenged Sevenfold – Lance in a tailspin of sleep deprivation, chemical burns and blistering rage.
- Chapter 63: *Black Flies* by Ben Howard – In the reckoning.
- Epilogue: *This is Why We Fight* by The Decemberists – Credits roll and curtain falls.

– Malcolm Ivey

Acknowledgments

Special thanks to the West Virginia Wolfords and McGuires; the Grundy Street Blakes; the Crawfordville Collins family and their Charlotte transplants; the Mission, Texas Trevinos; the Flomaton, Alabama Odoms; the Schwab Court Griffiths; the Pennsylvania Bairds; the Jeudevines, Conways, Eblens, Shimkowskis, Chancerys, Drivers, Hursts, Mattsons, Sieferts, McCauleys, to the Rhodes family, and the Peters family; to Tara Blackwell, Jacob Gaulden, Brittney Knapp; to my beautiful nieces, nephews and cousins. I am blessed to have so many amazing and inspiring people in my life.

To my beta readers in the Gull Point Chair Aerobics Class, Escambia County Master Gardeners, and the ladies who lunch at Piccadilly, Olde Seville Chiropractic; to Odie and Joker for always having my back; to Mitch for the crystal insight; to Sheena "Pixie" Law for allowing me to rant, preach, and lecture; to Mary Burger and to Cheryl; to the Raylas, Kevins and Weasels who populate my world; to the most kickass mom on the planet who sacrifices so that I may dream; to Marcus and Kelly "the book Shaman" Conrad for believing in a convict; and finally, to my great-nephew Jude who has shown more perseverance, more will, and more balls in his first few months of life than many men show in a lifetime. I'm honored to be related to such a warrior.

Made in United States
Orlando, FL
11 February 2025